To Amy,

Charlotte Ashby

Enjoy !

Girls Like Us

Charlotte Ashby

x

TwistedCountry ⑲ *Gloucestershire*

First published in 2013
by TwistedCountry Publishing
Filkins GL7 3HX

ISBN 978-0-9927820-0-9

A CIP catalogue record for this book is
available from the British Library

Printed in the United Kingdom

Acknowledgements

With thanks to my very dear friend, Lisa Tebbutt, for making me write this in the first place. Her intelligence, inspiration and constructive feedback sustained me throughout, not to mention the memories of our rented flat in Fulham…

To my mother, Catherine Cranna for her humour, support and uncompromising honesty. For Jude and Leila, for checking the swear words, all of which apparently they already knew. And for his endless help, Ryan Hadley, an incredibly talented and patient artist and graphic designer.

And above all, Jimmy, not so much my 'rock' as my 'rocket- propelled, refuse-to–take-no-for-an answer, relentless, human mojo machine', without whom I probably wouldn't even get out of bed in the morning.

For Jimmy

Hammersmith & Fulham Police
Ms Emily Brighouse and Ms Isabella Jenkins
53 Latimer Road
Fulham
London SW6 9BY

Dear Ms Brighouse and Ms Jenkins
Re: Anti-social behaviour/nuisance

Despite previous warnings we have received further complaints/information that you have continued to behave in an anti-social manner.
It is alleged that on repeated occasions between September 2011 and October 2012, you have been in breach of the Noise Abatement Act, causing harassment and distress to your neighbours and encouraging others to do so. We also have reports of intoxication and indecency at the above address.
We hope that having received this letter you understand that your behaviour causes distress and alarm to other people and we expect you to stop this behaviour immediately.
Please take this as a final warning that your behaviour is being monitored and should we receive further complaints we will start legal action against you, such as applying for an Anti-Social Behaviour Order (ASBO) or eviction from your rental property.

If you would like details of services that may be able to support you or if you wish to discuss this further with us, please do not hesitate to contact us on 0207 633 2941.

Yours sincerely
DW Thomas
Inspector, Hammersmith & Fulham Police

1

From a distance, Costas Vassiliadis could almost be mistaken for Danny De Vito. Right now he was in no mood for flattery. They wouldn't sweet talk him this time, with their fancy excuses and gifts of Greek wine… he meant business. It was going to take more than a bottle of Gerovasiliou to make up for another sleepless night, his wife's bloodcurdling shrieks as she opened the door and slid a slippered foot through the pool of vomit on the doorstep, the broken bottles and cigarettes strewn along their shared entrance.

'Those girls', which is how they were referred to in the Vassiliadis household, had been renting the Greek family's flat next door for over a year. The previous tenants had turned the flat into a cannabis factory. It had taken them eighteen months to regain possession and Mr Vassiliadis didn't think his wife's nerves could take any more.

So the nicely brought up English girls had seemed like the perfect tenants. Just like Lady Di, Mrs V had said. Isabella and Emily. Lovely girls.

He was all steely resolve as he hammered on the door. He looked down at the rubbish spilling over the step. There were 60, 70, maybe 80 empty bottles. No sound from inside.

'Girls! I know you are in there!' He knocked again. There were scuffling sounds inside. 'Girls, come out!'

He bent down to look through the letterbox, just as the door opened.

It didn't help that it was the blonde one. She had something of the Goldie Hawn about her, one of Mr Vassiliadis' particular favourites. 'Mr Vassiliadis! I can't tell you how sorry we are.' He had heard it all before.

He never knew quite what to say at this point. The blonde carried on. 'We just asked a few friends round for a quiet drink, to celebrate Bella's promotion. It got a bit out of hand to be honest. We didn't know half the people ourselves.' She managed to sound wounded and remorseful at the same time. 'Please forgive us Mr V. It won't happen again. We promise.'

He shook his head. 'Girls, it can't happen again. They were ringing on our doorbell all night.' He sounded defeated. 'The music was so loud our floor was vibrating.' He looked away for a moment, as if to gather his resolve. 'This is the eighth time this year. My wife is very highly strung. She hasn't slept. There's vomit on our doorstep again.'

The blonde winced as she glanced sideways at the step. 'Everything will be cleaned up by lunchtime Mr V.'

He looked past the blonde, into the flat. The brunette didn't seem to have anything to say at all, but stood completely still in a rather awkward pose, halfway down the hall.

Mr Vassiliadis walked in and looked tentatively into each room. Mrs V had insisted that he check for damage. The smell of stale smoke and alcohol was overwhelming. Every surface was crammed with bottles, cans, discarded pizzas, plastic cups and brimming ashtrays. It was a rubbish tip, but no permanent damage that he could see.

He had to admit that the flat was not exactly top of

the range. His wife had dissuaded him from replacing the threadbare carpet. The orange bathroom suite was at least 20 years old. But still, these girls! How did they hold down jobs? In his day, women never behaved like this. Why didn't they get some nice boyfriends and settle down? His feet stuck to the lino in the kitchen and he struggled to free himself. Still the brunette stayed fixed like a statue in the hallway, so that he almost had to push past her on his way out.

He shook his head as he walked towards the door. 'How can you carry on like this? You'll never find nice husbands if you don't start to behave.' The girls offered no response. He walked towards the door and turned round for one final parting shot. 'This is your final warning girls. I mean it. One more party and you are out. Do you understand?'

But even as he said it, he knew that this wasn't supposed to be the 'final warning'. Mrs V's instructions had been quite specific. 'Eviction' she had said. 'Give them notice! Nothing less.'

He retreated down the path, clutching the gift of a tea towel for Mrs V, which the blonde had pressed into his hand. It featured Princes William and Harry ('those poor boys' as Mrs V called them), and a bottle of Gerovasiliou's finest Domaine Carras, a Greek wine from the town where he was born.

He knew what his wife would say. 'Costas, you stupid old fool, laughed at by those English Sloaney girls.' He opened his front door and braced himself for what would surely be a shrill ear bashing, of Olympian proportions.

Emily closed the door and lent against it for a moment. She exhaled deeply, relieved that this time, it was just a warning. 'He's gone Bels, you can move.'

Bella shifted her feet to reveal two gigantic cigarette burns in the carpet. 'Do you think we got away with it Em?'

'Not really. I don't think he'll chuck us out though.' Emily picked up a plastic cup from the floor. 'We're getting a bit low on the Greek wine. I'll order some more.'

She collapsed on the sofa next to Bella and took in the full devastation around them.

As far as Emily could remember, the idea of a party had all happened without much warning. They had been in their local pub, the Dog and Duck, more commonly known as the 'Snog and Fuck', just round the corner from the flat. Emily had been persuaded to join Bella and a couple of her work mates. It was a nice enough, uneventful Wednesday evening, when the god like creature had joined their table, a friend of a friend apparently. She knew at once that he was just how Bella liked them. He was what Emily referred to as a 'knitting pattern cover boy'. She had visions of him perching on a sand dune, modeling a cream arran cardigan with leather buttons, all chiseled jaw line, olive skin and blonde hair. Emily looked across at Bella. He was gorgeous enough to cause them to exchange the very subtlest of raised eyebrow and for Bella to pipe up… 'You will all come to our party on Saturday won't you?' Emily wasn't really surprised, but she was well trained enough to say nothing. As soon as they were alone, walking home from the pub, she could finally ask. 'What party Bella?'

'The party we are going to have, so that we get to see that stunner again, party.'

'I see'. Emily paused and looked at her friend. 'And we have three days to make it happen'.

But they had. And 'knitting pattern cover boy', who had clearly missed the point entirely, had brought his boyfriend along with him.

Emily often thought how lucky they were, that they didn't go for the same men. Bella definitely liked pretty boys, while Emily preferred something altogether more rugged.

She had first met Bella at the age of 4, but it wasn't until they were six that the friendship really took off. Sitting in a DT lesson at St Xavier's Catholic Girls Primary, sewing buttons onto felt Easter bunnies and chatting so animatedly, they completely failed to notice that Emily had sewn her Easter bunny to Bella's tights. Sister Mary Evangelina had called Emily an idiot. She would never forget Bella's strident defence. She had been awestruck. That was the first of many detentions they would share.

While Emily was more often in trouble, it had quite often been Bella's idea in the first place. It occurred to Emily as she looked around the room, that nothing much had changed.

There had been an unfortunate period in their late teens when they had locked themselves in a battle for the blondest hair, only calling a truce when Emily's hair started to come out in handfuls. But in spite of the thick black eye make up, orange foundation, platinum blonde hair and seriously dodgy attitudes, they had both been clever. Bella had now reverted to her own glossy, gorgeous brown tresses, Emily still blonde, but a slightly more upmarket golden tone these days.

Emily stood up and started to shovel the remnants of the party into a black bin liner. She looked at her friend, sitting deflated on the sofa. Poor Bella. It had all been for nothing. 'Did you invite 'Bastard Ben'', she asked hesitantly.

'Yes. He didn't turn up,' Bella looked forlorn.

Emily frowned and put the bin bag down. 'Would a cheese and ham toastie help?'

'Yes please.' Bella paused. 'Do you think Mr V's right about us, Em?'

'How do you mean?' Emily was distracted, trying to tie up the bin liner.

'What he said about girls like us not finding nice husbands. I mean, why don't we have boyfriends Emily?'

Emily laughed a little sarcastically. 'I don't know Bella? Maybe because if we're not drunk, it's because we're hungover. Oh and we have a giant 'tube map of shame' in the hall, with colour coded drawing pins denoting the nearest tube stop, where we've each shamed ourselves.' She was warming to her theme now. 'And we live in a seventies tribute flat with shit brown sofas. We are 28, neither of us can drive a car and we are about to be served with an ASBO. Shall I go on?' Bella didn't respond. 'Anyway, I don't think either of us really wants a 'nice' boyfriend do you?'

'No. Well, maybe not.' Bella stared into space.

Emily ripped another bin liner from the roll and tried to open it up. A pained look flickered across her face. She was struggling to suppress an unwelcome flashback. She looked horrified suddenly. 'Did I streak Bella?'

'Yup, to the traffic lights and back this time.'

Emily closed her eyes and felt the shame wash over her.

Bella sighed. 'Do you think maybe it's time we grew up? Or at least started acting in a way that might give us a tiny chance of meeting the 'right kind of man'?'

'No!' Emily looked appalled. She was hit by another wave of shame and nausea. 'Oh, I don't know. Maybe. Why, what do you suggest?'

Bella thought for a moment. 'We could give up alcohol for a bit, take up some hobbies, go to the theatre, join a gym or something.'

Emily rolled her eyes. 'Bella, how long have you known me? Do you seriously think I'm going to meet the man of my dreams at a Scottish reeling class? I'm afraid, my ideal man does not attend self improvement evening classes.'

'Anyway', she concluded decisively, 'my last annual gym subscription averaged out at £250 per visit.'

Emily was silent as she pondered. She turned to Bella. 'It's a good question though, isn't it? Where would someone like me go, to find the man of my dreams?' They both looked at each other despondently, before Bella blurted out. 'God Em, maybe you already have and didn't realise it and now it's too late.'

Emily snorted. 'No chance, I think I would have spotted him.'

'Hang on Em, didn't you turn down the sexiest, most successful city broker, just because he wore a tie-dye purple t-shirt and stone washed jeans on the second date.' Emily rolled her eyes again. Here we go, Bella loved this one. Emily was a little bored of it, but she couldn't be bothered to stop her.

She watched her lips move, but didn't really need to listen. 'I mean' Bella carried on, 'you could've just gone out with him and bought him some nicer clothes. But oh no. That was that!' She had a tendency to come over a bit naggy sometimes.

Emily issued her standard counter attack. 'And don't you rush across London, whenever bastard Ben feels like a shag, whatever hour of the night. Am I mistaken or has the loser ever, actually taken you out to dinner, or bought you a drink?' She regretted it as soon as she had said it. It was hardly Bella's fault if everything in Emily's life seemed pretty hopeless right now. The job, the flat, the love life – all fairly laughable when she stopped to think about it. 'Bitch!' Bella muttered, staring at the floor.

'Sorry.' Emily knew she was right. She wondered if the imminent arrival of her 29th birthday was having this effect on her. It was looming, threateningly, like a big, black cloud, in a matter of days. It seemed to be lending everything a little too much meaning. She attempted to lighten the mood. 'Anyway Bels, Colin Firth would never wear purple tie-dye.'

'True Emily.' Bella smiled and Emily knew she was forgiven. 'But Colin Firth is married to a stunning Italian woman, who unlike you Emily, does not remove her pants and tights in one go and leave them, coiled behind the bedroom door for a week.' Emily laughed.

Bella was on a roll. 'No, she probably pops her designer undies into a Louis Vuitton laundry bag, with separate sections for light and dark washes.' Emily raised an eyebrow. Clearly her friend was very hungover. The laundry fantasy was very Bella, who had always had rather higher standards than Emily.

Emily smiled, 'I don't suppose she has supernoodles for dinner either, does she Bels?'

'No.' Bella looked wistful. 'And I dare say she always removes her make up before she goes to bed.'

They both sighed.

Emily looked at Bella intently. She hardly dared say it. 'What if I just got desperate Bella and ended up marrying an accountant from Hemel Hempstead?'

Bella stared straight ahead impassively. 'Or a quantity surveyor from Cheam…'

Emily felt mournful suddenly. 'I'd rather shoot myself.'

Bella was more upbeat. 'Seriously though, do you think it's possible to get to know a really old friend and suddenly find you're in love with them?'

'No!' Emily was exasperated. 'I mean, who on earth finds themselves 'suddenly' in love with an old friend? I know if I want to shag a man within two minutes.'

'Jesus!' Bella pretended to be shocked. 'You said that out loud by the way.'

'Oh come on Bella.' Emily was finding the mock prudishness a little wearing. 'I mean, do you think Mrs Firth was having dinner with old friend Colin one night, when suddenly it hit her like a ton of bricks. Good God, Colin my old chum! I hadn't noticed it before, but you are actually tolerably attractive. And didn't I hear you say that you were quite big in films these days…'

Bella laughed. 'Yes but Emily.' She pointed out accusingly. 'I bet Mrs Firth doesn't amuse herself by playing – 'which one would you shag if your life depended on it' on the tube in the morning, does she?'

'Only because, she's never been on the bloody tube!' Emily snapped back.

It was Sunday and she was feeling remarkably gloomy. She wasn't sure if it was the state of the flat, the birthday, the hangover or the thought of work tomorrow, but she needed to do something quickly, to prevent a slide into full blown melancholia.

She reached into her bag for her flat keys. 'Look at this globe Bella.' Emily spun the miniature globe on her key ring. Bella smiled. This was a well practiced routine. Emily swung the globe in front of her now, like an amateur hypnotist. 'Let's try to be logical Bella. Are you or are you not, a relatively normal, heterosexual female, who would like, at some point, to get married?'

Bella played along, nodding.

'Well then, the good news is, statistics indicate that you are 95% likely to achieve your objective.'

They were both mesmerized by the globe. Emily carried on. 'And Bella, are you likely to settle for anyone less sexy, devoted, gorgeous, witty and charming than the best boyfriend, crush or one night stand you have ever had?'

'God no!' Bella laughed.

'In which case', Emily continued, 'we are forced to conclude that we are both, 95% likely to meet a man who is sexier, more gorgeous, witty, charming and devoted to us, than anyone we have ever met before. And he is somewhere here on this globe, Bella, waiting …'

2

It was June 15th, another tiresome day in the office, except that today was Emily's birthday, her 29th. She had managed to convince herself that it was no big deal really. There was no need to panic yet. After all, she still had plenty of time to meet someone, before her ovaries shrivelled up entirely and spat out their last barren, desiccated egg. No panic then.

Often around her birthday, she would become more than usually preoccupied with Jane Austen heroines, particularly their age - Elizabeth Bennett, 20 at the start of Pride and Prejudice, the sensible and mature Elinor Dashwood, just 19. Thank goodness for good old Anne Elliot - an impressive 27, but 'wretchedly altered' in looks apparently. If she were a Jane Austen heroine, the arrival of her 29th birthday would spell disaster – the beginning of a spinster's life - stitching samplers and visiting the poor.

Emily didn't like the word 'spinster'. It was a terrible word. It summoned up images of cats, rocking chairs, sucking on toothless gums and years of knitting jumpers that no one ever wants to wear. 'Bachelor' on the other hand, was all about unfeasibly large HD TVs and empty beer bottles, copies of Nuts magazine, golf and lap dancing. Spinster or bachelor? She knew which she'd rather be.

She stared absent mindedly at her screen. Had she already been 'passed by'? There hadn't seemed any great sense of urgency in her 20s, until now. How did she get here, with these people, in this office? Stop, it's the hangover talking, snap out of it.

She tried some yoga breathing, just to keep the panic at bay. She'd read somewhere that men can actually smell fear. Anyway she had done the maths and it was all still fine. It was perfectly possible for example, that she would meet someone tonight, go out with him for approximately 2 years before he decided the time was right to propose. Say then, that she were to give up her high flying PR career, reluctantly of course, to start a family within 18 months, move to the Cotswolds and devote time selflessly to charity work and complete refurb of expansive Georgian rectory… she would only be 32 ½. The ovaries would still be chugging along nicely.

There was no need to panic then, but absolutely no margin for error either. NO ROOM for mistakes, any MORE mistakes that is. She felt strangely soothed by this calculation.

Next to her, she could hear Mean Monica stabbing away at her calculator. Monica was the same level as Emily, a Junior Account Director at Hobbs & Parker PR and desperately competitive. From the sound of it, she was working out her expenses; each receipt meticulously numbered, with a lengthy description, even the accounts clerk would be too bored to read. Monica's disapproval of Emily was palpable. She had never yet passed up an opportunity to point out that Emily was late, hungover, had missed a deadline or failed to achieve her coverage targets. God she was painful! She wondered if Mean Monica had ever woken up in a stranger's bed in Tooting

Bec, with absolutely no idea how she got there....
probably not. At least she would have been able to refer
back to her numbered receipts to work it out and calculate
the exact cost of the evening on excel. Emily sniggered to
herself at the thought. She never really understood why
Monica resented her so much. Every now and again, she
thought she might be getting somewhere.

She popped her head over the partition. 'Any plans for
the weekend Monica?' A lame attempt at small talk, but at
least she was trying to be friendly.

Monica stopped tapping for a second. 'Just a quiet one,
trying to save up – me and Debs are making curry at
home.' There it was - the inevitable reference to money.

Emily was finding it particularly hard to do any
work today. She stared aimlessly across the office. Dan
O'Shaunessy was spinning his Irish charms on some
unfortunate tabloid hack. Dan hadn't just kissed the
Blarney Stone, he must surely have shagged it, but the
trouble with Dan was that to be honest, he was actually
very attractive. Almost every female H&P graduate
trainee had succumbed to his leprechaun charms, as
indeed had Emily, she wasn't proud to admit. The man
had a completely brass neck. Dan O'Bullshit, more like.
She could hear him on the phone to a journalist right
now. 'Alright my darlin', I've got you Beckham – everyone
else has 5 minutes – I've got you 10.' It was nauseating
stuff. Dan's career to date had consisted of schmoozing
A-list sports stars and journalists 24 hours a day – the
booze flowed and not surprisingly, so did the media
coverage. Luck of the Irish, as they say.

She often wondered by what ill-fated planetary
arrangement, she had ended up with quite such shite
accounts. Her client portfolio consisted of Food Fayre,
with its 15 variants of fish based toppings, a new Poweraid
Cherry drink and not forgetting of course, Dewsbury
Pork Products, 'this year is going to be big for Dewsbury

Pork Emily' – or so her client kept telling her. And for some reason, probably some sort of unwritten rule if you want to do well in marketing, the clients were almost always called Martin, Neil or Derek.

She sighed rather too loudly as she flicked through Frozen Food Weekly. Nobody at H&P seemed to want to acknowledge, that gaining front page headlines for a canned fish paste is considerably more challenging than arranging a photoshoot of David Beckham, wearing nothing but your client's new range of tight fitting underpants. She tried not to be bitter.

She clicked on her inbox, just to look busy. Nothing very exciting there. The trouble was, her clients thought it was perfectly feasible, that Stella McCartney would want to turn up to the launch party of their new, bog standard cherry drink. The arrival at the last minute of Barbara Windsor and a lesser known member of the Holby City cast was nothing short of a PR triumph, but did nothing to appease them. As ever, Monica was always lurking in the wings, ready to dispense wisdom on how she had failed to 'manage expectations' - quite tricky when your client is delusional.

There weren't that many people in the office today. Normally it would be noisier, with more people to distract her. She really should do some work in a minute. She heard a roar of laughter and looked up to see Dan O'Shitster and his adoring sidekick, big Pete, guffawing away at something or other. Pete really was the kindest man in the building, although perhaps not entirely cut out for PR. He actually looked and sounded more like a tabloid journalist than a tabloid journalist – head to toe in crumpled cream linen, 22 inch neck, salty tidemark armpits and egg stained cuffs. He met Bella once, when they went out for drinks after work and claims to be in love with her, which of course is unrequited.

Emily had come to think of Pete as a cherubic guardian angel. On the frequent occasions when some new disaster had caused her bottom lip to wobble, his text was always waiting.

Em! pub? 5 mins?

Pete's client list was more like her own, in other words, not as glam as Dan's. He did his best to spice things up though. Pete's Little Black Book of contacts was almost exclusively populated by strippers and Page 3 girls. No press launch run by Pete would ever be complete without an appearance by Maria and Tracey – the glamour model duo, all spray tanned pertness, pouting on cue for the flashing cameras, as they clutched the latest client product. This was a hit and miss strategy really - it more or less guaranteed coverage in every tabloid, but didn't always impress some of H&P's more high brow clients. Emily had tried to explain it to him, but Pete didn't seem to appreciate that some of them had aspirations to reach a slightly more upmarket target audience.

The trouble was, last week Pete had 'gone too far' – to be fair, the gold nipple tassles the girls wore, as they burst out of the gold cake had been absolutely true to the brand colour. The personal finance journalists certainly loved it, even if the client didn't. They were supposed to be launching the AVA Investment All Gold savings plan, aimed at the affluent over 60s. It was considered inappropriate, so Pete was now on his second verbal warning.

They were off again, laughing away. Dan had obviously said something hysterical. At least someone was enjoying their job. An email popped up on her screen. Emails from Jemima were often the only thing that got her through the day. Jemima was a producer at Radio North and she had saved Emily from PR disaster many times over.

She always found a slot for her ludicrous surveys on the lunchtime news. Their email banter had started two years ago, when Jemima had complained about a particularly ridiculous PR survey. There was very little she didn't know about Emily, a sort of e-confessional, with disappointingly few revelations in return.

To: EBrighouse@Hobbs&Parker.com
From: Jem.im.a@RadioNorth.com
Subject: Jawdies...

Dear Emily Brighouse, can you tell your jaw droppingly stupid colleague Arabella/Anoushka/Araminta (I forget) to stop sending me 9 page press releases about hand held vacuum cleaners, referring to people from Newcastle as 'Jordies' – it's 'Geordie' you southern twats. Any more dirty stop outs you need to report – come on, get it off your chest, I need a laugh?

Your only Northern friend (I'm prepared to bet) and Jaaawwwdiiieee

Jx

Emily smiled to herself and started to type a reply. She quickly flicked back to her inbox when she realised that Clare, her director was standing right behind her, breathing down her neck.

'Emily, my office please…' She may as well have clicked her fingers. Emily trotted off dutifully behind her. Clare Forster Blair with the swishy hair, persisted in calling her small carpet tiled area an office - she had been with H&P for 13 years and had worked her way up from junior receptionist to Senior Group Associate Director, with her very own partitioned off section, complete with breakout table and chairs. The entire office could listen in on her very upmarket diary arrangements and her banker fiancee's daily 4pm call to find out what she was planning for 'sup sups'.

Emily always thought she had the distinct air of someone who doesn't really need to work. The Cartier watch, 5 bed house in Balham and generous trust fund, all suggested that this was more of a hobby than anything. She was adored by her clients for her 'nanny knows best' approach, just a whiff of the dominatrix about her. The other day, Emily actually overheard her on the phone, saying 'don't be silly Hugo' to one of the most senior Chief Execs in the country. Clare ran what was known as the 'Posh Division'. Her personal client list consisted of Champagne and Malt Whisky, a Bond St jeweller and luxury leather brand – Le Voisier.

'Come in Emily!' she said, as if you required permission to enter her domain. 'I'm going to need your help with a Polo tournament.' It didn't sound too bad so far.

'Just outside York in two weeks, Le Voisier are sponsoring the Final. It's the usual routine, Chief Exec presenting the cup, photography, branded pics out to society pages, that sort of thing. How does that sound?'

'Sure Clare, I'd love to. When is it?' Emily replied enthusiastically.

'Two weeks on Sunday.' Shit, a weekend! She walked straight into that one.

Clare saw her sudden change of expression. 'Dan's off at some golf do with a client, I can't take Pete for obvious reasons.' (Emily knew that she actually meant that she finds Pete a little bit common). 'So it's you and Anoushka. I'll give you a fuller brief, but pop it in the calendar for now, OK?'

Anoushka? Emily raised her eyebrows. Anoushka's catalogue of misdemeanours would normally have ended in dismissal by now, but it recently emerged (or rather, Pete's email hacking revealed), that she was in fact the

Chairman's niece. Bang on cue, Anoushka popped her head around the partition wall.

'Hi Clare, can I just check something with you? She was all cheerful efficiency.

'Yes Anoushka?' Clare sounded weary.

'You've asked me to label this envelope W. Fawcett Esq. but the client's name is Bill. Shall I just change it to 'B. Fawcett Esq.'?' Anoushka wrinkled her nose as if to indicate that it would be no bother at all.

Clare spoke calmly, but rather more deliberately than she normally would. 'No, don't do that. Anoushka, can you tell me what is Bill short for?' Anoushka giggled. 'No, sorry, not following you...' Emily looked at the floor.

'Bill is short for William isn't it,' Clare was still surprisingly calm, as this revelation was met with a blank stare. If it had been anyone else, Clare would have torn shreds off them by now. 'Ok, Anoushka,' she continued, 'someone might be called Bob, but their real name isn't Bob is it?' Clare's eyebrows were slightly raised at the futility of it.

'Well what is it then?' Anoushka was unabashed. 'I'm so not getting this am I?'

There was a loud snorting of suppressed laughter from behind the partition, where Dan and Pete were obviously listening in. Dan could no longer contain himself. 'Hey Anoushka!' He shouted, 'My Gran's called Peggy? Do you know what that's short for?'

At this point, most of the office was laughing. Clare had had enough. She gave one of her irritated hair flicks that indicate, you are no longer required in her presence. She raised her hand dismissively. 'Emily, just take her away and explain...'

They walked away and at a safe distance, Anoushka turned to Emily, 'I honestly don't know what that woman is on about half the time! Cup of tea Emily?'

'Yes please Anoushka.' Emily picked up a newspaper

and some celeb mags and trudged back to her desk. Time for a bit of media monitoring.

Reaching for The Guardian Jobs page, she spotted an article by Grania Wardman in the Arts Section, an interview with Kevin Spacey for God's sake. Grania had been in the same year at Oxford as Emily. They had both read English, but their careers had taken rather different paths. While Emily would spend the afternoon unravelling Anoushka's extraordinary attempt at a press release for National Sausage Week, Grania would probably be laughing with her editor about the new Director of the National Theatre, or planning her next cutting edge Arts feature.

Grania was such an irritating swot. What had her tutors said about Emily? She lacked 'application' apparently. Emily didn't even want to be Arts Correspondent at The Guardian, or go to Grania's intellectual dinner parties. She just didn't need a daily reminder of Grania's bucket loads of 'application' and her fabulous career.

She had completely forgotten that she had called a brainstorm for National Sausage Week, so was a bit surprised when Anoushka, Pete, Dan, Monica and a small group of graduate trainees gathered around her desk. She hastily put away the papers. At least it would kill a bit of time.

Her client, Derek Dewsbury had been 'disappointed' by their first round of ideas. 'Think bigger' the email had said. 'I want TV, national newspaper front pages, push the envelope Emily!'
'OK' she kicked off, trying to muster some enthusiasm. 'Usual rules apply, no idea too stupid, no negative comments and if anyone mentions putting anything on the fourth plinth at Trafalgar Square, they're sacked.'

A typical H&P brainstorm would normally generate 3 types of ideas – X-rated (Pete and Dan), safe and boring (Mean Monica) and impossible/ludicrous (all). This was going to be no different.

Pete got straight in there. 'How about we dress Anoushka up as a giant Dewsbury sausage and get her into the BAFTAs to hug celebs?' It wasn't completely ridiculous. Emily wrote it down.

'I know, a naked sausage flashmob storms Parliament!' Dan was on predictable form.

One of the braver graduates pitched in. 'Find the UK's biggest sausage addict! Unusual human interest story. Bob Smith has eaten nothing but sausages for 83 years...' Everyone was too polite to say anything and Emily pretended to write it down.

'Place a series of competitions in cookery magazines to win sausage themed hampers?' This was an absolute classic from Monica.

'Re-enact famous landmarks around Britain in sausages – the Forth Bridge, Angel of the North, Stonehenge in sausages, that kind of thing...' You had to hand it to the graduate trainees, for sheer enthusiasm.

Pete wasn't even trying to be helpful by now. 'How about a high profile celebrity angle - Prince William attacked by giant Chippolata – the Duchess of Cambridge fights valiantly to save him.' Emily raised her eyebrows and made a mental note, not to bother to turn up to his next brainstorm.

'Produce some recipe cards for food magazines, featuring favourite sausage casseroles from around the world.' Another vintage Monica suggestion.

Even Anoushka chipped in now. 'Lobby Parliament with a 'Campaign for more sausages!' She had heard this at another brainstorm.

Pete's turn again. 'How about we retrain that dog off 'That's Life' to say 'Dewsbury sausages'

'That's Life!' Dan snorted. 'Jeez, how old are you Pete? That dog probably died thirty years ago?'

The mention of the dog was enough for Emily. She knew

when she was beaten, 'Great, thanks everyone, that was a really good session, I think we've got loads of ideas there.' Crock of Shite, more like. It was going to have to be another bloody survey.

Hobbs & Parker
Draft press release for approval

Bangers, wieners, bratwurst - we all like a sausage

It's estimated that we eat 6 billion sausages a year in the UK. Women of Newcastle like a sausage on a Thursday, whereas their Brummie sisters like a bit of sausage on a Friday... A quarter of Welsh women like ketchup with theirs. Londoners like them small, but housewives of Hull like a larger sausage. So says a survey by Dewsbury Pork, to celebrate National Sausage Week....

She read it back to herself. It was predictable, nonsensical and offensive on many levels, but just as long as Derek from Dewsbury gave it the thumbs up, she would be home and dry. She looked at her watch. Only two hours to go till fabulous birthday drinks, in new, glamorous guest list only bar, organised by lovely Bella. Which meant, only one hour to do her make up, get hair blow dried, buy self birthday present - new snakeskin heels, spotted in Selfridges window this morning. This would have to do.

To: Derek.dewsbury@dewsburyporkproducts.com
From: Emily.Brighouse@Hobbs&Parker.com
Cc: Anoushka.marchwood@hobbs&parker.com
Subject: National Sausage Week PR exploitation

Dear Derek
Thanks for your feedback on our initial plans for NSW.
Please find attached a news release, which we believe
aims higher in terms of national press and TV coverage
potential. We estimate at least 3 pieces of national
coverage, 10 radio interviews, 25 regional pieces and
one TV opportunity, all branded 'Dewsbury Pork' and a
reasonable number featuring interviews or quotes.

We can commission the research on an overnight
telephone omnibus. Let me or Anoushka know if you are
happy to progress.

Kind regards
Emily

She pressed 'send' – job done. The targets were ludicrously high, but what the hell, tomorrow was another day. She could always enlist the help of H&P's new graduate intake. They were a precocious lot and it wouldn't do them any harm to eat some humble pie. Emily knew only too well what it felt like to phone up a national newspaper journalists, to tell them the 'good news', that it was National Smile Week or National Cupcake Week, National Nestbox Week or National Gnaw your Own Head off with Boredom Week.

Funnily enough, the journalists were not always completely receptive, especially the ones who particularly despised PR people and their gushing, inane phone calls. And sometimes Emily could see their point. Quite a few PR people had very little grasp of things like basic grammar, newspaper deadlines or the need for some kind of news angle. But she had come to the conclusion that the PR industry wouldn't even exist if the journalists didn't quite often print their fluffy, absurd press releases. She used to think it must be great to be a journalist. By removing every brand mention in your press release and printing it anyway, they could render weeks of work, entirely pointless. How they must laugh.

She tried not to dwell on the futility of it all, for fear of getting into an irreversible spiral of negativity. Mean Monica walked past her desk and glanced at the white board above her head, on which Emily had meticulously drawn up a chart, showing media coverage targets for National Sausage Week. Each column featured a line for coverage 'anticipated' and coverage 'achieved', a different coloured pen used for every branch of the media. She found it strangely reassuring to carry out this rather futile exercise at the start of each campaign, even though she knew it would have no bearing whatsoever on the outcome.

Emily hoped Monica would keep walking but she stopped and studied the white board for several minutes. 'You'll never make those targets!' She snorted.

Emily didn't give her the satisfaction of looking up. 'Thanks for your support, Monica.'

She looked at her emails, one from Pete. Maybe he was apologising for his less than helpful performance at her brainstorm.

To: Emily.brighouse@Hobbs&Parker.com
From: Pete.neville@Hobbs&Parker.com
Cc: Anoushka.Marchwood@Hobbs&parker.com
Subject: Sizzle my bangers...

Briggers,
Since your inspiring brainstorm on National Sausage
Week, I have hardly been able to think of anything else. I
am bursting out of my own sausage skin with creativity.
Have penned a quick press release for you - attached, but
here are the key findings...
'2/3rds of housewives from Hull like it long and meaty,
single women from Doncaster like a bit of girth to their
banger and half of Scottish lesbians admit to loving a bit
of sausage now and then...'
I'll alert the tabloids to clear their front pages and I can
brief the lovely Maria and Tracey to re-enact some of our
sausage findings for the tabloids.

Suck my sausage...
Pete

Since she started work on the Dewsbury Pork account,
Emily had grown used to Pete and Dan's ever helpful
suggestions. This time though, Pete had outdone himself
with a full press release, systematically targeting every
region of Britain with a sniggering sexual sausage
innuendo. It was inspired.

To: Pete.neville@Hobbs&Parker.com
From: Emily.brighouse@Hobbs&Parker.com
Subject: your wiener

Pete, you pathetic little man,
Loved your press release! After 3 years on National
Sausage Week I thought I'd heard them all, but even to

my jaded sausage palate, 'the queen loves a right royal porking' and 'Newcastle's Barmy Salami Army' were 'refreshing'...
Dust off your Braunschweiger and come down to Rocco's Bar tonight for my birthday drinks.

My flatmate Bella will be there!

Emily

3

Emily woke but kept her eyes firmly shut. This was definitely not her own bed and she could hear the sounds of an unidentified man, humming in the shower. Oh Holy Cow, where was she? She opened one eye at a time, enough to see that the pillow beneath her was a Turin Shroud of black mascara. A wave of nausea overcame her, accompanied by a dull ache in the small of her back. There was a sharp, searing pain in her chest and she looked down, to see a one inch diameter red ring, branded on her left breast.

She was lying naked in a double bed, on some kind of mezzanine platform, next to a bathroom from where the humming was now getting louder. As she sat up in bed, she could see some stairs that led down to a sitting room and an enormous chandelier, suspended from a double height ceiling. A piece of fabric hung from the chandelier, blue and white striped with a purple bow ...oh my God, her pants!

Clutching the sheet to her, she looked around desperately for some kind of implement with which to hook her pants. She knew she had to keep calm. Deep breathing. Focus Emily, focus! Whether to attempt a pant retrieval and risk being caught 'commando' mid-manoeuvre by unidentified one night stand man, or gather her belongings in stealth-like silence, leaving her pants to their fate. She could see her bra and handbag, just over there on a chair. She rolled silently out of bed and swiftly pulled on her tights, two small ladders, not too bad, dress, jacket and heels, all fine except, 'What the fu...' – her 4 inch snakeskin heels were not just snapped, an entire heel was missing. She was still wearing her watch – it was 7.48 am – everything might still be OK, just enough time to get into work, assuming of course that she was still in London.

She was breathless and terrified as she crept down the stairs, still undecided about the pants predicament. If she could just keep her head. To her right, she spotted a university boat club oar, resting on hooks on the wall. She could just see an engraving on the side - several names and 'Exeter University Coxless pair'. If she could lever it off the wall, she might just be able to identify the name of her one night stand and simultaneously hook her pants off the chandelier. Standing on a chair, she carefully lifted the oar off its hooks – B. L. Jones, C. J. Fanshawe were emblazoned down one side in large black letters – no clues there.

The oar was heavier than it looked, but with an almighty effort, she managed to balance it on her right shoulder, as she heaved it over to the stairs and pointed it in the general direction of the chandelier. She gasped as the paddle of the oar swung precariously around, very nearly smashing the chandelier.

Her breathing was heavy now. Even hanging over the banister, she was just a couple of inches short of her target – tantalisingly close. Straddling the balustrade, she leaned out and twisted the paddle. She had manoeuvred it perfectly into position, just under the crotch of the stranded pants. Oh my God, the sound of the shower had stopped. She must have a minute, seconds even, to complete the operation.

In one swift, desperate lurch of the oar, the pants were freed, but so was Emily.

'Fuuuuuuuuuuuuuuuuuuuuuck!'

The splintering, cracking balustrade collapsed and fell to the floor, sending her plummeting down, screaming as she plunged head first, into the double height sitting room.

She screwed up her face, braced for impact, but suddenly, the 15 foot freefall was broken, as the paddle of the oar she was desperately clutching, attached itself to the chains of the chandelier. She swung across the room, Tarzan like and landed face down in the nearest sofa.

Lying on the cushions, she must have had all of 3 seconds to catch her breath. As she looked up, the chandelier, now creaking and spinning was hanging by a single wire. The oar was still attached to the chandelier, but only because it was caught in her pants. It swung like a giant clock pendulum.

She lunged for her bag, the bathroom door handle now turning, the door opening. She grabbed her shoes, ran for the front door, just in time to hear the sound of splintering glass as the chandelier crashed to the floor and the voice of the still unknown man shouting...

'Holy shiiiiiiiitt!'

Outside, a sharp left hand turn took her onto a busy high street. If she raised her left heel 4 inches, she only had a slight limp. Her breathing was beginning to slow a little. This, she decided, must finally be rock bottom...no pants, make up smeared across her face, no idea where she was, who she had spent the night with, what to call him? Her faceless lover, 'in-cock-nito' so to speak. She stifled a giggle in spite of everything.

Here she was, doing a walk of shame that was surely being replicated throughout London this very morning. Thousands of twenty and thirty something women, limping shamefully down unfamiliar high streets, counting the cost of that extra bottle of Pinot Grigio. A sort of slutty sisterhood. If only men came with nectar points, you could at least claim a set of saucepans or Italian City Break. What a bloody brilliant idea…no, that's the hangover again… She tried to get a grip on herself.

Now where the hell was she? Keep walking, find the tube, any clues on passing buses, shop fronts. 'Chicken Cottage', discount hardware store, Costa Coffee…Bethnal Green! What in the name of all that's holy was she doing in Bethnal Green?

She rifled around in her handbag, but her mobile and house keys were both missing. She must have tipped them out. Oh God, how could she be so unbelievably stupid. Not to mention the extensive damage she had caused her faceless friend. As she limped along, she thought about the devastation she had left in her wake. She would have to offer to pay for a replacement banister rail…and chandelier… and replaster the ceiling. There was no point thinking about that now, keep the mind focused on the present, a short term survival plan…

Berocca, Nurofen, clean pants, face wipes, toothbrush, toothpaste, new shoes
Berocca, Nurofen, clean pants, face wipes, toothbrush, toothpaste, new shoes

Chanting the necessary items quietly to herself, she caught the central line in the general direction of the office. She sat, dejected, in the corner of the tube next to a man in a suit. She looked over his shoulder at the magazine article he was reading.

"Many people think of alcoholics as dishevelled, homeless winos who have lost everything, but there are people who meet the criteria for a medical diagnosis for alcohol dependence who are highly functional in society and still have their jobs, homes and families. This type of drinker is known as a functional alcoholic."

Oh God, was that her, 'a functional alcoholic'? But if she was an alcoholic, she wouldn't have a hangover this bad, would she? What if she promised out loud never, ever to drink again, to stay in for weeks at a time and only go out in order to attend self improving night classes and learn to cook Thai food or speak fluent Mandarin, volunteer in soup kitchens or read the complete works of Proust.

She rounded the corner and walked into the offices of H&P. By some miracle, she was only a few minutes late. Apart from the web of red blood vessels in both eyes and the pea green shoes she had found in a second hand shop in Bethnal Green, she might just get away with it. At the other end of the office, Pete and Dan were already amusing themselves by trying to get Anoushka to identify Paris on a map of the UK.

She started to examine the evidence. A receipt in her handbag - four bottles of Pinot Grigio, six Mojitos, two tequilas (tequila gold – classy!), four drambuies and two plates of nachos with melted cheese (how sensible to have had some food). She flicked on her computer. Maybe her emails would reveal more clues.

To: EBrighouse@Hobbs@Parker.com
From: Bella.j@hothouseproductions.co.uk
Subject: OMG...

Emily,
I've texted, I've called – PICK UP YOUR PHONE!!! Are
you OK? Phone me the second you get this? You were...
awesome, astounding in fact, but God you must be in
pain this morning – that burn looked really bad (the
flaming drambuie on the breasts trick is always a winner,
but not according to my colleagues here, if the glass has
been sitting on the bar for some time and is white hot!)
and I can't believe you didn't break anything when you
jumped off the bar. So did you really shag my friend–
Charlie 'Fanny' Fanshawe - he's actually really nice...
Phone NOW!

PS. Please don't tell your chubby work colleagues that I
fancy them!

So she had slept with someone called 'Fanny' who is
'really nice', probably not so nice when you've destroyed
his flat. Well, that explained the strange circular scar on
her left breast – a shot glass of course. She scanned down
the rest of her inbox.

To: EBrighouse@Hobbs&Parker.com
From: Jem.im.a@RadioNorth.com
Subject: You are wasted in PR...

Em – I have just had another of H&P's dubious surveys
land on my desk – imagine my astonishment when it
revealed that 80% of Geordie women (and congrats
on the correct spelling by the way) don't like washing
up! Well stone the crows...to add to my obvious

*astonishment, the news desk are actually going to
run it, unless of course a badger is run over before
we go live and your story falls off the running order...
and I can tell you that 3 women who may have once
been to Newcastle does not represent 80% of the local
population...
How are you doing slapper? How was the birthday
drinks? x*

Where to begin! She started typing her reply, a frank
and expansive appraisal of what she could piece together
of the evening – the crowd surfing, the flaming drambuie,
the chandelier and finally the purchase of the pea green
shoes. She was quite pleased with the subject line - 'I left
my pants on a light fitting in Bethnal Green'. She wasn't
exactly proud of her behaviour, but at least it would give
Jemima a giggle. Just as she pressed 'send' her screen
froze, but with a few random stabs of her keyboard it was
on its way.

She looked up and saw Dan O'Shagtastic wandering
nonchalantly towards her desk, taking his time, clearly
enjoying himself. 'Emily, I've the number of a taxi driver
here, he says he has your mobile...he rang just before you
got in. The bad news is, he won't give it back to you unless
you give him £50 to clean up the back seat. Here's the
number.' He presented her with a post-it note, smirking as
he walked away. 'Oh and Emily' he said, pausing for effect
and raising his voice for the benefit of the whole office,
'He says there was a text message on your mobile and it's
great news, your test result came back negative!...'

Emily closed her eyes to shut out the world. She could
feel a rash creeping across her neck.

'Nice shoes Emily', Clare Forster Blair swished past
smelling all fragrant and righteous – 'very retro!'

Monica popped her head over the partition. 'There's some guy called Charlie Fanshawe on the phone for you Emily...'

Shit! It was him. She wasn't ready for this, but she couldn't bear to ask Monica to make an excuse for her. She gestured to her to put the call through to the meeting room. It was not a conversation she wanted to share with the entire office.

Her mind was buzzing as she stumbled towards the meeting room. How to address a person who you don't actually know, have most probably slept with and whose home you have destroyed? It would be difficult to get the tone right. Do you ask for your pants back or gloss over, probably best to gloss over. She took a deep breath. Keep it broad and light hearted. Right then, time to face the music, with a quick burst of yogic breathing, she picked up the phone.

When Emily returned to her desk 5 minutes later, she was a little less downcast. Yes, things had definitely improved, maybe she wasn't a desperate, ageing drunk after all, but an amusing and attractive woman with every chance of meeting Mr Right .

So what if she was wearing second hand shoes and nylon, emergency purchase pants. Charlie Fanshawe thought she was 'hysterical' and would like to take her out to dinner. Charlie Fanshawe, an ex Guards officer, who now works in the City. Charlie Fanshawe was really a very sweet man! Desperately posh, so much so that he was quite hard to understand at times. Generations of marrying first cousins had rendered him almost unintelligible, but he was really very nice about the chandelier and balustrade and seemed to think it was 'hilarious'. No mention of pants at all – a true gentleman!

Her mind was drifting off now, to the future and their life together. Once they were married, she would probably have to spend summers on his estate in Scotland, being bitten to death by gnats of course, but she would respect his family heritage and devote herself tirelessly to restoring the family seat, hosting shoots, opening the estate to the public, and appearing reluctantly in six page Country Life photo spreads. She imagined the outfits, obviously a whole new wardrobe befitting the chatelaine of a small country estate, deep purple velvets, harris tweeds but with a slight military twist, nipped in at the waist, Spanish riding boots, windswept but gorgeous on the Scottish moors with a hip flask of homemade sloe gin. And it would all start with dinner next Thursday night… if only she could remember what he looked like…

She dragged herself reluctantly back to real life and sighed as she opened her emails.

What on earth! 30 new messages in her in-box and all received in the last 15 minutes …one of them from Anthony Jennings, chairman of Hobbs & Parker, for goodness sake, whom she had never dared speak to, let alone email…

To: EBrighouse@Hobbs&Parker.com
From: AJennings@Hobbs&Parker.com
Subject: Your email

Dear Emily,
With reference to your email entitled: 'I left my pants on a light fitting in Bethnal Green…'
I believe you may have pressed 'reply all' in error? By the way, – next time you go for a quick drink after work, I shall be sure to join you!

Tony
Anthony Jennings
CEO – Hobbs & Parker UK

Oh my God, please no, oh my God, oh my God…no, no, no, no, no, this isn't really happening, pleeeeaaaase…

To: *EBrighouse@Hobbs&Parker.com*
From: *Pete.neville@Hobbs&Parker.com*

Brighouse,
I have had my chandeliers reinforced, pop round for a drink anytime…

Pete

And so it went on and on. She hardly dared look, but a quick glance in her 'sent' box revealed that yes indeed, Jemima had received her email, but then so had every employee at Hobbs & Parker, a great deal of whom had seen fit to reply.

Neville from the post room, I left my pants on a light fitting in Bethnal Green - it sounds like the start of a great blues song, Emily!

Happy Birthday! Go Emily! From the girls on reception…

And Sheila the librarian had apparently had an assignation in Bethnal Green herself, just after the war…

To: *EBrighouse@Hobbs&Parker.com*
From: *CForster-Blair@Hobbs&Parker.com*
Subject: Your email

Emily,
Quite apart from making a fool of yourself in front of some very senior H&P bods, I was planning on putting your name forward for a promotion this month, which will clearly now have to wait until all this dies down.
Emily, can I give you some advice. You can tell me it's none of my business, but this kind of behaviour not

*only affects your career. I can't help noticing that you
are single and likely to stay that way if this is how you
behave. This is not how you will meet the right kind of
man.*

Clare

Emily's eyes narrowed. Prissy Cow! Sitting there all
smug, wearing her knuckleduster engagement ring and
flicking through My Perfect Wedding. Well maybe this
time Emily had met 'the right kind of man'.

She could hardly bear to look over at Mean Monica.
She didn't need to say anything - she was clearly exultant,
shaking her head slightly as she looked back at Emily.
How quickly life can change. She would do anything to
return to the safe, tedious, existence of 24 hours ago. If
only there was a vow she could take - good behaviour,
steady progress, predictable outcomes – why didn't other
people get into this kind of mess. Bella often said that her
'natural exuberance' was to blame.

It was way too early to go for lunch. There would be at
least another hour of professional humiliation before she
could slope off. She couldn't bring herself to do any actual
work. Maybe look up some ex-boyfriends on Facebook.
Maybe not, she hardly needed to intensify the feelings of
shame. She googled 'embarrassment at work' instead.

Are you yearning, or learning! Hey, so you mucked up?
What did you learn from it? Or are you too busy feeling
sorry for yourself, clothed in your own embarrassment?
Time to change the record? Lose the shame! Reject
the guilt! Instead, look in the mirror and say "this is my
learning experience".

What a load of shit!

Get real! Take responsibility for your mistakes!
Embarrassment comes because we are afraid of what others think of us. We think of ourselves as shameful in their eyes. Hey, they don't give a damn about you! They don't notice the way you behave, because they're too busy focusing on their own concerns. Take responsibility! Right now, you are letting other people determine how you appear to the world...

There was that 'being responsible' thing again. She understood the theory but applying it to her daily life was another matter. It was actually sweet Anoushka who lifted her spirits. Dear Anoushka who knew no other way than to speak from the heart.

To: EBrighouse@Hobbs&Parker.com
From: Anoushka.Marchwood@Hobbs&parker.com
Subject: Whoops!

Emily - I just want to say that I think you are absolutely fantastic. I was in Rocco's last night and I thought your break dancing was brilliant! I expect you must be feeling shitty today, so don't worry about National Sausage Week, I've got it all under control. Derek came back to me and said he loved your press release. I will handle everything – planning to send it out next week, Sunday for Monday morning.

Huge respect!
Anoushka x

4

Emily waited until Clare F-B had finally left the office, before she headed off home. With a sense of relief, she turned the corner into Latimer Road and walked up to the familiar front door. She had already forgotten of course, that she had lost her flat keys, but luckily Bella was already back and let her in. It was a comfort to be home at last and she threw her bag and coat onto her bed and followed Bella into the sitting room. She was dying to get straight down to business, a full post mortem of last night and the aftermath, but Bella was engrossed in an episode of *Antiques Road Show* and Emily knew she would have to wait.

'Hi Bels. What's happening?' She greeted her, but Bella didn't look up from the TV.

'Antiques Roadshow repeat.' Bella replied. They both loved it and Emily always enjoyed Bella's abusive comments, which were shouted intermittently at the screen. Fiona Bruce was introducing the show, on top sugary, school prefect form. Bella's particular favourite had always been posh Bunny, the toy expert with the pearl choker, while Emily had a soft spot for the one that looked like Einstein, who was on the screen right now, addressing an anxious looking couple.

'So what we have here is a more or less perfect example of a Georgian Country Oak Grandfather clock, inlaid with yew, brass finials, made between 1780 and 1800 by WM Hall of Grantham, only 10 miles down the road from where we are today. Really in pretty good condition. Can I ask how you came to have it?'

'Nicked it!' Bella was off. Shouting directly at the couple on the screen. It was almost as if they could hear her.

'Well we lived next door to a lovely old lady. We used to pop in and make sure she was alright. She gave it to us, just before she died.' The couple explained.

Emily thought they looked quite nice really, but Bella obviously wasn't convinced. She was shouting again.

'Yes, because you probably snuffed the life out of the poor dear, with her own pillow, you bastards!' Emily realised that Bella must be feeling hungover as well. Even for her, this was harsh.

Bella stopped shouting long enough to glance up at Emily. 'I'll be with you in a minute, Em.' But her eye was obviously drawn down to Emily's extraordinary green footwear. 'Blimey Em, where did you get those shoes?'

Emily threw off the pea green slip ons and flopped down beside her on the sofa. 'I bought them from a second hand shop this morning. Look what I did to my beautiful, birthday shoes!' She retrieved the wrecked snakeskin heels from her bag and waved them under Bella's nose, but she didn't look up.

'Hang on a second Ems, it's the valuation.' Emily knew better than to talk through the most important part of the show.

'£2000!' Bella shouted, confidently.

The camera closed in on the couple's expectant faces, as the antique's expert got to the bit they were all waiting for.

'And I think what we're looking at, is an insurance value of at least £2000.'

'Yessss! On the nose!' Bella turned to Emily, clearly pleased with herself. 'Sorry I just had to see that. What were you saying?'

'Take a look at my shoes!' Emily waved them in front of Bella.

Bella switched off the TV. 'Oh dear, where's the heel?'

'No idea.' Emily replied.

There was a pause, as if they were both taking in the full repercussions of the night before.

Bella shook her head as she spoke. 'I cannot believe you sent that email out to the whole of H&P.' She thought for a few seconds, before adding. 'Well, actually I can.'

Emily really didn't need another telling off. She tried to divert the conversation. 'Well at least I've got to know my colleagues a bit better. Did I show you the reply from the Chairman of H&P?' She held up her phone so that Bella could read the email. Bella gasped as she read it and started to laugh.

Emily pulled down the collar of her dress to look at the wound on her chest. She had forgotten all about it, but the small ring of fire imprinted on her skin was starting to sting again.

'Ouch! That looks sore.' Bella winced at the sight of it and went off to the kitchen. She returned with a bag of frozen sweet corn and Emily held it to her chest. They both started to chuckle. 'Seriously though Em, your dancing was incredible and to be fair, we were egging you on.' Bella started to laugh again as a vision of Emily popped into her head. 'You know I love it when you do that walking on your hands thing. You just need to make sure your shirt's tucked in first though.' Now they were both snorting with laughter.

Bella turned to her. 'Will we be drinking tonight?'

Emily looked at her wearily. 'Actually Bella, I really don't think I can!' She replied.

'God, OK', Bella looked slightly taken aback. 'Let's order from Pizza Palace then. Extra cheese meat feast?'

'Yes please.' Emily cheered up at the thought.

Bella went off to the hall to get the phone number. 'So Ems', Bella shouted, 'Chubby Pete from your office followed me round all night. Thanks for that!'

'Oh but he's really lovely.' Emily shouted back.

Bella popped her head round the door. 'So you go out with him then!'

Once the pizzas were ordered and they had opened two cans of diet coke, they settled into the sofa and prepared to dissect the evening in detail.

Bella kicked off proceedings. 'So how much of last night do you actually remember?'

Emily sighed. 'Not a lot. You'll have to fill me in.'

Bella sucked in air through her teeth and shook her head.

'Oh come off it.' Emily replied. 'I mean, how bad are we talking?'

Bella shrugged as if words were inadequate.

Emily tried again. 'OK, I mean, on a scale where 1 is sober and dignified and 10 is utterly mortifying, where would I have been?'

'You really want to know?' Bella looked earnest. Emily nodded.

'OK, I think I'd probably give you a 6 or 7. I mean, you didn't vomit, streak or get thrown out this time, BUT… you were asked to get off the bar several times AND you didn't come home last night.'

Emily nodded at what seemed like a fair verdict.

But Bella hadn't quite finished. 'And when you did come home, you appear to have borrowed some of the Queen Mother's old shoes.'

'Vintage Bella, the shoes are vintage.'

Bella's lip curled as she caught sight of the offending pea green items on the floor. 'Second hand shoes that someone died in are not necessarily vintage though are they?' Bella shook her head in mock despair. 'No, I'm afraid my friend, you've earned yourself a new blue drawing pin. Shall I update the 'Tube Map of Shame' or do you want to do it yourself?'

'Oh God.' Emily was laughing, but there was a weary note in her voice. How often had they sat on this sofa, analysing their behaviour, cringing as they recalled every last detail. She wondered if she would ever be mature enough to go out for a quiet drink, without bringing utter shame on herself.

Bella hadn't even really got going. She was off again with renewed enthusiasm. 'So come on? What happened between you and Fanny?' Tell me everything! I saw him catch you as you jumped off the bar, then I couldn't find either of you. Do you like him? Has he called? Spill the beans!'

Emily paused, enjoying for a moment, the fact that Bella didn't quite know everything.

'He did.' Emily smiled enigmatically.

'Did what? Texted? Called?' Bella was gasping. 'This is so exciting. What did he say?'

'He called and we chatted. He was really nice actually, about the damage and everything. He seemed like a laugh.' She paused for a second. 'Is he really called Fanny though? I mean how could I ever go out with a man called Fanny?' Bella rolled her eyes. 'Don't be petty, Emily. You see you're doing that thing again - getting hung up on the detail. You said you liked him, isn't that the main thing?

Anyway, you might be interested to know that he's titled and has a castle in Scotland?' She obviously enjoyed delivering the last bit of information.

'Really? Emily checked herself. 'God, listen to us. What do we sound like? Desperate Aristocrat wannabee WAGS!'

At last the pizza arrived. They carried the boxes into the sitting room. Emily realised she was starving and ripped off a large triangle, dripping with cheese. She was aware of Bella watching her as she rolled it up and crammed it in her mouth, chilli oil dribbling down one side of her chin. 'What's the matter? She said, as she finally managed to swallow it. 'Am I looking too gorgeous for words?'

Bella looked slightly disgusted. 'No, I was just thinking, that you make me sick.'

'Thank you.' Emily replied, reaching for another slice. 'That's just what I needed to hear.'

'No, I meant, why aren't you fat?' Bella replied.

For all Emily's lack of exercise, she was in fact not quite a size 10. Bella always thought it was a travesty that she had been given an athlete's body, all that untapped potential, apart from the dancing of course.

'It's my supernoodle and tequila diet.' Emily replied in between mouthfuls. 'And all that nervous tension I get, from making an absolute tit of myself. Anyway, never mind that.' She said impatiently. 'Tell me more about my future husband?'

Bella cast her mind back. 'From what I can remember at Exeter, he was a nice bloke.'

'Nice!' Emily nearly spat out her pizza in indignation.

'OK, he's not going to set the world on fire, but he's a funny, attractive kind of guy.' Bella thought for a moment, not wanting to put her off. 'Very hooray though, you'd have to be prepared for that. He was quite keen on the signet rings and primary coloured corduroys.' They both pulled a face. Bella got up from the sofa. 'Stay there, I'll get my laptop, we need to Facebook him.'

Annoyingly, Charlie had a picture of a Jack Russell in Ray Bans as his Facebook photo, so she couldn't really find out what he looked like, but that didn't stop them scrutinising every friend and friend of a friend he had. Most of them were Bufton-Tufton, Farquharson-Smythe army chaps, with the odd girl called Cosima thrown in and an awful lot of them were pictured with either a horse or a spaniel. Bella was sniggering. 'Looks like you're going to have 'rahhly good fun' with his friends, Em!' She was enjoying this rather too much. 'Blimey, look at this lot!' She was off again. 'It looks like we've stumbled on the final of 'Upper Class Twit of the Year.' Gosh yes! It'll be back-to-back Hunt balls and Point to Points for you from now on.' Her face lit up. 'You're going to need a whole new wardrobe!'

Emily was beginning to get a bit annoyed. If the tables were turned, she knew she wouldn't be allowed to be quite so insensitive. 'I thought you said I was the one who got hung up on detail. You said he was really nice!'

'He is Em, I'm only joking. I'm sure his friends aren't all diehard hoorays and I seem to remember he was really funny.'

'Anything on the telly?' Emily interrupted before Bella could go on. She was actually feeling exhausted and rather touchy. She didn't want to hear any more about 'Fanny' and his 'really funny' friends.

'Not really. Have a look.' Bella handed her the controls. She had been putting off the moment when she told Emily about the postcard. It had arrived in this morning's post and after all the hilarity, she had forgotten all about it. She couldn't help herself, of course, she had already read it. She picked it up from the table and handed it to her. 'Em, this came for you.'

It was from Emily's mother and Bella dreaded the inevitable reaction. She had watched Emily's face crumple at the age of 9, as she was told yet again that her mother wouldn't be home for Christmas. Emily was an only child, the product of one of her mother's shortest marriages and clearly not a priority, as she flitted from one love affair to the next. No one could believe she had gained custody, but then Emily's father was a travel writer and was hardly ever in the UK for more than a few weeks.

As Emily grew into her early teens, her mother would be absent for large parts of the school term and pretty much every holiday. Bella's parents had become like a second family to her. And now, over 20 years later, her mother hadn't changed a bit. Her main priority would always be her latest, doomed romance.

Bella would happily have strangled the woman, but she was always careful not to be too rude. She had never once heard Emily criticise her mother. She had come to realise that Emily longed for her mother's approval and she also knew that her worst fear was that she might end up, just like her. Bella anxiously watched her face as she read it.

Emily darling fabulous weather here. Sorry to do this to you, but Benoit says he needs some space to paint. It's just not going to work out for you to come to France in August. Have a fun summer! Catch up soon.

Mummy

Emily sighed. Benoit was her mother's current love interest, the latest in a long list of hopeless affairs. She cast her mind back to some of the more memorable ones. There was Artem the Czech photographer, complete lech, tried it on with Emily when she was 15 – she never told her mother. Then there was Johnny Rathbone, total twat

– a perma-tanned, middle-aged Chelsea playboy, who picked up Emily's mother in a bar on the King's Road, the night his wife was giving birth. And oh God, Peter Braithwaite, one of Emily's tutors at Oxford. It was skin crawling. Her mother had come up to see her for the weekend. To be honest, that was probably the worst.

She reread it a couple of times. That was that then. There was no mention of her birthday. Her flight to the south of France had already been booked, but it might not be too late to get her money back. Even though she was quite used to this kind of thing, Emily felt a familiar lurch of disappointment. Why couldn't she have a normal mother, one of those ones who fussed around after you, worried about your fruit and veg intake, made cakes, put plasters on your knee, that kind of thing. Even one who occasionally wanted to see her would have been nice.

When Emily's father died and she thought her heart would break, it was Bella who had held her hand at the funeral. Her mother had swanned in dramatically in dark glasses, arm in arm with her latest love.

Bella folded up the pizza boxes and attempted to chivvy away the gloom. 'Never mind Ems, we'll plan something exciting instead.' Emily didn't reply, but Bella kept going. 'Anyway, back to the matter in hand. Your future husband. I want to hear more details. I mean, did you… you know…'

'Did I what?' Emily replied with mock innocence.

Bella rolled her eyes. 'Did you shag him, Em?'

Emily gave her a weary look. 'I think we can assume from the position of my pants on the chandelier that there was indeed a union of some kind, yes.'

'And will you be seeing him again?' Bella was loving this. She pressed on.

Emily paused for effect. 'Yes, as a matter of fact. We're having dinner next Thursday.' She looked quietly pleased with herself.

'That's good then isn't it?' This was almost too much for Bella, but Emily sounded less convinced.
  'Is it?'

5

It was Thursday night and she was desperately nervous as she walked into the restaurant. 'Hamilton's' was Charlie's suggestion and everything was just as she had imagined. Traditional British with a Scottish twist, claret coloured walls, antlers, lots of leather and tartan and a choice of 26 malt whiskies. The air was thick with the gentle braying of ex public school boys and the occasional guffawing outburst.

She had broken Bella's golden rule of first dates, or rather 'first dates where you are a little fuzzy about what your date actually looks like'. 'Make sure you get them to come to your home or work', she had said, which now made perfect sense.

She hovered by the entrance, but luckily the Maitre D' was one of those bossy types who instantly took charge with an, 'ah yes, the gentleman is waiting for you, the table in the corner' and swept her through the restaurant. It was packed and noisy as he led her across the room, to where Charlie was sitting. She had decided for obvious reasons that she wouldn't call him 'Fanny'. There he was, better looking than she remembered. Once the first awkward air-kissing 'hellos' were out of the way, she had a chance to survey her date. Thomas Pink shirt, purple knotted cuff links, pinkie ring no doubt featuring Fanshawe family crest, no surprises there, but actually quite a cool suit, nice eyes and a very sexy smile.

The worst bit was out of the way, she sat down and started to relax. Bella had advised her not to bring up the damage to his flat or the stray pants unless prompted, but they had 'role played' a number of possible responses just in case. All things considered, she actually felt surprisingly calm. Perhaps it wasn't too late to redeem herself. Having already shown him some of her more leftfield party tricks and of course, woken up naked in his flat, with her pants on his chandelier, Bella had suggested that it was time to show him a more demure, sophisticated side.

That was easy for Bella to say, she was born sophisticated. Emily on the other hand, needed instruction. 'Keep asking questions about him, they love that…' she had said. 'Cultured conversation, a genuine interest in his career and family, that sort of thing.'

'Oh my God, I've already had sex with this man' – a quick panic attack threatened her poise, but she held it together and kept firmly to the script.

'So what do you actually do in the City?' She smiled sincerely.

He didn't answer immediately, but summoned the waiter and without asking her what she wanted, ordered her a large glass of Sancerre. A touch 'old school' possibly, but right now she was grateful and tried her best not to gulp it down.

He sat back in his chair before answering. 'Mainly bonds and fixed income derivatives. We've got a Hong Kong basket of securities in a collaterised credit wrapped structure, so obviously today's announcement by the Hang Seng was interesting.'

She tried not to look baffled. None of Bella's instructions had prepared her for the scenario 'what to do when your date spouts incomprehensible bollocks'. She was going to have to improvise from Bella's approved list of responses.

'God yes, it must have been amazing, how fascinating.' Please God, don't let him ask her about the Hang Seng, whatever that was.

'Yah, bloody good fun! What about you?' He leant towards her. Yes, he really did have very nice eyes.

She dropped her guard a little. 'Oh I fell into PR really. I've been trying to leave Hobbs and Parker for 7 years now!' She blurted out. She could almost hear Bella's voice - steady Emily, not so bitter, don't scare the man, less about yourself. She needed to get back on track. 'No, no, I mean it's great fun really. Never a dull moment it has to be said.'

She paused for a moment and couldn't help adding. 'Listen, I just want to say sorry about the chandelier and leaving your flat the way I did.'

He looked slightly startled. 'The chandelier, oh yes, no problem, don't worry about it.' He paused and she thought that was it, but then he opened his mouth again. 'So how did it happen exactly?'

'Sorry?' She wasn't expecting this. She started to flush.

'The chandelier?' He continued. Why on earth had she even brought up the subject, Bella had expressly forbidden it. She started to feel slightly sick. She had caused major structural damage to his flat, of course he wanted to discuss it.

Luckily just then she heard her phone buzz. Normally she would ignore it, but she was grateful for the diversion and made a great fuss of rooting around in her bag to retrieve it.

It was a text message from an unknown number **'sitting at corner table'**. 'Oh, it's from you', she laughed nervously.

'Yes probably.' He smiled.

Probably? What did that mean? This supposedly relaxing dinner to get to know Charlie was turning out to be very stressful. Emily took a gulp of her wine. She could feel one of her nervous rashes creeping up her neck. How could she get the conversation back on track again. She thought about Bella's list.

'So you rowed for Exeter University?' It was inspired, a swift digression, back to his interests. Bella would be proud.

'Do you like rowing?' he passed it back to her.

'Yes, love it!' She lied. She knew nothing about rowing, except that you seem to have to do it at 5am, which ruled her out.

'So, the chandelier…' Charlie continued. Oh my God, Jeremy bloody Paxman, will he shut up about the bloody chandelier.

She took a gulp of her wine. 'Shall we get some menus?' She was getting desperate now. 'I love Haggis', another lie.

But Charlie wasn't listening. He leapt to his feet and kissed an elegant woman who was rushing forward to greet him. She was in her early seventies, clutching what looked like some very expensive shopping bags.

'Henry, darling, sorry I'm late.' She noticed Emily and raised her eyebrows. 'So, are you going to introduce me?'

He looked completely flummoxed. 'Oh yes, Mother, this is…? He hesitated. He couldn't seriously have forgotten her name.

He said nothing, so she stood up and filled the gap. 'I'm Emily…Emily Brighouse.' At least he wasn't talking about chandeliers for a moment. But who the hell was Henry? This was now seriously bizarre. And bringing your mother on a first date? Emily was now feeling very uncomfortable. Was she supposed to act like this was perfectly normal?

She stood awkwardly between them and it was just at that moment that she spotted him - the real Charlie Fanshawe. He was sitting on his own at a corner table, just a few feet away from them. And he was laughing so hard, he had turned the colour of the walls.

Emily was no longer smiling as she turned to the imposter, 'Is there any sane reason why you let me make a complete arse of myself?'

He looked a bit sheepish. 'Sorry. You came and sat down and I guessed you were on a blind date. It was just too good.' He sniggered.

'Oh how divine, a blind date?' Henry's mother joined in.

'It's not a blind date.' Emily snapped back. 'Just a little hazy.'

Henry looked apologetic. 'I don't suppose you'll tell me what happened with the chandelier?!'

'No chance.' She replied as she grabbed her bag and attempted to saunter as casually as possible, over to the corner table. She only hoped the entire restaurant hadn't spotted her bizarre speed dating antics. Henry raised his glass to Fanny in an infuriating gesture of male camaraderie. Fanny raised his hand in a sort of 'no harm done mate' acknowledgement.

The real Charlie stood up and helped her into her chair. 'So sorry Emily, I couldn't help myself. Should have come over to get you, but I haven't laughed so much for years. I did try to text you...' His voice trailed off.

'Yes, I know.' She replied, stiffly. 'I got the text.'

There was an awkward silence. 'Well, shall we try that again?' Fanny was off again, snorting with laughter, spitting and every time he half recovered, another snort. Her nervous rash was beginning to subside – it seemed she simply couldn't embarrass herself anymore than she already had. She consoled herself that at least she was now at the right table, with the right man and his inability to stop laughing gave her time to size him up.

Bella had been right. Whichever way you looked at it, he was indeed a diehard Hooray. He could have been plucked off the Kings Road, circa 1982 and cryogenically frozen. Red socks, regulation pinkie ring, silver cufflinks embossed with a pheasant. His weekend wardrobe would definitely include a pair of canary yellow cords and velvet monogrammed slippers. She would have put money on it.

But if you looked at the total package, he was definitely attractive - a little chinless perhaps, but very blue eyes, not bad at all. She wasn't really listening to what he was saying. She found herself strangely mesmerised by his mouth. Just like Prince Charles, he barely moved his lips to speak and all the sound came from the bottom right hand corner.

The next glass of Sancerre arrived and she found herself relaxing and really rather enjoying herself. How could she have been so nervous.

He placed a package on the table in front of her. 'I believe this belongs to you, Emily.' She let out a little gasp. Please God no, not the pants.

He saw her appalled expression. 'It's your heel, Emily. You remember, it snapped off in the taxi, when you tried to force the cork out of the bottle?' Of course she didn't remember. He carried on. 'I suppose it's just as well the bottle smashed, we didn't really need any more to drink. The taxi driver wasn't too impressed though!'

Her head was spinning, this was all good news. Maybe she hadn't been sick in the taxi after all and she might now be able to mend her snakeskin heels. Tonight was getting better by the minute.

Her steak and kidney pie arrived and a glass of Claret. She had forgotten Bella's instruction to order a small plate of manageable food, that would be easy to eat. The conversation was flowing and if she crossed her eyes just enough to slightly blur her vision, he was actually very attractive.

'Emily? Are you alright, your eyes?' He was looking at her strangely.

She forced herself to focus properly again. 'Oh sorry, yes, carry on…so what do you do in the City, exactly?' They were back on track.

Well my working title is 'Head of Structured and Collaterised Emerging Market and Index Linked Debt Origination'. She stared at him blankly. Bloody hell – here we go again.

'Wow, you must have a very long business card!' It was all she could think of to say, because by now, she was not feeling at her absolute sharpest.

She realised that she might have sounded slightly sarcastic. 'What does that actually mean exactly?' She added hastily.

'Oh sorry, lot of jargon.' He smiled. 'Basically it's a proprietary trading unit which develops statistical and econometric based models, which can be real-time traded. Generically structured vehicles, that correlate to illiquid individual vehicle entities, that sort of thing.'

'Quite.' She replied. 'You know something Charlie, I've never met anyone in the City, who could describe their job, so that anyone outside the Square Mile could understand it. Is it a conspiracy?'

'You're probably right', he nodded.

She was feeling brave and foolhardy now. 'And, what exactly is the Hang Seng?'

He was off again, it was like a wind-up toy. 'Well crudely speaking, it's a freefloat-adjusted market capitalisation-weighted stock market index, based in Hong Kong.'

She snorted. 'That makes it much clearer, thanks.'

Her mind wandered off again as he spoke. Should she snog him at the end. On a normal first date, she might not, but this was a tricky one. Having already slept with him, a quick snog might effectively 'take it back' a level or two, which wouldn't necessarily be a bad thing, but then he probably already thought she was a bit of a slapper. How to play it - difficult one.

"To snog or not to snog, that is the question:
Whether 'tis nobler in the mind to suffer the gropes and
lunges of outrageous hoorays…"

He had that funny look again. 'Emily, are you with me?'
'Sorry, what?' She really must pay attention. God knows their first encounter hadn't exactly created the best impression. He had nice hands, she noticed. It was quite hard to concentrate on what he was saying. What had Wikipedia said about him?

```
Lt Colonel Sir Roger 'Fanny' Fanshawe,
7th Baron Sir Roger has 3 children by
his wife, Sarah, the eldest of whom,
Captain Charles Fanshawe, is heir
apparent to the baronetcy and followed
his father into the City.
```

She took a sip of water and tried to focus. 'So do you come from a long line of Fannies?' She regretted it at once. 'Sorry, that was pathetic!'
He was still smiling though. 'Don't worry, I'm used to it! Actually my father and grandfather were both called 'Fanny'. It started in the army.'
'Ah Sir Roger?' she blurted out, before she could stop herself.
He looked at her for a moment. 'Good Lord Emily, have you googled me?'
'Of course I have.' There was not much point denying it. They both burst out laughing. Charlie shook his head . 'So

how is the lovely Bella these days? Tell me she's not still hooked on dreadful Ben.'

'Afraid so'. Emily replied. 'Bastard Ben' is still very much around.'

Charlie pulled a face. 'What a shame! Can't we find her some nice chap?' This was all getting a bit smug and cosy, matchmaking their friends already.

'Trust me, I've tried. What did you have in mind?' She rather liked talking in this slightly self righteous way, about other people's disastrous love lives – it was refreshing.

Charlie swirled his wine in the glass, 'I don't know, some decent bloke, nice house in the country, couple of sprogs and a John Lewis account – isn't that what most girls want?'

Did he just say that? Emily only just managed not to spit her wine across the table. 'Or a quantity surveyor from Cheam!' she blurted out.

'Sorry, what?'

'I'm sorry, I was being sarcastic.' She explained. 'Actually some of us would rather live in a council bedsit with Javier Bardem and shop at Poundland.'

'Javier who?' He looked baffled.

'Never mind.' She smiled. Bread and butter pudding and a glass of port and Emily was in no state to argue.

The Maitre D' was hovering by their table and he rather theatrically placed a tumbler of malt whisky in front of each of them. 'Our sincere apologies for the most unfortunate misunderstanding earlier, so glad you found the right table. Please accept this on the house – our fault entirely.' He retreated.

'You see Emily, it wasn't your fault at all', Charlie added. He really was a lovely man, she decided. She tried to pay the bill, to make up for the damage she had caused to his flat, but it turned out he had already settled up while she was in the loo.

He was definitely a true gent! Did it matter that his views on women were fixed somewhere in the 1930s, or that his wardrobe contained quite so much corduroy. She shouldn't be so quick to dismiss a man on the strength of his clothes. Hadn't Bella said that she needed to stop being so superficial – something along those lines anyway.

Outside the restaurant, as she swayed on the pavement, there was no getting away from the fact that she was astonishingly pissed.

*To snog or not to snog…*it was now on repeat in her head.

At the awkward moment of truth she decided 'not' and aimed her lips ineptly at his right cheek, but he had opted for her left cheek and their lips met clumsily at the halfway mark. And suddenly, the aborted air kiss had turned into a full, impromptu, tongue-sliding snog. Charlie pulled her towards him and she surrendered herself to the inevitable. It was too late to back out now, try to make the best of it.

But as his hold tightened, it was Colin Firth's lips on hers, his hand on the small of her back, pulling her closer, until Javier Bardem pushed Colin aside and claimed her lips for himself, pressing her into his body, his fingers wrapped in her hair, bruising her lips with the force of his latin kiss.

'Emily!' Charlie sounded startled as she pulled away from him.

The yellow light of a black cab caught her eye. 'Taxi!' She screeched, lurching into the waiting cab. Seeing his bewildered face, where he stood, abandoned on the pavement, she lowered the window.

'Thank you Charlie, lovely dinner, early start, speak soon, got to go…' She stammered as the taxi pulled away.

The driver switched on the intercom and looked in the mirror. 'Seemed a shame to break it up there, love – nice dinner was it?'

'Confusing actually.' She replied.

'Didn't look that confusing from where I was looking.' She could see the driver's shoulders shaking. Luckily he was so pleased with this comment that he took some time to recover and there was no further questioning.

There was no sign of Bella when she got home. The answer machine blinked with a message.

'Hells Bels come over here, I'm looooonnneeely. Waiting for you...' The unmistakeable sound of Bastard Ben's slurred speech. *'Message left at 11.37pm today.'*

So Bella had no doubt donned her best underwear and raced half way across London to be there for him when he got out of the pub. Bastard!

Emily swayed slightly in the entrance hall. Here she was, staring in the mirror, chapped lips, stubble rash on the chin and the hangover already kicking in. Dear God, what a hopeless pair they were!

She slept fitfully that night, in and out of strange, disturbing dreams...

''Lady Fanshawe, your taxi is here' announced Colin Firth's wife, as a monocled Fanny in full shooting gear galloped past on a stag, laughing like a demon and shouting 'couple of sprogs', 'house in Cheam'...

SUMMONS ON APPLICATION FOR AN ANTI SOCIAL BEHAVIOUR ORDER Crime and Disorder Act 1988 IN THE INNER LONDON COMMISSION AREA

Hammersmith and Fulham Magistrates Court: June 30th
To the tenants: Ms Emily Brighouse and Ms Isabella Jenkins
Address: 53 Latimer Road, Fulham SW6

You are hereby summoned to appear on the 29th July, before the Hammersmith & Fulham Magistrates' Court to answer an application for an anti-social behaviour order, which application is attached to this summons.

Justice of the Peace
By order of the Clerk of the Court

Note: Where the court is satisfied that this summons was served on you, within what appears to the court to be a reasonable amount of time before the hearing, or adjourned hearing, it may issue a warrant for your arrest, or proceed in your absence.
If an anti-social behaviour order is made against you, and if without reasonable excuse, you do anything you are prohibited from doing by such an order, you shall be liable on conviction to a prison sentence, not exceeding 5 years or to a fine or both.

6

There was still no sign of Bella the next morning. Emily was just walking out of the front door, late for work again, when she spotted the typewritten envelope on the mat. She ripped it open and hastily ran her eye down the page. It sounded more serious this time, but she would just have to deal with it later. She stuffed it into her handbag and set off for work, trying not to think about it as she walked to the tube.

A Summons to appear in a Magistrate's Court! An ASBO! Try not to panic. She had a whole month to sort this misunderstanding out before the court appearance. 'A warrant for your arrest.' Shit. As the train pulled up to the platform and she took her seat, she wondered if anyone else in her tube carriage had received an ASBO for breakfast. Probably not, all decent law abiding citizens by the looks of things…apart from that weird looking axe murderer bloke in the corner…

She tried to block it from her mind. A Magistrate's Court! She had only ever seen them on TV. She knew it was a trivial and immature reaction, but couldn't help thinking about what to wear at the court appearance and what type of shoes conveyed both regret and professionalism.

She battled with a rising sense of panic the entire way to work. It would be fine, she had a month to sort it out. No problem. By the time she rounded the corner to the offices of H&P she was a little calmer, but still distracted enough not to notice the TV cameras and studio van parked right outside the entrance. As the lift doors opened and she approached her desk, a deluge of yellow post it notes almost completely obscured her computer. She didn't even have time to read them. Clare Forster-Blair was behind her in an instant. She looked furious.

'Emily, my office NOW!' She practically spat…

Emily followed her, wondering how she could be so wound up already. It was only 9.15. She gestured to a chair. 'Sit down Emily. God knows I need to.'

What on earth had come over her! This was dramatic, even by Clare F-B's hair swishing standards.

'Emily, you are of course aware that today is the start of National Sausage Week.'

Emily relaxed a little. 'Yes, of course Clare.' Maybe this wouldn't be so bad after all, she just wanted a progress update. 'Anoushka issued the press release last night and we are following up for coverage today.' She was pleased with her response.

Clare's steely face gave nothing away. 'But you might not be aware Emily, that last night, Anoushka issued a press release to the national daily newspapers, national and regional TV newsdesks, consumer mag food pages, national and regional radio & TV, online food journalists and food bloggers entitled: 'Lezzers love a wiener!'

Emily was confused. What on earth was she talking about now? She had clearly got hold of completely the wrong end of the stick. She opened her mouth to correct her, but Clare was too quick.

'Anoushka was extremely thorough in her distribution of the release, Emily. It goes on to insult almost every region and minority in Great Britain, and I quote

'Doncaster lovelies like a bit of girth, whereas Geordie women want it long and hard. Derek Dewsbury is quoted in full in the most obscene detail.'

Emily was actually shaking her head now and smiling, 'No, no it's fine Clare. I've seen the release.' But Clare ignored her and carried on.

'I can assure you it's not fine. There are TV cameras downstairs Emily, wanting to interview the Chairman of Hobbs & Parker about 'unethical PR practices'. ITN News are running a piece every hour on the hour about how the desperate PR industry has finally gone too far. Women's groups on Twitter are calling for a complete ban on Dewsbury Pork products and you have been personally invited to appear on Radio 4's Woman's Hour to defend the PR industry and how it portrays women.'

For the second time that day, Emily thought she might be sick.

There simply was no explanation. 'I just don't understand it'. Was all she could mutter. The words in the press release sounded strangely familiar, but the draft press release they had prepared for NSW was just the usual nonsense. A survey of 100 people, if that, a few weak innuendos, some less than fascinating regional differences in sausage consumption and a rather mundane quote from Derek Dewsbury, so bland in fact that it was unlikely to ever appear in print. This felt like one of Emily's cheese dreams. She would surely wake up any minute in a cold sweat.

Just then, Mean Monica popped her head around the partition, barely disguising a smirk as she looked at Emily. 'Clare, I've got Derek Dewsbury holding for you on Line 2.'

'Tell him I'll call him back in 20 minutes.' Clare snapped, before returning her icy glare to Emily. 'I could happily kill you.' Yes, this was definitely the most angry that Emily had ever seen Clare. She had one of those bizarre flashbacks where an incensed Herbert Lom, one eye twitching with fury, was addressing Peter Sellers in Return of the Pink Panther.

Clare's voice forced her back to reality. She was speaking very deliberately. 'Hobbs & Parker is a laughing stock nationally, we will have lost the Dewsbury Pork account when I return his call and no doubt any other self respecting H&P client in the food industry. We may even be sued for loss of business if the public boycott Dewsbury products. You are as good as sacked Emily and I find it hard to believe that you will ever work in this industry again. Any thoughts?'

Emily found herself strangely elated by the last threat. Silence. She sat open mouthed. There didn't seem to be anything helpful to say.

'Anything Emily? Say anything!' Clare waited, Emily stared straight ahead.

'Anoushka.' Emily finally whispered.

'Anoushka?' Clare repeated, shaking her head, 'I hardly think she has the cerebral capacity we are looking for right now, but if you really think she has something to add.' Clare summoned her. Anoushka appeared, a picture of cheery innocence.

Emily mustered every bit of poise she had left and tried to keep her voice steady. 'Anoushka,' she explained breathlessly. 'Our press release for National Sausage Week has attracted some negative responses.' She explained with staggering understatement.

'We have apparently insulted large parts of the population with sexist obscenities, which did not appear in the approved press release. Can you shed any light on the situation?'

'I sent it out last night, just as we agreed.' Anoushka replied.

'But what did you send out, Anoushka?' Emily was still struggling for breath.

Anoushka gave Emily a look, as if she was being a tiny bit dim. 'The revised version, the latest one.' She was oblivious to any sense of panic.

Emily thought her heart might stop. 'What do you mean, latest one? There was only one version. The client approved it with no changes.' Her voice was higher now.

Anoushka was quite enjoying having the upper hand for once. 'Yes, but there was a version saved in the file, with Pete's amendments, which was more recent than the original, so I sent out the latest version.'

'But Pete doesn't work on the Dewsbury Pork account, Anoushka', Emily was whispering now as the full scale of what had happened began to come clear to her.

'Anoushka?' Emily could hardly dare to ask, because she already knew the answer. 'Did you send out a press release saved as 'Pete's version' in my files?'

'Yes, Emily. I dated it and checked the contact details, just like you always say. And I remember, because Pete came over to borrow my stapler and I said to him...'

'Anoushka!' Emily cut in. 'That was a joke press release, a spoof written by Pete to take the piss out of National Sausage Week. It was completely obscene, pornographic. Did you read it before you sent it?'

'No, Emily.' Anoushka began to pick up on an atmosphere in the room.

'Oh my God, this is even worse than I thought.' Clare flopped into her chair.

Mean Monica was back. 'Derek for you again, Clare.' She had heard every word and was all chirpy efficiency.

'Right.' Clare's face was now white with anger. It lent her a chilling calm. 'I am now going to take this call from probably the angriest client we have ever had. I suggest that the two of you and Pete get together, the triumvirate of morons that you are, and work out what the hell we are going to do. Make no mistake, your jobs are already history, but the very least you can do, if you ever want to work in this industry again, is to save H&P from legal proceedings.'

Mean Monica followed Emily out of Clare's area and back to her desk. Never one to miss an opportunity to rub someone's face in it. 'God Emily. Why didn't you check the press release before she sent it out - I mean that's just basic isn't it?'

'Go away Monica!'

'Right.'

Emily sat down at her desk and peeled off enough of the yellow post it notes so that she could see her computer screen. There were 72 unopened emails in her inbox. She went straight to the one from Jemima.

To: EBrighouse@Hobbs&Parker.com
From: Jem.im.a@RadioNorth.com
Subject: Wieners?

Good God Em, I know I said that your press releases were dull, but you didn't need to take it this seriously. Your latest survey is quite a change of direction. I loved it of course, but there's a whole load of 'hot and hungry Geordie lezzers' who are not so impressed! We've covered it twice this morning and The Evening Chronicle are going to press with a call to boycott Dewsbury products! Shall I see if there's anything I can do to help?

Jx

To: Jem.im.a@RadioNorth.com
From: EBrighouse@Hobbs&Parker.com
Subject: All help gratefully received...

Hello my lovely northern friend,
Yes, I do appear to have committed PR suicide. Anoushka
sent out a joke press release penned by our very own
Porno Pete and which I, for some lunatic reason, decided
to file next to the original. The three of us are sacked as
from the end of the week, so any thoughts on alternative
careers gratefully received? Oh and I had a summons
to receive an ASBO through the post this morning, so
somewhere to live as well might be good. Fuck it, let's
just go for the full change of identity shall we! Anyway,
must dash, a few statements to write, busy, busy...

Ex

One by one, she read the emails and the post it notes.
The words 'appalled', 'disgusting', and 'shocked and
saddened' leapt out at her. Clare was right, Anoushka
had indeed been most thorough in her distribution. She
closed her eyes and took 12 breaths, exhaling deeply
with each one. There was nothing for it but to set about
responding to each one.

Statement in response to Look North TV enquiry

Hobbs and Parker apologises unreservedly for the offence caused. Our press release was not intended to suggest in any way that women from Hull have lower moral standards than the rest of the country. The use of the word 'slapper' was an innocent attempt at humour, which we now recognise was deeply offensive.

Statement in response to the Scottish Gay & Lesbian Society

Dewsbury Pork Products and Hobbs & Parker take the rights of Scottish Gays and Lesbians very seriously. Our press release did not mean to suggest that lesbians are secretly attracted to male genitals, although of course they are perfectly entitled to embrace a full range of behaviours. Hobbs & Parker celebrates diversity and apologises wholeheartedly to the lesbian and gay community.

Statement in response to Liverpool Radio PM programme

Hobbs & Parker would like to apologise wholeheartedly for any offence caused. We recognise that the phrase 'fat scouser lasses' could be construed as offensive and we fully appreciate that mobility scooters are used by a wide variety of people with very serious and debilitating conditions and not just by people with weight issues. We recognise the challenging nature of weight conditions, which are not as our press release may have suggested, as a result of the over consumption of sausages or any other food products.

Statement in response to query from the Midlands Evening Post

Hobbs & Parker would like to apologise unreservedly to all women in Birmingham. We recognise that the phrase 'Bang my Brummie Bratwurst' was an ill judged attempt to create a topical, regional news slant and particularly offensive to the Muslim population.

Statement in response to Wales Today programme – BBC Radio

Hobbs & Parker apologises unreservedly for any suggestion that Welsh men are less well endowed, or in any way, below the national average in that area. The phrase 'woeful welsh wieners' was entirely innocent and in no way intended to suggest any kind of shortfall on the part of Welsh men.

It was a relief to have the distraction of hard work. There was simply no time to stop and think. She could only concentrate on right now and getting through the relentless list of statements. She had covered off most of the post it notes, now only News at Ten, the Daily Mail, The Telegraph, Sky News, the Vegan Society, the Matthew Right Show, Loose Women and the Archbishop of Canterbury's office to respond to. Emily looked at her watch. She had been churning this stuff out for 3 hours.

It turned out that writing statements was a doddle compared to the gut wrenching humiliation of the live phone interview. This was the bit she was really dreading and no one else was going to take the flack. She could hardly ask Anoushka to do the interviews. She felt physically sick as she went down in the lift. The journalist led her into the cramped studio van, parked outside the offices of H&P, the same van she had completely failed to spot on her way in this morning. The interview would be 'down the line', the journalist explained and syndicated to radio stations across the Country. She felt like a convicted criminal, taken from the dock to the cell. She may as well have been in handcuffs. 'Three, two, one…' they were live, on air…

'You're listening to Liverpool Sound at Drive Time. We've got Emily Brighouse live in the studio with us this afternoon, well she is at the moment anyway! (haha). And Emily is going to tell us why she called you lovely women out there 'Fat Scouser slappers'. Emily?'

'Yes, well we would like to apologise unreservedly for our ill judged and inaccurate press release…'

Emily, you are from the South I believe, from London? I think I'm right in saying? Have you ever been to Liverpool before?

'No I haven't.'

'So this was in fact, just a cheap and shoddy stunt really? To get your products some free publicity?'

'Well, I, yes, no…'

Over a number of years, the DJ had suffered countless calls from 'southern PR twats', selling ludicrous, survey based press releases - it was payback time.

Within 10 minutes of the end of the interview, some clever little geek at Liverpool Sound had turned her flustered ramblings into a rap…

'My name is…my name is…my name is…Emily Brighouse, live in the studio' 'Ever been to Liverpool', 'No I haven't', 'cheap and shoddy stunt', 'well, I, yes, no'.

Played every half hour and available on Youtube, she was fast becoming a minor celebrity. Back at her desk, the online coverage was coming through thick and fast. The worst one featured her face, taken from a rather unflattering H&P website shot, next to the headline 'What a chump'.

It was time for the dreaded update with Clare, who had been in talks with Hobbs & Parker's lawyers and CEO for most of the day. She traipsed into Clare's area, a resigned expression on her face. It couldn't really get any worse.

Clare looked slightly less white-faced than before. 'Sit down Emily. I expect you will be relieved to know that the lawyers think the press release is so ridiculous, that it would be dismissed in court as nothing more than a poor attempt at humour. So it looks like we won't have a discrimination court case with every minority in the country on our hands after all.'

Relief was not the word. None of this had actually occurred to Emily.

'Tony Jennings has managed to pull a few strings on News at Ten and most of the nationals, so we are hoping this will die down after today's coverage.' The mention of the CEO's name caused Emily a fresh wave of shame.

Her cheeks reddened, but Clare carried on oblivious. 'The Board are calling each client individually to explain, so that just leaves Dewsbury Pork and whether or not they will sue us for damage to their brand.' Emily didn't reply and kept her eyes fixed on the floor.

'Oh and Emily, you, Pete and Anoushka are to hand back your entry cards and company mobiles and leave by 5pm on Friday. HR will be in touch about the details.' Clare was back on ruthlessly efficient form. 'We are willing to offer you positive references, provided of course that you remain professional and don't further damage the name of Hobbs & Parker in any way. Is that all perfectly clear?'

God, she was actually loving this. Emily could tell.

Emily looked up and tried to form a sentence. 'Look I just want to say...'

Clare snapped back. 'I'd leave it at that, if I were you, Emily.' She paused for a moment, before adding. 'I did try to warn you that this kind of behaviour would not help you in the long run.'

Bitch!

The unexpected cruelty of this last comment, gave Emily just enough nerve to respond. 'Look Clare, I can understand if I have to go. It was my client, my team and my stupid fault for saving a spoof press release in a client folder, but I really don't see why this has anything to do with Pete. He sent me that release as a private joke, with no intention that it would ever be issued. This has nothing to do with him and you know that. Given the right type of client, he's great at his job.' Clare didn't interrupt, so Emily carried on. 'And Anoushka can hardly be blamed. She tries so hard to please – she has a heart of gold. And you've said yourself, she's brainless, so she can hardly be blamed. You can't sack her anyway, she's the Chairman's niece.' Emily felt some satisfaction at this last revelation.

Clare didn't flicker. 'I know she is Emily, which is why she will be moved sideways to one of H&P's sister companies. Pete on the other hand was already on his last warning after the AVA disaster. He lacks versatility and we don't have enough clients in the soft porn industry to make full use of his specific talents. I will need a full report in the morning and I mean every piece of coverage Emily - press, radio, TV, online, national and regional - everything. You'd better get started. Good night. ' She was dismissed.

By the time Emily had finished the report and trudged her weary way home, it was shortly before 11pm. As she opened the front door, she was praying that Bella would still be up and thank God she was. Her cheerful voice greeted her from the sitting room. 'Hi lovely. How was your day?' Sudden kindness after today's ordeal caught her off guard and her bottom lip began to wobble uncontrollably.

Bella looked startled when she saw Emily's face. 'What's happened? Are you OK?'

Where to start? And she hadn't even had time to tell her about the court summons. 'It's been a shocker Bels. I can't really begin to explain. Look at this.' She flipped open Bella's laptop and googled 'Dewsbury Pork.' Bella flicked through the articles open mouthed, before Emily played her Liverpool Sound's 'Pork Rap' on Youtube, which by now had a creditable 127,000 hits.

'Oh my God, Emily!' They looked at each other for a few seconds before the sudden explosion of laughter. The relief of it was immense, a build up of pressure released into uncontrollable, hysterical, doubled up, red in the face laughter.

They were both gulping for air. 'I'm sacked of course', Emily managed after a few minutes.

'You're joking.' Bella looked shocked. 'So what now?'

Emily shook her head. 'I don't know. A swift marriage to a stonking hooray called 'Fanny' and exiled to a draughty Scottish Castle for the rest of my life?'

Bella smiled and put an arm around Emily. 'Don't be dramatic. I'd never let you marry him anyway. Shit, Em, I'm so sorry about your job. Drink?'

'Yes please...'

7

Under the circumstances, Emily felt surprisingly buoyant as she approached the office the next day. There was no sign of any radio vans, not a live broadcast in sight. Of course, she had already lost her job and had been humiliated in large sections of the UK media. But the worst was surely over. It was just a case of turning up, she told herself, putting on a brave face. She would spend the day updating her cv, clearing her desk and going through the motions, without giving anyone the satisfaction of seeing how she really felt.

Dan and Pete were both hovering expectantly by her desk as she approached, Pete grinning madly and Dan frenziedly waving a copy of The Times around as he spoke. 'You bloody genius, Brighouse! You lucky, bloody genius! Look at this in The Times! Media Guardian has described it as the most brilliant PR campaign for a decade!'

Dan read out loud…

'Dewsbury Pork, until yesterday, a little known Cumbrian meat packing business, has been propelled into the national consciousness by a PR campaign, just short of genius. After first offending almost every colour, creed and religious persuasion in the UK, quick thinking PRs negotiated a deal with Sainsburys and the Radio Sound network...'

Emily snatched the paper from Dan. Her eyes widened as she continued to read in slightly less theatrical style...

'Shoppers brazen enough to utter the words 'Sizzle my Dewsbury Bangers!' are being rewarded with a 50% discount on all Dewsbury sausages for the duration of National Sausage Week. The discount deal was initially negotiated with Sainsburys, via Dewsbury's PR agency and promoted heavily on Radio North Sound and its sister radio stations up and down the Country. Following early success in the Radio North Sound area, it has now been adopted by almost every supermarket in the UK.' Her voice trailed off in utter astonishment, before Dan snatched the paper back and continued to read it to her.

'Listed on AIM, shares in Dewsbury Pork have increased tenfold. Speaking last night, Derek Dewsbury CEO said, 'We are delighted with the public's response. British housewives clearly have a sense of humour...'

Emily sat back in her chair, unable to comprehend the turn of events. She read it and reread it. It just didn't make any sense. She hadn't negotiated any deal or radio promotion and Clare F-B was too busy enjoying the crisis to have thought of anything so brazen. But then she kept seeing the words 'Radio North' and Jemima's 'shall I see if there's anything I can do to help?'

Pete was exultant. 'You see Emily, the British public have spoken. Genius will always be recognised in the end. They loved my press release after all! She can't sack us now, can she?'

'I wouldn't be surprised.' Emily checked his enthusiasm. 'Let's just see what CFB has to say before we start cracking open the Champagne shall we Pete?'

Clare's face popped round the partition, 'Ah there you are! Emily, my office please...' The voice was a little clipped this morning.

She shuffled into her office, head still bowed, in spite of this latest news.

'Well Emily,' Clare began. 'It seems the tide has turned in your favour. Derek phoned me last night and told me that you had instigated a deal. Representatives from Radio North and Sainsburys contacted him yesterday afternoon and so far it seems to be a great success. He is a happy man. I don't know how you pulled this off Emily, or how it's possible to set up a major radio promo in less than one day. Quite frankly, I don't care, but as your line manager, I would have appreciated being told about the plan. Anyhow, you apparently have very good friends up north.' She delivered this last line with an insincere attempt at a little laugh.

'Well done Emily.' The words almost choked her.

Pete's face appeared. 'Derek Dewsbury called to say the Sainsburys buyer has tripled their order…' much whooping and cheering from behind the partition.

Emily hardly dared say the words. She had a nervous neck rash and her voice was slightly hoarse as she spoke. 'So the job situation, Clare. How is that affected?'

'Well of course', Clare now attempted to sound blasé, 'it goes without saying that all three of you would be welcome to stay at Hobbs & Parker. In fact Tony brought up the subject of your promotion only last night.'

'Thank you Clare', Emily tried to sound calm. 'In that case, with your permission, I would like to take Anoushka and Pete out for lunch, courtesy of the Dewsbury Pork account.'

Clare smiled. 'I'm afraid that won't be possible Emily. It won't come as a huge surprise to you that Anoushka is having one of her sick days today, which is unfortunate really. She was due to be dropping press releases to the national newsdesks for the launch of Zappit insect repellent.'

Sounds quite fortunate then, Emily was thinking.

'So unfortunately, that means, that you will have to deliver the press releases this afternoon instead.'

Shit. But nothing could dampen Emily's joy at this point. Look on the bright side, a bit of shopping in between journalist visits and straight off home afterwards.

'Oh and Emily,' Clare paused as if wondering how to phrase the next bit. 'I forgot to mention that you will be dressed as a mosquito. You'll find the costume on Anoushka's desk. You'll need some help getting into it and we need it delivered back here tonight when you have finished, with a full, written report of which journos you met and when they intend to publish our press release.'

Double shit. But still nothing could touch her. She bounced back to her desk, her head still spinning with the dramatic turn of events. What was it Clare had said -'Representatives from Radio North'? She needed to talk to Jemima.

To: *Jem.im.a@RadioNorth.com*
From: *EBrighouse@Hobbs&Parker.com*
Subject: *a thousand thank yous could never cover it...*

My gorgeous friend
In the words of my director 'I don't know how you pulled this off', but I will never be able to thank you enough. I take it you did the deal with Derek D and Sainsburys. Inspirational! Thanks to you, the three of us still have our jobs. This is written in haste as I have to leave the office. Clare F-B is exacting her revenge by dressing me up as a giant mosquito and sending me round the national newsdesks. It took me 20 minutes to get into the costume – you can't even begin to imagine - red tights, a floor length proboscis, brown fur abdomen and a six foot wing span...

I owe you big time sweetie. Let me know when you are going to be in London and I will take you out for the biggest night ever. Have sent you a little something in the meantime to say thank you.

Ex

Emily pulled on the brown fur slippers that accompanied the rest of the ludicrous outfit. One last thing before she could go. She hastily arranged to have a huge bouquet of pink champagne and lilies sent to the offices of Radio North. Just as she put the phone down, an email popped up in her inbox.

To: EBrighouse@Hobbs&Parker.com
From: Jem.im.a@RadioNorth.com
Subject: a thousand thank yous could never cover it...

Any time, my southern friend. Anyway, I couldn't have you getting sacked, could I? What would I do for laughs?

I told Derek D (great bloke by the way) that you came up with the plan and our promotions dept were more than happy to take some money off him.

Not sure how I can help you with the ASBO though! Good luck out there...

Jx

8

Emily sat on a bench outside the offices of yet another national newspaper. She was resting her brown slippered feet on a concrete planter. The red tights were now heavily snagged and the Velcro, which held the three foot proboscis onto her face mask, itched terribly. She was sweating profusely under the heavily padded fur abdomen and with a piece of thick black netting in front of her nose, her breathing was laboured.

Most of the women's magazines had greeted her with baffled stares, the odd snigger and a couple of saucy remarks from security guards. The tabloids were another matter. She took a wrong turn in the corridors of the Sunday Mirror and ended up in the middle of the Sports Desk. It was a skin crawling 5 minutes before she could find the exit. The Daily Sport had been the worst, chasing her round the office shouting 'strip' and then a terrible scene with her wings in the revolving door.

By the time she reached the foyer of ITZ magazines, quite a lot of the stuffing had come out of the red proboscis, which was now flaccid and dragging along behind her. It was understandable if the woman on reception was not taking her seriously. She gave her the name of the journalist she was booked in to see. The receptionist raised her eyebrows before lifting her phone. 'Linda, there's a 5 ft 7in turkey in reception, that says it wants to speak to you…' she stifled a giggle.

Emily, hot and irritated by this stage, attempted to explain that she was a mosquito and not a turkey. Her response was an incomprehensible muffle, behind the stifling head gear.

'Sorry love, I really can't hear a word.' The receptionist was not being helpful.

'I said I'm not a turkey! And I have an appointment with Linda Goodman.'

'What was that? Gobble? Gobble?' The receptionist was thrilled by her own wit.

Emily wrenched the massive headgear off. 'I'm not a fucking turkey, I'm a mosquito alright!'

The receptionist didn't hesitate. She raised one hand in the air. 'Security please!'

Emily really didn't see why it needed two security guards, one on either side, to eject her from the building. 'Come back at Christmas love!' they had laughed, as they lifted her off the ground and deposited her on the pavement outside the building. She had gathered up her bag of press releases and limped off to the next appointment.

Now, sweating and exhausted, she stretched out on the bench, just outside the offices of The Guardian. She was dragging heavily on a menthol cigarette, for the first time in two years – driven to it, she decided, by the accumulation of disasters, humiliations and impending fuck ups which currently affected every aspect of her life.

Of course she couldn't find a decent man! Who wants to go out with a giant, fucking chain smoking mosquito with an ASBO – a walking bloody disaster zone. It was fair to say that the initial euphoria of this morning had now worn off.

Emily tried to work out what positive comments she could put in her report. Even with her extensive blagging experience, this was going to be difficult. She flicked her ash into the plant pot. 'Daily Sport – 'greeted enthusiastically by the news desk." She sniggered to herself at the thought.

Just at that moment, Grania Wardman, Guardian Arts Correspondent, stepped out of a taxi at the entrance to the building. She was fresh from attending a fascinating exposé at the V&A – The influence of the Victorians on punk culture. Brian Sewell had hosted it. He had been on brilliant form.

By the time Emily spotted Grania, it was too late. She was a few feet away and there was nowhere to hide. She just had time to stub out her cigarette and take her feet off the plant pot like a naughty school girl.

'Emily? Is that Emily Bwighouse?' Grania had a speech impediment – a slight lisp and difficulty pronouncing her 'r's' , but this of course only increased her intellectual gravitas in media arts circles.

'Hi Grania, how are you!' Emily did her best to sound sincere.

Grania was standing right in front of her now. 'How gweat to thee you Emily.' She paused, looking her up and down.' But why are you dwethed as a turkey?'

Really no point going into the mosquito thing at this point. Emily was faced with a dilemma. Should she tell the super-bright and meteorically successful Grania, her Oxford graduate contemporary, that her career was not in fact flourishing in quite the same way as her own and that she was dressed like this in the hope of promoting an insect repellent to Grania's colleagues. She decided not.

'Oh God, this!' She tried to sound unphased. ' I'm not actually at work today. Mad fancy dress party, hilarious story, not worth going into.'

Grania seemed convinced. 'I don't think I've theen you thince gwaduation! I heard you were doing weally well in public welations.'

'Yah, no, really good.' Emily was almost nonchalant. 'I'm with Hobbs & Parker International Division, mostly corporate comms, a lot of clients in the City, that kind of stuff.'

Grania was impressed. 'God, thounds weally glamwus. Listen, I'd love to meet up. Let's thwap details. You mutht come to dinner!'

Forgetting for a second that she was dressed as a mosquito, Emily reached into her bag, to retrieve her mobile, but her enormous black mosquito mits made this impossible and instead, she tipped the bag off the bench, scattering Zappit Mosquito repellent press releases and promotional fly swatters all over the pavement.

'Let me help you.' Grania bent down and started gathering up the press releases.

Emily hastily stuffed them into her bag, but a few had made their way onto the flower beds next to them. She watched in horror as Grania retrieved the mud splattered pages.

'Here you are.' Grania handed them back to her. 'I've left my mobile on my desk, but I'll just scwibble your number down on the back of this shall I?' Emily nodded as Grania held onto one of the pages and wrote down Emily's number.'

'Tho lovely to thee you Emily, it'll be weally gweat to catch up.'

Emily watched Grania as she disappeared into The Guardian offices, clutching the back page of a Zappit press release. It was inevitable that Grania would at some point turn it around, read the moronic content and Emily's contact details at the bottom. The shame of it was almost too much to bear.

She heard her phone buzzing in her bag - a text from Pete. He had phoned Anoushka at home, to tell her the good news and they both wanted to celebrate.

'Emily where r u? We need a drink! A and I will come to u. Find the nearest pub and txt us'

Emily slung her headgear under her arm and went in search of a pub. She reckoned she'd seen enough journalists for one day. Anyway, what harm would a couple of drinks do….

To: EBrighouse@Hobbs&Parker.com
From: CForster-Blair@Hobbs&Parker.com
Subject: Zappit press coverage…

Emily
I am sitting at my desk looking at a press picture of you, spread-eagled over the wind screen of a taxi, in the act, it appears, of being run over. You are dressed in the Zappit mosquito outfit and the company's logo is clearly visible on your bottom. The client has just emailed me the Evening Standard cutting, which features the headline 'Splat!' – it's attached, in case you haven't seen it yet. I saw you come in this morning, so I take it your injuries are not serious. Emily, yet another client is furious and I am left to sort it out. I suppose it was naïve of me not to anticipate that you would get drunk, wearing the client's costume, but did you really have to do so in the nearest pub to one of the biggest media organisations in the UK?

Your career at H&P very much hangs in the balance Emily. Luckily for you, Derek called yesterday afternoon to say that he is doubling our fee on the Dewsbury account next year. But you really are on very thin ice at the moment.

I am too upset to speak to you today and there is little explanation you can give. I shall see you at the Le Voisier polo on Sunday. You and Anoushka need to be there on time, dressed smartly and remain sober throughout – all the top bods from Le V will be there. Look upon it as the opportunity for a fresh start, but I cannot emphasise enough, that you really cannot afford to put a foot wrong.

Clare

To: EBrighouse@Hobbs&Parker.com
From: Anoushka.Marchwood@Hobbs&parker.com
Subject: Splat!

Hi Emily

Have u seen the coverage – wow, fully branded! Sorry I couldn't stay with you longer in A&E. I gave the taxi driver £50 for his windscreen wipers – shall I charge it to the Zappit account? Hope you are not too bruised this morning. A x

To: EBrighouse@Hobbs&Parker.com
From: GWardman@guardianarts.co.uk
Subject: Dinner!

Hi Emily
Great to bump into you again! I found your email address on the bottom of your press release! So lovely to see you yesterday. Can you come for dinner on July 25th? Just a few media chums. You might remember Tasha Stevens from Oxford, who also has a column at The Guardian,

Marcus Lockwood from the Economist and Alistair Hollis,
who has just finished a superb biog of Pope Cedric IVth –
I'm hoping Gideon, a sculptor friend can also come down
from Scotland - should be a fascinating evening. We can
all catch up and find out what everyone's up to!

Can't wait!
Grania

Emily was actually rather relieved that Clare wasn't talking to her. It could be worse. As for the email from Grania – 'Can't wait!' Oh God, an evening with Grania and her 'media chums'. That really did go into Emily's 'Top Ten Situations To be Avoided at All Costs'. Straight in at No. 3, dinner with a bunch of condescending twats, handpicked to make her feel even more hopeless than she did already. She could regale everyone with stories of her career, promoting insect repellent, dressed as a cartoon character mosquito, while they swapped high powered stories about North Sea oil or the price of nickel or some other random world issue that Emily, quite frankly, knew fuck all about.

She stared at her screen. Too early to go home – how to amuse herself? Facebook or some random googling? She decided to google 'career issues.' There was certainly no shortage of advice.

Five strategies to deal with a career plateau…
Own Your Career. *It's your career – so take responsibility for it! You should set goals and create a strategy for moving forward and check each week that you are right on track!*

Perhaps she could ask Mean Monica to prepare a spreadsheet to measure her goals.

Consider Your Options. *This is a great time to determine what you really want. Do an honest assessment of the workplace behaviours that got you "here."*

Getting pissed mainly, if she was brutally honest.

Ask for Feedback. *Finding individuals in the workplace willing to provide honest and constructive feedback can sometimes be a challenge – remember to be open and receptive to their comments.*

That'll be Monica and Clare. She imagined they would be more than happy to provide 'constructive' feedback.

Develop your brand. *Constantly work to broaden your skill set; get actively involved in professional organizations, volunteer with non-profit groups, and seek board opportunities.*

Shag Tony Jennings…?

Form Authentic Relationships. *Move outside of your circle to connect with less familiar individuals. Ensure that your network is diverse. Allow others to really get to know you.*

Shag Neville from the post room…?

Crock of shite anyway…

She sighed. Maybe the answer was obvious. What she really needed to do was get out of this place. If she could make a fresh start in a new agency, she could reinvent herself and become the well thought of, professional, senior player she always knew she could be. How could she ever be taken seriously, doing PR for sausages and insect repellent.

To: EDunwoody@prsolutions.com
From: EBrighouse@Hobbs&Parker.com
Subject: Career opportunities...

Dear Elspeth
I have been with Hobbs & Parker for five years now, during which time, I have worked on some amazing, international brands across a diverse range of markets. We launched Kittybits Catfood into the UK market – you may remember our campaign around Gordon the talking cat? I have particular strength in the laundry and detergent market, having worked on a groundbreaking project for Dazzle White tabs and the 'Who does the housework in your home?' campaign for Vylux Handheld vacuum cleaners. I have full responsibility for the annual Top-ums Fish paste communication programme and most recently handled National Sausage Week for Dewsbury Pork. Rewarding though my time here has been, I feel it may now be time to move on, develop my skill set further and explore other opportunities. I am currently a Junior Account Director. I attach an updated copy of my CV and look forward to discussing any suitable opportunities you may have.

Many thanks
Emily Brighouse

To: EBrighouse@Hobbs&Parker.com
From: EDunwoody@prsolutions.com
Subject: Career opportunities...

Dear Emily
Great stuff! Good to hear from you! No problem at all.
It's a really strong market right now and we have loads
of opportunities for someone of your experience. I'll be in
touch with a list of options.

Elspeth

Well, that was heartening at least. She would soon be snapped up by another agency. As she traipsed the well trodden route from the tube to the flat, she was feeling a little weary, hungover and unusually for Emily, a bit depressed. The events of the last 48 hours had taken their toll. She still had her job and a place to live, for the moment at least, but life just seemed a bit more of a struggle for her than it was for other people. They were all problems of her own making - she realised that. Oh God, why did it feel like Clare F-B's voice had crawled inside her hungover head.

She opened the door to the flat, no sign of Bella yet. She glanced at the Tube Map of Shame. By rights, she should probably pop a blue pin on Kings Cross, near enough the exact spot where she had spread-eagled herself across the windscreen of the black cab in her mosquito suit and slid slowly off, still clutching the windscreen wiper. Yes, that should indeed qualify her for a new drawing pin, but it was looking a bit crowded to be honest. If they carried on like this, they'd need a new map.

Her phone buzzed in her bag – 1 new message.

Where the hell r u? I'm in the S&F with YOUR date.
u were supposed to meet Charlie here at 7! he came
round to the flat to find u. running out of things to say.
Come quick! Bels x

Shit! That's all she needed. She had completely forgotten. He had emailed her a couple of times since the unfortunate snogging debacle outside Hamilton's. She had arranged to meet him for an early evening drink at the Snog & Fuck – noisy, packed bar, unromantic venue, close to home, potential for quick getaway – perfect.

She looked at herself in the bathroom mirror. Dear God, the strain of being Emily was beginning to show. She reached for the bronzer and brushed it liberally over her face. A quick squirt of Bella's new perfume and she grabbed her bag and headed off for the pub.

Charlie and Bella were sitting in the beer garden. She tried to sound upbeat as she approached them. 'So sorry Charlie! I got held up at work. Hi Bels! What can I get you both to drink?'

Charlie wouldn't hear of being bought a drink and insisted on going to the bar himself. Such a nice bloke! He was wearing a pale blue open necked shirt, beige chinos with a pronounced crease down the front and very shiny brown brogues. It had obviously been smart casual day in the City today.

He was safely out of the way, but Bella still lowered her voice. 'Did you forget you were meeting him?'

'Yes I did.' Emily replied, genuinely grateful. 'Thanks for bringing him to the pub.'

'That's OK.' Bella smiled. 'I'll leave you after this drink.'

Emily looked horrified. 'No you will not.' She spoke through gritted teeth. 'You stay exactly where you are.'

'No way Em, I'm knackered.' Bella was not to be swayed. 'I'm not playing gooseberry. I was looking forward to a night in.'

'Please Bella!' Emily was starting to sound desperate. 'He's as much your friend as mine.'

'Hardly sweetie. I haven't slept with him for a start.' Bella smirked.

Emily knew she was losing the battle. Bella could be very stubborn, but she honestly didn't think she could get through this without her. 'OK. Let's cut to the chase here, Bella. What will it take to make you stay?' She pleaded.

'Nothing, I'm off in five minutes.'

Emily tried to think of something, anything to give her some leverage. 'My new Zara dress. It's yours.' She knew she was clutching at straws.

Bella rolled her eyes.

'With the shoes?' Emily added, desperately.

'No. Emily.' Bella was adamant. 'You created this situation. You didn't have to agree to meet him again. Deal with it!' It occurred to her that Bella was rather enjoying this.

'Oh God, Bels he's coming back. I've got a massive hangover. You can't do this to me. I'm actually begging you.' Emily shot her a last desperate look.

Bella leant towards her. 'He's come all the way over from the other side of London to see you. The least you can do is talk to him for an hour or so.' Her face softened a little. 'He's really nice Em. Give him a chance.'

Charlie was walking back towards them. Emily only had a few seconds. 'OK, here's the deal. You can go in ten minutes, but only if you promise to text me in one hour, with a bloody good reason why I have to leave immediately. And try and make it believable.'

Bella muttered 'I'll see what I can do.' He was back at the table with a tray of drinks.

Bella seemed to drain her glass of wine with unnecessary haste and finally she left them. They watched her walk away. There was a pause. Emily struggled for something to say.

'How was work?' She knew it was a crashingly dull start.

Charlie smiled benignly. 'I was at an FSA compliance training session all day.' It was at this point, that she would normally reach for her wine and knock back most of the glass, but the hangover was slowing her down.

'Oh right. What was it about?' This was desperate now. She stifled a yawn.

'It was all about implementing the Alternative Investment Fund Managers' Directive. You'd have loved it.' He laughed. 'What about you? Been on any blind dates recently?'

Oh thank God, anything to get off that subject. 'No, no I've managed to avoid them.' She tried to keep it light. 'Did you notice how quickly I recognised you this evening?'

'Yes, I was impressed.' He paused. 'But then I was sitting with your flat mate, so you did have a sporting chance.'

They smiled at each other and suddenly it was all OK. The conversation was playful and if she wasn't mistaken, mildly flirtatious. Two plates of nachos and a couple of glasses of wine later and they were giggling like old friends. So much so, that she hardly noticed her phone buzzing on the table.

'That's yours I think.' Charlie passed it to her. Only ten minutes later than instructed, Bella's text came through. She took it from him and read the message.

mr tibbles has been run over. a neighbour found his body. can you come home now. Bels x

'Oh NO!'

'What is it?' He looked concerned.

As if too pained to speak, Emily showed him the text. She was almost not acting, because by now she was really rather enjoying herself and had forgotten her desperate plea to Bella.

'God, that's awful.' Charlie looked appalled.

She looked at the ground. 'Thanks Charlie, I think I'd better go.' She pecked him on the cheek.

'Yes of course. I'm really sorry about your cat, Emily. I'll call you.'

'Sure, thanks.' She actually felt quite guilty now, as she trudged back home.

Five minutes later, she walked into the flat. Bella was sprawled across the sofa watching TV.

Emily sat down beside her. 'Mr Tibbles, Bella?'

Bella shrugged her shoulders. 'I was tired, it was the best I could do.'

'You're a very sick woman, Bella Jenkins.' Emily started to laugh.

'He'll probably buy you a kitten now!' Bella snorted.

'Well, we'll know what to call it, won't we!' Emily replied as she headed onto the patio with her handbag.

Bella eyed her suspiciously. 'Have you started smoking again Emily?'

'No I haven't' Emily lied . 'I'm just going out to bury Mr Tibbles.'

9

It was Sunday, the day of the all important polo match and Emily was feeling quite proud of herself. She had gone to bed early on Saturday night, after only one glass of wine and was almost cheerful, considering that this was a working weekend. They had been picked up at the train station by a very smart, chauffeur driven 4x4. And now, as the black Range Rover swept around the corner into yet another field, Emily thought she had never seen such a beautiful sight. Wintersbourne Polo Club shimmered in the morning sunshine. Fields of bright green, perfectly manicured polo pitches, horses tethered to a string, encircling a picture perfect oak tree. Row upon row of shining silver trucks lined up, while skittish ponies were cantered up and down by their grooms. Le Voisier's purple logo fluttered proudly above the largest silk lined marquee she had ever seen.

A day which had begun without promise, a luke warm coffee with Anoushka on the 8.31 from Kings Cross, was suddenly looking rather wonderful. Hob-nobbing with a few journalists at lunch, a glass or two of Pimm's and the fast train home. No wonder Clare so jealously guarded her client list – this was how PR should be!

Bella had insisted on 'styling her'. Important to get the look just right, she had said, after the disasters of the last few weeks. Apparently you have to try very hard to look like you haven't tried too hard. Bella should know of course – she got to go to film premiers as part of her job. In the end, Bella's pale grey chiffon dress, matching pashmina and killer heels struck just the right note – sexy but not tarty. 'Emily you look beautiful!' Bella had declared triumphantly.

Of course walking required quite a lot of concentration, teetering just high enough above the ground, to prevent 4 inch heels from sinking into the grass. At least she only had to make it the short distance from the car to the picket fenced VIP area.

She was studying the ground so intently that she hardly noticed the sound of hooves a few feet in front of her. 'Get out of my bloody way' shouted an angry voice on horseback. Emily lurched backwards just in time to see a stunning girl cantering past.

She looked back at Emily with pure contempt, mouthing 'for fuck's sake' in her general direction.

With some relief, she made it to the safety of the tent. Clare was already there of course, clucking around, air kissing and barking orders at the photographer. Anoushka was hovering over by the seating plan. Emily walked up beside her and quickly scanned the board for their names. At least they were on the same table, that was OK then. But her relief was shortlived when she realised that Clare had placed her right next to the CEO of Le Voisier - Hector Braun no less. Clare breezed past, just close enough to breathe down her neck, 'Remember what I said Emily, best behaviour!'

'Of course, Clare.' Emily replied, through fixed smile and the three of them walked off to find their seats.

She looked around the table. Anoushka had assembled a motley group of the usual hacks – all there for the free champagne and luxury brand Le Voisier goody bags, except perhaps for that very horsey woman from Polo News. To her right, the shopping editor from Your Style magazine, Roisin O'Donnell. She was a larger than life Irish lady, bright red lipstick and jet black 'monk's fringe', accessorised to the hilt, a barrel of a body swathed in yards of printed silks.

Brimming over with good intentions, Emily once again mustered her sincerest PR smile and turned to Le Voisier's CEO, 'It's Hector isn't it? I'm Emily Brighouse. Very good turnout from the media, we should be able to get some great coverage for Le Voisier.' She gushed.

He was a good looking man, short grey hair and a slight tan, mid 50s she guessed and perfectly groomed in a pale blue shirt and a cream linen suit. He kissed the air rather theatrically either side of her face. 'Stuff that my darling,' he whispered, 'We don't sponsor the polo for the media, we do it for the gorgeous bums! Isn't that right John? Where is he? John, come over here and meet Ms Emily Brighouse. Emily, this is John, my partner.'

Emily shook his hand and felt herself relax. Oh thank God, this was going to be so much more fun than she had thought.

Hector gestured for her to come and sit down and reached over for a bottle of Champagne. 'Now tell us all about Clare,' he said in a stage whisper. 'John and I are absolutely petrified of her – we think she's a dominatrix in her spare time. Do you think she keeps her fiancée in a cupboard, all dressed in leather and zips?'

He poured her a glass of Champagne. She knew she shouldn't, but already good intentions were slipping away as she turned to Hector. 'Actually Hector, I think it's worse than that…' she whispered, to the obvious delight of her companions.

Their conversation was interrupted by a voice over the loudspeaker, announcing the start of the first chukka and they ambled out together into the sunshine. The game was underway and Emily couldn't help laughing to herself, when she thought how much she had been dreading today. Instead, here she was in seventh heaven, sipping champagne under a silk lined awning, giggling with two gay men and watching eight god-like creatures galloping past, sticks flying. There was no need to listen to the official commentary, with Hector right beside her, who seemed to know the inside story on every player. He was also quite adept at following her gaze.

'Now La Piru's number two is a bigger queen than me, so don't bother with him. Ah, but I can see your eye has already been drawn to the big prize, Hacienda's No.3. Jerome Armstrong - beautiful isn't he!'

Emily, awestruck, found herself nodding silently in agreement, unable to take her eyes off the field.

Hector carried on. 'I believe his mother was Portuguese. Father has a farm and polo yard in Northumberland. I presented him with the trophy last year and he actually kissed my hand.'

Hector and Emily looked at each other and sighed simultaneously, before bursting out laughing.

It was the third chukka now and Hacienda were just ahead of La Piru. The voice on the loudspeaker was going berserk. A brilliant nearside shot to goal from No.3 nudged them into the lead and more importantly, afforded Emily a very good close up. He galloped past, grinning and pumping the air in triumph with his stick – 'Good God', muttered Emily and even Hector and John were momentarily silenced.

Hector broke the spell. 'Come along Emily, follow me! I find one cannot stomp a divot, without something to drink in the hand'. She didn't have the slightest clue what he was talking about, probably best not to ask. He handed her a glass of pink Champagne and she followed dutifully as he strode off towards the polo pitch.

It was all quite confusing really, some kind of strange ritual. Apparently the spectators were expected to go round treading any loose turf back into the ground. She couldn't keep up with Hector, on account of her killer heels, but once she'd got the hang of it, she happily teetered around pressing in the soil with her toes and trying to stay upright.

It could have been muscle fatigue in the calves or just the quantity of pink Champagne she had drunk, but halfway across the polo field, she could no longer hold her heels the necessary one inch above the turf. As she felt 4 inches of Jimmy Choo stiletto sink slowly into the soft ground, she had to try quite hard not to panic. A glass of Champagne in one hand and her feet firmly rooted to the spot. Think Emily, think! There must be a logical solution - surely just a question of co-ordination. She was strapped firmly into the shoes - three buckles on each ankle. If she dropped the glass down by her side and then very discreetly bent her knees, she might be able to squat long enough to undo each of the six buckles. The only thing was, the dress was actually rather tight.

Clare sauntered past with the horsey woman from Polo News. Emily sometimes thought Clare had a sixth sense for when she was about to let the side down. 'Hi', said Emily weakly, raising her glass – Clare shot her a warning look. Again she struggled, pulling first on one heel and then the other – nothing. Bugger! What she really needed was some leverage, something or someone to hold onto. But by this time the commentator was urging everyone to leave the field. She could just about make out the voice on the loudspeaker.

Thank you Ladies and Gentleman for helping us preserve this magnificent polo ground. The players are about to start. If you could please take your seats for what promises to be a thrilling second half of the Le Voisier Cup Final.

She was pretty much alone now on the pitch, a hundred eyes in the stands and VIP tent watching her. Any minute now, they would want to start the game. She began to panic. There was nothing for it, but to attempt the downward slide towards her feet. But just as she almost reached the squat position, her fingers tantalisingly close to the ankle straps, she lost her balance and lurched forwards, arms flailing like a turbo powered windmill. She only just managed to get her hands down in front of her to stop herself from headbutting the turf. She was on all fours now, trapped in position, like a sprinter in the blocks. Oh God, the front of her dress drooped open, revealing flesh coloured bra – if she tried to lift one arm, she risked rolling sideways and breaking an ankle. All eyes on her, she cut a lonely figure in the middle of the field.

It occurred to her that if she walked her hands backwards, she could roll herself up again into standing position. She was sure she'd done this in a yoga class once, but obviously not with her heels fixed in position and her toes pointing skyward. Oh my God, excruciating pain in both calves. The net effect of the hand walking was that her bum was now pointing right up in the air and her entire body was balancing on the tips of her fingers. There was no longer a discreet way out of this. Lifting her head as much as she could, there was nothing for it but to muster a tiny and pathetic 'help', 'help'.

And then through her legs she saw them, her saviours, Hector and John. Like camp superheroes, they sashayed at an impressive pace across the field. Linen jackets flapping like caped crusaders, they ran to her assistance, heaving her out of the grass and hoisting her into a fireman's lift.

Hector was clearly delighted. 'Really Emily, no need to get into doggy position just yet!' He sniggered.

They held her aloft, unnecessarily high she thought and delivered her across the pitch and back to her seat, to the sound of applause and cheers from the watching crowd.

Clare was there in an instant. 'Oh well done, Emily, well done. I believe you've stolen the show again', she spat out under her breath, clearly incensed. Emily imagined she would hear more on the subject from Clare, when they were back at work. 'Best behaviour, Emily!' She had said. The words were still ringing in her ears. Strictly speaking, being carried across the polo pitch in a fireman's lift, by the CEO of your client company was probably not what Clare had meant.

Mercifully, the players cantered onto the pitch and play commenced.

By the sixth chukka Hacienda were well ahead. Emily, Hector and John sat spellbound as No.3, cantering up to the string of ponies, leapt from one horse to another mid-chukka, and galloped back onto the field, to secure a final triumphant goal.

Champagne flowed and the volume increased. Hector was easily the loudest. 'Clare!' he shouted across the table, 'We demand to have Emily on our account. Why have you kept her from us for so long?' Emily winced. She was sober enough to realise how this would go down. Clare was tight lipped but smiling. By this time, the larger than life 'Your Style' journalist was out cold, her cheek resting on a side plate. Hector was decorating her hair with strawberries and asparagus spears. He turned to Emily, clearly pleased with his efforts. 'Rather Rubenesque don't you think?'

Emily made a half hearted attempt to sound professional, 'Hector, I think you should treat members of the press with a bit more respec…' but her voice trailed off.

What could only be described as the most beautiful man she had ever seen, strode towards them. It was No.3. Shoulder length curly dark hair now damp with sweat, green eyes flashing, muscular thighs straining out of white jeans. He stopped at their table and looked around. She realised her mouth was open and she made a determined effort to shut it and muster some composure.

When he spoke, his voice was not what she expected. It was deep and sexy, but with a hint of a Northumbrian lilt. 'I heard you lot were from Hobbs & Parker, is that right?' How on earth did he know the name of her Company. How bizarre. The whole table stared inanely, no one thinking to answer him.

He tried again. 'Is Emily Brighouse here?' Every head turned towards her and for a moment, she forgot that she was in fact Emily Brighouse.

Anoushka was also unable to speak, but managed to point to Emily.

Seconds later, to the astonishment of the entire table, he lifted her out of her seat and swept her up towards him. Emily was rigid with shock as he deposited her on the ground next to him. If she hadn't seen him play polo, she could easily have believed that he was a stripper-gram. Or maybe she was being secretly filmed, for a reality TV show. The way her life had been going recently, nothing would surprise her.

He was grinning at her like he thought he knew her. 'Emily this is long overdue.' His tanned arms outstretched, he folded her into his damp, warm chest and just there and then, she wanted to die of happiness. Whatever mistake had led to this, she didn't really care, no need to clear up the confusion just yet. Eventually emerging from the paradise of his torso, her face clearly betrayed complete astonishment.

'Emily, it's me! It's Jem!' He looked at her searchingly.

'Who?' She replied, still utterly baffled.

'What do you mean who?' He was sounding quite affronted now. 'It's Jem, Radio North Jem, you're only northern friend, remember?'

So now this polo player, this quite obviously male polo player, was claiming to be her email confidante, Jemima. Why would he do that? She felt like Alice in Wonderland. Maybe someone had slipped something into her drink.

'Are you OK Emily?' He looked concerned.

Her mind was starting to explore the smallest possibility that this could be Jem. What if it was true and she had in fact been emailing a six foot polo player for two years. How else would he know any of this? And then horrified, she started to recall the emails, the explicit subject lines, the confessions, her innermost fears. She had treated her, him, the remote northern friend she thought she'd never meet, like some sort of virtual confidante. She didn't even know it, but her hands instinctively covered her mouth. The hairs stood up on the back of her neck. How could she have made such a mistake?

'But Jem?' She uttered weakly. 'You're supposed to be a girl!'

'I hardly think so darling!' Hector sniggered from the seat behind.

And still, she couldn't get to grips with it. Her friend Jemima, her girlfriend Jemima from Radio North, with whom she had shared everything, every one night stand, Mosquito outfit, ASBO summons, frustrated romance, career low, in fact every thought and deed, was in fact a six foot bloke. She played back some of the emails in her head. Where were the clues? How had she missed them?

'Any more dirty stop outs you need to report – come on, get it off your chest, I need a laugh?'

The words went round and round. Why had she thought he was a girl, how could she have been so stupid?

'But hang on a second. You said your name was Jemima? And you're supposed to be a journalist?' Slowly a little clarity was returning.

'I am a journalist', he replied, 'but it's Jerome. I play polo at the weekends.' He was looking at her very strangely now.

She realised she needed to regain some composure. She wasn't very good at looking cool at the best of times, let alone when she was genuinely gobsmacked.

'But why didn't you say that you were a man?' Emily's voice trailed off as she realised how pointless that sounded.

'Why would I? I didn't know you thought I was a girl' he threw his head back laughing. 'Emily, you're a mad woman.' But he saw her face had drained of colour and poured her a glass of water. 'Come over here and sit down, he gestured to a bench by the entrance.

She sipped slowly on her drink, still trying to find flaws in his story. 'How did you know I was here?'

I heard someone say that Hobbs & Parker were organising this and when I saw you on all fours on the polo field, I just thought 'that's got to be Brighouse!' and sure enough, it was you!'

In between staring open mouthed, she scoured her memory for clues, but all she could think of were lines in her emails.

'You know everything.' Her face flushed. 'There's nothing I didn't tell you.'

'I'm so sorry Emily, I genuinely didn't know that you thought I was a woman!' He put his hand on hers. 'Look, I love hearing about all your adventures. I hope it doesn't change anything.' He looked slightly crestfallen.

'Of course not.' She lied, still racking her brains. Then it came to her. 'But your email address? It says something like 'Jemima@radionorth'.'

'Oh I see, yes, that's true! It actually stands for Jerome Ignacio Marques Armstrong. I think some smart arse in Radio North's IT department thought it would be funny, when they set up my email.'

She knew she needed to snap out of it. Maybe this was another monumental cock up in the life of Emily Brighouse. But quite frankly, the most beautiful man she had ever seen was sitting right next to her, his hand squeezing hers – this was no time to get hung up on gender. Time to pull herself together and make the best of it. And try not to think about the enormous nervous rash, which must by now be spreading across her chest and neck.

'Well thanks very much for saving my job anyway.' She said, attempting a little nonchalance.

'Any time, my love. And thank you for the lilies and champagne by the way, now half the news desk thinks I'm gay!'

Hector, who had tipped his chair back so that he could hear them better, raised his eyebrows and inhaled deeply at the thought.

'Oh God I doubt it!' Now she was laughing, a little hysterically. She didn't notice the whole table straining to hear them.

'So how did it all work out with sausage-gate?' He stared, smiling, straight into her eyes.

'Very well, actually. Derek Dewsbury doubled the size of the account and we're up for a PR industry award, which should be yours really. I'll let you know if we get shortlisted.' She was gabbling a little breathlessly now.'

He looked over to the table and lowered his voice. 'So that must be Clare Forster Blair with the swishy hair and Anoushka I think?' He turned back and looked at her intently. 'In fact Emily, you are the only one I had got completely wrong. You are not at all what I expected, from your descriptions of yourself, you're far more…'

'Jem!' A voice shouted from the other side of the marquee. His sentence was cut off in mid air, as a stunning brunette strode resolutely towards them. Emily realised immediately that it was 'stunning bitch, canter girl'.

'Jem! There you are!' She wrapped her arms around his neck, her cool gaze meeting Emily's as she spoke. 'Well aren't you going to introduce us, Jem?'

'Oh yes sorry Frankie, this is Emily Brighouse!' Jem replied. 'And Emily, this is my girlfriend, Frankie.'

Emily felt herself flush as Frankie looked her up and down. 'Oh how hilarious! Emily Brighouse no less!' She sneered, before turning her back on Emily. 'Jem darling, they want to give you your trophy. They've been waiting for ages. They need you and Hector outside.'

Jem gestured as if to say, 'I'll be back' and offered an arm to a delighted Hector.

Frankie turned back to Emily, 'Well it's good to finally meet you Emily. Jem has told me so much about you.' There was a stilted silence, before Frankie continued. 'He can't believe your antics, none of us can. You're quite famous at Radio North you know! I think we're all waiting for the press release, 'Emily Brighouse wakes up in her own flat!'

Emily, stunned, could offer no reply, but once again Frankie filled the gap.

'Jem hates things like this – ghastly, drunk punters dressed up to the nines. None of them know anything about horses. Do you ride?' She smiled sweetly.

'Absolutely.' Emily replied.

Absolutely not, would have been closer to the truth.

Frankie obviously thought she'd made her point. 'Well, lovely to meet you and keep sending us the ridiculous surveys!' She strutted off out of the marquee, leaving Emily staring after her muttering "I will" to herself. She felt like she had just sustained some kind of assault and was almost grateful when Clare F-B swooshed up.

'Emily, I need you and Anoushka to leave immediately and take that Your Style journalist with you.' Clare was stage whispering again. 'She's blind drunk and I think she's wet herself. For God's sake get her out of here. There's a taxi waiting. I'll help you get her in.'

Between the three of them, they just about managed to heave her up and into the car. As the journalist slumped onto her, Emily looked longingly out of the window. Luckily the effort of delivering a semi comatose 16 stone woman into a train seat preoccupied her for much of the next hour.

It was only when Anoushka went to the buffet car that she finally let the tears slide down her face. Catching sight of her mournful expression in the train window, she reflected on Frankie's words, 'He can't believe your antics', she had said. She was the laughing stock of Radio North and the friend she had confided in thought she was ridiculous. Maybe Clare F-B was right. She didn't deserve a decent man. And now there wasn't even any Jemima to console her when she got back to work.

'I'm really sorry love, I think I'm going to be sick.' Roisin lurched forward and all Emily could think of was to throw off her wrap and offer it to the stricken journalist. Roisin was true to her word. 'Oh Jesus love, I've puked on your genuine, feckin' pashmina!' she exclaimed as the next wave of nausea overcame her.

Roisin finally stopped being sick as the train entered Peterborough station. 'Oh God, I'm utterly mortified, Emily!'

'Don't even think about it Roisin, honestly. 'There but for the grace of God go I' and all that!' Emily smiled, handing her a bottle of water. The train pulled into Kings

Cross. They said goodbye to Anoushka, who was catching a tube and Emily flagged down a taxi, so that she could drop Roisin off at her Hampstead flat.

'You're a lovely girl, Emily, thanks for looking after me. I owe you one.' Roisin stumbled gratefully out of the taxi and waved to Emily as the taxi turned round and headed off to Fulham.

Clutching a plastic bag containing her vomit soaked scarf, Emily opened the door to her flat. No sign of Bella to lift her spirits. She stared at the 'Tube Map of Shame' pinned to the hall notice board.

Inspired by those WW2 films, where uniformed WRAF women with perfectly coiffed hair, move flags round a map at Bomber Command. Theirs was a shoddy version indeed - a diary of ignominy – a few one night stands here and there, but mostly just shameful episodes involving some sort of alcohol fuelled, public humiliation. Every incident had been carefully recorded with a drawing pin in the appropriate tube stop – red for Bella, Blue for Emily. She noticed that Bella had updated the map with Bethnal Green in blue – the whole map was looking decidedly blue. Not as blue as she felt right now.

Of course, Jem Armstrong knew all about the 'tube map of shame'. In fact, he knew about every date she had been on for the last two years. He knew about every confrontation with their long suffering landlord, he even knew about their orange bathroom suite.

And every detail of her desperate, sad, single existence as it now seemed, was probably cc'd around the offices of Radio North, for the amusement of all.

Well that was that. She would bring an end to the email confessional and she realised sadly, to the friendship. And not, she decided, because he was a man. He may have gone out of his way to help her, but meeting him today changed everything. She felt betrayed and humiliated and strangely bereaved.

It would be radio silence from now on, at least no more revelations would be coming his way, for the entertainment of all. At very least, she could try to be dignified.

Her phone buzzed – here we go, a telling off from Clare F-B no doubt.

To: *EBrighouse@Hobbs&Parker.com*
From: *hectorbraun@levoisier.com*
Subject: *No.3!*

Darling girl,
How dare you leave without saying goodbye! We're in the car now. Couldn't help myself - did some detective work! No. 3 works at Radio North as a producer. Has been with Frankie for 6 months, she's his boss! A she-devil apparently! She was watching when you buried your head in his sweaty pecks by the way! He did a journalism scholarship in Canada and was offered a job on Newsnight. Turned it down to be close to his sick mother, who died last year. So he's a doting son and going places in journalism! Surely he must be gay! You looked so good nestled in his chest, I nearly wept with envy...this could be the start of something gorgeous...he was looking for you after the cup presentation!
Lunch soon? Will be in touch

Hector x
Sent from my iphone

10

Emily and Bella were still slightly shell shocked. It was 11 o'clock and they had both taken the morning off work to attend the court hearing. They walked together down the steps of Fulham and Hammersmith Magistrates Court, neither of them speaking.

Bella broke the silence. 'Well, that was humiliating. I wasn't expecting the photographic evidence, were you?'

Emily shook her head. 'No I wasn't! All those photographs and a log of our activities! I'd forgotten we even had some of those parties. And I thought some of the descriptions of indecency and intoxication were a bit OTT, didn't you? I mean, I can accept that we caused 'distress' playing loud music, but 'alarm' seemed a bit far fetched.' She was upset and gabbling.

'I don't know Em,' Bella looked at her. 'Have you seen yourself topless?'

They both burst out laughing, but quickly stopped themselves, conscious of showing appropriate remorse so soon after leaving the court. True to form, Bella was taking it rather better than Emily, who was still affronted by some of the judge's comments. 'It made us look like we were having some kind of orgy.' She was flustered. 'I mean, I only did it for the bet. It was £100 for God's sake.'

'I know', Bella smirked. 'But I don't think the Judge felt that was a legitimate defence, Em.' Emily had always admired how composed Bella remained in these situations. There had been many, severe reprimands over the years and Bella's cool indifference could still provide a subtle note of defiance.

Silence again, before Bella began, 'Seriously though, did you check out the police officer?'

Emily pretended to look shocked. 'Bella, for God's sake! There's a dating website for people like you.'

'He was gorgeous though, wasn't he!' Bella laughed.

The judge had found no extenuating family circumstances to take into account, nothing to be done but lower their heads in shame, as DI Thomas read out the humiliating list of 'unbecoming incidents' to the magistrate, in mortifying detail.

'At least we didn't get a criminal record though'. Emily tried to sound positive.

Bella was more realistic. 'Yes, but we will if we break the ASBO restrictions and I don't see how we're going to manage not to break them.'

'It'll be fine, we'll just have to make a few changes.' Emily was ever the optimist.

'A few changes! Are you kidding?' Bella raised her eyebrows. 'No music after 9pm, no drinking of intoxicating liquor within 100 metres of the flat, no more than 2 guests in the house at any one time... for two years!'

'Yes, well.' Emily tried to think of something to say. 'We're just going to have to be very selective from now on.'

'Selective! We're going to have to move, Emily!'

Now it was Emily's turn to be realistic. 'Oh yes and I'm sure our future landlord won't be at all put off, when the routine checks bring up the conditions of our ASBO. And Mrs Vassiliadis is bound to give us a glowing reference!'

Bella was looking at her watch, not really listening. 'OK, Em, I've got to get back to work. We'll talk about it later.'

'OK. See you Bels.' They stood at the bottom of the steps, about to go their separate ways when Emily remembered. 'Oh shit, I forgot. I have to have a quick drink after work with sausage lord Derek Dewsbury. He's coming in for an update and we're supposed to be celebrating after. Nightmare!'

Bella smiled. 'Well, try not to come home drunk or topless. I'll see you later.'

Back at her desk and Emily avoided opening her emails for a while. The magistrate's words were still playing in her head and she hadn't even let herself think about the humiliation of the polo. Her response to this morning's events, would normally have been an email to Jemima and she immediately felt sad at the thought. She wondered if she would hear from him and what he would say. Finally she opened her inbox.

To: EBrighouse@Hobbs&Parker.com
From: Jem.im.a@RadioNorth.com
Subject: Manhood...

Emily
Very good to meet you on Sunday. You left before I could say goodbye properly. Forgive me if I gave you the impression I was a girl! It honestly wasn't intentional. I hope this doesn't mean you won't tell me every salacious detail of your latest escapades. How's it going with 'fanny' the chinless hooray? Derek Dewsbury? Did you have your court appearance today? Tell all...

Jem x (just to be clear, that's Jerome)

It was just as she had expected. He could carry on as normal. She on the other hand, was clearly just an object of ridicule. She had been rehearsing her reply in her head most of the night. How to sound unaffected, dignified and slightly less the comedy buffoon? How strange – a week ago that same email address popping up in her inbox would have given her an instant smile.

To: *Jem.im.a@RadioNorth.com*
From: *EBrighouse@Hobbs&Parker.com*
Subject: Manhood...
Jem,
Really good to meet you too! The court appearance is in a few weeks. Going quite well with Charlie actually, another dinner this week, I suppose we're pretty much an item. Thanks again for all your help – looks like I'm being promoted next month! One step away from the Board – who would have thought!

Em x

She was pleased with her response. The tone was just right, slightly less tragic. A couple of white lies to put a spin on her otherwise pitiful love life and career – she was in PR after all. She imagined Charlie would be quite bemused by the description of them as an 'item'. She felt a sense of satisfaction and went to make a cup of tea. She tried not to look at her inbox when she returned. Why should she care if he replied. No new emails for a while. Twenty minutes later, still nothing, she pressed 'refresh'. Finally a new message appeared.

To: EBrighouse@Hobbs&Parker.com
From: Jem.im.a@RadioNorth.com
Subject: Manhood...

Em, that's great about your promotion and Charlie!
Sorry I didn't mean to sound rude about your man – your
descriptions are too good. Don't get too senior – send me
a survey at least...

Jx

Dignity restored. There, that was easy. A high flying PR executive, board director in waiting, with a steady and increasingly serious relationship, with a boyfriend who happens to be heavily involved no less, in running the international money markets, or something along those lines. She almost believed it herself. Laugh no more my northern pen pal! She took a sip of tea. There was an unopened email from headhunter, Elspeth Dunwoody. No doubt it would outline a series of lucrative career options. She settled into her chair to review them in detail.

To: EBrighouse@Hobbs&Parker.com
From: EDunwoody@prsolutions.com
Subject: Career opportunities...

Hi Emily,
Listen, I had excellent feedback on your cv, from a couple of HR contacts in some really great companies. In fact, they were both so impressed by your cv that they googled you, which seems to be the norm these days! Unfortunately they both came back to say that you are not really the candidate for them.

Having reviewed the online content they were talking about, I think we need to look at some Search Engine Optimisation for you – I can get my IT guys to look into it. The Youtube stuff we might have to live with - I think it was the taxi windscreen shot that caused the real problem.

I think our best bet is for you to hang fire for a while. Stay put for now, look at consolidating your position at H&P, broaden your client base, really network those senior colleagues – you must be in line for a promotion in the next couple of years?

Be in touch.
Elspeth

In other words, Emily was forced to conclude, she wouldn't touch her with a shitty stick. Promotion? Oh yes, in the unlikely event that she were to hold onto her job and stay out of trouble, she might be looking at a promotion to the appropriately titled SAD - Senior Account Director - in two years. Or she could just shoot herself now. Oh my God, if one of the most pushy recruitment consultants in London wouldn't touch her, she really was up the creek.

'Morning Emily!', Clare F-B wafted past her desk, looking at her watch. 'I hope you haven't forgotten we are going out with Derek Dewsbury tonight. I'm going to give him a quick update and then I'll get reception to buzz you when we're finished.' She started to walk off before stopping right by her desk. 'Oh and Emily, Tony Jennings has decided to join us, so do be very careful what you say. Bear in mind what I said about your promotion last week.'

Randy Tony! Emily winced at the thought of the infamous CEO of H&P. The plummy, perma-tanned silver fox. Famous for appearing without warning at the side of your desk and whispering slightly too close to your ear.

'And what exactly do you do for us, my dear?'

Emily had so wished she had the gall to reply 'Bugger all, Tony! But just like every other graduate trainee, she had blustered her way through her list of clients, at which point the pervy old saddo had uttered his stock response, 'I do believe you're blushing, Emily'.

Everyone at H&P knew what it meant to be asked to join him for drinks, in his penthouse office on a Friday night and partake of his generous minibar facilities. By some miracle, Emily had managed to stay under the radar, until that is, the 'Pants in Bethnal Green 'reply all' email disaster'.

This would be fine though, she told herself. She would have nanny Clare as chaperone and northern sausage magnate, Derek Dewsbury in tow. She hadn't met Derek, but her mental picture wasn't great. She had only met Dennis Dewsbury, Derek's dad. He was a short, plump, jovial man with a massive, red veined nose, looking uncannily like one of his pork products. Dennis was a lovely client. A couple of articles a month in Pig Farmer magazine and he was a happy man. But now that Derek was in charge, everything had changed. He insisted on daily phone updates, weekly email round ups of national press coverage secured and anticipated. If she got him in The Times, Derek wanted to know why it wasn't on the front page.

She had hoped that last week's coverage would have shut him up for a while. One morning he gave 15 radio interviews in 3 hours. Most people would have had to lie down in a darkened room, but not Derek. He phoned straight afterwards to discuss the next day's 'plan of action'. She had unleashed a media monster. The National Sausage Week debacle meant that 56 million potential sausage buyers had now heard of Dewsbury Pork Products. Was he satisfied? Was he hell. The man now thought he was Branson. 'But how are we going to keep up this momentum, Emily?' A couple of Mean Monica's Pork hamper promotions in Good Housekeeping were clearly not going to cut it. That was the trouble with PR, if you got it wrong they were 'disappointed', if you got it right, it was almost worse. Bloody nightmare.

She realised she was getting into a negative spiral. The key to this job was to give off an air of self confidence and optimism. She tried to think upbeat thoughts.

By the time Clare phoned from reception and told her to come down, she had three words imprinted on her brain – 'sober, dignified, professional'. This is how she would behave tonight, in front of her biggest client and her CEO. She mouthed them to herself as the lift descended to the ground floor.

She felt her stomach lurch slightly as she saw them all gathered in reception. There was Tony Jennings and Clare F-B already fawning over Derek. She walked towards the three of them.

'Ah Emily my love, our resident PR genius,' Tony was looking particularly orange and bouffant today, 'I believe you haven't actually met Derek Dewsbury. Derek, Emily…'

At this point Derek turned round to shake her hand and Emily nearly choked. She tried hard not to look flustered. Who would have thought, Derek Dewsbury was an absolute stunner. Dressed in an expensive suit, he was all aftershave and knotted cufflinks. A tad too smooth for Emily's liking, but undoubtedly blessed physically.

What had she expected? A pork pie hat and striped apron, stained with the remnants of a hard days butchery? Apparently the man was worth £30 million. She really hadn't counted on the bright blue eyes, perfect teeth and beautifully manicured hands. But all beauty has a flaw she realised as he opened his mouth to speak to her - face of Brad Pitt, alas, voice of Fred Dibnah.

Tony led the way as they walked up the road to the restaurant. The conversation was punctuated by the traditional agency to client outbursts of insincere laughter, at almost anything Derek said.

Hamasan was a fabulous new Japanese, celebrity hang out. Emily looked around delighted. She spotted Pixie Geldof and Alexa Chung giggling in the corner, while Hoxton media types feasted on Dim Sum and Kumquat Mojitos.

Tony clapped his hands together. 'Is everyone happy to start with a couple of bottles of Cristal?'

Good old Tony! Emily tried hard to look nonchalant as she nodded her head.

They took their seats in the restaurant. She needn't have worried, the conversation was light hearted and dominated by Tony's anecdotes. Plates of Dim Sum and bottles of Champagne were replaced as quickly as they were emptied. Tony and Derek were clearly getting stuck in. Clare sipped politely, taking care, Emily noticed, to alternate with water. Tony and Derek swapped stories about shooting parties in Cumbria.

She was looking around the restaurant when Tony turned to her. 'Well I think we should all raise our glasses to young Emily Brighouse and her fabulously successful campaign for National Sausage Week. I trust you won't mind Derek, if we enter the campaign for a PR industry award.' Emily tried not to blush at the sudden attention.

'You're not wrong Tony. Derek grinned. 'Emily, you did us proud.'

Emily was elated, but tried to sound modest and professional as she replied, 'Well, our contacts at the Radio Sound network were very helpful.'

Derek was having none of it. 'It was a stroke of genius Emily. When that radio producer phoned me, he said you were the brains behind the operation. He spoke very highly of you.'

'Really?' She felt herself flush and was desperate to question him further, but held herself back.

She tried to tell herself to just enjoy the moment. For once in her life, everything seemed to be going well. Unlimited supplies of Champagne, glowing praise from her CEO and the thought of Jerome Ignacio Marques Armstrong speaking highly of her. It was all making her feel rather giddy. If only Bella was here to enjoy it with her. She had an idea and headed off through the archway and up the stairs to the loo. Maybe she could get hold of her before she left work. She reached for her phone.

BELS! URGENT HOT BLOKE ALERT! *come 2 Hamasan NOW... free champagne & Derek, yes Derek D... is hot sausage magnate stunner! usual routine...hurry hurry x*

As Emily walked back to the table, she was feeling a tiny bit smug. Maybe PR wasn't so bad after all. If only Grania Wardman could see her now, sipping Cristal, modestly brushing off the compliments, planning her submission for top PR industry award. Elspeth Dunwoody, headhunter from hell, wouldn't be playing so hard to get, if she could see her now. Sober, dignified, professional – well obviously not entirely on all counts.

Tony and Derek were guffawing with laughter when she sat down, just in time to catch the tail end of another hilarious Tony anecdote.

Tony was obviously savouring the punchline. 'And the email entitled 'I left my pants on a light fitting in Bethnal Green' was delivered to 1,200 H&P employees!' The two men roared with laughter as they looked over at her.

'You bastard Tony.' Emily muttered under her breath. But neither of them heard her, they were laughing so much. Clare F-B heard of course and shot Emily a look of pure venom, as she gallantly attempted to steer the conversation back onto safe ground.

Clare had to shout across the table to be heard. 'So, Derek, how did you start off at Dewsburys.' No one answered and she tried again. 'Did your father make you start at the bottom?'

You had to hand it to Clare, Emily couldn't help thinking. She really was a diehard PR professional.

'No, no.' Derek replied politely. 'I was a Management Consultant for a few years, before I did an MBA at Harvard. It took Dad a few years to persuade me to come back and run the family firm.' Emily sighed as she sipped her Champagne. The man just got better and better.

Another plate of Dim Sum arrived and they all tucked in. Emily was starving and looked around to see if anyone was watching her, as she struggled to cram the sticky rice and wind dried pork into her mouth. This place was achingly glamorous. The crystal chandeliers above each table had by now been dimmed. Tony was alarmingly close, thigh pressing into hers, hand intermittently on her knee to demonstrate a point. She could smell his Champagne breath as he turned to her. 'So Brighouse, where were you educated? Tell us what fine academic institution turns out clever girls like you!'

She attempted to edge away from him as she replied. 'St Xavier's Catholic School for Girls in Putney and Oxford.'

His cheeks were already quite pink. 'Ah, a convent girl – I might have guessed! And Oxford! Secretarial college was it?'

'No Tony, I did English at Oxford University.' She replied, but Tony wasn't listening.

'My son's at Durham, daughter's going to secretarial school in Oxford, always good for a girl to learn to type don't you think, Emily?'

She felt Clare's eyes drilling into her and kept a fixed smile on her face as she replied. 'Oh God yes Tony. Sixty words a minute and a decent soufflé, ought to be the backbone of any girl's education.' Clare shot her another look, but there was clearly no danger of Tony picking up on any sarcasm.

Emily helped herself to a steamed crabmeat dumpling and looked up to see Bella walking into the restaurant. Gorgeous Bella. Sometimes she forgot quite what a head turner she was, 5 ft 9" of beautiful skin and glossy, brown hair. It was probably only Bastard Ben that wasn't in love with her. And she always looked so elegant, that old fashioned quality that was clearly having a mesmerising effect on Derek right now. His eyes hadn't left her as she walked across the bar towards them.

Bella was word perfect as she approached them. 'Emily? Emily Brighouse? How nice to see you?' They air kissed theatrically. 'What are you up to these days?'

'Oh hi Bella! I haven't seen you for ages.' Emily tried not to laugh as she spoke. Tony and Derek were looking expectantly at them, waiting for an introduction. 'I'm with some friends from work.' Emily turned back to the table. 'Bella, this is Tony, Clare and Derek. This is my old school friend, Bella Jenkins.' No one replied, so she carried on. 'Actually, we're having a bit of a celebration.'

Tony was on his feet in an instant. 'Is this one of your gorgeous secretarial friends, Brighouse?'

'Bella's in film production actually.' Emily replied.

Tony's cheeks were glowing. 'Delighted to meet you', he said kissing her hand. 'I insist you join us for a glass of Champagne.'

Emily was very pleased with herself. Mission accomplished. Bella was installed between Derek and Tony's other thigh.

When Tony and Derek went to the bar to order more Champagne, Bella and Emily had a quick exchange, under the suspicious glare of Clare F-B.

'Good God Ems,' Bella whispered. 'Who's the randy Satsuma with the bouffant wig?'

Emily struggled not to laugh. 'Tony Jennings, our CEO.'

Bella looked over at the bar as she spoke. 'And why have you never mentioned gorgeous Derek before?' Bella spoke quite loudly now and Emily threw her a look.

'I just found out myself. I've only ever talked to him on the phone.' Emily spat back under her breath. 'I thought he'd look more like a butcher!' They were both really struggling to keep a straight face now. Emily thought it best not to mention the £30 million Dewsbury family fortune. Bella looked flustered enough as it was.

Derek and Tony returned, carrying a bottle each. Clare was still stone cold sober, taking miniscule sips of her drink, just enough to wet her lips and pretend to join in, but all the time her eye trained on Emily and Bella. Nothing was going to shift her.

Maybe it was the Champagne, but Emily was feeling a little bit like Paul Newman in Cool Hand Luke. Her eyes narrowed as she maintained eye contact with Clare. Which of them was going to crack first? Maybe she had drunk a tiny bit too much. She was all bravado as she shouted across at Tony, 'I think Clare needs a top up!' Clare's lip curled.

Derek turned to Bella. 'So Bella, you're an old friend of Emily's?'

Emily watched as Bella stared back at him. A crimson rash creeping up from her chest to her cheeks.

'Yes', she managed after what seemed like an hour.

'Would you like a glass of Champagne?' Derek tried again.

An even longer pause and finally.... 'Yes' Bella replied.

Emily didn't know quite where to look. Her normally articulate friend appeared to be stupefied. As Derek handed her the glass, she seemed to have lost all fine motor skills and gestured at the table with her head, for him to put the glass down.

Derek continued valiantly on. 'Have you been to Hamasan before, Bella?' You had to give the poor man credit.

Bella swallowed hard before replying. 'Yes'

Emily could stand it no longer. 'Do you know Bella's a film producer, Derek.' It was random, but she couldn't let her struggle on.

'Is that right?' Derek replied enthusiastically.

But Emily watched horrified as Bella, reaching now, with a trembling hand for her Champagne glass, sent it shooting across the table, the glass intact, but the contents pouring neatly into Clare F-B's handbag.

'Bella! Go to the loo. Now! I'll follow you up in a minute.' Emily whispered. 'It's through the arch and up the stairs.' Bella nodded as she got up.

Tony slipped an arm around Emily. 'So Brighouse, we've got a big pitch coming up. Old contact of mine in the Territorial Army in fact. Bit hush hush. How would you like to be on my bitch team?'

Emily leaned away from him. 'I'm sorry Tony?' Had he just said what she thought he said?

'My pitch team Emily.' Tony leered at her. 'For the Army account.'

'Great Tony, I'd love to.' She smiled back.

'Good girl.'

Emily excused herself and raced up the stairs to the loo.

'Bella Jenkins, are you in there?' She knocked on the loo door. 'What on earth's the matter with you?'

Bella came out looking shaken. Emily shook her head. 'For God's sake Bella, I've never seen you like this. Did you have a few drinks before you arrived or something?' Bella started to splash water on her neck to try to calm the rash.

'No I did not. I came straight from work when you texted me.

I don't know what's the matter with me, Em.' She smiled, slightly unhinged, into the mirror. 'Well actually I do, it's him! He's just gorgeous. What am I going to do? I can't even speak in his presence.'

Emily rolled her eyes. 'Well you're going to have to Bels.' She rummaged around in her bag. 'I think I've got some rescue remedy somewhere.' She pulled out a bottle and clumsily aimed a few drops into Bella's open mouth. They missed and Bella grabbed the bottle from her and snapped off the top. As Emily watched her gulping it down, she noticed a large patch of wine on the back of Bella's dress. 'God Bella, it looks like you've peed yourself.' Emily unravelled the snakeskin scarf from her neck and started to drape it round Bella's waist to hide the offending patch. She spoke slowly as she tied the scarf.

'Right, now listen to me Bella, you have got to keep your cool. I want you to take 12 sharp inward breaths and then breathe out deeply and slowly for 20 seconds.' Bella nodded. 'Keep doing it for a few minutes, until your breathing calms down.' Emily was not at all sure that any of this had gone in, as Bella continued to look at herself in the mirror. She carried on. 'Now Bels, you know the rules about conversation. They're your rules for God's sake.' She was getting a little impatient now. 'Three simple, open questions. 1. Tell me about your job? 2. Where do you live? 3. What was National Sausage Week all about?'

Bella looked at her blankly. At that moment, the door to one of the loos opened and they both stared incredulously as Alexa Chung walked out. She looked Bella up and down as she flicked the water from her hands and ran a hand through her shiny dark hair. 'I love what you've done with that scarf,' she winked and flounced out.

'Oh God Em, do you think she heard us?' They both started to laugh. 'Probably.' Emily knew there was nothing more to be done.

Bella looked at her blankly. Emily knew there was nothing more to be done. 'Now Bella, I am going back to the table. You follow me down in a couple of minutes. OK?'

'OK. No, you're right Em. I'll be fine.' Bella started to compose herself.

'And Bella?'

'Yes Emily.'

Emily held her by the shoulders, so that she was forced to look at her. 'Repeat after me. I am a beautiful, successful, witty and intelligent woman and any sane man would be desperate to go out with me.'

Bella repeated. 'I am a beautiful, successful, witty and intelligent woman and any sane man would be desperate to go out with me.'

'Good girl. See you in a minute.' Emily returned to the table.

'Is she alright?' Derek looked concerned.

'Oh yes, she's fine. Just spilled a drop of wine on her dress. She's giving it a bit of a rinse.'

Another plate of Dim Sum arrived. By this time Clare had worked out that Derek knew banker boyfriend Rupey. They were flinging names of mutual friends across the table, like a manic game of posh happy families. Tony was up at the bar and Emily could sit back and relax for a moment. She sipped her drink contentedly and looked around the noisy restaurant, trying to spot any famous faces.

Seconds later, the happy buzz was silenced. The entire restaurant stopped in its tracks. Every table looked up towards the archway. A massive crash of metal and splintering glass cut through the air, as first a tray of cocktails banged and splattered down the stairs, followed almost instantly by Bella, who shot like a rag doll down the entire length of the stairway, screaming loudly as she went.

'Oh my dear God', Clare mouthed silently.

Derek was by Bella's side in an instant, helping her up, brushing olives and lemon slices off her dress. Waiters hovered around, offering napkins. Amidst all the fuss, Emily couldn't help noticing that Derek held onto Bella's hand, for just a little longer than was absolutely necessary. They looked deeply into each other's eyes, both now smiling.

Derek finally let her go and Emily rubbed her back, as she whispered into her ear. 'Perfect Bella! That was just what I had in mind. You only went slightly off brief there!' Bella started to giggle. 'I'm sorry Ems, I think all that yoga breathing made me light headed and then I smacked straight into the waiter on the way out.'

Clare F-B was at their side and Emily couldn't stop thinking of three words - sober, dignified, professional. 'Emily.' Clare whispered firmly. 'I've flagged down a taxi – it's waiting outside…I suggest you and your friend get in it NOW!'

They gathered awkwardly outside the restaurant. Derek kissed Bella on the cheek. Tony pressed himself into Emily and whispered into her ear. 'Goodnight Brighouse, my little convent girl. Get Clare to brief you on the army account. I'll see you at the pitch. Wear your shortest skirt!'

11

To: EBrighouse@Hobbs&Parker.com
From: Derek.dewsbury@dewsburyporkproducts.com
Subject: PR Award entry

Emily
Great to meet you and the team last week. Just to say that I was more than happy with your suggested content for the PR Award consumer campaign entry. Have signed and posted back. Look forward to the Awards dinner ...
On another subject, I know I'm probably being very unprofessional, but I think you said Bella was an old friend of yours and I wondered if you might be able to track down her contact details for me. No problem at all if not appropriate.

Best
Derek

BINGO! Emily smiled to herself as she forwarded the email to Bella. She thought about Derek and Bella's first date. How was that going to work? It was going to take something considerably more effective than yoga breathing and a couple of drops of rescue remedy this time. She wondered if Beta Blockers might do it, but how would they react with alcohol. She googled 'Beta Blockers and alcohol'.

'Both alcohol and beta-blockers can reduce your blood pressure, so mixing the two increases your risk of collapse.'

Oh dear, that was no good then. Emily looked at her inbox, desperate to hear Bella's response.

To: EBrighouse@Hobbs&Parker.com
From: RoisinOD@yourliving.com
Subject: Mortification...

Hi Emily
Just to apologise once more for my desperate behaviour at the polo event last week. I was so grateful for your understanding – so sorry about your scarf. Let me know if there is anything I can do to repay your kindness.

Cheers
Roisin x

Roisin was sweet. Emily started to think about the duff press releases she could persuade her to print. Monica walked past her desk. 'Emily, I expect you've forgotten about the TA brainstorm?' Emily sighed. Yes indeed she had. And the unavoidable had finally happened. She was going to have to work directly with Mean Monica on the pitch document – just the two of them. Mean Monica had a laminated A4 diagram pinned above her desk, a give-away from some new business course she had no doubt attended. It was entitled 'The Perfect Pitch Pyramid' and featured all sorts of helpful steps in the pitching process.

Emily particularly liked the blindingly obvious, 'take a thorough brief' and the inspirational 'gather ideas'.

Emily screwed up her face at Monica's back as she walked away. Monica was a great fan of process. It didn't seem to bother her if she didn't have the slightest hint of a good idea, just go through the motions, plough on regardless. Emily thought Monica's pitch process was a pile of crap. Quite frankly, if you didn't have any good ideas, then no amount of bullet points, graphs and powerpoint slides were going to disguise it. Of course she had to admit, that Monica's approach had the benefit of making you look terribly busy, as opposed to Emily's method, which mainly involved looking out of the window, waiting for an elusive bolt from the blue.

Emily sighed at the inevitability of it all. The next level on Monica's 'Perfect Pitch Pyramid of Success' was a brainstorm. For some reason, H&P had decided that the best way to come up with the next award winning PR campaign, was to sit the entire team in a children's activity centre style ball pit. It was an impressive 30 foot structure, surrounded by netting and reconstructed on the top floor of the H&P building. Random words, like 'GRASS' and 'FIRE ENGINE' had been sellotaped rather badly to a job lot of plastic balls in primary colours.

It often occurred to Emily, as she took her shoes off and slid reluctantly into the ball pit, that this was about the least likely place you would ever come up with a good idea. It sometimes felt like the whole PR industry had gone completely bonkers in its effort to appear creative. An epidemic had swept through London – if you didn't have a sand pit or a caravan in reception, you might as well pack up and go home. One agency famously had a 20 foot long slide to enter their reception area. 'How creative!' the clients were presumably supposed to think, as they shot down towards the crash mat, nervously clutching their laptops. Crock of shite more like.

'Emily – I'll see you in the Ball Pit in 5.' Clare F-B breezed past, irritatingly chirpy this morning. Emily couldn't face it just yet. She lingered at her desk, waiting for a response from Bella. An email popped up in her inbox.

To: *EBrighouse@Hobbs&Parker.com*
From: *Jem.im.a@RadioNorth.com*
Subject: *Where have you gone?*

Emily
I haven't heard a word from you for a week and when you do email, you sound like a stilted stranger. No smut? No visits to A&E? No stories from the H&P creative powerhouse? Do I have to book in a sex change to be your confidante? If that's what it takes, just say the word...

I miss you Emily.
J

The last four words made her catch her breath. She just had time to type a quick reply.

To: *Jem.im.a@RadioNorth.com*
From: *EBrighouse@Hobbs&Parker.com*
Subject: *Where have you gone?*

Jem,
Don't intend to sound like a stranger. No smut stories, new boyfriend keeping me well and truly under control. Work really quite interesting for a change and quite busy with big pitch coming up. Have to go - brainstorm in ball pit!

Em x

She was pleased enough with this. Not unfriendly, but very much in control. The reference to a boyfriend and new business pitch, continued to build a picture of personal and professional success, or slightly less hopeless individual anyway. She read it again before pressing send. It might be weeks ago, but his bitchy girlfriend's words were still ringing in her ears. What was it Frankie had said? 'I think we're all waiting for the press release 'Emily Brighouse wakes up in her own flat!" Evil cow!

She rummaged in her bag for a pad and pen to take to the brainstorm. No doubt there would be numerous, mould breaking ideas to note down.

Ping. There he was again. Emailing her straight back.

To: *EBrighouse@Hobbs&Parker.com*
From: *Jem.im.a@RadioNorth.com*
Subject: *Where have you gone?*

For fuck's sake Emily! Will you come up and stay with me in Northumberland? Just one weekend. Then you can never reply to my emails again if you so wish.

Jem

Emily didn't even realise that she had let out an involuntary yelp of joy. So much happiness, in one day. She read and re-read the email. Wasn't this more than friendship? It was charged with something else. Something that was making her heart race. She started to type.

She didn't trust herself to say anymore. Already she was imagining them, arm in arm, walking across the dales, or whatever they were called up there, laughing as he lifts her effortlessly over a stile and then holding onto her slightly too long, a brooding Portuguese Heathcliffe to her Catherine. He was of course dressed in full polo kit, busting out of grass stained white jeans, but what should she be wearing? Oh who bloody cares, blessed great bollocks of unbridled joy!

Her phone rang. Internal call. The sound of Clare bloody Forster Blair, like a bucket of cold water on her state of rapture. Clare was obviously cross. 'Are you coming to this brainstorm or not. We're in the ball pit.'

She wandered over to the lift, in a trance-like state, transported as she was to the hills of Northumberland. She, Emily Brighouse, was going to spend a romantic weekend with the sexiest man she had ever met – 'just one weekend' he had said. She wondered if he spoke Portuguese. This could actually be an epic, life changing moment. Suddenly the planets had aligned and for once, everything in her life had gone absolutely right. She didn't even feel the familiar embarrassment on entry into the ball pit.

She was vaguely aware of the presence of Dan, Pete, Anoushka, Mean Monica, a couple of graduate trainees – the usual suspects.

Clare was sitting on a yellow, soft foam sea horse, her tone impressively business like, given that she was up to her knees in multi-coloured plastic balls. 'Right, Monica and Emily, if you could both take notes, let's get started with some warm up exercises. Pick up a ball everyone and shout out the words.'

'BIG BEN…PENCIL CASE…LAWN TENNIS… WASHING MACHINE…LUNCH BOX.' This was the bit where Emily, Dan and Pete would normally get the giggles.

'WANKER!' Pete shouted out. Everyone tittered.

'Thanks Pete, if I could have that one?' Clare confiscated the offending ball and popped it into her bag. A few weeks ago, an unidentified H&P smartarse had gained unlawful entry into the ball pit area and added their own balls, featuring some interesting additions, such as 'LABIA, SCROTUM and PUNANI.' The first brainstorm after that was a lot more fun than usual.

Clare had immediately ordered Anoushka and Pete, who was the main suspect, to rid the pit of every offending ball, but some had clearly slipped through the net.

'SANDCASTLE…FRYING PAN…PONY… BUTTPLUG!' Clare held out her hand for the last one. They carried on.

Polo…white jeans…grass stains… Emily, oblivious to everyone else, was having her own little brainstorm. She was clearly in another world and Clare shot her a look.

'OK, that's a great warm up everybody. Now each of you is going to put on one of these thinking hats.' God Clare loved this shit. 'We'll do some role play exercises, just to get us focusing on target audiences.' She reached down into a dressing up box full of hats and started to hand them round.

If you didn't feel like enough of a tosser, sitting in a child's play area full of plastic balls, then wearing a flat cap, nylon headscarf or policeman's helmet to help you get in character, would normally do the trick. Today, Emily didn't care. She had nothing but benevolent thoughts as Clare soldiered on. 'Anoushka, you are a school teacher and a working mum, Dan, you are a travelling salesman.' She passed him a moth eaten brown Homburg. 'Monica, you are a student.' Obligatory baseball cap for the student, demonstrating, Emily often thought, just how out of touch H&P was with Britain's 'yoof' culture.

'And Emily!' Clare spoke quite loudly now, 'You are a 30 year old immigrant factory worker.' She rooted around in the box, obviously a bit troubled by the headgear for this one. Emily wasn't even really surprised when Clare passed her a Fez. She couldn't look Pete in the eye as she put it on.

'Now, let's talk about why each of you might want to join the Territorial Army.' They all sat in their hats, staring blankly back at her. Emily wondered how confident the Major General would be, if he could see his PR team right now.

As she wiggled her toes distractedly, moving the plastic balls around, her thoughts turned back to Jem and the weekend up north. Back to that bracing weekend in the country, collecting eggs from wherever you are supposed to collect eggs from… a tractor ride sitting next to Jem, his arm slung casually around her. Later as they stroll across the dales, he sweeps her over a low stone wall, their lips tantalisingly close… a hearty pub dinner with a flagon of red wine, a roaring fire, the two of them stare at each other, no need for words…

'OK, thanks everyone.' Emily was snatched from her dreams. 'I think that was a really useful session.' Clare snapped her notebook shut. There was an unspoken H&P rule that you had to end every meeting with a positive comment. An insincere summing up of a completely pointless meeting, justifying your colleagues' wasted time.

They stepped one by one out of the ball pit.

Emily looked down at her blank notepad. She really didn't have a clue what had been discussed in the brainstorm. She had missed the usual 45 minutes of heart stopping boredom, suspended instead in a state of catatonic ecstasy. It would pain her of course, but she was going to have to ask Mean Monica for her notes. She drifted back to her desk. She couldn't wait to catch up with Bella. More emails in her inbox – and another from Jem.

To: EBrighouse@Hobbs&Parker.com
From: Jem.im.a@RadioNorth.com
Subject: Where have you gone?

Emily
So glad you can come. Frankie is really looking forward to seeing you again. How about either 1st or 2nd weekend in October. Bring Charlie by the way – would love to meet him.

Jx

Aaaaagghhhhh. Plug pulled on catatonic state of ecstasy. Frankie was so 'looking forward to seeing her'. How could she have got it so spectacularly wrong. There would be no sexual frisson on the hills of Northumbria, not with bitch stunner Frankie around. And her mystery boyfriend, Charlie! That was the biggest joke. In fact she couldn't even go now, due to inconvenient non-existence of said boyfriend.

To: Bella.j@hothouseproductions.co.uk
From: EBrighouse@Hobbs&Parker.com
Subject: Fwd: Where have you gone...

Bella
Shit! Now what do I do? Crushing disappointment aside,
I don't really want to spend the weekend watching
bitch canter girl snuggling up to dreamboat boyfriend.
Gutted doesn't cover it! Need to respond fairly soon with
blasé email to at least maintain sense of dignity. Off to
lunch with Hector from Le Voisier – will ask him what he
thinks....
For a moment there I thought things were looking up -
bollocks!

Em x

If anyone knew what to do, it would be Hector. Emily
put on her coat and got in the lift. Emily and Hector
had discovered that his favourite Italian restaurant was
exactly halfway between their offices. He had been going
to Il Paradiso for at least 20 years. The waiters danced in
attendance and always kept his favourite table for him.
Hector and Emily had decided there was really no need to
tell Clare F-B about their fortnightly gossip lunches.

Hector could tell something was up as soon as she
walked in. He had two glasses of pink Champagne
waiting, as usual.

'Spill the beans, Emily. Tell Uncle Hector what's been
happening.' He handed her a glass.

Emily showed Hector the emails on her phone.

'Ah, I see! Quel dilemme!' He raised his eyebrows as he
handed the phone back.

'Well, what do you think I should do, Hector?' Emily

was hoping for something more tangible. He wasn't usually short of opinions.

Hector put on his reading glasses and looked at the menu. 'And what were you planning to do?'

'Write him an email this afternoon and say that I can't go.' She replied.

'I see.' Hector looked unimpressed as he continued to scan the menu.

Silence.

This was infuriating. 'Come on Hector. What do you think I should do?'

Hector beckoned the waiter over. Once they had ordered their food, he put down the menu and looked at her over his reading glasses. 'Emily, I wouldn't of course presume to tell you what to do. You're a grown woman, who can make her own decisions.'

Silence. She knew there would be a 'but'.

'But I can tell you one thing my darling.' He leant over the table towards her. 'At the risk of sounding like a self help manual, 'you've got to play to win".'

'Win what?' Emily replied. This really was most unhelpful. 'I don't really see how playing gooseberry for a whole weekend, with a man who just wants to be good friends, is really going to win anything.' She looked forlorn. 'You know Hector, I am so tired of making a complete tit of myself.' She managed a weak smile.

For an embarrassing moment, she thought she might cry. She hadn't even known Hector for that long, but sometimes he seemed to know her more than her oldest friends. He saw her expression and changed tack.

'If you want my opinion, there is more going on in that email than friendship. Men don't send emails like that if they want to be your best buddie.'

She didn't reply and Hector carried on. 'At least, go up there and find out what's what, Emily!' He cajoled. She shook her head.

Hector looked a little exasperated. 'Take Charlie with you then. You'll probably have to share a room and suffer him dry humping your back all night, but it's a price worth paying.' Hector snapped a breadstick in half, decisively. 'Look, if you want this man, Emily, you have to go and get him. Stop letting life happen to you!'

'Do I do that?' Emily looked surprised.

'Yes you do, my Oxford educated, sausage promoting little friend. Have you ever thought about aiming a little higher?'

'What do you mean?' Emily was taken aback, but at least it shook her out of her gloom.

Hector was on a roll now. 'I mean, for once in your life, you need to decide single mindedly what it is that you want and go out and get it.' He was jabbing his breadstick at her as he spoke.

This was all a bit much. Emily started to get defensive. 'It's all very well Hector, but sometimes it's incredibly hard being a woman.'

He raised his eyebrows in mock disbelief, but let her carry on.

'I mean, you know, the prejudice, lecherous bosses, biological clocks, spinsterhood, being labelled a slut if you sleep with half as many people as a man does. I don't even really care about all that crap. ' She paused for a second, as if gathering her thoughts. 'It just seems quite hard being me sometimes.' She trailed off, a little ashamed at her own self pity.

Hector was clearly unmoved. 'Prejudice Schmejudice!' He shot back at her. 'Listen sweetie, I'm a gay jew - I think I know a little bit about this subject. Use your brains Emily! I thought you were supposed to be clever. Show some gumption!'

'I thought you weren't going to tell me what to do.' Emily couldn't help but smile.

'Well, bugger it darling, someone's got to!' They both started to laugh. He ordered them both a glass of wine and she thought about what he'd said, as she played around with the fusilli on her plate.

'But Hector, what if Charlie won't come?' She was relieved to have found a flaw, in his rather forthright argument. 'I mean, he might be a bit surprised by my sudden invitation. I haven't exactly been keen, have I?'

Hector took a sip of red wine and dabbed his chin with a napkin. 'Of course he'll go with you. I dare say he'd go on a train spotting mini break, if you suggested it.'

But she was quite determined now. 'No. I'm not going Hector. It's just not fair on Charlie. He's a lovely bloke. Anyway, Bella and I have made a pact, to start getting real. If I spend my life fantasising about unavailable polo players, I might miss the person I'm supposed to be with.' Hector was laughing at her, but she was steadfast. 'I'm not going and that's it.'

He was looking at her and shaking his head. 'Oh Emily, Emily. Can't you see? You are Maria in the Sound of Music.' Emily looked bewildered, but he carried on.

'Captain Von Trapp has just brought the Baroness home to meet his children. Maria flees the Von Trapp house, fighting a torrent of new and unfamiliar feelings for the Captain. Her emotions in turmoil, she returns to the Abbey.' Emily was none the wiser. 'And what does the Reverend Mother tell her to do Emily?'

'I have no idea Hector. Make some lederhosen out of curtains?' She sniggered.

Hector leant across the table, speaking in a loud, stage whisper. 'Maria…Emily! These walls were not meant to shut out problems. You have to face them.' He clenched his fist rather dramatically. 'You have to live the life you were born to live.'

'Good God Hector.' She laughed. 'How many times have you seen the film?'

'Sixteen.' But he would not to be put off. 'Climb every mountain, Emily, search high and low!' She realised to her horror, that he had actually broken into song.

'Follow every highway, every path you know.' The singing was getting louder.

She looked around the restaurant. 'Please stop! Hector!'

He ignored her and rose to his feet. 'Climb every mountain, ford every stream, follow every rainbow, till you find your dream.'

He was loud enough now for the whole restaurant to hear him. In spite of the shame, she noticed he actually had quite a good voice, an unexpectedly rich baritone. He gestured dramatically to the waiters as he sang, who were now gathering round, starting to applaud.

'A dream that will need all the love you can give, every day of your life, for as long as you live.' It was all directed at her and some of the waiters were starting to join in.

She stared down at the napkin on her lap. 'What will make you stop Hector?'

He broke off from his song. 'Agree to go to Northumberland.'

He was off again. 'Climb every mountain, ford every stream, follow every...'

She closed her eyes. 'Sit down, I'll go.'

He instantly obeyed. 'Good, that's that settled then.' Hector smirked, dabbing his mouth with a napkin.

She looked a little shell shocked. 'Hector, you know this could be a disaster.'

'Of course it could my darling. But the question is, could you live with the not knowingness of turning it down?'

She smiled, knowing that he was right. Hector was triumphant. 'You know Emily, John was living with a 26 year old male model when I fell in love with him. Do you think I gave up?'

'No I don't Hector.' She was forced to concede, wishing he would now just drop the subject.

'Correct answer. Now pass me your phone and we'll email him straight away.' Hector reached his hand out across the table.

'No, no, I'll do it later.'

Hector put his head on one side. 'Do I look like I just rode in from Bumfuck Idaho, my dear? Hand over the phone, Emily.' He was overwhelming. Slowly she reached for her phone. She could hardly believe it as she dropped it into his hand.

'Good girl!' He flicked onto her emails, typing as he spoke. 'How about this - *'Looking forward to it. Thanks, will bring Charlie. Em x'* There, sent!'

It was just not possible to turn Hector down, he was insufferable. As she walked out of the restaurant, he blew her a kiss. She waved at him, smiling through the window as she walked down the street. 'Go get him!' he mouthed and clawed the air.

She laughed most of the way back to work, still not quite believing what he had talked her into. Back at her desk, she flicked through the incomprehensible scribbles in her notepad – the meaningless TA brainstorm. There was nothing for it, she was going to have to ask Mean Monica for help. They were supposed to be working on this together anyway, but Emily had hoped to avoid any direct contact. She was a few desks away, picking at her homemade lunchbox.

Emily tried to sound casual. 'Monica, I seem to have got a bit confused with the TA ideas. I don't suppose you were taking notes?'

She was over in a flash, notepad in hand. 'Did you not take notes Emily? I think Clare told us both to take them down.'

Predictable.

'Yes, I did Monica, but there were so many.' She was brisk and upbeat. 'I can't really make up my mind which was the winning idea. I'd love it if you would take me through your notes and tell me what you think?'

Mean Monica was very rarely asked for her thoughts. She was secretly delighted.

'Well, Pete suggested a photocall with Maria and Tracey in camouflage bikinis, driving a tank. I think it was Dave who came up with the naked TA calendar idea. Oh and someone suggested a performance artist, spray painted half as a city worker and half in army uniform. We'd put it on the forth plinth in Trafalgar Square.'

'Of course they did.' Emily was now feeling slightly less chipper. 'I'm surprised there's no mention of a survey?'

'Oh there was one.' Monica scanned down her notes. 'Quite a good one actually. A survey to find out how many of us fancy men in uniform. Great regional spin…80% of Geordie women would fancy their other half more in army fatigues, etc, etc…'

'Absolutely not.' Emily looked horrified.

'Really? I thought that was quite a good one. Nice regional coverage.'

'Keep going, what else?' She was keen to move off the subject of stupid surveys about Geordie women.

Thankfully Monica moved on. 'OK, where were we? Oh yes, challenge key business people – Lord Sugar, Richard Branson, Nicola Horlick, etc to join the TA.'

Familiar feelings of exasperation. Emily chewed her biro. 'It might just be me, Monica, but I'm not really hearing anything that will convince large parts of the UK to race down to the recruitment office and join the Territorial Army.'

'No.' It was the first thing they'd ever agreed on.

'And what about you Monica?' It was disgraceful sucking up, but she was desperate. 'You normally have some very practical ideas.'

Monica snorted in agreement. 'Well I did think my idea was probably the most workable.'

'Remind me what that was again?' Emily's pen was poised.

'Placing a series of TA themed reader offers and competitions. We'd target key lifestyle magazines and give away six 'army style' boot camp weekends in the Lake District.'

No kidding. Why had she even asked. 'Brilliant Monica. I really like that. Is that it then?'

Monica hesitated. 'Well there was one more, a bit silly really. That new grad trainee suggested we recruit 5 top journalists into the TA for six weeks, measure their fitness levels at the start and finish and get them to write about their experiences. Sounds risky to me.' She snorted again.

Finally an idea that might actually work. Emily mustered a smile. 'Thanks Monica, I'll type those up if you like and email them to you and Clare.' Job done.

Her email pinged. Jem.im.a@RadioNorth.com What now?

To: EBrighouse@Hobbs&Parker.com
From: Jem.im.a@RadioNorth.com
Subject: Your trip to the North...

Hi Em,
Good to hear that you and Charlie can make it. Come up after work on the Friday night if you can. Does Charlie shoot? Dad and I can take him out if he's interested and Frankie says you're a keen horsewoman? Bring your gear. Will email you directions.

Look forward to it.
Jx

Thrice shite! Oh what a tangled web we weave, blah, blah. So just a devoted boyfriend and an urgent riding masterclass to sort out. Emily felt sick again. Right now, she could kill Hector. The main thing was to stay calm. She could worry about the riding stuff later, first of all she would need to sort out Charlie.

To: cfanthorpe@hutchinsons.com
From: EBrighouse@Hobbs&Parker.com
Subject: Weekend away?

Hi Charlie
It's been ages! Just wondering if you would like to come up to Northumberland with me for the weekend. A friend of mine has a farm near Hexham. Lots of shooting and bracing walks I expect. Two weeks on Friday – short notice so no problem if you are already busy. Hope international money market movements are favourable.

Emily x

She sat back in her chair and slowly exhaled. It was done. Let fate decide. Please say no, please say no. Please say yes. He's probably in a meeting anyway.

Could be a long wait. She was gnawing the end of her pen now. No point just staring at her inbox. She stared at her inbox. Four minutes and 36 seconds later. Ping. A new email in her inbox. It was from Charlie. She bit through the biro, without even noticing.

To: EBrighouse@Hobbs&Parker.com
From: cfanthorpe@hutchinsons.com
Subject: Weekend away?

Emily
Of course, I would love to come - thank you. I'll bring my guns. Shall I drive? We can discuss international money market fluctuations on the way up – I know what a keen interest you take.

Charlie

The fates had decided. She felt breathless, elated and petrified. The reality of what she had agreed to, began to dawn. 'Bring your riding gear!' Holy cow, what had she got herself into this time. This was insanity. Bella would have some sound advice. Emily brightened at the thought. Bella was always logical. They had two weeks to work it out. It would be fine.

To: EBrighouse@Hobbs&Parker.com
From: Bella.j@hothouseproductions.co.uk
Subject: Weekend with northern dreamboat couple

Em
Have been mulling this over and absolutely don't think you should go. We know from previous experience that you are not good in the countryside. Remember that shooting party!? You'd have Charlie to deal with, that bitch troll stunner of a girlfriend trying to make a fool of you, ruddy cheeks and frizzy hair, totally inappropriate

footwear, etc – impossible. If you are going to win this man over, it needs to be on your turf. Say no to this, but come back quickly with an invitation to London. I don't know how we wangle it, but hopefully without the girlfriend? On no account agree to go. Speak later.

Bella x

Bloody marvellous! Emily put her head in her hands.

To: Bella.j@hothouseproductions.co.uk
From: EBrighouse@Hobbs&Parker.com
Subject: Weekend with northern dreamboat couple

*Thanks for nothing my friend. As you can clearly see from the emails I forwarded to you **4 hours ago**, events have slightly moved on...*
I think we can safely say that I am up a Northern shit creek without a paddle.

Does Jimmy Choo do a hiking boot?
I want you to know that I forgive you.

E x

Pete sauntered past her desk. 'Alright Brighouse? How's your flatmate?' He stopped and looked at her up close. 'Bloody hell Brighouse, what happened to your face? It looks like you've been shot in the mouth with an exploding fountain pen.'

To: *EBrighouse@Hobbs&Parker.com*
From: *CForster-Blair@Hobbs&Parker.com*
Subject: *TA progress*

Emily

I hope the TA pitch is coming along well. Tony is very old friends with the Major General, so he will want to personally vet the ideas before we put the pitch together. Can you have them ready for me to show him by close of play today please? Tony also had a fabulous stunt idea for the start of our pitch presentation. Can you let me know if you and Monica have any abseiling experience?

Clare

12

Bella and Emily had debated the 'Northumberland problem' for almost two weeks. In the end, they had come up with nothing and here she was, hurtling up the motorway, with no plan, no line of attack, nothing.

They had left London at 4pm. Charlie at the wheel of his black Audi, Emily sitting next to him. She imagined they looked like any normal young couple, heading off for a weekend in the country. How simple life would be, if she could only fall in love with him. Safe, affable and tolerably attractive in his canary yellow weekend cords. Bella seemed to think he was the perfect man for her. He was almost certain to have checked the oil and tyre pressures before they left. Life could have been so straightforward.

They chatted easily at first, but now as they sped relentlessly up the M1, Emily fell silent. The road signs were becoming distinctly northern - Rotherham, Pontefract, Wetherby – she had visions of flat caps, whippets and toffee factories. Surely they couldn't be that far off. Drawing closer and closer to their destination, where he was waiting for them.

She stared out of the window, silent and panic stricken.

'Cat got your tongue?' Charlie asked cheerfully.

How much would she have given for a burst tyre and a train ticket home.

Bella would be leaving their flat for her first date with Derek any minute now. No need for beta blockers, they had decided, just a pep talk and a carefully chosen, familiar restaurant with loos on the ground floor - they had checked every detail. Look who needed the beta blockers now!

This weekend had of course prompted a significant retail investment. Luckily Elle were running a 'get the country look' feature this month – Emily had bought everything in it. Brand new 'international ladies' Barbour with biker twist and tartan cuff, mid calf Hunter wellies in plum, cashmere snood, moleskin bootcut hipsters – a small fortune to be honest. Not too rural, not too urban - country but with a nod to the city. The only problem was, it all looked a bit too brand new.

She tried to remember what calm felt like as she hurtled inexorably towards almost certain humiliation. Less than one hour until they arrived and she still hadn't broached the subject of bedroom arrangements. Where to start? She searched for the elusive opening line.

'I hope you didn't mind me asking you to come away for the weekend.'

Charlie turned and smiled at her. 'Not at all. Delighted!'

'I hope you won't be, you know, disappointed.' She stammered. 'I mean, in terms of…you know, I'm not sure if we'll be sharing a room, I expect we may be, but basically I just felt, you know…' She flushed with the effort of getting the words out.

Charlie laughed. 'Don't worry Emily, no need to be shy. After the night of your birthday party, I don't think you've got much to hide!'

Oh my God, shocking wave of nausea…she was breathless. What to say?

'Yes, well things moved quite quickly that night.' She attempted a little laugh. 'I thought it would be a good opportunity to sort of, you know, take things back a level, get to know each other, sort of thing.' He didn't reply, she soldiered on. 'I mean, I know we've already spent the night together and I mean…it's just that, I'd rather not… until, you know.'

'Understood, Emily.'

But had he understood her inarticulate ramblings? They both stared straight ahead. She could only hope.

It was dark now and past 8pm as they turned off the M1 and headed up towards Hexham and on towards Corbridge.

She had texted Jem half way there and bang on time, they swept up the hill and then left, through a gate into the entrance of Haydon Mill Farm. They were seconds away. She could hardly breathe. Ten sharp inward breaths and a long exhalation, repeat six times. Absolutely useless, having no affect whatsoever on her rising panic levels.

They drove up a mud track between endless fields. Charlie looked at her. 'Are you alright Emily? You're breathing sounds a bit odd.'

'Yes, yes, fine.' She really must pull herself together. 'I think the house is left at that barn.'

Outside lights came on as they drew up outside the Farmhouse. Any second now she would see him.

And then there he was, tousled black hair, white shirt, ripped jeans. 'Insanely good looking', she found herself repeating the words in her head, which made her want to giggle.

She climbed shakily out of the car. 'Emily!' He drew her towards him and kissed her cheek. He smelt of soapy sandalwood. It must have been his father standing behind him, a tall, 60ish, handsome man, not so dark, but strikingly similar to Jem. He was shaking Charlie's hand and taking their bags.

Jem of course, was completely at ease. 'Charlie, delighted to meet you.' He shook his hand. 'Emily, Charlie, this is my father John.'

She reached out a trembling hand, but never made contact, because just at that second, she spotted it coming down the track - a snarling, diabolical beast, hurtling along the path, its ears pinned back and clearly heading for her.

'Jesus!' She shrieked. She wanted to turn and run. Show no fear. 'Here, boy.' She mouthed, feebly.

With one massive leap, the enormous hound flung her against the bonnet of the car. His paws were on her shoulders and she teetered backwards until he had her fully pinned down. Shit! She grimaced as she braced herself for the inevitable bite to the neck. For a split second she was struck by the irony. She had been so frightened all the way here and now she was going to bleed to death, before even making it into the house. But instead of biting her, the hound, who was dribbling profusely now, set about vigorously licking her face and hair. She was so relieved she didn't even really mind.

'Oh there you are!' Frankie appeared now, 'I really wouldn't let him do that Emily, he might have worms.' The dog now spread-eagled across her and starting to hump her leg, was well over six foot when fully extended. Emily marvelled at Frankie. She hadn't even said 'hello' yet, but had already managed to put her down.

'Get down Pilot!' Jem pulled him off her. 'I'm so sorry Emily, he seems to have taken a shine to you.' She tried her best to look unflustered.

Frankie made a token gesture of kissing her cheek at least a foot from her face, which was understandable, given that her ears and hair were still damp with saliva.

'Pilot'? An Irish Wolfhound called 'Pilot'. Now why was that so familiar? Emily tried to recall as she followed them inside the house.

They were led through a wide, flagstone hallway. A huge open fire crackled and spat on one side, providing most of the light in the dark corridor. She could just make out the unfamiliar detritus of country folk all around. Every wall crammed with antlers and stuffed wildlife, saddles stacked in rows. Every corner was piled high with riding boots, fishing rods, polo sticks, dog leads and old copies of The Field.

John caught her looking around. 'You'll have to forgive us Emily, Jem and I have become quite undomesticated since my wife passed away.' He turned to Frankie. 'Would you mind showing them to their room? I expect you two are exhausted. Why don't you get settled and come down for a drink and something to eat when you're ready.'

Frankie flounced up the stairs ahead of them and led them into a small, low beamed bedroom. They put their bags on the bed and suddenly she was alone with Charlie, standing silently in front of a particularly small double bed.

There was an awkward silence. 'Here we are then.' She offered, pointlessly. 'Which side of the bed would you prefer to sleep on?' Oh God that was lame and no doubt in sharp contrast to the last time they had shared a bed, if she could even remember.

'No preference. Shall I go by the window?' Charlie was breezily casual.

She laid out her flannelette drawstring pyjama bottoms and a T-shirt on top of the pillow. Bella had decided that a double knotted drawstring with T-shirt tucked in, would provide an adequate first line of defence.

Feeling her way along the corridor, she found the bathroom and washed the dog saliva off her face. She stared at her flushed expression and dishevelled hair in the mirror. So much for looking calm and in control. It was so dark, she could barely find the stairs back down to the hallway, but followed the voices until she found the dining room. Charlie was already there, chatting animatedly to Jem's father. Another huge, open fire and low beamed ceiling, which made the men look particularly tall.

Jem greeted her at the doorway. 'It's so good to have you here Emily.' He looked genuinely pleased to see her. 'Have you recovered from the dog assault? Pilot's nearly ten, but you wouldn't know it.'

'Oh yes, it's fine' she tried to sound blasé, as if being humped by an oversexed Hound of the Baskervilles was an everyday occurrence. Suddenly it occurred to her why the dog's name seemed familiar. 'Did you say his name is Pilot? Isn't that Mr Rochester's dog from Jane Eyre?'

Jem smiled. 'Yes exactly. My mother had a thing about Mr Rochester. Apparently that's why she married Dad.'

She could see it now. Jem wasn't quite Darcy or even Heathcliffe. Of course not, he was Rochester! She smiled at the realisation, even though she couldn't quite picture herself as Jane Eyre. But Frankie as mad, bad Bertha in the attic, Rochester's deranged first wife. Now that was perfect!

And here came bad Bertha now, between them in an instant, offering Emily a glass of wine. She was conscious that her hand was shaking as she took it. If only she could get it to her lips, she might be able to calm down a little.

'Shall we sit down and eat.' John started carving a side of beef and passing plates around the table.

Emily noticed that Frankie sat herself at the head of the table, next to Charlie. She smiled sweetly at him as she spoke. 'So tell us how you two met, Charlie?'

Charlie laughed and Emily braced herself for his reply. 'Well, to be honest, she literally fell into my arms,' he looked affectionately at Emily. 'Jumping off a bar!'

'Oh how hilarious!' Frankie managed to look scornful even though she was smiling.

'Now why doesn't that surprise me Emily?'

They were laughing at her already. 'Charlie is actually an old friend of my flatmate Bella.' Emily countered. 'What about you and Jem?' She asked unthinkingly. She wasn't sure she wanted to know.

Frankie looked delighted. 'Well, shall I tell it Jem?' He opened his mouth to reply, but she had already launched in. 'I was competing in a Team Chase near here. My horse, Desperado belonged to a friend of Jem's, so he came along. He watched me win the race and we got chatting afterwards. It turned out that he had worked in TV and had just finished a radio course in Canada.' She was gushing. 'I offered him a job on the spot and the rest, as they say, is history.'

Emily found herself silent and awestruck. 'Oh right.' She muttered, inadequately.

'Frankie is a brilliant horsewoman, utterly fearless' John added like a proud father.

'And News Editor of the biggest radio station in the North.' Jem pitched in.

'Oh stop!' Frankie attempted to be coy.

John turned to her. 'So tell us about your job Emily. It sounds fascinating, though I can't say I understand it at all.'

They all looked at her expectantly. She took a deep breath before replying. 'Well, I do consumer PR, actually.' She saw John's blank face. 'Our job is to try and publicise literally any product you might buy in a shop.' For a moment she couldn't think of any. 'Like washing powder, cherry drinks, sausages, that kind of thing. We try to get them on TV, in newspapers, radio, online, that sort of thing, to help them sell more stuff really.' She trailed off weakly.

'I see', said John politely, 'so that's how you came in contact with Jem.'

Emily was grateful he didn't ask more. 'Yes, I think he was on the receiving end of one of our sillier surveys.'

Frankie was happy to elaborate. 'They actually have a thing called 'National Sausage Week' John.' She bellowed across the table. 'And Emily is apparently up for an award for the campaign. Isn't that right Emily?' She paused for a moment before adding. 'Although by rights, I believe it really should be Jem's award. Don't you think Emily?'

'I hardly think so Frankie.' Jem came to her rescue. 'It was Emily who came up with the survey and got the media talking in the first place. I just made a couple of phone calls.'

Frankie raised her eyebrows. 'You are too modest, my love.' She carried on, seeing John's confusion. 'We're talking about surveys, John. It's when PR people tell the media that they've spoken to 1000 Newcastle women, whereas in fact they have probably spoken to 3. Why did you choose PR, Emily?' It sounded like an accusation.

Emily stammered through her response. 'Well to be honest it chose me really. I ran up so many debts at University, you see. It was the first job I was offered.'

'Poor you.' Frankie put her head on one side. 'However did you manage to get in such a mess?' It astounded Emily, how she managed to be quite so condescending.

'Probably just like everyone else, Frankie!' Jem laughed.

Emily was finding it increasingly difficult to concentrate on defending herself, because by now the amorous hound was back and under the table, wrapping his front paws around her lower leg in readiness for his next assault. She was hoping that no one had noticed, but Frankie missed nothing, of course. 'How disgusting!' She said loudly. Emily wasn't quite sure if she meant her or the dog.

'I'm so sorry Emily,' Jem stood up from his chair. 'I'll put Pilot outside.'

But as they chatted, the dog whined and scratched at the door. Emily looked at Frankie's inscrutable expression. Yes, Bitch Bertha was perfect. She wondered if she had sprayed her with some sort of dog attracting pheromone, as soon as she arrived.

After dinner, they were ushered over to sit by the fire. Emily walking beside John, stopped beneath an oil painting. 'What a stunning portrait. Is it your wife?' she asked, without thinking. 'Oh Gosh, how insensitive of me.' She added hastily.

John smiled warmly. 'Not at all, I'm glad you ask actually. Yes that's her. I had it done just after we met.' They both stood silently, admiring the portrait, before John added. 'That's what people don't understand you see. They don't mention her in front of me, but I like to talk about her.'

Emily relaxed for the first time that evening. 'She's so beautiful. How did you meet her?'

She could see that John enjoyed retelling the story. 'I first saw her in a bar in Lisbon. She was dancing on a table. I was touring Europe with some chums at the time. I had never seen anyone quite like her.' He sighed. 'I found out later she was Maria Theresa Marques, the daughter of a Portuguese aristocrat, way out of my league naturally. I never thought she'd agree to come and marry an English farmer and live somewhere as remote as this.'

'But she did!' Emily was awestruck.

'She did indeed' He replied. 'And she ended up loving Northumberland as much as me.'

Emily was choked. 'It must have been a terrible loss for you.'

'Yes, devastating.' He replied. 'I don't know what we would have done without Frankie to help us. She kept everything going for us really.' She felt a pang of regret at this last disclosure and immediately felt ashamed.

John turned the conversation back to her. 'What about you Emily? Where do you hail from?'

She was acutely aware of Jem listening to every word on the sofa behind them. Frankie was draped around his shoulders by now, his hand resting on her arm.

'All over the place really.' She replied and seeing the confusion on his face, she explained. 'Well my mother and father divorced a long time ago and I used to split my time between them. And my mother now lives in the South of France, with her fourth husband.' Her voice trailed off and she gave a little laugh, desperate not to sound tragic. She could tell that Bitch Bertha was listening in and no doubt forming her own conclusions about Emily's behavioural influences.

'And your Dad?' John asked.

'He died 8 years ago.' She tried to sound matter of fact.

'Oh I am sorry to hear that.' John looked at her kindly. 'Brighouse - it's quite an unusual name. I've not heard it before, apart from Jack Brighouse, the travel writer of course. No relation?'

'He was my Dad.' Emily replied proudly.

'Good grief, really! He was one of my favourite writers. Brilliant chap, very funny! I used to read his column out to Jem. I think that's what got him interested in journalism.'

Emily loved it when people had heard of her father. Eccentric, witty and usually broke, he may not have had much ambition, but his readers and fellow journalists universally adored him.

John was still getting over this revelation. 'So, you weren't tempted to follow your father into writing then?'

Emily shook her head. 'Too broke after University and then I got sidetracked, I'm afraid.'

'Shame.' John checked himself. 'So tell me more about this PR business, Emily. It sounds like a terrific lark.'

Frankie had called Jem into the kitchen and Emily couldn't help her gaze following after them. A few minutes later, they strolled back in. Jem came over and sat down. 'Oh Em, you've got to tell Dad the Zappit mosquito story.'

She wasn't allowed to get away with a thing. No detail could be edited out. 'Tell him about the bit where the windscreen wiper was flicking across your nose, Emily!' Jem was animated. Emily was less excited. 'Ha bloody ha!' she was thinking, as John who was laughing uncontrollably by now, got out a hanky to wipe his tear stained cheeks.

And here she was, right back in comedy buffoon territory, despite every effort to seem interesting and dignified. Emily did her best to divert the conversation. 'How close are we to Hadrian's Wall?' She asked, pleased with her effort to change the subject.

'Only about five miles in fact.' It had worked and John was off. 'Funnily enough, this house is made from part of it.' John topped up her glass. 'Come outside and have a look! I'll just grab a torch. We've actually got some ancient 'Cup and Ring' marks in the walls of the house.'

When they returned, Charlie was engrossed in a conversation with Jem, no doubt talking about shooting or fishing or some other mysterious country pursuit. She realised that she had neglected poor Charlie, but he was clearly fine.

Jem stood up. 'Well, I'm off to bed.' Don't rush to get up tomorrow Emily. Dad and I were planning on taking Charlie shooting in the morning, if that's OK with you.' She nodded, relieved that she wasn't expected to go. 'You can have a lie in if you like, or Frankie mentioned that she could take you for a gentle hack around the farm after breakfast. We've got loads of riding gear hanging around if you need it. I'll see you in the morning. Thanks for dinner Frankie, it was delicious as usual.'

As he walked by, he bent down and kissed Emily on the head. She resisted a strong urge to grab his shirt, with both hands and keep him there. He whispered in her ear. 'Thank you Em. I haven't heard Dad laugh like that for a long time.'

'I'll be up in a minute.' Frankie looked up at Jem. The words stabbed Emily in the stomach and she bowed her head unable to watch them.

Charlie moved over and sat with John and Emily. They sipped John's homemade Kumquat liquor and swapped recipes for damson vodka and sloe gin. Emily was suddenly conscious of the approach of bedtime and all that it might entail. She downed another shot of Kumquat liquor and didn't resist as John filled it up again.

Once Jem was out of the room, Frankie leant towards her. 'Actually Emily, I've got a surprise for you - a bit of a treat. I ride with the North Hexham Hunt and it's their Opening Meet tomorrow. It wasn't easy, but I've managed to get you in as a guest. I've got a fabulous horse you can ride.' Seeing Emily's face, she carried on. 'Oh God, sorry, you can ride can't you Emily? Or were you in PR 'lala land' when you told us that?' She gave a little laugh.

Emily looked Bitch Bertha straight in the eye, or as straight as she could manage, given quite how much kumquat liquor she had now put away.

'Of course I can ride Frankie.' She replied. 'Sounds fantastic, thank you. Be great to be back in the saddle.' She added, with unnecessary bravado.

'Good'. Frankie looked delighted. 'Did you bring your own kit, or do you need to borrow some?'

'Kit?' She tried not to look confused.

'Yes, you know' Frankie replied, 'Breeches, stocks and pin, hunting jacket, that sort of thing?'

Emily saw a way out and grasped it. 'Oh no, what a shame! I forgot to bring it with me. Would have been such fun.'

Frankie met her gaze evenly. 'No worries,' she smiled. 'I thought you might say that. I've got some stuff you can borrow, which is more or less your size. I'll wake you at six then.' She got up from the sofa. 'Sweet dreams.

13

It was pitch black when Emily heard what sounded like scratching on the bedroom door. Still half asleep, she wondered if Bad Bertha had set fire to Mr Rochester's curtains again. She looked around for a pitcher of water to douse the flames.

'Emily, it's Frankie.' A voice whispered through the door. 'I've got some clothes here for you. You'll need to be ready in 20 minutes.'

Why on earth was Frankie offering her clothes in the middle of the night? She got up and stumbled to the door. A pile of bizarre apparel lay neatly folded in front of her on the floor. It all came sharply back into focus. It was 6am, she was very hungover and it occurred to her, that this was probably as far up shit creek as she had ever ventured.

If there had been any amorous fumblings from her bedfellow last night, she had been blissfully unaware. His gentle snores were the only sound now. There was a whiff of mothballs as she pulled on the most extraordinary pair of trousers. She had not seen anything like it on the high street, that was for sure. Enormous comedy breeches, snug round the waist and ballooning alarmingly at the thighs. This and an oversized fleabitten navy jacket, made an unflattering combo.

Once she had attached the hair net and Kirby grips, she crept silently along the corridor and looked at herself in the full length bathroom mirror. She grimaced at the sight - Nora Batty meets WW1 field officer. If she was going to have to die, did it really have to be in fancy dress?

Ten minutes to go. There was only one thing left to do. She started to apply her make up.

Charlie was half awake now. 'What are you doing up Emily?' Then he caught sight of her. 'And what in God's name are you wearing?'

'I'm going hunting Charlie.' She replied, as if it was perfectly obvious.

Charlie rubbed his eyes. 'What? I didn't know you rode?'

She decided not to address this directly. 'How hard can it be?' She replied casually.

Charlie sat up at once. 'Now seriously Emily. Are you sure this is a good idea?'

'Yes, of course. Should be fine. I can ride well enough and Frankie says she has a lovely horse for me.' She thought it best not to be specific about her exact number of 'hours in the saddle'. He'd only fuss. 'Have fun shooting pigeons and things.' She sounded as cheery as she could. 'I'll see you at lunchtime.'

Charlie shook his head and smiled. 'Well at least let me tie your stock for you, so you look the part.'

Her legs shook as she walked down the stairs, dignified on her walk to the gallows. Frankie was waiting for her in the kitchen. She was immaculately turned out and Emily noted that her sleek, cream jodhpurs and perfectly tailored black jacket, bore no resemblance to her own bizarre concoction of an outfit. She also realised, that the hairnet was only meant to go round the bun area, as opposed to the complete 'Nora' look she was now sporting.

Frankie had lined up riding hats on the kitchen table and Emily tried each one on for size. 'Come on then, let's go!' Frankie led the way. 'Our horses have already been taken down to the meet by a friend of mine, so we'll drive down.' She looked at Emily's face. 'God, how much make up are you wearing, Emily? Honestly, I've never understood how some people can be bothered.'

Emily was tempted to say something about not wanting to die looking like a minger, but instead she slid, silent and stony faced into the Defender.

Frankie didn't look at her as the car pulled out of the drive. 'You'll be riding Titan, one of my horses. He's a fantastic hunter.'

Shit. Emily blanched. That didn't sound good. She had been hoping for something called Mr Chips or Snoopy.

'He's a fabulous horse.' Frankie carried on. 'Been out of work for a bit. Try to keep a loose rein. He likes to go and you're better off just letting him. You should be fine, as long as you don't yank him in the mouth.'

She wanted to ask what other methods there might be to stop a horse, but by now she was in far too deep.

Frankie gabbled on with one incomprehensible instruction after another. 'I'll be upfront with the first field, but a friend of mine, Biffy will be looking after you. You'll be in the second field, so no need to jump if you don't want to and when you've had enough, she'll bring you back.' Emily had heard none of this. Frankie drove through a gate and turned to Emily. 'And do remember to say 'good night' to the Master of the Hounds.'

Emily nodded. 'Of course, yes.' What the hell was she on about now? Good night? It was 7.30 in the morning. How long was this nightmare going to last?

They pulled up in a field and Emily stayed in the car and looked around. Camilla Parker Bowles was obviously some kind of major style icon round here. Those on foot were mostly wrapped in large amounts of tweed and enormous fur hats. She decided that the Northumbrian Sloane was a slightly ruddier version than the southern equivalent, more weather beaten perhaps.

Reluctantly, she climbed out of the car. Frankie appeared leading Titan. The sight of him took Emily's breath away.

'Oh my God, he's enormous.' She blurted out.

Frankie was business like. 'He's only 16 hands Emily. Now come on, I'll give you a leg up.'

Keep calm, keep calm, remember the basics, one rein in each hand, one leg either side. It was all she could do not to turn and run.

'One, two, three…' She was on the horse and miles off the ground. Frankie was off again. 'Now, when you start off on the gallop, I would let him jump forward on a semi-loose rein, before you spring up into position and bridge your reins.'

'Sure.' She felt sick.

'How are your stirrups?' Frankie looked at her.

'Great thanks.' How the hell were stirrups supposed to be?

Frankie broke into an uncharacteristic grin. 'Emily, this is Milo DeVere Jones, the Saturday Secretary and this is Biffy, who will be looking after you.'

Emily wondered if people actually got christened 'Biffy'. They nodded to each other. Biffy was a very pretty, slightly plump blonde, with an astonishingly deep, horsey voice.

Frankie was in her element. 'Good to see your gorgeous girls out today Milo!' Emily was introduced to Cosima and Venetia Devere Jones, his precocious 10 year old twins. She smiled, relieved to see some children, but they stared blankly back at her.

'Morning Emily.' Milo greeted her. 'Welcome to the North Hexham Hunt. We're a pretty friendly bunch really.

Gosh Frankie, I didn't know Titan was back in work?!
Hope you like 'em fast Emily...'

'Absolutely!' How much worse could this get.

Frankie trotted past on a beautiful chestnut mare.
She remembered the last time she had seen Frankie on
a horse, practically mowing her down at the polo. She
hadn't quite managed to kill her that time, but Plan B was
certainly looking more promising. Emily wondered how
on earth she had got herself into this? She decided to try
some horsey small talk with Biffy.

'I like the red ribbon on Titan's tale. Is that to show
where the horse comes from or something?'

Biffy looked surprised. 'No, that's to warn other riders
that he's a kicker.'

'Oh' Emily replied, feeling foolish.

Venetia Devere Hunt overheard them. 'You're holding
your crop upside down!' She sneered and cantered off
theatrically, turning round in order to mouth, 'loser!' at
Emily.

'Stirrup cup?' A large tweed and fur lady popped up
next to her with a tray of drinks.

'Yes please.' She reached gratefully for a glass of port
and downed it in one.

The sun was struggling to break through a low mist. If
she hadn't been so frightened, the colours and muffled
sounds of the hunt might have seemed beautiful,
romantic even in the early morning fog. She thought of
Bella, snoozing happily in her bed. What wouldn't she
give, to be at home in bed right now.

Titan was snorting with excitement and literally
foaming at the mouth. Unable to stay still, he was
prancing around in circles.

Frankie watched her efforts to control him. 'Don't
snatch at his mouth Emily, you're winding him up.'

'I don't think he likes the dogs.' Emily answered weakly.

'Hounds Emily, not dogs.' Biffy boomed.

'Face the hounds!' Somebody was yelling at her. These people were utterly deranged.

The Field Master was addressing the crowd now. She missed most of it; something about newcomers staying at the back. She was actually relieved when the Master sounded the horn and finally it began.

Her lips moved silently as the hunt moved off. She was doing frantic deals in her head. Please God, if I can just stay alive for the next two hours, if I can just live, I'll go back to London and be really nice to Charlie and do my job really well and I promise I'll just be grateful to be alive.

A huge bottleneck of riders and horses formed at the bottom of the field, as one by one they trotted through the open five bar gate. This is OK, she thought. If I can just do this trotting thing all day. It was very uncomfortable, but manageable.

Biffy was beside her again. 'Emily, don't you do a rising trot?'

'No' Emily shouted back. 'We don't believe in it where I ride.'

Biffy shrugged. 'It's just that Titan will think you are asking for canter all the time.'

'Have fun Emily!' shouted the Saturday Secretary. 'You'll be absolutely fine!' He cantered off after the evil twins and jumped over a low wall. She finally made it through the open gate, just in time to see him tearing up the headland, smack straight into a large branch and fly to the ground. He must have been on his horse for less than a minute's hunting. Brilliant. How she envied him. As she looked behind her, he was stumbling round the field, clearly concussed.

Biffy was next to her again. 'Barrister from London. Only comes up at weekends. Crap rider!' She bellowed.

A small child fought valiantly to stay on his bucking bronco of a pony, but finally succumbed, flying through the air like a rag doll. 'Back on the horse Inigo!' shouted Mother.

This was like some sort of Total Wipe Out for toffs. And it was her turn next.

Titan was snorting and prancing. He started to canter, throwing her bottom out of the saddle with every stride. The Port was sloshing around alarmingly in her stomach, with the remains of the Kumquat liqueur. Shit, this was petrifying! She had no control now whatsoever. Hold on, she mouthed to herself, but what to hold onto?

Biffy was right beside her. 'Check your horse Emily.'

'Check him for what?' She managed as she shot past.

And now Titan was heading through a small copse, down towards a stream. He had at least stopped cantering, but branches and twigs whipped her in the face. She looked around hopefully for a low hanging branch. If only she could be knocked out cleanly and wake up in her bed in Fulham.

Frankie was next to her now. 'Keep back Emily, keep back! You've ridden over the scent!'

'Sorry!' She was mystified. Even if you had any control of the wayward beast you were clinging to, how were you supposed to know where the bloody hell the scent was anyway.

They were out of the copse now, sweeping up through a field and cantering full pelt up a main road. The B4045 Emily noticed rather randomly as they stormed along. If this was a race, she was closing in on the front runners.

And here was Venetia, back again. 'Hi loser!' she shouted at Emily and even managed to form an L with her fingers as she cantered up the road. Sweet child!

A sudden sharp left and she was very nearly thrown off, clinging desperately to Titan's neck, as he launched them across a ditch and into another field.

And now they were in open countryside, the sun shone through patches of cloud hanging low over the

Cheviot hills in the distance and miles of open landscape stretched before them, bathed in a kind of magic light. Purple heather, copper bracken and what must have been Hadrian's wall, snaking through the landscape. What a staggeringly beautiful place to die.

No time for romantic reverie, they were cantering again and evil twin was now neck and neck with her, staring straight at her, smirking, inches away, reins in her right hand, to allow the fingers of her left to maintain a constant 'L' as she rode past.

And now something akin to lunacy gripped Emily. With an all too familiar feeling of reckless abandon, she actually kicked Titan on, urging him to go faster with whatever strength she had left in her shaking legs. As they started to gallop, she turned and shouted to Venetia, 'What's the matter Verruca? Can't keep up with the big girls? Looooser!'

But the last word was lost in the air, as Titan pulled away with such force, it took her breath away.

Leaving Venetia well behind, hooves thundering, she was charging up, right behind the Master of the Hounds. Great clods of mud came flying through the air, off his horse's hind legs.

'Hold hard woman!' he shouted as she overtook him. 'Someone get that idiot woman to slow down!'

'Tell the sodding horse!' She replied as she thundered past, wiping a large lump of mud from her eye.

They were galloping along the brow of a hill. She tried standing up in the saddle in a desperate imitation of something she'd seen on Channel 4 racing. Her legs were solid with fear, lactic acid coursing up her thighs and no vision at all in her left eye. The phrase 'breakneck speed' kept popping into her head. And then suddenly, like one of her strange cheese dreams, she thought she could hear Jem's voice.

'Emily, can you hear me?' There he was, tucked in behind her, galloping along on a horse so big it even dwarfed Titan.

'Yes Jem!' The relief was inexplicable.

'Listen to me Emily! I'm not going to ride alongside as he'll try to race me, but try to do exactly what I say. OK?'

'OK.'

She could hear his voice behind her. 'Sit back down as deep in the saddle as you can. Take one hand and anchor it on the neck and hold onto the neck rein. That's it. Now try to use the other to pull on his mouth, then release, then pull again.'

She tried to do as he said.

'OK, that should do it, but not so hard that you swing his neck.'

They were galloping downhill into a valley now at a terrifying speed.

She pulled and pulled again. There was a slight decrease in speed, but nothing that suggested an end to this terrifying nightmare. She was heart stoppingly frightened now, but still painfully aware of Jem right behind her, with a perfect view of her backside, bouncing around in balloon thighed breeches. She had to make this stop.

Trying to sound confident, she glanced briefly behind her. 'I'm fine.' She shouted. 'Just going to steer him over to that gate, to make him stop.'

'God no, Emily! Don't do that!' It was the last phrase she remembered hearing. A second later, she came face to face with the folly of her plan. Titan hardly broke stride as he obediently propelled himself off the ground, hurling them both over the five bar gate. For a long time afterwards, she could visualise the exact second that she and the horse finally parted company, her feet flying out of the stirrups and the rest of her starting a slow motion somersault through the air. She crashed into the ground and rolled down a steep, grassy riverbank, picking up speed until at last, she hit the water.

Jem was there in an instant, running down the river bank.

'Jesus Emily, are you OK?'

'Never better!' She struggled to get up, out of the water, but her legs were so weak, she fell backwards again. Giddy with relief, she started to laugh uncontrollably.

'Where am I and who are you?' She made another attempt to get up.

'Well that's the River Coquet, you were sitting in.' Jem smiled.

'Lovely! Very refreshing!' She felt a bit light headed.

'And I am your friend Jem.' He walked down towards her.

'Ah Jemima, it all makes perfect sense now.' Emily was laughing again, mainly with relief.

He looked at her strangely. 'Are you sure you're OK, Emily? Did you hit your head?'

'No. I'm fine.' Water ran down the inside of her breeches, but she didn't care. It was over and she was still alive.

Jem cupped her chin in his hand and turned her face towards him. 'Your eye looks quite bloodshot and your lip's bleeding. Let me have a look at you.'

'Just a bit of mud that hit me in the eye.' She smiled. He lifted her out of the water and carried her up the river bank. It was almost all worth it, she decided, just for this.

As he gently released her at the top of the river bank, he sounded serious for a moment. 'Now I've got a question for you Emily. Have you ever actually sat on a horse before?'

'Of course I have!' She started to laugh. 'But I was six and I believe the horse was called Biscuit.'

'Oh God, Emily!' He sighed.

Frankie had caught Titan and was leading him behind her horse. She rode up to the gate and had clearly heard every word.

She looked furious. 'Emily, I cannot believe you. You could have killed yourself and my horse and you actually think it's funny. You've ruined the day for everyone and I shall never be able to hunt with the North Hexham again.'

Jem tried to calm her down. 'OK, enough Frankie. The main thing is everyone's fine.'

'No, not OK Jem!' She snapped back at him. 'What exactly is her problem? Doesn't it bother you that she's a disastrous liar?'

Emily shrank under her icy glare, but Jem seemed unruffled. 'Frankie, calm down. It was an accident. Look, why don't you take Titan back to the farm and I'll take Emily back on Ted with me.' Frankie gave him a look that could curdle milk and cantered off with Titan by her side.

Emily stared after her. She gasped as Jem, with one swift movement, lifted her onto his horse and leapt up behind her. Her breeches were damp and extremely itchy by now. He was so close behind her that she could feel every muscle in his body.

'I suppose she's just pissed off that I'm alive.' She immediately regretted saying it.

Jem didn't reply for a moment. 'She's right you know. That was a lunatic thing to do. How was she supposed to know you couldn't ride.'

'She knew.' Emily muttered just loud enough for him to hear her.

'Look, I don't know what's going on.' For once he sounded at a loss. 'I think she thinks you're some kind of love rival.' He paused long enough for her heart to feel like it had stopped. 'Which is ridiculous.'

'God yes, ridiculous!' She replied a bit too quickly. Ridiculous was the word. Ridiculous, because she was a damp arsed comedy buffoon, or a 'disastrous liar.' She stared straight ahead. At least he couldn't see her face. Neither of them spoke.

'Is it far?' She broke the silence.

'About an hour, at a walk. And don't worry, we won't be going any faster than this.' He held the reins with one hand and the other arm circled her waist.

Completely alone, they were following the line of Hadrian's Wall. A sunny autumn morning had burned through the mist to reveal a river running through copper coloured hills. A pheasant shot out from behind a tumbledown wall, but his horse ambled on oblivious.

She was suddenly glad that she and Titan had covered quite such a distance. 'This is so beautiful! Where are we?'

'The Northumberland National Park.' He pointed down the valley. 'That's Hadrian's Wall down there and just over there, the edge of Greenlee Lough. You can just see a pair of greylag geese on the water.' She nodded. 'There's a family of otters living on the Lough. Next time you come up, I'll take you over to see them.'

'Next time you come up.' The words made her want to sing. She thought she was going to faint.

'Are you OK, Emily?' His arm tightened around her.

She started to think about how she had pictured this weekend, her ridiculous fantasies. Even she couldn't have dreamt up this one. But then she remembered that he belonged to someone else and she was an imposter. She sighed to herself. Here she was, spoiling the moment. Enjoy it while you can, she tried to tell herself.

'So, how did you know I had gone hunting, anyway?' She did her best to sound jovial.

'Charlie and I went out shooting. He seemed a bit worried. I thought you were still asleep at the farm and then he told me that you'd gone hunting.' Jem paused. 'We were going to call you, but he didn't have your number in his phone.'

'Oh.' She hadn't thought about that one. Of course it must look odd.

'He really cares about you, you know.' This was all she needed.

'Yes I know.' She replied half-heartedly.

'Brilliant bloke by the way.' She really wished he wouldn't go on. 'I thought he might be a bit of a chinless twat, the way you described him, but I like him. I can see why you two got together.'

Emily rolled her eyes. Any minute now and he'd be asking to be best man. She thought that was it, but Jem hadn't finished. 'But does he make you happy, Em?'

'Yes, I guess so.' It was a weak response, but what else was she supposed to say? Actually no, I brought him here as a decoy. It's you I want.

She really needed to get him off the subject. 'So why aren't you wearing a hat then?' It was random, but it did the trick.

'Well I left in quite a hurry. Actually, I had quite a hard time trying to catch you. You were fast. Pretty good, considering you've not really ridden a horse before.' She could tell he was laughing at her, but she didn't care. 'I guess all that breakdancing and jumping off bars, must have done something for your balance.'

She could laugh about it now. 'Yes, it was just the stopping bit that was the problem. I couldn't seem to find the brakes.'

'Well it's not quite the same as driving a car Emily.'

'I wouldn't know, I haven't passed my driving test.' She winced as she said it. Why did she always have to do that? Just in case her loser status was in any doubt. She swiftly changed the subject. 'Why do you have to say 'Good Night' to the Master of the Hounds? What's that all about?'

He laughed. 'I don't know, one of those hunting traditions I suppose.'

They lapsed into a comfortable silence for a while. She looked around her. 'When you're on horseback, the wildlife doesn't seem so scared of you, does it? Look at that sparrow on the wall.' She knew she was babbling.

'It's a Skylark.' He paused. 'Have you really not passed your driving test Emily?'

'No.' At least she managed to stop herself, from telling him how many times she had failed.

'And how old are you?' He sounded quite bemused.

'29.' Time for another change of subject. She was becoming quite adept. 'Do you ever hunt Jem?'

'God no! I'll stick to polo, much safer.'

She spoke without thinking again. 'I'm not sure I even agree with foxhunting.'

'Well I wouldn't worry, Emily. Thanks to you, I don't think any foxes were actually harmed today.' They both laughed but he suddenly sounded quite sincere. 'Emily Brighouse. Are you not scared of anything?'

She thought about it for a while. 'Your girlfriend, actually.' Realising she had gone too far, she tried to lighten the tone, 'and bloody hell, some of those ruddy cheeked, horsey women!'

He didn't answer, she chattered nervously on. 'I forgot to tell you. In a bizarre twist, my flatmate Bella and Derek Dewsbury have got together.'

'You're kidding. How did that happen?' Relief, they were back on safe ground. It felt a bit like Jemima and Emily again, relaxed and laughing. They were heading down a lane now, on the outskirts of a village.

She had an awful feeling they were nearly home. 'At the risk of sounding like a complete alcoholic, I don't suppose we could stop at that pub could we?' What on earth did she go and say that for?

'Of course. We'll call Charlie and stop for lunch. In fact, we should call him to let him know you're OK. Did you bring your phone?'

As Jem tied up the horse outside the pub, she reached into her inside top pocket, where remarkably, her mobile phone was still intact.

'I haven't got his number, though.' She blurted out.

'Oh, OK.' Was that a slightly odd look that flashed across his face. 'I'll call Dad. You go in and dry off by the fire. I'm going to stick Ted in the stable round the back.'

She sat by the fire and very soon Charlie and John drove up to the pub. Their initial concern soon faded as they settled in with pints in hand, to hear the full story. John insisted on a detailed account and Jem was happy to interject with anything she had left out. John was shaking his head. 'Good God woman, were you not tempted to admit you couldn't ride at any point!'

'It didn't occur to me.' She realised on reflection, that it did seem rather odd.

'Emily, you are too much!' She was tempted to agree as he reached for his hanky, to wipe his eyes once again.

Jem left before them, to take Ted back in daylight. The sun was setting as they drove into the farm and suddenly she was exhausted. She wasn't sure she could face the full force of Frankie tonight.

Her phone buzzed in her pocket. A text from Bella.

Hope u r having fab time. I managed not to blow it. Derek is a dream. Stay away from horses, cows, sheep, etc. Look forward to full run down tomorrow night. Bx

She smiled. Bella was going to love this.

They ate supper in the kitchen. A sober affair compared to lunch – Emily struggling to stay awake and Frankie silent and sulking. She could hardly manage any food, let alone wine and she made her excuses and went up to bed as soon as she could, leaving Charlie and John by the fire. Jem walked with her to the door.

'You know, Dad hasn't stepped inside a pub for two years and like I said last night, he hasn't laughed like that since my mother died. You seem to be having a magical effect, Emily.'

'It was worth the near death experience then,' she smiled, wishing she could have a magical effect on Jem.

'Good night Emily.' He kissed her on the cheek and she walked, exhausted up the stairs.

14

It was 2am and it took her several seconds to remember where she was. Woken by the pressure of a warm body pushing against the small of her back. Oh shit, here we go. Pretend to be asleep and maybe he'll give up. More insistent now and a face, pressing into the back of her neck. Don't move a muscle. And now damp, heavy breathing right into her ear.

'Oh for fuck's sake Charlie!' She swung her body round to face him and found herself staring straight into Pilot's panting jowls. Charlie slumbered on regardless at the other end of the bed.

She pulled on Pilot's collar. 'You! Out now!' But every attempt to eject him from the room was met with loud whimpering and scratching at the closed door. She let him back in. Bloody dog! In the end, they struck a compromise and he settled at the end of the bed.

3am. Wide awake now. Fretting, going over every word he had said. How ridiculous that Frankie should see her as a rival! Isn't Charlie a brilliant bloke! I can see why you two are together! Why had she put herself through this agony. So much harder to forget him now, than it would have been if she'd never come here. She stared at the back of Charlie's head. Poor, sweet, tolerant Charlie. 5am and sleep finally overcame her.

At very least, she could get up in the morning, wear her own clothes and try to regain some kind of composure, before they left this place. That was until she saw her face in the bathroom mirror.

Charlie sat up in bed. 'Emily, have you seen yourself?' It seemed uncharacteristically harsh, but he was right. One black eye, completely bloodshot and a split lip that she hadn't even noticed last night. She carefully made up the one eye, but that just made it look more weird and she certainly didn't need anything to plump the lips this morning.

Jem, John and bitch Bertha were already up when she walked into the kitchen and braced herself for the inevitable exclamations.

'You look awful!' Bertha was predictable.

John was kinder. 'Gosh, your face has really taken a battering hasn't it, my love. What can we get you to eat?'

He made her a slice of toast which she nibbled tentatively out of the corner of one side of her mouth. 'That looks a bit painful Emily. Come on, I'll make you some porridge instead.'

Frankie clucked around the kitchen like she owned it, stirring a huge pot on the aga and fussing over John.

She was conscious of Jem watching her as she struggled to spoon the porridge into one side of her mouth. 'Right, come on, Emily, when you've finished that. I've got a surprise for you!' Emily was appalled. What now! She wasn't sure she could take any more surprises.

She couldn't disguise her lack of enthusiasm. 'Don't tell me, something to do with cattle? I know, milking a crazed cow? No? Sheep shearing?'

'Wrong season. A driving lesson in fact. We can't let you get to 30 without being able to drive a car Emily.'

He saw the look on her face. 'Don't worry, we're taking the Land Rover, you can't do too much harm, it's nearly the same age as you.'

'Thanks for the reminder.'

'And nearly as many miles on the clock.' Frankie muttered, just loudly enough so that Emily and no one else could hear.

She followed Jem out of the house. The ancient Landrover was parked at the front door.

'I think I should probably drive till we get to the field,' he said, leaping into the driving seat.

He had laid out six straw bales in a large field behind the farmhouse. As they swapped places and she focused on all the levers and buttons in front of her, she started to think that this could actually be worse than the hunting.

'Right then' she tried to sound positive, 'this driving lark, is it anything like riding a horse?' The gears roared as she released the handbrake and attempted to move off.

'Clutch down Emily!' He actually looked quite alarmed.

'And that's where exactly?' They slammed straight into the first straw bale and the car juddered to a halt.

'OK. Perhaps I should outline the basic workings of the car first, Emily'. They were both laughing and it felt like old friends.

She smiled. 'Go on then, but keep it snappy, you know I'm easily bored.'

They were off again. Better this time, same screeching of the gears as she only half pressed the clutch, cleared the first bale but crashed straight into the second. 'How about I just go round the outside of the field for a bit', she suggested, weaving her way out of the straw bales and dangerously fast towards the fence. Jem leaned over and grabbed the handbrake.

They both flew forwards. 'How am I doing?' She shouted over the sound of crunching gears.

'Jesus woman, you're a fucking liability!' he grinned.

'Is that right? You're not frightened are you Jem? I thought you were hard as nails up north?' It was like talking to Jemima again and she was giddy with the feeling that she had refound her friend. 'What was it you called me in that email? Southern, shandy drinking poofter? Let's see how hard you are now then, shall we?'

With that, she slammed the car into gear and put her foot flat down on the accelerator. The car leapt forwards. He had one hand over his eyes and with the other he hastily released the handbrake. They were tearing round the field now, the car lurching and bouncing, laughing and shrieking so loudly that Charlie, John and Frankie had come out to watch.

'I think you'll be fine to take it out of 2nd gear now!' Jem shouted, before she finally brought them to a halt next to John.

Once they had both recovered enough to speak, she turned to him. 'So how was my first lesson?'

'Christ Emily, I think you need professional help,' he said laughing. She wasn't sure if he meant generally or just for the driving lessons.

The sight of Frankie's face brought her back down to earth. In just over 3 hours, she would be sitting in Charlie's car, heading back down the M1. She felt a sinking feeling in the pit of her stomach, as she got out of the Land Rover and watched Jem drive off.

She didn't see him again until lunchtime. At least Frankie was also off somewhere. Charlie and Emily chatted to John as they helped him make the lunch. He talked about the countryside around the farm and she recognised some of the names Jem had talked about, as they rode home yesterday. John was brimming with enthusiasm. It seemed there was nothing he didn't know about the history and wildlife of this place. He suggested they go for a walk after lunch, to Green Lee Lough. In the end, they only had time to do a 2 mile loop of the farm.

There was a favourite view of the Cheviot Hills he wanted them to see, at the far end of the farm land.

After lunch, they set off and Emily noticed that her brand new plum, mid calf Hunter wellies suddenly looked very shiny. She tried to scuff them as they walked along, deliberately walking through any kind of slurry she could find. A cold wind whipped their faces and thick clouds were settling in.

They had been walking now for half an hour and John led them over a stile and up a steep hill. Her eye stung a bit in the wind. Charlie linked arms with her as they walked up the slope and she couldn't help thinking how different this scene was from the breathless Brontë-esque scenario she had envisaged; just Jem and her, passion in the heather. Instead, the five of them trudged onwards, through misty, damp air and spitting rain.

In spite of the cloud, the view from the brow of the hill was breathtaking. It felt like they were on top of the world and they all stood silently, taking it in. Endless rolling hills in copper and green, tinged with purple heather.

On the way down, she found herself at the back, walking alongside Frankie, who waited until they had fallen well back behind the others before she piped up.

'Emily, I would just like to say that I don't think I have ever been as embarrassed as you made me yesterday.' Emily was taken aback by the sudden, candid outburst. She couldn't think of anything to say.

Frankie carried on. 'I mean, why on earth didn't you say you couldn't ride at all?'

They were well behind the others now, but Emily still lowered her voice. 'We've been over this Frankie. I don't know why.' There was a silence and she tried to lighten the tone. 'You're a very persuasive woman Frankie. Anyway, it was OK actually. Once I got going, I quite enjoyed it.'

Frankie slowed to a halt, staring straight at her. 'I am persuasive Emily... and very competitive. I hate to lose.'

'Good for you.' Emily smiled insincerely and carried on walking. Bloody hell, this woman was a lunatic. Lose what exactly?

No eye contact. They both looked straight ahead.

Frankie broke the silence. 'It's so funny Emily, because Jem and I were just saying that you have completely lived up to expectations.' Emily felt her whole body tense as she waited for the inevitable explanation. 'Jem couldn't believe some of your emails you know. The way you behave! He used to forward them to the whole Radio North team. You actually achieved a bit of a cult following.' Frankie giggled insincerely. Emily felt like she had been winded. She couldn't speak. Frankie carried on. 'Jem's promised them all a full run down of this weekend. Hilarious! I expect he'll be emailing them all first thing tomorrow morning. I must say, you haven't disappointed.' Frankie shook her head, smiling.

It might as well have been a well aimed body blow. Emily was crushed by a familiar feeling of choking disappointment. What had she really expected after all? Tears began to prick her eyes, but she wasn't going to give Frankie the satisfaction. She took a deep breath and tried her best to sound calm. 'I'll tell you what Frankie. Would you do me a favour?'

'I beg your pardon?' Frankie replied, all innocence.

'Would you do me a favour and just shut the fuck up.' It was Frankie's turn to look taken aback as Emily spoke very deliberately. 'You have been on my case, more or less non-stop, for about 48 hours, making out I'm some kind of floozy, a liar, too much make up, shit job, blah blah and that was shortly before you tried to kill me. And now it turns out I'm the laughing stock of an entire radio network.' Frankie didn't reply, but Emily had found her voice. 'To be honest Frankie, I don't really give a shit if you don't wear make up, because you think you're too pretty to bother, you're riding in the sodding Olympics or you can pluck a whole fucking pheasant with one hand tied behind your back. What would be fabulous though, is if you could just fucking shut up. I'll be gone forever in less than one hour, so that would be great, OK?'

'OK.' Frankie whispered her response.

They walked along in stony silence on the way back to the house, both adopting slightly studied smiles as John pointed out the names of distant landmarks and local wildlife.

'Girls, can you see Great Whin Sill over there. It's the natural rampart that the Romans used when they built Hadrian's Wall. It was formed about 295 million years ago.'

They nodded and made suitably appreciative noises. John, completely oblivious to any atmosphere, pressed on. 'And we've got some very rare species of birds and reptiles around here, 230 metres above sea level.' Luckily Charlie was at his side, full of questions and enthusiasm.

As they walked back to the house, Emily was feeling physically sick. They had packed their bags and put them in the car before the walk. Charlie was already making noises about leaving and stood at the entrance, shaking John's hand. Without really knowing where she was going, she slipped off towards the stables, needing just 5 minutes to be alone and maybe harden her heart for the six hour journey home.

She found Titan in the stables and went up to him. Wrapping her arms around his neck, she kissed his velvet nostrils one by one.

'I'm probably not supposed to kiss you, am I Titan? Not very horsey, I know. Thanks for looking after me, gorgeous boy. Sorry I'm such a crap rider.' Titan nuzzled into her arm and she rubbed his neck.

At that moment, she felt the weight of a stare behind her and turned round. Jem was sitting on the stable door, framed by the archway, watching her intently. She stared back and for a moment, neither of them broke eye contact. Without a word, he slid off the door and walked towards her. They stood now, a foot apart, still staring at each other.

'What do you want me to do?' he asked.

'What?' Her breath was shallow.

'Tell me?'

Maybe she was imagining all this. 'What do you mean?'

'You know exactly what I mean.' He wasn't laughing now.

She bit her lip, it hurt but she didn't move. They were now only an inch apart, not touching. She could feel the warmth of his body.

'They're waiting for you at the house. You should go.' He said, but stayed exactly where he was, blocking her way.

Still she didn't move. She watched his hand, as if in slow motion, come up from his side and reach behind her as he slid his fingers up her back and up inside her shirt.

'What do you want Emily?' His voice was hoarse.

She closed her eyes and gasped as he pulled her to him.

'Emily, Emily', he muttered as he kissed her so hard she was reeling. His hand moving up her stomach now, they staggered backwards like some kind of dance as they kissed so urgently. Through his shirt, she felt the muscles of his back. He lifted her up, her legs wrapped round him and they tumbled backwards onto a stack of straw bales. He was on top of her now and she thought he would crush her, his body now touching every part of hers. Her fingers were tangled in his hair. They rolled onto another stack of bales, his leg between hers. Both breathing heavily as he pulled open her shirt and kissed her throat and down between her breasts.

They didn't hear the door click as it opened, but the movement in the stable made them both look up.

Charlie was standing watching them in the doorway, confused and crestfallen. 'Oh, I see. I'm sorry.' he said. 'I just thought. I just thought we should be off soon Em. So sorry, I hadn't really realised, you see.'

Jem leapt to his feet. 'No I'm sorry Charlie, I'm really so sorry mate. That was really never meant to happen, believe me.' He strode out of the stables, leaving her sitting on a straw bale, staring after him.

'I just, I just came to say it was time to go', Charlie sounded apologetic.

She was motionless, her head in her hands.

'Your lip's bleeding' he said, handing her his handkerchief. He came over and sat next to her in silence and picked a couple of strands of straw from her hair.

'You're right', she said, 'it's probably time to go' and took the hand he now offered.

As they stood at the farmhouse entrance saying their goodbyes, she noticed that Jem didn't even move towards her. He didn't try to kiss her cheek, but managed a brief handshake and pat on the back for Charlie. John's warm hug almost made her cry. Frankie bristled as they exchanged a stiff air kiss. At the last minute, Pilot galloped down the track towards her and the mood lifted a little, as she received the inevitable slobbery goodbye.

'Goodbye Emily Brighouse, brave, beguiling woman! You are your father's daughter, I'm glad to say.' John kissed her cheek as she got into the car. 'Come back and see us soon.'

If she could just manage not to look back. She forced herself to stare straight ahead as the car pulled away, but just as they rounded the corner, she looked in the wing mirror to see the three of them, still standing at the gate. Her eyes started to well up, but the pain in her lip seemed to sharpen her resolve not to cry.

They were silent, no attempt at conversation from either of them. Just past the outskirts of Newcastle now.

Charlie had filled the car up with petrol after yesterday's trip to the pub so that they could drive to London without stopping. They should be home in 5 hours. She stared out of the window, seeing nothing. It had started to rain. Please God, don't let me cry. They reached the outskirts of Sheffield and Charlie pulled the car into the inside lane and drove into a service station.

She looked up, surprised that he was stopping. 'Are you OK?' she said.

'Yes, but you're not', he replied, switching off the engine. 'Come here.'

He hugged her and her silent tears soon gave way to great big convulsions of weeping. Her shoulders shook with painful gulps of air as she sobbed loudly into his shirt.

'That's it, let it all out.' He stroked her head and waited for the worst to subside before he took a handkerchief out of his pocket.

'Poor love', he said, wiping the tears from her cheek and dabbing carefully around her blackened eye. 'It will be alright you know. And you won't believe me, but I do understand how you feel.'

She watched him as he got out of the car and went into the petrol station shop. Two minutes later he was back, with two coffees and a packet of menthols.

He took the wrapper off and handed her a cigarette. 'There you are, have one of these.' He lit it for her.

She stood outside the car and dragged on the cigarette. 'Oh God, Charlie, I have no right to even call you a friend. How can you be so nice? I'm so sorry. I've treated you so badly.'

'No, you haven't. I enjoyed myself. It's all fine.' He smiled benignly.

'Why are you being so kind about this?' She looked at him disbelievingly.

'I'll explain one day.'

'Oh Charlie.' She sighed. 'Do you think you might be able to forgive me?'

'It's done. Forgiven. No harm done. And you're going to have to trust me on this one. It will be OK. Come on.' he said, sounding more businesslike, 'We'd better get going, we've got a long way to go.'

They drove on, mostly in companionable silence and conversation when it came, was easygoing.

'Where's Gloria Gaynor when you need her', he said, flicking through radio stations for something uplifting. 'Anything interesting at work next week?'

'Oh yes.' She said, suddenly getting a sinking feeling. 'I'd completely forgotten. We're pitching for the Territorial Army. First thing tomorrow morning.'

Charlie laughed. 'Well you'll look very convincing with a face like that.'

'Thanks.' She smiled.

There was a pause, before Charlie added. 'Who are you pitching to?'

'Major General Sir Johnny 'Jock' Strapp. And I didn't make that up. Have you heard of him?'

'Can't say I've come across him.' Charlie replied.

She realised that in her massive bout of self pity, she hadn't asked him anything about himself. 'What about you?' She asked. 'Busy week in the City?'

'Oh yes.' He smiled as he glanced briefly at her. 'Meeting first thing tomorrow on EMEA high yield diversification.' He carried on, satisfied that it had drawn the inevitable blank look. 'You know Emily, the index linked bond market, the affect on cross border primary origination, that kind of thing. Any thoughts you might want me to share with the team?'

'Crock of shite.' She smiled back.

'I'll pass that on.'

He reached into the glove compartment. 'Here,' he said, chucking a road map of Britain onto her lap. 'See if you can find any rude place names. We've got 3 more hours to kill.'

'OK.' She opened the map and studied it carefully for a while. 'There's a Shitterton in Dorset. And a Titty Ho in Northamptonshire.'

'Not bad, not bad at all, carry on.'

She knew he was just trying to distract her, but she was grateful nonetheless. 'Lickfold in West Sussex? Oh hang on, I've got Rimswell in East Riding here.'

She was silent for a while, before shouting, 'Cockmouth!' triumphantly.

'Well done!' He sounded genuinely impressed.

Pause.

'Twatt in the Shetlands.'

'And Horton-cum-Studley in Oxfordshire.'

'Good work Emily.' He sounded like a school teacher. 'Have you tried Wales? That's always useful.'

'You're right. Brynbugga!' She shouted.

A little while later.

'Piddlebottom, Butteryhaugh and Hooker's End.'

'Excellent!'

It was 10 o'clock, when she eventually walked through the front door of the flat. The hall light was off and the answer machine flashed – one message.

'Bellaaaaaa, it's Ben. Pick up the phone. I'm loooneeeely. I miss you. Come over and cheer me up.'
Beep.

Twat.

Oh God, that meant Bella was out. No doubt perfumed and primped and racing across London by now. But just at that moment, Bella appeared from the kitchen door, smiling. Her expression changed very quickly when she caught sight of Emily.

'Flaming Nora Ems! What happened to your face? Is that a black eye? I think you and I have got some serious catching up to do. Wait a second while I open a bottle.'

Emily tried to get Bella to start, but it was no good. Bella could sniff the drama and wanted immediate satisfaction. It was a slow process, with frequent interruptions to clarify every last detail.

'So he's been sending my emails out to the whole radio network and I think he may even have invited me up there, just to get another instalment for his colleagues, which of course, being me, I provided.'

Bella winced as she watched Emily dribbling. Her attempts to suck the wine out of the glass, while avoiding her painfully puffy, split lip were unsuccessful. It really was a pathetic sight. 'Wait a minute, I think we've got a straw in the kitchen.' Bella returned with a pink, bendy party straw and settled back onto the sofa.

'Well, Good God.' Bella exhaled loudly. 'I did tell you.' She added unhelpfully. 'See what happens when you leave London. Poor Charlie, poor you.'

'Indeed.' Emily replied, abandoning the wine glass and applying the bendy straw directly to the bottle. 'And less of the 'I told you so' thanks very much.' She was less keen than usual to conduct a full post mortem. 'Now let's hear your tawdry tale. Did you manage to get any words out this time, or were you just speaking the language of love?'

'Well.' Bella could barely contain herself. 'It did threaten to go quite badly at first and I was monosyllabic for the first few minutes. Honestly Em, I could barely look at him. But then I asked him about National Sausage Week and we were off. From then on the conversation just sort of flowed.' She looked rather wistful. 'I did nearly forget a few times that you and I are supposed to be distant friends and that we don't live together.'

'More importantly, Bella, did you go to the loo?' Emily had to ask, given the thorough research they had conducted.'

'Yes, all OK. On the ground floor as planned.' Bella was off in dreamland again.

'And then?' Emily urged.

'Well he was just really lovely.' She sighed.

'Oh stuff that Bella! I think we've established that he's a demi-god and 'really lovely'. Did you or did you not snog him?'

'Did I what?' Bella smiled. 'We snogged the entire way from Soho to Fulham. Obviously I couldn't bring him back to our seventies tribute flat, with photos of you and me everywhere. I made him drop me off three streets away.'

Emily looked surprised. 'That IS impressive.'

'Well I didn't have any choice, did I?' Bella raised her eyebrows. 'I kept visualising the Tube Map of Shame hanging in the hallway as we were kissing.'

Emily laughed. 'And are you going to see him again?' She asked tentatively.

Bella paused for effect. 'Yes, he phoned the next day and he's coming down again next Friday.'

'That's brilliant!' Emily burst out. 'I'm really pleased Bella.' But she couldn't help adding. 'Of course if you say he's 'really lovely' again, I might have to kill you. Did you notice my restraint in not mentioning the word 'porking' all the way through your story?'

Bella shook her head, laughing. 'I really can't ever bring him home can I?'

'Nope.' Emily was matter of fact. 'Not if you want to keep him.'

Bella picked up a postcard from the coffee table and handed it to Emily. In all the excitement, she had forgotten about it. 'This came for you. I haven't read it.' She lied.

Emily started to read.

Emily darling,
Benoît has left me. We had an awful
row. He went off last week on one of his
painting retreats and hasn't returned.
Spend Christmas with me in Paris! It will
be such fun and I need some one to lift
my spirits. Only six weeks - can't wait.

Mummy

15

It was first thing Monday morning and for once, Emily actually wished she was at her desk. A biting wind whipped around her as she stood, shivering next to Monica on the 21st floor of H&P's London Headquarters. They were decked out in full combat gear, but mercifully not in the camouflage mini skirts that Tony Jennings had suggested. Clare had persuaded him that they were not entirely suitable for abseiling.

She thought of Grania Wardman sitting in the warmth of her editor's office across town, Charlie in a high level meeting on some emerging market instrument or other, Frankie and Jem, about to be live on air with the morning news, no doubt sniggering about her weekend antics, a thought that made her wince. And here she was, stepping into some sort of nappy harness device, preparing for her descent, hundreds of feet down the side of the building and into the 7th floor boardroom of H&P, where the Territorial Army pitch team would be waiting. She couldn't really remember agreeing to this bizarre stunt, but it was clearly way too late for those kinds of thoughts. Her mouth was completely dry.

She allowed herself the briefest of glimpses below and could see a dizzying aerial view of Oxford Street, Hyde Park in the distance, the Serpentine. She could just see Marble Arch out of the corner of her eye – cars and buses scooting round like tiny toys. Shit, this was high up!

They were waiting for a text to give them the green light. The Major General in place, Pete and Dan in similar combat gear, poised to make their entrance by breaking down the meeting room door accompanied by a cloud of smoke and the sound of sirens, Anoushka on standby, on the dry ice machine and Emily and Monica, with military precision, to burst in through the boardroom window seconds later.

Two windows left open next to the boardroom table would allow them in, simultaneous access, feet first. Once the dry ice had subsided, Dan would begin the presentation. Anoushka was in charge of the details. It was never going to be easy to get all of this to happen at exactly the same time. But the feeling was, if they got this right, that the lack of any tangible pitch idea in the presentation might go unnoticed.

Emily glanced at Mean Monica, who didn't look remotely scared. She was whippet thin, sinewy even. Not surprising really. She spent her weekends mountain biking and was far too tight to buy any food.

At last, the text came through.

The Eagle has landed, commence your descent.

Pete had got slightly too into this.

The abseiling instructor had been through the safety drill, but to be honest it was quite dull and Emily hadn't been paying much attention. The harnesses were tightened around them and the instructor clipped them onto an alarmingly thin rope, attached to a metal bar. Emily and Monica shuffled out backwards, out onto the scaffolding. For the second time in 48 hours she realised that she might die wearing fancy dress.

He gave them the signal to let go. Mean Monica shot straight off. White knuckled, Emily stayed put, clinging to the bar.

'Let go of the scaffolding now, Emily!' The instructor shouted.

'No, no I can't.' She looked at him pleadingly.

'You've got to let go. Take hold of the rope, one hand at a time and step backwards.'

'I just need a second, if you don't mind.' She was frozen with fear, clutching onto the scaffolding, the wind whipping around her as she glanced between her legs and caught sight of the tiny cars below. She imagined her limp body, lying in the road.

He was shouting again. 'Step backwards! Don't look down and let go of the bar after three. One, two, three…'

'No, not quite ready yet.' She realised she sounded absurd.

'Let go of the bar! Now!' He was actually sounding quite angry.

She could see Mean Monica, already snaking half way down the side of the building like some crazed stuntwoman. Never mind the fact that they were supposed to arrive at the bottom together. Monica had never seemed like an 'all for one and one for all' type of girl and clearly, it was every man for himself this morning.

The instructor actually started to prize her fingers off the metal bar. Instinctively, she tried to lash out at him, but that only weakened her grip.

'Bastaaaaaaard!' she shouted, as she flew backwards off the side of the building, shooting down four floors, screaming all the way, until the safety harness brought her to a jolting halt.

Once the shock had subsided, she realised she had stopped freefalling and was still alive. She recovered a little and tried to breathe normally. There was nothing to do but start lowering herself, releasing the rope painfully slowly, inch by inch, down the side of the building. As long as she didn't look down at the miniature lines of buses and taxis far below and kept looking straight ahead through the windows of each floor, she actually managed to calm down. By the tenth floor, she was feeling cocky enough to wave at Neville in the Postroom. He waved back, slightly startled and mouthed something which she couldn't understand. By the eighth floor, she was humming the theme to Mission Impossible as she bounced confidently off the windows with every step.

She must concentrate now. What had they said? It was crucial not to overshoot the 7th floor. But that was the thing. Where exactly was the 7th floor? She'd lost count. And where were the two windows that were supposed to be open, to allow them to slide in dramatically and start the presentation. Monica's rope was still dangling, but no sign of her or where she had disembarked. Panicking now, her eyes ran up and down the side of the building. Not surprisingly, in mid-October, every window of the H&P building, right down to the ground floor was shut tight.

From outside the window, where she was suspended, Emily could just make out the familiar words of the start of the presentation. She slowed her pace and listened, lowering herself towards the sound of the voice. There they were, she could see all the faces inside. The meeting had started, but no one noticed her, hanging limply the other side of the window. It suddenly occurred to her that she must look like some crazed, window cleaning terrorist. What if pedestrians below saw her and called the police? She had visions of a helicopter police swat team swooping down and taking pot shots at her. Should she knock on the window and ask to come in? She was tempted to slide discreetly down to the car park and slope off somewhere for a coffee and a menthol.

She squinted through the window again. Dan O'Shagmeister was giving it his dramatic all.

'The outcome of recommendations of the FR20 Commission, to examine the future shape and role of the UK's Reserve Forces, predicts an integrated, trained Army of 100,000 by 2020, comprising 70,000 full-time and 30,000 part-time soldiers.'

This was the bit where she was supposed to come in with the strategy part of the presentation. She could see Mean Monica, relishing the moment, preparing to save the day and present Emily's slides. There was nothing for it but to knock sheepishly on the glass. She tapped as hard as she could. Clare F-B was the first to spot her, as she dangled helplessly, too tired now to keep her feet wedged on the window.

But instead of coming to her rescue, Clare frowned and mouthed something at her, flicking her hand away. The words were lost on Emily, but the tone was fairly clear and she made no attempt to let her in. Emily was forced to knock again. No one looked up. Her breath fogged up the glass and she started to spell out 'HELP!' in mirror writing on the window.

At last, Anoushka caught sight of her and let out a scream. The Major General was first to his feet and Tony and he struggled to open the window. With a great effort they caught hold of a leg each and manhandled her through the gap in the window and into the building.

Tony offered her a hand. 'Ah Brighouse! Nice of you to join us!' He was obviously loving this. 'We wondered what had held you up.'

Emily got up off the floor and attempted to release herself from the harness. Clare F-B's face was unimaginably angry.

Tony was jocular. 'Good God Brighouse, are you sporting a black eye?'

The whole room was tittering now. 'Emily went up north for the weekend.' Dan added helpfully.

'Haha! Hard night on the town was it Brighouse?' Tony was beside himself.

'No, a hunting accident actually Tony.' She tried to sound dignified.

'Splendid! Splendid!' That obviously went down very well with the Major General, who nodded enthusiastically.

Clare F-B's stare was searing into her and she didn't dare look up as she took her seat next to Pete. Mean Monica carried on regardless, she was halfway through her part of the pitch, standing under a powerpoint slide bearing the giant words 'Chalenge Briton!' Anoushka had obviously been allowed to type up the title slides herself. Emily looked at the floor and tried to recover herself, grateful just to be inside the room.

'And we will then challenge five leading members of the UK media, all of whom are longstanding contacts of H&P, to experience the Territorial Army for themselves......
Roisin O'Donnell from Your Life, Frankie Blake and Jerome Armstrong from Radio Northsound...'

The list went on, but Emily wasn't listening to the rest of the names. Last time she had seen the presentation, the names of the journalists were still blank.

Hearing their names read out like this felt like some kind of cruel joke.

Clare turned to her. 'Now that you've joined us Emily, perhaps you would like to present the last few slides?' She stood up and stumbled her way through Monica's last few predictable ideas.

And then each member of the media will receive a press release with a pot of black- out camouflage face paint, an airfix model tank and an army themed hamper, with a discount voucher for a bootcamp work out session.'

She sat down and Dan took them through the budgets, but by now the Major General wasn't paying any attention to the presentation. He turned to Tony next to him.

'Brilliant work Tony, you didn't disappoint. That bit where the girl pretended to be stuck outside the window was pure genius – bloody funny.' Addressing the whole room now, the Major General stood up.

'I would like to start by thanking you all for the hard work and detailed operational logistics that have obviously gone into this very thorough presentation. I dare say it's not very PC of me, as I haven't told the other two agencies on the pitch list yet, but I can honestly say that as long as none of you has a criminal record or an ASBO, you can consider yourself hired!'

Much laughing and cheering all around. Emily's stomach lurched violently at the mention of the ASBO. As they all shuffled out of the meeting room, she was the only one who didn't queue to shake the Major General's hand. The mood was jovial as they all crammed into the lift together.

'So who were you hunting with up north Emily?' the Major General inquired.

'Oh, I believe it was the North Hexham Hunt.' She replied.

'Good stuff! My daughter Biffy quite often hunts with them. Emily Brighouse is it? I'll mention your name when I see her.' Emily blanched at the thought.

Tony, Clare and the Major General were planning on a long, celebratory lunch and the rest of the team got out of the lift at the fourth floor. They walked back along the corridor. By now, Emily had a thumping headache and was in a very bad mood. She turned to Monica. 'Did you deliberately shut the window so that I couldn't get into the board room?'

'Of course not!' Monica looked defensive. 'What happened to you anyway, we were supposed to arrive together.'

'Yes, well you shot off like a bloody rat down a drainpipe. Tom Cruise would have had trouble keeping up.'

Pete cut in. 'Girls, girls. We won it remember. Let's not bicker, we should be celebrating.' At least his patronising outburst temporarily united them, as they shot him a collective evil stare.

Emily wasn't quite finished. 'And Anoushka, where did you get that list of journalist names?'

'From your contacts list, Emily. Did I do wrong?'

Emily's tone softened. 'No Anoushka, it's not your fault. I'm just not sure we can count on some of those journalists to join the TA. I meant I don't know if you remember, Roisin O'Donnell from Your Style, but she's at least 16 stone. Can you just run these things past me before you go ahead next time.'

'Sure Emily, sorry!' It was much harder to be mean to Anoushka than Monica.

Still in combat gear, Emily took herself off to the square round the corner and found an empty park bench. She rooted around in her handbag for the packet of menthols Charlie had bought her and lit one up. A tear ran down her cheek as she dragged on the cigarette. She was struck suddenly by the absurdity of how she must look - military camouflage fatigues, crying, with a black eye and a cigarette hanging out of her mouth. Right now, she didn't know what to think about anything. She just knew she wanted Jem so much it hurt.

Anoushka walked into the square. Emily looked down and thought she hadn't seen her. No such luck.

Anoushka bounced cheerfully up to her. 'Emily! Are you OK?' She spotted the cigarette and the tearstained face. 'I didn't know you smoked.' Emily didn't reply. 'Would it help to tell me what's wrong?'

Emily laughed wryly. 'Oh you know, Anoushka, just the usual! I think I'm in love with someone else's boyfriend, who actually finds me ridiculous and I've also really hurt the lovely guy who was pretending to be my boyfriend for the weekend. I've just made an arse of myself at work. I've started smoking again. That kind of thing.'

'Ok.' Anoushka looked perplexed. 'Actually, I don't really understand at all. Do you think you could start from the beginning and explain in a bit more detail.'

Emily lit another cigarette and dragged deeply. Keeping it fairly simple, she started from the beginning. 'Do you remember a journalist called Jemima at Radio North, who I thought was a girl and was actually a man?'

'No not really, but carry on, it sounds great.' Anoushka looked enthralled.

Emily recounted the whole story. If she had thought it would help, it didn't. By the end, she felt even more hopeless.

'So let me get this straight.' Anoushka was frowning. 'You were just pretending that you were going out with Charlie.'

'Yes Anoushka.'

'Why?'

'Because Jem is going out with Frankie.' Emily answered flatly.

'And you were just pretending you could ride?'

'Yes.'

'OK.' Anoushka appeared to be taking all of this in. 'And then you ended up rolling in the hay with him, so to speak!' She looked at Emily. 'God that's awesome Emily.'

It didn't feel at all awesome. In fact it felt a bit shoddy when you came to think of it. Emily examined the evidence. Maybe, given her reputation, he couldn't resist having a go himself, a quick romp in the hay before she left for London. She wondered if he would include that bit in his Monday morning Emily Brighouse newsflash.

Anoushka was still looking rapt. 'Well if it helps Emily, I think you're fabulous.'

'It does and thank you Anoushka. You are very kind.'

It didn't.

Anoushka went back to the office and Emily stopped off at the station to buy a sandwich and a card, a thank you card for John and Jem. Now that one was going to be a challenge to write. She eventually found one featuring an English hunting scene. Back at her desk she drew herself and Titan into the picture in biro. The wording was a little trickier to work out.

Dear John, Jem ~~and Frankie~~

Dear John and Jem,
~~Charlie and I would like to thank you~~
~~for a wonderful weekend~~

Dear John and Jem
Thank you for a wonderful weekend.
Northumberland is beautiful ~~and I hope~~
~~to see it again soon~~

Dear John and Jem
Thank you for a wonderful weekend. ~~In~~
~~spite of my tumble, I very much enjoyed~~
~~myself.~~
~~Much love~~
~~Kind regards~~
Emily

Dear John and Jem
Thank you for a wonderful weekend. The
doctor says I should be back on solids
soon. Northumberland is beautiful.
Much love
Emily

She ran down and posted it quickly before she could change her mind.

It was past 4 when Clare F-B came back to the office and she actually looked mildly pissed. Maybe this was a good time to strike. Emily took a deep breath and approached her desk. 'Clare, could I have a quick word?'

'Sure Emily! Come in.'

Emily braced herself. There was no point skirting around the issue. 'It's about that ASBO thing that the Major General brought up in the pitch. I didn't realise it, but of course, there are certain rules involved in working with the MOD.' She laughed nervously as Clare looked at her expectantly. 'Clare, I think there's something you probably need to know...'

The entire fifth floor looked up from their desks when they heard Clare scream. Her reaction was quite a lot less controlled than usual, but then she'd had a few drinks at lunch. Emily noticed that she sobered up quite quickly.

She crawled back to her desk, relieved at least to have made her confession. It didn't take very long for Clare to recover herself.

To: EBrighouse@Hobbs&Parker.com
From: CForster-Blair@Hobbs&Parker.com
Subject: The ASBO situation...

*Emily. I will somehow square it with Tony and the Major
General, which will be tricky, as he particularly asked if
you would be working on the account. You can at least
work on the campaign for the first six weeks, to make
sure we get it up and running. I am not sure at
this stage, how the ASBO affects your contract with H&P.
If you want
to keep your job, and by God I mean it this time Emily,
you had better get me 5 top tier journalists signed up to
join the TA by close of play Friday. This was pretty much
our only real idea in the entire pitch document anyway.
Make it happen.*

Clare

To: RoisinOD@yourliving.com
From: EBrighouse@Hobbs&Parker.com
Subject: Favour...

*Hi Roisin
I don't know if you remember me, we met at the polo in
York a few months ago? You mentioned at the time that
I might be able to call in a favour at some point. We've
just won a project to promote the Territorial Army and I
wondered if I could call you for a chat about an idea we
have?
Emily*

16

Nearly a week had passed. Not a word from Jem, nothing from Charlie. At least Clare had calmed down a bit and stayed off her back since their last little chat. Emily flicked through her emails.

To: EBrighouse@Hobbs&Parker.com
From: hectorbraun@levoisier.com
Subject: Well, did Captain Von Trapp blow his whistle?

Did the Baroness bow out gracefully, leaving you and the Captain to forge a successful and enduring career on Austrian Talent Shows? Is that the distant sound of two people singing Edelweiss I can hear coming from the North? The Reverend Mother needs an urgent update. Come to the Abbey at 12.30.

The hills are alive with the Sound of ….what exactly?

Hector x

To: hectorbraun@levoisier.com
From: EBrighouse@Hobbs&Parker.com
Subject: Brace yourself Reverend Mother...

Captain Von Trapp blew his whistle indeed. What they don't tell you is that in real life, he has a quick 'how's your father' with Maria and then goes running back to the Baroness. Bastard! See you in the Abbey at 12.30.

Maria

To: EBrighouse@Hobbs&Parker.com
From: hectorbraun@levoisier.com
Subject: Brace yourself Reverend Mother...

Oh dear! I am assuming the brace position as we speak! RM

As Emily walked into Il Paradiso, she had forgotten the state of her eye, now faded to a purplish, yellow tinge and still slightly bloodshot. Hector was waiting for her. 'Good God darling you look rough!'

'Thank you Hector', she said sitting down.

He scanned the menu. 'Quick let's order, before you start. Am I going to lose my appetite?' Hector looked at her over the top of his reading glasses. 'Have you been eating properly Emily?'

'Not really.' She looked deflated. 'And I've hardly had a drink.'

'Oh Lordie!' Hector handed her a glass of Champagne. 'Well drink that and tell me everything.'

Emily recounted the weekend's events. This was the third time and she now had the exact sequence of conversations, dog assaults, bitchy one liners and weeping car journeys off pat.

Hector leant forward, captivated. When she had finally finished, she sat back in her chair, waiting for his reaction. 'So what do you think Reverend Mother? Do you feel bad now, for making me go?'

'I do not!' He exhaled loudly. 'Mark my words. This is the start of something big Emily. Suppressed passion will always out!' He studied her for a moment. 'I must say though, I have never heard you sounding so negative. Perk up Emily! This is fabulous.' She looked unconvinced. He carried on. 'So tell me! If Heathcliffe is mad, Darcy is repressed and Rochester is brooding and attractive, where would you place Jerome Armstrong?'

'Oh Rochester, definitely! A little less brooding obviously, but you won't believe this, he even has a dog called Pilot.' Hector was relieved to see her animated at last. 'And of course his other half was just like mad, bad Bertha. Just a pity she wasn't restrained in the attic this weekend.'

'Too wonderful.' Hector was practically swooning.

Their starters arrived and Emily seemed to rally a little. 'You know Hector, Bella thinks I should give Charlie another chance, if he'd have me.'

Hector nearly spat out his bruschetta. 'What! Don't be ridiculous!'

Emily couldn't help but smile. 'Girls like me don't get the leading man, Hector. You have to be a perfectly poised, non-smoking virgin, with a curtain of shiny hair. I'm afraid I just don't qualify.'

'No dear.' He shook his head, undeterred. 'That's only if you want to marry royalty, which I don't think we're talking about here.' He took a sip of wine. 'Besides, any man worth having, would be bored rigid in minutes by a girl like that.'

They both smiled. She had one final card to play. 'Do you know something Hector? I don't want to break your romantic little heart, but in real life, Maria Von Trapp

was not in love with the Captain? Did you know that?'
She waited for a reaction to this shattering revelation,
but none came. 'She fell in love with the children straight
away, but apparently she had to learn to love the Captain
later. I meant how realistic and depressing is that?'

Hector shrugged. 'Well maybe she wasn't a passionate
creature, Emily.' He leant across the table. 'But I can assure
you, that you are.'

'Think about it Hector!' Emily carried on. She loved
it when they disagreed. 'I mean, think about the women
who created Heathcliffe, Rochester and Darcy. Look at
where their passion got them!'

Hector nodded indulgently, glad to see her back on
full form. 'Jane Austen only ever loved a penniless Irish
Barrister and was forced to break off with him, because
he was too poor. She never married. Miserable! Charlotte
Bronte was depressed all her life, married a man she
disliked, starved herself to death. Emily Bronte, died at 30,
a loveless recluse. Do you see what I'm getting at Hector?'

'Oh I think so Emily.' He replied, mocking her gently.
'And I can also see that you are in a very bad way.' Hector
gestured to the waiter to bring her another glass of wine.

He adjusted his napkin and addressed her very
deliberately. 'Now you listen to me Emily Brighouse. I will
not have you poo poo passion. It is the glue that holds us
together, when everyday life makes us nearly hate each
other.' He spoke as if he were delivering an ancient truth.
'This might not be a straightforward situation, but you are
going to have to keep the faith.'

'I'm sorry Hector.' She wasn't convinced, but she knew
he meant well. 'I don't mean to be so self pitying.'

He nodded. 'I can see that you're suffering, Emily.
Anyway, enough of your heartbreak, I need you to do me
a favour. Le Voisier are sponsoring a series of classical
music concerts in two weeks. It's an annual thing, at the
Albert Hall. Lots of stiff directors from the US and some

crashingly dull journalists. You must please promise that you will come to the opening night?'

'Of course I will Hector.'

'Bring Bella and her meat packer millionaire if you like.' She laughed. 'I'll ask them.'

'And that other thing Emily?' He added enigmatically, as she got up to go. 'Leave it with your Uncle Hector.'

As she walked to the tube she smiled at the thought of Hector and his rousing words. He really was better than any therapist or self help book. She decided that everyone should have an Uncle Hector.

She got back to her desk, long absence undetected. Mercifully little to do this afternoon, which was just as well as the wine had made her rather sleepy and even less focused than usual. Technically, Clare's deadline to recruit the world's media into the TA had come and gone, but she hadn't said anything about it. Maybe she would try to sign up a few more 'top tier' journalists this afternoon. Well, 'top tier' was going to have to be open to interpretation.

To: peter.king@britishfrozenfoodbulletin.co.uk
From: EBrighouse@Hobbs&Parker.com
Subject: Exciting opportunity

Dear Peter
I loved your article, on the increase in sales of imported frozen sausage meat in the last 2 quarters – really interesting. I was just wondering if you were interested in running a piece on the army's frozen food operation. Army marches on its stomach and all that. Only thing is, you would have to sign up to the TA for six weeks. Might be quite fun for your 'what's in the freezer this month' column?

Best regards
Emily

To: EBrighouse@Hobbs&Parker.com
From: RoisinOD@yourliving.com
Subject: Favour...

OMG Emily, that is actually what's known as a massive favour! Are you serious? I know I puked on your pashmina, but this is harsh. You may have noticed that I don't have the most athletic of bodies! But feck it, if I absolutely have to, I will.

Cheers
Roisin

Yessss!! She almost punched the air. Thank you Roisin, my little leprechaun angel. One down, four to go.

To: tanyawilliams@goodlooks.com
From: EBrighouse@Hobbs&Parker.com
Subject: Exciting opportunity

'How do female soldiers cope with the stresses and strains of army life on their skin? Is the day job taking its toll on their complexions? Cleansing, toning and moisturising in the field of combat? What sort of foundation would we recommend in dry, sandy conditions? We challenged our beauty correspondent, Tanya Williams to join the army and find out.'

Hi Tanya – see above for suggested beauty feature - let me know what you think.
Thanks
Emily

Clare F-B swooshed past her desk. 'How's it going with the journalists Emily? The Major General is waiting to hear. Needless to say, he is very keen that our first activity for him is a big success.'

It was good timing. Emily replied with cheery professionalism. 'Really well, actually Clare. Your Living has confirmed and six more are really interested, just waiting for confirmation.'

'Great, keep on top of it. And remember they have to be absolutely top tier journos.'

'Sure Clare.' Emily's smile faded as she walked off.

To: *gaz.t@dailysport.co.uk*
From: *EBrighouse@Hobbs&Parker.com*
Subject: Exciting opportunity

Hi Gaz
Just had an idea for a photo spread for the Sport. How about your regular Page 3 girls, Maria and Tracy, join the Territorial Army. Cheer up the troops, cheeky pics with the boys, full photoshoot in camouflage bikinis, girls draped over tanks, etc
Let me know what you think.

Emily

She knew it was getting desperate, but if she could just bump up the quantity, the quality bit might go unnoticed. Anyway, Mean Monica was being singularly useless in her attempt to get any journalists. So far she'd only managed a lukewarm response, from the TV critic of the Oxshott Gazette. She opened her inbox, hoping for one more 'yes' from a halfway decent journalist.

To: EBrighouse@Hobbs&Parker.com
From: hectorbraun@levoisier.com
Subject: The twin poles of passion & practicality...

"By and by I learned to love him more than I have ever loved before or after." Maria Von Trapp

So there misery guts!

See you at the concert next week. Chin up!
Hector

Emily smiled. Bless him! He was never going to give up.

To: hectorbraun@levoisier.com
To: EBrighouse@Hobbs&Parker.com
Subject: The twin poles of passion & practicality...

Hector
Very impressed by your research, but then I had forgotten that you probably have a signed copy of the Von Trapp family biography on your bookshelf. Thanks again for a lovely lunch. Sorry for being so grumpy – I shall bounce back no doubt. Will definitely come to the concert next week – I shall ask Bella and Percy Pig.
xx

There was an email from Charlie in her inbox. Not surprisingly, she hadn't heard a word from him since the ill-fated weekend.

To: EBrighouse@Hobbs&Parker.com
From: cfanthorpe@hutchinsons.com
Subject: Can we meet for a drink?

I really need to talk to you Emily. Need to set a few things straight really. If we can't be totally honest with each other, then I can't really see how we can continue to be good friends. I've got some things I'd like to get off my chest, if you can bear it, things I probably should have said at the time. Are you free at all next week, after work?

Charlie x

Oh God, here we go, she thought, the inevitable telling off. She knew he was too good to be true. Prepare for a giant ear bashing session. Well he could stand in the bloody queue at this rate. Oh well, she guessed she deserved it and he, of all people, deserved the chance to have a rant.

To: cfanthorpe@hutchinsons.com
From: EBrighouse@Hobbs&Parker.com
Subject: Can we meet for a drink?

Of course Charlie –I've got a couple of things I have to go to next week, but could meet on Friday night, after work. Is that any good? Just let me know where and what time. E x

In the old days, that is before her heart was broken and Bella hooked up with Mr Perfect Porker, she would never have suggested a Friday night. But now that Bella was out with Derek all the time, she knew she would be facing another night in by herself and quite frankly, even

an ear bashing was preferable to another repeat episode of
'Come Dine with Me.'

To: EBrighouse@Hobbs&Parker.com
From: cfanthorpe@hutchinsons.com
Subject: Can we meet for a drink?

Thanks Em. In the bar at Hamiltons. 6.30pm, next Friday.

See you then,
Charlie x

When she got home, Bella was getting ready to go
out. Every window was misted up with steam from the
shower and wafts of expensive perfume drifted from her
bedroom. She was playing her romantic power ballads
again and joining in loudly at intervals.

'Hey Em, are you staying in again?' She called from
her room. Emily winced slightly. Even a devoted, life
long, best friend could become just the teensiest bit
patronising, in that way that only the newly in love can
be.

'No no, I've got loads on next week actually. Grania's for
dinner, Albert Hall concert and then I'm meeting Charlie
next Friday. Quite grateful for a night in really.' She tried
to sound upbeat. 'By the way, you and Derek are invited
to a Le Voisier concert, at the Albert Hall. It could be your
first public date!'

Bella was shouting over the sound of the hair dryer.
'That sounds great, I'll ask Derek. Did you say you're
meeting Charlie? That's really good Em. I'm so pleased
you're going to see him again.'

Emily pulled a face behind the door. Pleased in what
way exactly? Pleased that she had given up on the silly
idea of finding the man of her dreams and settled instead

for Mr Nice, which of course Bella had not had to do. She knew she was being mean-spirited. She decided not to tell her that she was meeting him, so that he could give her an earful.

Bella came out of her bedroom. She looked gorgeous, apart from the inevitable neck rash, which she had unsuccessfully tried to disguise with too much skin coloured powder.

Emily brushed it off. 'So now that you've waited an appropriate amount of dates, Bella, presumably tonight is the night? North meets south for the long awaited inaugural shag-a-thon!'

Bella was coy, 'Well, I don't know. I mean, we'll see. I can't bring him back here can I? I still haven't told him that you and I live together and he can never ever be allowed to see this dump of a flat, that's for sure. He's just not a 'burnt sienna' bathroom suite, cigarette burn on the carpet kind of guy. Anyway, he normally stays at Soho House when he comes to London.'

'Of course he does.' Emily replied sarcastically. 'Well don't forget a clean pair of knickers and some face wipes. And remember to nick the sewing kit and toiletries before you leave in the morning.'

Bella left in a waft of expensive perfume. Emily couldn't help shouting after her. 'Of course you know you'll never see him again if you shag him, don't you!' She could be forgiven for feeling a little warped.

It wasn't so tragic, she decided as she settled in front of the TV with a family sized pizza and a bottle of Pinot Grigio. Maybe a single night in wouldn't be that bad after all. Bella normally insisted on University Challenge, a documentary or the News.

Tonight, she could watch all the things, that were normally banned. She flicked through the channels. 'Obese and six months to live' or a documentary about immigrants stealing all our jobs and English people being too lazy to work, or a rerun of Grand Designs. She opted for 'Obese and six months to live.'

'Adrian is morbidly obese. If he can't dramatically reduce his body mass within the next few weeks, doctors have given him less than six months to live. Adrian is now too large to get out of his house unaided.'

An air ambulance crew, crane operator and team of builders were working together to remove the roof and winch the enormous man and his unfeasibly large abdomen, out of bed and up out of the roof. He was now enveloped in a large section of tarpaulin, attached to ropes and awaiting the signal from the ambulance crew to commence winching.

'I don't understand it,' His girlfriend, who clearly liked a few pies herself, was pleading.

'He eats quite normally really...'

'…if you consider 8 packets of jaffa cakes a normal breakfast that is,' Emily was talking directly to the TV screen now.

The winching was a success and Adrian was now in a hospital bed, having lost a spectacular 3 lbs in a week. But just as she was tucking into her second slice of pizza and with no warning to viewers, the camera zoomed in on some running sores under the folds of his flesh. Bloody hell! Emily tried not to retch and reached hastily for the TV controls. She switched onto a documentary about immigrant workers.

'Until last week, British worker Shaznay had been employed as a seasonal fruit picker at this East Anglian fruit farm. Her job has now been filled by a Polish worker.

'So Shaznay, why did you quit your job at the fruit picking farm...'

'Because you're a lazy cow by any chance?' Emily shouted at the screen.

'The thing is wherever I work, right, they've got to respect me and I felt that the management at the farm were disrespecting me...'

'I don't respect you Shaznay! No one does!' Emily started to yell.

The TV presenter turned to Shaznay. 'Isn't that because, out of your five day a week contract, Shaznay, you only turned up for two of those days?'

Enough of that, no longer entertaining, she was getting too angry. In the absence of anything calming with Alan Titchmarsh or Monty Don, she quickly flicked onto a house restoration programme. That's better. She could feel her blood pressure drop.

'Chris and Tanya had no intention of ever living in a disused concrete water tower, but 8 years ago they fell in love with the space it offered. It was surprisingly cheap at £50,000.'

'Of course it bloody was! Because it's a fucking, ugly ruin you morons!' She had drunk nearly all of the bottle by now.

'Chris and I could never live in a 'normal' house again.' Tanya did that particularly annoying thing in the air with her fingers, to suggest speech marks around 'normal.'

'Pretentious twats!' Emily was shouting again. She carried on watching though, only because the presenter had the hint of a soft and very familiar Geordie accent and if she closed her eyes, she could almost see Jem's face.

The phone rang. She decided to leave it, as it was just getting to the bit where soft Geordie accent TV presenter had returned 'out of the blue' to see the finished build. He swept up the drive in a brand new Landrover Defender. The camera zoomed in on the car, just long enough, she noted, to secure the presenter's free Landrover deal for another year. She could hear Bastard Ben's voice in the background talking into the answer machine.

'Bels are you there?'

Emily hesitated for a moment, but emboldened by the wine, she couldn't help herself. She sprang up off the sofa and ran to the phone.

'Hi Ben.' She had hardly ever spoken to him. 'It's 10.45, what can I do for you?'

'Can you put Bella on.'

'Why?' She replied in mock innocence. 'Did you want to take her out for dinner tonight or something? It's just that it's a bit late now and she might need a bit more notice, that's all.' Who cares if she was slurring a little. This was fun.

'Just get Bella thanks Emily.' He insisted.

'Say please!' She knew she was getting childish now.

'Alright, get Bella Emily… please.'

She paused for effect. 'I can't.'

'Look, just stop mucking around Emily and go and get her, OK?' As well as being a total tosser, he was actually quite aggressive.

Emily took her time. 'I would love to Ben, but I'm afraid she's out for dinner with her boyfriend.' She waited a second for this to take effect. 'I'll give her your message, but she said she'd probably be staying with him tonight.'

'What?' Ben suddenly didn't sound quite so overconfident. 'She hasn't got a boyfriend.' He paused. 'When did she get a boyfriend?'

'Oh God, ages ago! Did she not tell you?'

'No, she didn't.' He sounded crestfallen.

Emily felt no compassion. She had never liked the way he treated Bella. 'Oh, OK. Well, the upshot is that she won't be needing your services from now on. Thanks for everything. So long fuckbuddy.' She didn't really know why she added the last bit.

She put the phone down and went back to the TV, a little giddy with her own boldness. On reflection that was a bit rash. She probably shouldn't have done that without Bella's permission. What if she came back in tears tonight, having split up with Derek and wanted to run back into Bastard Ben's arms. Oh well, he probably wouldn't object, he was one of those men who find indifference a turn on – wanker.

'Bollocks.' She had missed the end of the water tower restoration programme and would never now know how Chris and Tanya had turned their monstrous, concrete eyesore into a 'unique and funky space.' She didn't really give a toss either. She wondered what Bella and Derek were up to. It was hard not to be jealous, as she imagined them sitting in their boutique hotel bed. After a marathon shagging session, they would probably be showering, using bespoke, luxury toiletries, wrapped in white fluffy robes and waffle slippers. Or maybe they were still at dinner, holding hands over the table, sipping Limoncello and giggling.

And here she was alone, watching shite telly and eating pizza in this crappy flat, on a threadbare brown sofa. Maybe in time, she would buy a couple of cats for company. This was how her life would be, nothing but catfood, supernoodles and Pinot Grigio in the cupboards and maybe some Febreeze for the sofa.

She eventually gave up on the TV and stumbled into bed. She allowed her mind to wander, as it so often did, to the first time she had ever seen him. That brief, wonderful moment, before she had decided to typecast herself as a sexually incontinent, comedy buffoon. It was a vision of Jem striding towards her at the polo match, smiling at her, a moment of untainted joy, which she savoured and frequently played back.

It must have been the extra cheese on her pizza, but that night, as she drifted in and out of sleep, she reluctantly accepted Bastard Ben's hand in marriage. In the absence of her father, Jem had agreed to give her away. Derek and Bella arrived at the wedding in matching butchers aprons, in a pink, Dewsbury Pork branded Hummer. She only had the short trip up the aisle to tell Jem that it was all a mistake. 'Can't you see? It's you I want Jem, not Bastard Ben. It's you I want to marry!'

'For goodness sake, Emily, that's disgusting, on your wedding day.' He replied. 'I would never marry someone like you anyway. You're very lucky to have Ben, you don't deserve him. He's a lovely bloke, you know.'

Charlie had retrained as a vicar and was taking the service. The bridesmaids were gothic, in ripped black lace, Frankie, Clare F-B and Mean Monica, a trio of cackling witches, backcombed hair and black lipstick. Charlie turned to Emily and asked her if she would take Bastard Ben as her lawfully wedded husband. 'I will' she sobbed through her red veil, at which point the gothic bridesmaids started chanting 'liar, liar, disastrous liar' in unison. The whole congregation joined in now, laughing and chanting, even Derek and Bella…

17

It was Wednesday night. Emily had turned down Grania's dinner party several times already, with one excuse or another, but the bloody woman was relentless. She had the bit firmly between her teeth and finally the day had come. Whoever has a dinner party on a Wednesday night anyway. Bella had said she might meet someone, but the idea that Grania 'media lisp' Wardman might be the provider of Emily's perfect man was way beyond plausible.

Rejected outfits lay scattered on her bed as she once again reflected on how the hell she had agreed to this tiresome dinner party. Grania was in the same halls of residence as Emily at university. They had absolutely nothing in common. On one occasion, Emily had agreed to be in a play directed by Grania, for the sole reason that she fancied the leading man and temporarily needed to remodel herself as a keen, arty farty, thespian type. She had in fact secured a quick snog, but instantly went off him and had to endure another four weeks of Grania's rather overbearing style of directing and the now unwelcome attentions of twatty leading man. She never really understood why Grania continued to pursue her.

She always introduced her as the 'hillaaaawious girl in my corridor'.

While Emily held the College record for the number of shots downed by one person while still standing, Grania had started a poetry workshop and was president of the debating society. She also wrote for the University paper, presented an arts show on University radio and was fluent in Ancient Greek, which she apparently spoke at home to her parents and brother, Ptolemy.

What to wear? Black seemed like a good option, serious, intellectual even, but maybe accessorised with some slightly funky, arty jewellery - tribal meets funeral. Why was she even trying to be like these people.

Grania's friends always peppered the conversation with references to 'Walter Mitty' and 'Pavlov's dogs', which was unsettling if you hadn't heard of either. Tonight was going to be a struggle, especially if she didn't manage to change her attitude in the next few minutes. Emily had scraped through her exams, just about managing to read the minimum number of books required, but it hadn't exactly given her the most extensive knowledge of English literature in its broadest sense.

She walked slowly to the tube. Grania lived just north of Ladbroke Grove, inevitably. She would never live in Fulham or Parsons Green. An arty intellectual needs to live with 'real people' of course. So much edgier to live in an area, with the highest possibility of being routinely mugged in broad daylight. The attitude really wasn't getting any better. No delays on the tube of course. She was standing at Grania's front door in less than 20 minutes. She hesitated before ringing the buzzer and tried to think upbeat, arty thoughts.

'Hi Emily, this is Emily everyone!' Grania was effusive. 'Now, Emily and I bumped into each other again after a long time. Emily works as a very glamwus and high flying PR for major international corporwates and loads of very exciting City firms, isn't that wight Emily.' She'd forgotten that particular little lie. Oh well, should be alright with this arty lot.

Grania started to introduce them all. 'Emily, this is Marcus, Business Editor for The Economist. Marcus is just back from the G8, Emily.' Marcus looked petrifying.

'And Alistair! Now Alistair, what do we call you these days.' Grania was almost flirtatious. 'Architect or historian?' Grania turned to Emily. 'Alistair is a very well wespected architect, but he has another stwing to his bow. I'm sure he won't mind me telling you that he is just about to launch the most fascinating biography of Pope Cedric the Inscrutable.'

Alistair was fiendishly ugly, one of the ugliest men that Emily thought she had ever seen. He couldn't be more than 30, but he looked like someone's grand dad – pot belly, little round glasses, unruly eyebrows. There was more hair attempting to escape from his nose and ears than on his head. Nature had been cruel, but it didn't look like he had put up any kind of fight. She realised she was staring, mesmerised, so she smiled. He smiled back and she noticed that he had very poor oral hygiene.

Grania steered her towards a seat. 'Emily, this is Tasha. And Tasha, would you believe it, is standing as the next Tory party candidate for Greenwich. Ithn't that exthiting!'

As Grania went round the table, the horrifying thought began to dawn on Emily, that this was Grania's attempt at an upmarket, artsy singles party.

'And Gideon, who is one of the most exthiting contempowawy artists and sculptors around at the moment. Gideon spends motht of his time on the Isle of Skye, so it was waarlly bwilliant he could come down.'

Shoot me now, was Emily's first thought. She was overwhelmed by a desire to leg it for the door and just keep running, like Forest Gump, until she got home.

She was sitting between petrifying Marcus from the Economist and ugly architect Alistair. Marcus was on her case in seconds. 'So which city firms do you represent Emily?' Was she being paranoid or was there more than a hint of contempt in his voice? She chose to completely ignore the question and instead, join in the general gushing as Grania struggled in with an enormous Paella dish.

'That looks amazing Grania.' Emily enthused.

'Oh well, you know, I thought I'd cook Paella as I've just got back from Thpain.'

'Oh whereabouts', asked Emily.

'The Alhambwa.'

'Oh I love the Alhambra, Grania.' Tasha was effusive. 'Was it work or play?'

'Work actually. Researching a feature on how the Reconquista affected Thpanish art, which is pwoving quite challenging.'

Alistair piped up now. 'Probably because the Reconquista tends to be subsumed into the wider context of crusading generally.' He was snorting with laughter at what he clearly thought was quite clever or funny, she wasn't sure.

'Well quite,' agreed Grania.

Emily had no idea what they were talking about, but her spirits lifted at the sight of the enormous helping of paella on her plate and the realisation that she was in fact very hungry. Grania's cooking, like everything else she did, was perfect. She tucked in. Tasha raised the subject of the Tate Modern's latest installation, which prompted aggressive debate. Emily pretended to be very involved with the business of peeling a prawn.

The state of Alistair's mouth really was shocking. 'So Emily', he turned to her. 'I've never really understood PR. What exactly is it that you do?' He might have a sound working knowledge of Iberian peninsula politics in the

15th century, but brushing his teeth seemed to have completely eluded him.

Luckily Gideon interrupted before she could reply. 'Has everyone seen Jez and Jonathan's new installation at the White Cube, Hoxton Square?' Not another lisp! She wondered if it was contagious and she would actually have one herself by the end of the evening.

Grania replied, 'Yah, I interviewed them at the opening. Emily have you theen it yet? They've constwucted a giant papier maché vulva uthsing only John Lewith receipts. It's a comment on post feminist middle class women… weally insightful!'

'Sounds great.' Emily enthused. 'I must go and see it!'

But Emily was mesmerised by Alistair's mouth. She couldn't stop staring, as his arguments became more insistent, he curled back his upper lip, exposing a badly capped front tooth, blackened at the edges, receding gums, red and inflamed. And as she stared, with ghoulish fascination, something inexplicably awful happened. A morsel of food, of uncertain origin or decade, dislodged itself from between Alistair's teeth and soared in an arc, inexorably towards her.

Unblinking, she studied its perfect trajectory as the stenching morsel climbed through the air and then plummeted, like a toxic kamikaze, heading straight for her plate of paella.

Oh my God, my God, keep watching, don't lose sight of it, Emily was intent. It was unthinkable that it should land on her plate and she should not be able to ring fence precisely, the area where it landed.

But just at that moment, Marcus tried to engage her again, 'So Emily, Grania tells me you read literature at Oxford. What do you think about Graham Greene's assertion that Proust was the greatest novelist of the 20th century…Emily?'

Nooooooo! Distracted for just one second, she had lost sight of the offending particle which had landed somewhere, anywhere, in her plate of paella. She pushed the plate away, devastated and turned to Marcus.

'No, he wasn't.' She replied.

'Based on what evidence, Emily?' Pedantic tosser, she thought.

'Based on the fact that there were loads of better ones.' Emily looked desperately over to Grania. 'Could you point me in the direction of your loo?' She didn't even need the loo, of course and knew that it would now look weird when she did.

She sat on the loo seat and looked at her watch. Shit - only 9.15! How long before she could make an excuse and leave. She checked her phone. No texts from Bella. She and Derek were going to Pietro's tonight, a gorgeous little subterranean Italian restaurant in Soho, probably just about to order their first course, sipping Chianti, holding hands and feeding each other bread sticks dipped in some heavenly sauce. God she was hungry and here she was dodging stenching missiles and trying not to reveal quite how stupid these people made her feel. The wall was packed with clip frames featuring Grania in various poses. Grania with Lucien Freud – luckily that one was titled, Grania with Tracey Emin, she recognised her at least, Grania with Kevin Spacey of course, Grania collecting a gong from Mariella Frostrup at the UK press awards, oh my God, was that Grania with Nicole Kidman? 9.18 now - how much time could she kill in here without being noticed. 9.24 - she returned reluctantly to the table.

'Emily, you've missed a heated debate! Gilbert and George or the Chapman brothers? You have to choose!'

'Then I suppose I'd have to say the Chapman brothers', she replied as confidently as she could, making her way back to her seat. She didn't know who they were and she only picked them because for a second she had thought they meant, choose your favourite Eastenders characters and that Grania might have meant the Mitchell brothers. Please God, no one ask me why I chose them!

Tasha had obviously started this one. 'Do you know, I went to a dinner the other night with a fairly urbane group of people and not one person out of the eight guests, knew who the Chapman brothers were, I mean can you imagine the ignorance?'

'Shocking!' Much general mirth at the cultural shortcomings of those not in the cognoscenti innermost circle.

Emily was conscious that she hadn't really joined in at all. Fortified by dry white wine and confident now that they were at least talking about culture, she piped up. 'I suppose it's a question of popular versus esoteric culture. I mean we might be able to name the Chapman brothers,' (and God, now she hoped they were in fact people with names, as opposed to an installation of some kind) 'but is it not also an intellectual imperative to keep abreast of popular culture, at least to offer some sort of cultural context.' She was very pleased with this insight. People seemed to be nodding. 'I mean, can anyone here in fact tell me the names of the more popular Mitchell brothers, for instance?'

Silence

'Well quite Emily,' Grania was the only person to answer.

'Nobody?' She should really have dropped it at this point.

'It's Phil and Grant. Phil and Grant Mitchell, from Eastenders.' Her voice trailed off.

They all stared at her. Tasha was quick to divert the conversation. 'So what does everyone think of the new director of the V&A?' Mercifully the table was animated once again, giving Emily's cheeks the chance to return to their normal colour.

Alistair was spitting again. 'Of course the V&A is all about design, but I've been saying the same thing for donkeys Grania! Architecture has historically been grossly under represented at the V&A. Don't you think Emily?'

'God yes!'

'I'm so glad you agree. There's absolutely no cohesion.' Alistair looked delighted.

'None whatsoever.' She added, grateful for his approval.

Grania started to clear the plates, 'Oh dear, Emily , did you not like it?' She looked at Emily's almost untouched paella.

'Oh no it was delicious, just not that hungry for some reason.' Emily replied.

'Gosh, well I hope you're OK and not coming down with anything.' Emily saw an opportunity and started to clear the plates, ignoring Grania's plea to stay in her seat.

Grateful for the blessed relief of a few minutes in the kitchen, she started to wash up the plates. Scrubbing the paella pan, she glanced at her watch. Only 10.09. How much more of this before she could start planning her exit.

Grania came into the kitchen with the rest of the plates. 'Oh Emily, that's weally thweet of you, but Alistair's started a debate on architecture – such fun! We're going round the table. You've got to take your turn now.'

Oh God, what new torture! She returned, grimly to her place.

Alistair was clearly very excited. 'Come on Emily, we're taking it in turns and each person has to nominate a piece of iconic architecture, what they think of it, why it's iconic and so forth. You can only talk for 3 minutes, tell us who designed it and why it's iconic. Call me a walking architectural cliché, but I chose Paul Baumgarten's glass addition to the Reichstag. Marcus won't accept that it's iconic, of course. Tasha chose Filippo Brunelleschi's

'Basilica di Santa Maria del Fiore.' Spoken in a very pronounced Italian accent, which exposed more of the oral horror story.

'Gideon you're next.' Alistair continued. 'Absolutely no prizes for guessing that Gideon is going to pick a Zaha Hadid structure.' Hilarity round the table now.

'OK, you've got me! Zaha Hadid's Phaeno Science Center in Wolfsburg.' The table was now borderline hysterical. Emily hated herself for laughing along, in spite of the fact that she didn't know what they were laughing at.

'Seriously though', Gideon was not to be put off, 'I hardly have to say why it's iconic. The way that the thpace beneath the building has been left to become part of a wider dialogue with the urban community. The distortion and how it communicates movement, change, twansformation. And the design itself, its inhewent wit, harking back visually to the early days of computing.'

'OK Gideon, we'll let you have that one!' The laughter slowly subsided and Alistair turned to Emily.

'Your turn Emily!' Oh my God, what was she supposed to say. Too late to run to the loo and google postmodernist architecture.

'Come on Emily, I know it's hard with so many to choose from.'

'Hadrian's Wall' she replied without really thinking.

'Oh.' Alistair replied and the rest of the table fell silent.

'Hadrian's Wall?' Marcus sneered. She realised she might as well have said Tellytubbyland. He looked at her with utter scorn. 'I mean, what does that owe to design? It's hardly iconic or a great piece of architecture.' They were all tittering now. You absolute wanker, Emily was thinking.

'Do you mean iconic in more of a quasi religious, ancient gweek sense Emily?' You had to love Grania sometimes.

'Thank you Grania, but no I don't.' She felt the stirrings of defiance, in the face of Marcus' derision. 'I meant iconic, in its more mainstream definition, as an important and enduring symbol, a symbol that continues to command attention. Hadrian's Wall was the most fortified border of the Roman Empire, so I don't think we can doubt its importance and as for endurance, it was started in 122 AD. Its purpose may have changed but it is still the most visited tourist attraction in the north of this Country.' She finished grandly, knowing she was indebted to Jem's father for this one.

'Bravo Emily!' Alistair was delighted and it seemed to have shut Marcus up.

She took a swig of wine and tried to look nonchalant. She had passed the test. Buoyed up by her triumph, she turned to Marcus. 'So how was the G8 summit', she offered.

He looked surprised. 'Oh, just the usual, you know, the international aid agenda, some minor progress on environmental collaboration, agreements on debt relief and trade justice, Germany, Russia and France intransigent as ever.'

Silence. Emily knew she should say something wise, but was now at a complete loss.

'And what about Spain?' She regretted it as soon as she said it.

'What do you mean, what about Spain?' He almost spat his answer.

'How did they react?' This was agony.

'Spain isn't one of the G8 countries, Emily, nor indeed the G8+5. I'd have thought with all your high flying international PR clients, you'd have known that.'

'Just need to go to the loo.' At this point, he was either going to think she was a massive coke head or had a bad dose of diarrhoea, but quite frankly she didn't care. She got up from the table again.

Just as she was leaving the room, Grania came in, carrying a tray of glass bowls, which were passed around the table.

'I hope everyone likes Jasmine Tea Granita.'

'Ah, Granita di Grania!' Alistair's OTT Italian accent again.

'Grania, this is absolute heaven.' Tasha enthused.

'Thanks, I got it from Mary Taylor Simeti's bwilliant book 'Pomp and thuthtenance: Twenty-five Thenturies of Thicilian Food.'

'Where did Emily go?' Alistair asked.

'In the loo again, I do hope she's alright.' Grania replied. They looked at each other.

10.57. She returned to the table. Marcus and Gideon were arguing about third world debt. It turned out that Gideon spent his days sculpting in the Scottish isles, subsidised by a generous trust fund and clearly didn't have much of a debt himself. He was on a sticky wicket, but pressed on regardless.

Grania was trying to arbitrate, 'Gideon, what Marcus is saying is that there is a 'Weal Politik' at work here.' Emily marvelled at Grania. Certain phrases should surely be off limits with quite such a pronounced lisp.

Grania decided to change the subject. 'Did you know, everyone, that Emily's father was the twavel witer, Jack Bwighouse.'

Just for a second, she thought Marcus looked slightly less contemptuous.

Alistair turned to her. 'I used to love his articles, Emily. There was a particularly brilliant one on Cuba, I seem to remember. Did you ever get to go on any of his adventures with him?'

'Not really.' She replied, wishing she wasn't once again, the centre of attention. 'He would just disappear off for a few months. We never really knew where he was.'

'How fabulous!' Tasha joined in. Emily didn't think it was that fabulous. Not if you were his daughter anyway.

'So you chose PR, Emily?' It was difficult to tell if Marcus was sneering or not. 'Not interested in academia or following your father into journalism?'

'It wasn't really an option.' She really didn't want to talk about any of this. She looked around, desperate for someone to change the subject.

'But PR? For an Oxford graduate? I never really understand what it is you people are supposed to do?' Marcus could not have sounded more condescending.

'Well I suppose it's the opposite of an academic really.' There was something about him that just made her want to take him on, or maybe she had drunk too much.

'How so?' Yes, it was definitely a sneer.

She turned round to look him in the eye. 'Well you could say, that an academic takes something potentially fascinating and newsworthy and makes it sound dull and ordinary to your average person. My job, on the other hand, is to take what is dull and ordinary and make it sound fascinating and newsworthy to normal people.'

Absolute silence.

'Touché Emily!' Alistair was chortling in response.

Quick glance down at her watch. 11.02. Home run. End in sight. Start planning exit.

Grania appeared with a tray of coffees. 'I've got an idea, everyone! Let's google each other!'

The need to leave was now absolutely critical. Emily started to reach in her bag for her phone.

Grania had her laptop open on the table. 'Tasha, loads of photos of you and DC! An article here describes you as 'formidable'. Oh my God Tash, apparently you are a 'Cameron Cutie'!'

'Oh how embarrassing' Tasha was clearly delighted.

'Emily, there's quite a lot about you here. You've even got something on Youtube, some sort of song from a

Liverpool radio station. Have you seen this Emily? Let's listen to it! Oh hang on, huge picture story here with the headline 'Splat!' God there's loads, Emily!'

Grania started to read out loud from one of the articles. It was The Guardian. Emily knew it off by heart. 'Snatching PR triumph from the jaws of disaster. One of this year's most shameful PR episodes has got to be the Dewsbury Pork's National Sausage Week Campaign. Perhaps the most surprising detail to emerge is that its creator is not a misogynistic male PR, but a woman. Attempting to defend the campaign, Emily Brighouse, of Hobbs & Parker, said…'

'My taxi's here Grania!' Emily blurted out. 'Lovely to meet you all.' She picked up her bag, grabbed her coat from the sofa and without looking back, walked swiftly to the front door.

Grania followed close behind. 'But Emily, there's no taxi outside. Why don't you wait inside till we can see it.'

Emily was desperate. 'I told it to wait at the end of the road. Thanks Grania. That was a lovely evening. Fascinating bunch of people. Never had so much fun. Thank you.'

And with that, she walked off down the street, trying hard not to break into a run. There was of course no taxi, but once she turned the corner and was safely out of sight, she almost cried with relief. She was gasping for the air of ordinary Londoners. She walked and walked in no particular direction, looking for a taxi, not knowing where to find a main road, just desperate not to double back and find herself once again at Grania's front door.

She lit a cigarette and wondered if she might be mugged at any minute. Quite frankly if her assailant didn't talk about postmodern architecture, she'd have given him everything she owned.

In the distance, a yellow light. Thank God, a taxi. She flagged it down and got in gratefully.

They were half way home, when the taxi driver broke the silence.

'Nice evening out love?'

'Yes, great.' She paused, worn out with the effort of insincerity. 'Actually no, it was pretty awful if I'm honest.'

He smiled into the mirror. 'Sorry to hear that.'

'Thanks.' She thought for a moment, before leaning forwards. 'Can I ask you something?'

'Depends what it is love?'

'Do you know who the Chapman brothers are?'

'Course I do love, Jake and Dinos! Took Dinos to a show in Hoxton Square just last month. Nice chap actually.'

She was none the wiser. 'Yes, but can you tell me who they are, as in what they do?'

'Two of the most provocative, talented and experimental artists of our generation. Not everyone's cup of tea, I grant you.'

'Oh, yes I see. OK. Thanks.' She was silent for the rest of the journey and had never been quite so grateful to open the door to the flat. She peeled a post-it note off the phone from Bella and read it as she walked to her room.

Your mother called. She's looking forward to Christmas with you in Paris. She says she's booked a couple of rooms in Montmartre and a table at Hotel Costes for Christmas lunch!'

Emily's spirits lifted a little and she climbed, exhausted into bed.

18

Anoushka, her newfound confidante was all ears
the next morning. She had moved desks, to be closer
to Emily. She claimed that it would help her get more
involved in client work. In fact it was to ensure she was
kept abreast of every aspect of Emily's latest adventures,
even if she didn't always understand the finer detail.

Emily looked at her inbox. The responses to her
Territorial Army emails were not an unqualified success.

To: EBrighouse@Hobbs&Parker.com
From: peter.king@britishfrozenfoodbulletin.co.uk
Subject: Exciting opportunity

Dear Emily

*To be honest, I was a little confused by your request. I
am not sure how relevant the Territorial Army is to the
readers of British Frozen Food Bulletin. I am struggling to
see how sending one of my reporters to join the TA for six
weeks will generate a suitable article for 'What's in the*

Freezer this month.' As you know, we are always happy to interview Derek Dewsbury. Good luck with it!

Peter

To: EBrighouse@Hobbs&Parker.com
From: gaz.t@dailysport.co.uk
Subject: Exciting opportunity

Emily
I think you're on to something here! The Sport will pay for the girls if you can provide the tank and troops. Happy to include a plug for the TA in the caption - our readers will expect the girls to be topless. How about camouflage thongs? Let me know timings. Say cheers to Pete.

Gaz

Emily chewed the end of her biro and wondered what to do. So far, their combined efforts had produced a 16 stone Irish fashion writer, a soft porn double page spread in The Sport and a lukewarm response from the TV critic of the Oxshott Gazette. He had promised a tiny mention in his 'on the box' column, read by about 6 people in Surrey. Emily smiled wryly. It was technically 3 out of Clare's target of 5. Probably not what Major General Sir Johnny 'Jock' Strapp would call a resounding operational success.

Emily
Wonderful to see you last night. Hilarious as ever! I hope you don't mind, I gave Alistair your email address. He thought you were an absolute hoot and would really like to see you again!

Grania x

Shit, shit, shit.

She exhaled deeply and sat back in her chair. At least she could leave early today. It was Hector's concert tonight at the Albert Hall. The opening night of Le Voisier's classical music week. Clare had bristled when Hector insisted that Emily attend, but the name 'Derek Dewsbury plus one' on the list hadn't seemed to phase her at all. Emily was looking forward to seeing her face when she realised who the 'plus one' was.

She left the office at 4.30 to go home and get ready. An email from Hector had instructed her to make an effort. Flipping cheek.

Bella was already home. She obviously hadn't heard Emily's key in the door and was blasting out a power ballad at full volume over the sound of the hair dryer. Painfully off key, even by Bella's standards.

'Where have all the good men gone, and where are all the gods?
Where's the streetwise Hercules, to fight the rising odds?'

Emily stuck her head round the bedroom door and joined in.

Isn't there a sausage knight, upon a pork based steed?
Late at night I toss and I turn, and dream of what I
need...'

They chorused triumphantly together, a seasoned double act, both blasting the words out, Bella into a hairbrush and Emily picking up a pair of hair straighteners.

'I need a hero, I'm holding out for a hero till the end of the night,
He's gotta be strong, he's gotta be fast, and he's got to be fresh from the fight,
I need a hero, I'm holding out for a hero till the morning light, he's got to be sure, and it's gotta be soon, and he has to be larger than life.'

And now both perfectly on cue...

'Doo doo doo doooooooooooo
Doo doo doo doooooooooooo
Doo doo doo doooooooooooo
Ahhhhhhh Ahhhhhhhh'

Bella switched off the hairdryer. 'Good day at work Em?'

'Nope, not really. You look gorgeous Bels. Is that new?'

'Zara sale. Bit tight, just about OK with magic pants.'

Emily pulled a face. She tried to shrug off the mental image of Derek wrestling with the magic pants later. She noticed that Bella's room was fast becoming a shrine to pale grey cashmere. Every date with Derek seemed to spawn some new 'handwash only' item.

Now, what to wear? She had been saving her new little black dress for something special. Your gay friend's work do didn't technically qualify, but still, she needed to make an effort for Hector and prove to herself that she wasn't a total write off. She stole some of Bella's perfume from the bathroom cabinet and put on some unfeasibly high heels.

Of course, they had to meet Derek there. The flat was still very much off limits. It was a particularly cold December evening as their taxi pulled up at the front of the Albert Hall and they shivered as they walked up the steps towards the entrance. Derek was hovering in the foyer, strikingly handsome in black tie and as he rushed towards Bella and greeted her, Emily felt an unexpected twinge of jealousy.

Hector appeared with arms outstretched. 'Emily darling, you look absolutely stunning. Come and have a drink! Not all the journalists are here yet, but most of the US directors are already half cut. John is sick in bed and I need some moral support.'

Emily kissed his cheek. She could tell he was nervous. 'Hector, this is Bella and Derek.'

'Oh glorious!' Hector looked them up and down. 'We meet at last! Follow me and let's get you all some Champagne.'

Hector had reserved six boxes in the Grand Tier for Le Voisier's guests, three on either side of the orchestra. He led them towards the one closest to the stage. It was just as she imagined the Moulin Rouge might look, beautifully lit, all deep red and plush, thick velvet curtains, gold brocade and chandeliers. The box was already swarming with slightly red faced Americans, intent on getting their fair share of the endless supply of Champagne before the performance began. As far as she could make out, they all seemed to be called Bob or Buddy. Derek saw her eyeing up the huge chandeliers.

He turned to her, grinning. 'Checking out the light fittings Emily? I've heard about some of your antics. I'd be careful with that one though, doesn't look like it's attached to a joist.'

She rolled her eyes. Marvellous! Now Derek had assumed the role of joshing older brother. What is it with men that start shagging your best mate, she wondered. They somehow think they've earned the right to start poking fun at you, like some old, familiar friend.

'That's really funny Derek.' She replied through gritted teeth. 'Just remember who got you onto the 10 o'clock news and found you the woman of your dreams.'

And there was Clare F-B, like a heat seeking missile. She had locked onto Le Voisier's US CEO and was attempting to engage him in light hearted, professional banter.

Hector was next to her now, whispering in her ear. 'Now Emily, be particularly careful of that one over there!' He said, nodding towards a short American with a particularly red face. 'He's over here for the first time without his wife. He appears to be on some sort of cock-led mission. He's actually the US Finance Director, so it's all a bit embarrassing.' It was too late. Red faced FD had spotted her and was over in a second. He held out a plump, sweaty hand. 'Hi, I'm Randy.'

'So I've heard.' Emily replied, smiling sweetly, but Hector grabbed her, turning her on her heel.

As he led her swiftly away, he whispered in her ear. 'Oh now look Emily, strike me down if that isn't Jerome Armstrong walking towards us?' Emily let out a little gasp, which only Hector heard. 'I think he's seen you, Emily.' He squeezed her shoulder. 'Try not to look so petrified.' Hector was clearly very pleased with himself. 'Did Uncle Hector do well?'

If she thought that Derek looked good in black tie, Jem was on another scale. He strode towards her. She couldn't look up. He was in front of her now, smiling, completely unruffled. 'Emily, you look beautiful.'

She dragged her eyes from the floor. 'So do you.' She replied. Jesus, she had actually said that out loud. For once, he looked a little flustered.

He looked around the room. 'No Charlie?'

'He's busy tonight.' She replied, struggling to keep her voice steady.

There was a pause before he looked her in the eye. 'How've you been?'

'Really good thanks.' She answered a little too quickly.

'We should…' 'I didn't…' They both tried to speak at once. Just then Randy spotted her. 'Hey Hector' he slurred, lurching towards her. 'This one's sitting next to me.' She didn't have time to protest.

Ladies and Gentleman, please take your seats, the performance is about to begin.

She and Jem were still facing each other. He leant towards her and for a split second, she thought he was going to kiss her. 'Shall I see you in the bar in the interval?'

She held his gaze. 'Yes'.

She watched him walk away as Randy patted the seat next to him on the front row. Sitting down between Derek and Randy, her heart was beating furiously and she pretended to be busy flicking through the programme.

The orchestra were tuning their instruments. She scanned every row, seeking him out, until Hector, moving behind her to find his seat, leant forward and whispered helpfully. 'He's over there Emily. I put him in the box opposite, so you can stare at each other all night.'

The orchestra struck up. The opening movement of Carl Orff's Carmina Burana. A 200 strong choir and the insistent beating of a drum. It was captivating, it felt like her whole body was vibrating in time to the music.

Randy turned and shouted in her ear. 'Hey! I love this tune. Didn't they steal it from the Omen!'

She allowed herself the odd glance across the stalls to the box opposite. There he was. Her mind was working overtime. If she could just have a drink with him, she could tell him that she'd split up with Charlie. Maybe there was still a chance. She looked hastily down at the words in her programme. She was beginning to wonder if Hector had planned the music for her, as well as the seating arrangements.

O Fortuna
Meus amicus? Hinc equitavit, eia, quis me amabit?
Where is the lover I knew? He has ridden off! Oh! Who
will love me? Ah!
(Chorus)

Floret silva undique, nah min gesellen ist mir we
The woods are burgeoning all over, I am pining for my
lover!

(Small Chorus)

She was awe struck. Randy was also clearly moved by the music. Emily smiled politely as she removed his hand from her thigh. In any other circumstance she would probably have punched him, but the music, the fact that he was Hector's boss and their position on the front row of the Grand Tier box tempered her response.

Chume, chum, geselle min

Chume, chum, geselle min,   *Come, come, my love,*
ih enbite harte din,   *I long for you,*

ih enbite harte din,	*I long for you,*
chume, chum, geselle min.	*come, come, my love.*
Suzer rosenvarwer munt,	*Sweet rose-red lips,*
chum un mache mich gesunt	*come and make me better,*
chum un mache mich gesunt,	*come and make me better,*
suzer rosenvarwer munt	*sweet rose-red lips.*

The music was frenzied, erotic even and she found herself watching him intently. He must have felt her gaze as he turned to look at her. They stared across at each other, eyes locked, neither one breaking the spell.

Randy broke into her trance. 'Hey. Who's that guy staring at you Emily? Do you know him?'

'Yes I do', she said smiling. 'We were lovers'. What on earth did she say that for! It wasn't even true! It must have been the music. This did nothing to dampen Randy's fervour. He was by now quite breathless.

Emily watched as Clare F-B sitting directly opposite, on the same row as Jem, reached for her binoculars and scanned the Grand Tier box. She stopped suddenly when she reached Bella and Derek. Emily could see her brow furrow. She looked over at Jem again, but he had turned back towards the stage.

Now it was Derek's turn to drag her gaze back from the opposite box. He chose his moment and whispered intently in her ear, 'Emily, I really need to talk to you privately. It's quite urgent. Can we have a chat in the interval?'

'Sure Derek.'

Bugger! This was infuriating. What the hell did he want to talk to her about anyway? Emily knew what she wanted to say. Sure Derek, why not Derek. I could be exchanging breathless pre-coital banter at the bar with Jem, but no, let's have a fucking chat instead shall we? What did you want to chat about then Derek? The future of frozen bloody pork products? She knew she was being unkind, but this was too much. The awful agony of staring, longingly at the man of your dreams, trapped between a middle aged, oversexed yank on one side and Derek on the other, like a couple of armed guards.

It was very nearly the interval. She looked down at her programme. No. 10, Were diu werlt alle min (Were all the world mine). The choir and violins reached a massive, crashing crescendo.

Now Jem was staring straight at her. Smiling. God he was good looking! He was grinning and pointing sideways towards the bar.

Stuff Derek! If she could just give the armed guard the slip and make it to the bar. 'Just need to pop to the loo!' She muttered, loud enough for Derek and Randy to hear. It worked like a charm. She grabbed her bag and there she was suddenly, free! She almost jogged round the circular corridor as fast as her 4 inch heels could carry her, guessing whether to go clockwise or anti clockwise. Past entrance L, M, N and O. God she wished she was wearing trainers. At least her shoes prevented her from breaking into a run, which might have looked a little over keen. Slightly dizzy now, P Q, R, S, damn, where was she? Getting brisker and beginning to panic, no sign of Jem or the bar. The interval was only 20 minutes long. H, I, J, K – bugger it, she was back exactly where she'd started!

'Ah Emily, there you are.' Derek's head shot out of a curtained alcove. 'Come in here! I really need to talk to you.'

'Oh God. Hi Derek!' She was quite out of breath now. 'Listen, you'll have to be very quick, I haven't found the loo yet...'

'OK, sorry! It's just that… you have to swear to answer me truthfully.'

'Of course I will. What is it Derek?' She replied impatiently. He released the curtain cord, so that it was half shut. What on earth was he playing at?

'I don't know how to put this.' He sounded quite dramatic.

'Come on Derek, spit it out for God's sake!' She was desperate now and quite snappy.

'OK.' He seemed to be having trouble finding the words. 'Is Bella living with another man?'

'What?' She was genuinely taken aback.

Derek carried on. 'You see, I think she likes me Emily, but I strongly suspect that she is living with another man. I know you don't see her that often, but I just thought you might be able to find out. You see, I've fallen for her in a very big way. I can't carry on like this.' He looked imploringly at her.

'For Fuck's sake, Derek!' Emily raised her voice.

He misunderstood. 'Oh I know I sound like some deranged, jealous boyfriend, but if you only knew what she's been like. Her behaviour is really strange Emily. She would do anything rather than let me drop her home. I know she stops the taxi several streets from where she lives and she won't tell me her address. The other day I was trying to get it out of her, so I could send her some flowers and she got really angry…'

'Derek, stop!' She held up her hand in exasperation. 'Look, I'm going to keep this very simple and when I've explained, don't make a big deal of it in front of Bella, OK? And then I really have to go.'

'Alright.' He looked at her expectantly.

'Bella isn't living with another man Derek. I can guarantee you that, because for the past seven years she's been living with me.'

'Oh thank God!' he exhaled slowly.

'The night you met, she was nearby and I texted her to come down and join the party, drink free champagne, etc. We pretended to be old friends, meeting by chance, so that Clare F-B wouldn't know that I had in fact just texted my freeloading flatmate.'

'I see.' He didn't look at all enlightened.

'And the second reason Derek.' She spoke quite slowly and deliberately, as if he was a little hard of hearing. 'Would be the state of our flat. You see, it's a dingey, 70s inspired shithole in Fulham, featuring a dark orange bathroom and threadbare carpets.' No need to mention The Tube Map of Shame, she felt.

He didn't answer, so she tried to explain. 'It's a far cry from the sorts of places where you generally hang out and she thinks if you see it, you'll dump her on the spot. I guess that doesn't say much about how superficially you may be coming across, Derek.' She knew that last bit was mean, but she was getting pissed off with him by now.

'I see your point.' Finally the penny had dropped.

'So that clears that up. No other man. All fine.' She moved towards the curtained exit, to make her escape, but he was still blocking the way.

He was shaking his head. 'This is such good news. I can't tell you. Such a relief! I really didn't know what to do.' He actually looked like he might burst with joy. 'Emily Brighouse. I honestly think you have made me the happiest man alive. Come here, I want to kiss you.' As distracted as she was, she couldn't help but laugh and they embraced.

'We need to celebrate Emily. I'll get you a drink at the bar!' He pulled back the curtain and strode off eagerly to find Bella. He was too elated to notice Jem, who had been standing the other side of the curtain, just long enough to catch the tale end of Derek's heartfelt outburst. He stood watching as they parted and waited for Derek to walk away.

'Emily. I was looking for you.' His voice was cold.

'And I was looking for you.' She replied, weakly.

'Yeah, it certainly looked like it.' He nodded.

'I'm sorry? What?' But she could see from the look on his face, just what he thought it looked like.

She was about to explain, but he carried on. 'You really can't help yourself can you?'

'What do you mean?' She stammered.

'You and men. You don't hang around do you? I guess I shouldn't be surprised, based on past performance, but Jesus Emily! Your life's like some kind of farce?'

She had been thinking of an explanation, 'that it was not what it looked like' or some other lame response, but that last comment, hit her straight in the gut.

She was still in shock, but somehow found enough resolve to look him in the eye. 'Well I'm so sorry to let you down Jem. At least my 'past performance' as you put it, gave you and your colleagues some great entertainment.'

He didn't hesitate. 'Not really, it was just a bit sad.' He looked away for a second before adding. 'I don't even know why Hector invited me.'

Emily looked at the floor. She felt like she was going to choke. 'So why don't you just go then?'

'Don't worry, I'm planning to.'

Randy appeared, swaying down the corridor. 'Hey there Emily, I've been looking for you!' And then to Jem, 'Hey buddy, so Emily tells me the two of you were lovers. Am I breaking up the party, here?'

'What?' The mix of disbelief and contempt on Jem's face was hard to bear. He looked at Emily and then back to Randy. 'Fuck this!' He said and strode off down the corridor.

'Easy buddy, only joking', Randy shrugged his shoulders.

She watched as Jem turned the corner and was gone.

'Look's like it's just you and me, babe.' Randy slurred.

'Just go away, will you!' She turned and walked slowly back to the box. Bella was already back in her seat.

'Emily, are you alright? You look like you've seen a ghost.'

Emily explained, a breathless gabble, but Bella got the gist. 'My God Emily! Is he still here? I'll get Derek to talk to him.'

'No, Bella. You've got to promise me you won't. He's already made me out to be a complete slut, I couldn't bear to look desperate as well.'

Bella looked concerned. 'Are you absolutely sure, Emily?'

'I am. You should have heard the things he said. I'm just going to have to get over this.' Bella slipped her hand into Emily's.

She saw Hector looking over at Jem's conspicuously empty seat. Poor Hector, she thought. Such a kind man. He could have done no more. Thank God now the lights were going down. Her eyes were swimming, as she once again pretended to take a keen interest in her programme.

No 12. Cignus ustus cantat (The Roast Swan)

Olim lacus colueram,	*Once I lived on lakes,*
olim pulcher extiteram,	*once I looked beautiful*
dum cignus ego fueram.	*when I was a swan.*

(Male chorus)

Miser, miser!	*Misery me!*
modo niger	*Now black*
et ustus fortiter!	*and roasting fiercely!*

(Tenor)

Finally the concert came to its crashing finale. Her breathing was just about back to normal. Bella and Derek stood either side of her as they said their goodbyes.

'Maria, what on earth have you done with Captain Von Trapp?' Hector shook his head in disbelief.

'Hector, I'm so sorry,' she said. 'I totally cocked it up. It was a brilliant evening though, a huge success!' She tried to sound upbeat, but Hector was frowning and unconvinced as he kissed her goodbye.

The three of them got into a taxi, Derek, for the first time, invited to spend the night in Fulham. As they pulled away from the Albert Hall, Emily clung on to the thought that, in less than 10 days she would be in France with her mother. Right now, her mother's encounters with the opposite sex bore an uncanny resemblance to her own. Paris for Christmas, the chance to escape and try to recover herself. Although at this point, she was tempted not to come back at all.

19

7.10am. The alarm went off and Emily's head was thumping, most likely due to the large amount of white wine she had drunk, once the three of them had got home. Still, she must have been fairly sober when she walked through the door. She noticed she had whipped The Tube Map of Shame off the hall notice board and jammed it hastily behind her bedroom door, along with two empty pizza boxes and one of Bella's rather unfortunate, flesh coloured bras.

The post fight analysis had gone on for some time. She remembered Bella's slurred summing up. It had been damning. Jem, she concluded, had been perfectly prepared to be unfaithful to his girlfriend, he had sent Emily's emails out to all his colleagues and made her a laughing stock. And now, he had topped it off by making her out to be a bit of a slut. Undeniably a bastard.

Derek, who was considerably outflanked, had tried meekly to chip in. 'But hang on girls, didn't he gallop after her, when she nearly killed herself on that horse?'

Emily was tempted to add that Jem had also saved her job and turned the total cock up of National Sausage Week into a triumph. But pissed though she undoubtedly was, she had to remember that this was Derek Dewsbury sitting on their crappy brown sofa, one of H&P's biggest clients and maybe she should keep that to herself.

She eventually went to bed, the words 'Hypocrite!' 'Bastard! and 'You deserve better!' ringing in her ears. But that was just it, she wasn't sure she did.

At 4am, she decided that there are few things so likely to make you feel like a loser than being forced to listen to your best friend having noisy and enthusiastic sex in the next room. It had gone on for most of the night. Nobody had got much sleep.

She crawled reluctantly out of bed and made marmite on toast and three cups of tea. She left theirs on a tray outside the door. Derek Dewsbury, H&P client and leading player in the frozen meat sector, in Bella's bedroom. She smiled wryly to herself. It didn't seem right at all. There was a brief lull in the noise from the bedroom and she knocked and shouted. 'There's tea and toast outside.' She couldn't resist adding, 'I expect you're exhausted.'

'Thanks Em!' Bella shouted from inside.

When she left for work, there was still no sign of them. She was late again and tried to look breezy and efficient as she walked past Clare's area. Mercifully no sign of her. She scanned quickly through her emails. No more news on the TA front.

To: EBrighouse@Hobbs&Parker.com
From: Alistair.H@Hollisandpartners.com
Subject: Jez and Jonathan's at Hoxton Square?

Hi Emily

Grania was kind enough to give me your email address. Wonderful to meet a kindred spirit! I think you mentioned that you hadn't yet seen Jez and Jonathan's

splendid new installation. How about we go next week?
Dinner after in Hoxton?

Alistair

Grania's architect! And he was talking about the papier maché vulva! The idea of staring up a giant fanny, with possibly the ugliest man she had ever met, prompted an uncontrolled wave of nausea. She had in fact wretched loudly enough for both Monica and Anoushka to look up.

'Are you OK Emily?' Anoushka looked concerned.

She couldn't even begin to work out how to reply to this email. Some things just need to be vacuum packed and put away in a box, until you are ready to deal with them.

To: Alistair.H@Hollisandpartners.com
From: EBrighouse@Hobbs@Parker.com
Subject: Jez and Jonathan's at Hoxton Square?'

Thank you for your email. Emily Brighouse is out of the office today Friday December 17th. She is unable to access her emails, but if your request is urgent, please contact her colleague Anoushka.Marchwood@ Hobbs&parker.com

She supposed she could have typed up a few more pleading TA emails, but decided against it, in favour of lunch in the pub with Anoushka and Pete. It was December 17th and most people in the office were on a pre-Christmas go slow. That afternoon, she was overcome by a wave of guilt and sadness for Hector. He had tried so hard to make things work out for her. She spent the rest of the day looking for a gift for him, scouring ebay for Von Trapp family memorabilia. There was a giant canvas of Julie Andrews and Christopher Plummer, a signed first edition of The Trapp Family On Wheels, the less successful sequel to The Sound of Music, an A4 sized Von Trapp family jigsaw and a signed poster from a 1948 Von Trapp Family US tour. She settled for the jigsaw and the poster.

Her thoughts turned to Christmas in Paris. The perfect place to waft around looking tragic. Sitting in cafes, wearing large black sunglasses, a beige trench coat, nipped in at the waist and black heels, drinking coffee and smoking. She could seek religious solace in Notre Dame or sit staring at some great work of art in the Musée D'Orsay depicting an abandoned, lovelorn heroine. Her mother would no doubt have an uncompromising opinion on her latest woes. Maybe their shared calamity would bring them together.

She must remember to buy some very large black sunglasses for Paris. Maybe they would come in handy tonight as well. She was meeting Charlie after work. She was looking forward to seeing him but apprehensive too, after his mysterious email. Maybe he was planning to lecture her about her behaviour in Northumberland. But if he was, why wait til now? She thought she had been forgiven, but he'd gone very quiet since the fateful weekend. She would find out soon enough.

She grabbed her bag and headed to the ladies loo. Her puffy, hungover, sleep deprived face in the mirror didn't quite match up to the vision of her wafting, haunting and beautiful through Paris. This was going to take some work. She rooted around in her bag for her make up. There was no sign of it. She tried not to panic, it must be at the bottom. It wasn't. Oh my God, 50 minutes exactly till she was due to meet Charlie half way across town - lovely Charlie, who was feeling like her last hope right now. No make up, perfect. She thought for a moment. If she left immediately, she might just be able to make it to the make up counter at Selfridges and then back to Hamilton's in time.

She half walked, half jogged down Oxford Street. Arriving breathlessly in the beauty hall, she found the only counter without a huge queue, which should have been a clue.

She walked up to the till. 'I'm thinking of a whole new look; foundation, mascara, lipgloss, blusher, everything...' She told the sales assistant. 'What do you recommend?'

Kerching! The sales assistant was thinking about her Christmas bonus. She was only 6 mascaras away from making the regional Bijoux finalists' sales conference in Brighton. Within seconds Emily was stripped of make up and lying back, defenceless in the black leather chair. The sales assistant had perfect skin, orange but flawless. 'Do you remove your make up and moisturise daily?' She looked in disdain at Emily's face.

'Oh God yes', replied Emily.

'Your skin is very dehydrated and your t-section is excessively oily.' Her eyes narrowed. 'Is your moisturiser oil or water based?'

'No idea.' Oh for fuck's sake. She now had less than half an hour to get there.

'At your age, you probably need a moisturiser with a higher elastin content.'

'I'm actually in a bit of a hurry.' Emily interrupted.

The sales assistant wrinkled her nose. 'What are you using to remove your make up? Not those alcohol based face wipes I hope, they really strip the skin's natural protective layers.'

'Certainly not' she replied. To be honest it was a rare occasion, when the make up was actually removed at all.

It always amazed Emily, the quasi-scientific shite these girls could spout. What a piss take, the NHS wasting all that money training top consultant dermatologists, with access to this kind of specialist knowledge.

The sales assistant starting sponging something over her face. 'I'm using a tinted moisturiser, applied with our new range of Bijoux heart-shaped sponge applicators, achieves a much more flawless finish than using your fingers, which retain too much heat. Do you like a natural or slightly darker look?'

'Not too natural.' That seemed to miss the point of make up entirely Emily always thought.

'OK, I'll take you up a couple of shades. Have you tried our new 'luscious lips' miraculous lip plumper – it actually works with your own natural collagen to promote maximum lip volume.'

'Yes, I think I read that in The Lancet.' Emily replied sarcastically.

'Sorry?' Oblivious, she applied the next layer of lip plumper.

'I'm putting a line of 'White Dazzle' on your inner lid for instant definition.'

'OK, great!'

'And I'm using our bestselling mascara, Fabulous, which is guaranteed to add 60% more length to your lashes.' Emily's lashes were already quite long and she had visions of her eyes looking like a couple of distressed spiders.

'Fabulous.' Emily mouthed through lips now coated in a slick of something that felt like golden syrup. 60%! That did seem very specific. No doubt rigorous scientific tests had generated that figure.

'Have you ever tried false eye lashes? They've come on a lot in the last few years and I can put some on you in seconds.'

'No, no that should be fine thanks.'

Finally, she held up the mirror and allowed Emily a hasty glance at her reflection. Bloody hell! No time to tone it down. Hamilton's she seemed to remember, was quite dark and she could wipe most of it off in the loo when she got there.

'That's great, thanks'. She lied, then steeling herself. 'I'll just take the lip gloss.'

'Is that it?' She looked genuinely shocked. Her heavily lined lip was curling in contempt.

'OK, how much is the tinted moisturiser and lip liner.'

'The moisturiser is £36 and the lip liner is £20.'

'OK, I'll take those two.' Shit £56!

'What about the Fabulous mascara? We've a special offer on, which means that the mascara is only half price if you buy one each from our lip and cheek range.'

'Yes, OK!' Emily was already reaching for her purse.

'So you'll take the tinted moisturiser, lip liner, healthy glow blusher, lip gloss and Fabulous mascara at half price. Oh and you'll need the Bijoux sponge applicators.'

'Ok.'

'Do you need any brushes?'

'No.'

'Shall I pop in the 'White Dazzle' instant definition liner, to complete the look?'

'No, thanks.'

'What about our new Eau de Parfum, Inoubliable. Here, let me spray some on you.'

'No, no, please. That's all, really.' Good God, they needed this girl in PR.

'If you're sure. OK. So, that'll be £94.99 please.'

'What! Jesus!' Too late to argue now. She handed over her card. 10 minutes to make it halfway across London to Hamilton's.

'If you'd like to pop in your PIN!' The sales assistant could barely wipe the smile off her face. She waited until Emily had left the shop to give a little 'whoop' and mouth the words 'Brighton here I come!' to the girl opposite on the Guerlain counter.

Emily stumbled, shell shocked through the revolving doors and back onto Oxford Street. Fuck! How had she let that happen? In the taxi, she was forced to reflect, heart still pounding that she seemed to be doing all this for Charlie. What was going on? Something to do with the fact that he was the last living male on the planet, who appeared to want to go out with her? They pulled up outside Hamilton's. Remarkably, only ten minutes late.

There he was. She realised how fond of him she had become. Gorgeous boy. Sitting at the same corner table, just like the last time. The Maitre D' recognised her at once. 'He is waiting for you in the corner, if you would just like to check this time.' Yes, yes very funny. She rushed over to join him.

'Emily!' He stood up when he saw her and sounded a little surprised. 'You look really… well, healthy, yes, really well.' He seemed nervous as he kissed her on the cheek. They ordered a bottle of wine and raised their glasses to each other.

Charlie sounded hesitant. 'Look Emily, I told you I had something, that I wanted to tell you this evening and… this is really quite awkward. I don't know where to start.'

Whatever it was, he was having real trouble. The telling off was going to be even more awkward than she had imagined. She wished he'd just get on with it. 'God, Charlie, I think we know each other well enough by now. I don't think you need to worry about what I'll think.'

'Look, it's… it's… it's not that you're not my type…' Was he trying to dump her or something? They weren't even going out!

'Of course Charlie, no worries.' This was excruciating. She reached for her wine.

'No, I mean, I really want to explain. The night we met, I almost thought you could be my type and you almost were.' He was looking down at the table.

'God, OK. No, I really do get the picture Charlie. You don't need to go on.' There was definitely some kind of conspiracy going on here, to shrink her ego down to nothing.

'No you really don't.' He looked exasperated. 'This is so difficult. I've never had to do this before.'

She actually felt sorry for him, even though she was the one being dumped. 'Look, it's really fine Charlie. You don't have to explain. You don't fancy me. I'm not your type. To be honest, I've treated you appallingly. I really wouldn't expect you to want to go out with me.' He didn't answer, so she carried on. 'If I'm honest, I'm a tiny bit gutted you don't fancy me, but I'll survive.' She tried to inject a bit of levity into the situation.

'I'm gay Emily.'

'Bloody hell!' She didn't exactly spit her wine, but certainly a lot of it left her mouth unexpectedly and ran down her chin. 'What?.....'

She reached for her napkin, shaking her head. 'No you're not!'

'Yes I am.'

'You're not, you can't be.'

He managed a smile. 'I'm quite sure I am, Emily.'

Her mind was playing back every scene since they'd met. 'But Charlie, we kissed. In fact, we slept together. Not precisely in that order obviously.' She was gabbling.

'Actually, we didn't sleep together.' He sounded quite calm. She couldn't speak. 'Emily, nothing actually happened that night.'

'But my pants.' She shook her head in disbelief. 'They were on your chandelier.'

'Yes, very impressive.' He smiled. 'By the time you'd actually finished spinning your underwear above your head, you were out like a light. It was kind of a relief to me, as you can imagine.'

'Oh.' She paused for a moment. 'So, what were we doing going home together in the first place?'

He laughed. 'I don't know. You threw yourself off the bar. Someone had to catch you I suppose.' He lowered his voice and grinned at her. 'And I thought you were the most fun person I had ever met!'

She ignored the compliment, as she struggled to make sense of it all. 'Hang on a second. What about the snog outside here?'

He sounded almost affronted. 'You snogged me, actually.'

'I did not snog you!' She was adamant. You lunged at me.'

'Dream on sweetheart.' He was laughing now and she couldn't help but join in.

She looked at him for a moment. 'So why didn't you say any of this to me before?'

He shrugged. 'I don't know, I suppose I was putting it off. Maybe I thought you could turn me Emily? You're half bloke after all.'

'Oh thanks!' She snorted sarcastically. 'Why do you have such a problem being gay anyway?' She said it without thinking and realised at once, how crass she sounded.

'That's easy for you to say.' He looked away for a moment. 'You try being the Honourable Charlie Fanthorpe, son of a baronet, Captain in the army, job in the city.' He gave a hollow laugh. 'It might be ok if you're Elton and David, but some of us are still struggling you know.'

This was momentous for him. She could see that now and she cringed at her flippant response. 'Charlie, is this the first time you've ever told anyone?'

'Yes. I guess this is the first time I've been totally honest.' He smiled ruefully. 'I wasn't always sure, you see.'

She could see the pain in his face. She hesitated to ask. 'Have you ever been in love?' He didn't seem to mind.

'Well there was someone in fact. In the army, but he was straight and you can imagine.' He trailed off.

'And your parents don't have a clue?' She imagined Sir Roger and Lady Sarah were not the most enlightened pair.

He shook his head. 'That's not even an option. It would kill them. Although I think my sister knows.'

'That's ridiculous.' Emily blurted out. 'For God's sake, it's the 21st century!'

He sipped his wine and looked at her. 'Not where I come from.'

She struggled to find the right words. 'I'm really flattered… I mean, glad… whatever it is I'm trying to say, that you chose to tell me.'

He put down his glass and stared at her intently. 'Do you know how good it feels to tell someone!'

'I can imagine.'

He shook his head and laughed at her again. 'No, you can't Emily.'

'Well, my gay friend.' She raised her glass to him. 'Another gay friend! Bloody hell, how many does a girl need? Here's to love! And all the adventures we'll have trying to find it.'

He raised his glass and smiled, as she went on. 'Do you know though, there was one comment you made that just kind of stuck in my mind.'

'What was that?' He smiled indulgently.

'You were tuning the radio in the car, on the way back from Northumberland. And you said 'Where's Gloria Gaynor when you need her.' A straight man would never have said that!' She was triumphant.

'So now you're all female intuition.' He laughed.

'No, to be fair, I clearly need to retune my Gay-dar!' Her eyes narrowed as she looked at him. 'Am I really half bloke?'

'In some ways, yes. I meant to be flattering.' He studied her face. 'Talking of which, what's with tonight's drag queen look?'

'What do you mean?' She hastened to the loo and on closer inspection, she could see his point. Her face was the colour of the burnt sienna bathroom suite – a deep orange that ended abruptly at the neck line. And the eye brows! The poor boy had been forced to come out, staring at a cross between Katie Price and Joan Crawford. It was ten minutes of splashing and blotting with loo roll before she could safely return to the table.

The waiter was hovering and Charlie called him over. 'Shall we order?'

Once they had chosen and the waiter had disappeared off, she leant across the table. 'So what are you going to do Charlie? I mean, you can't go on pretending to be straight just to please everyone else.'

He laughed at her. 'Look who's talking? What are you going to do Emily? You can't go on pretending not to be in love with Jem Armstrong!'

'Fuck off.' She was taken aback, but couldn't help smiling.

'Ditto!' He replied, looking smug. 'I don't suppose you want to come up to my parents' for Christmas and pretend to be my girlfriend.' He looked at her pleadingly.

'That's a very kind offer but I'm afraid I'm in France with my mother for Christmas.' She paused before adding. 'Anyway Charlie, I think you should stop pretending?'

'Oh come on.' He was indignant. 'I did it for you! I think I was a very convincing boyfriend, although I guess if I was pretending to be straight, I should have punched him when I found you in the stables!'

She tried to change the subject. 'I'm going to phone your parents and tell them you're gay.'

'In which case.' He replied without hesitation. 'I'm going to phone Jem Armstrong and tell him you're in love with him.'

'Oh,' she smiled. 'In that case, perhaps we should just make a pact, that we are going to sort ourselves out sometime soon?'

They held hands across the table and she started to laugh uncontrollably.

'Now what!' He asked.

'I was just thinking that things are never quite what they seem at Hamilton's – it should be their new ad campaign.'

The goodbye kiss was less troublesome this time. They hugged for a moment and as she held him, she couldn't help thinking, what a fucked up world they still lived in, if a brilliant bloke like this could still not be happy.

Bella was up when she got home. 'This came for you. From your mother', she said, handing her a postcard. 'I'm really sorry, I read it.' It was from the South of France. Emily turned it over.

Emily,
Great news - Benoit is back! Spending Christmas with him in Paris to celebrate. Sorry darling! Another time! See you some time in the New Year!
Love Mummy

Bella was hovering. She could tell that Emily was choked. 'Are you OK Em?'

'Yes great! Happy Bloody Christmas!' She was trying hard not to cry. Too much emotion for one evening. Maybe she hadn't realised how much she was relying on the trip to Paris to sort herself out.

Bella hesitated before asking. 'Will you come to my parents' for Christmas?'

'That's really kind.' Emily struggled to keep her voice from wobbling.

'How was your date with Charlie anyway? Did he declare his undying love finally?' Bella attempted to lighten the mood.

'He wanted to tell me that he's gay.' Emily replied flatly.

'What? My God, right. Well I didn't see that coming!' Emily was tempted to say something mean minded, about her not always being right, but she resisted. 'No, nor did I.' She looked around. 'Where's Derek?'

'He had to drive back up North after dinner.' You could see Bella was shocked, still trying to work things out. 'Hold on a second, if Charlie's gay, I thought you two, you know?'

'Apparently not.'

'Wow, OK. Well it's Friday night and we have no wine. Do you want a shot of that vile liqueur with the twig in it from Ibiza?'

'Yes please. And guess what?' Emily shouted to Bella, who was rummaging through the kitchen cupboards in search of the bottle, 'That ugly architect, Alistair, you know, from Grania's dinner party emailed me for a date. How depressing is that!'

Bella reappeared with 2 shot glasses and the offensive liqueur. 'Is he that bad?' she said breezily, 'Maybe you could just go for a drink with him.'

'I'm sorry?' Emily wondered if she was just supposed to ignore a comment like that.

'Well, you never know, you might find it entertaining. He might end up having interesting friends or something. I'm just saying, don't dismiss him.'

'You're just saying Bella! You're just saying that you think I should go on a date with someone I find physically repulsive?' Emily felt tearful suddenly. 'Weren't you listening when I told you he had a stenching black hole where his mouth should be?' It would normally have made them laugh.

'I'm just saying Emily, that maybe you need to help yourself.' Emily had drunk the best part of a bottle of wine. She wasn't in the mood for Bella's slightly self-righteous advice.

'What's that supposed to mean? By going out with really ugly men I don't fancy? That's rich coming from you Bella. I mean, you wouldn't even consider going out with anyone with less than model good looks.'

'I didn't say go out with him.' Bella sounded exasperated. 'Just have a drink with him! God, Emily, don't take everything so literally.'

'God, Bella! Since you've been going out with Mr Perfect Pork Millionaire, you've become really smug and patronising. Did you know that? Don't forget you picked him up in a bar, thanks to me.' She was slurring slightly now. 'I'm beginning to wish I hadn't bothered texting you.'

Bella, who was slightly more sober kept her cool. 'So now you're pissed off that I've found a man I like?'

'To be honest Bella if I wasn't stuck with your fucking boyfriend at the Albert Hall, explaining that you weren't living with another man, I might be with my perfect man right now, instead of standing here, listening to your patronising bullshit!'

Bella had had enough. 'Oh! That's right! Your perfect man! I thought we'd established that the man's an arsehole. For God's sake Emily, he called you a slut and emailed details of your one night stands all round his office for a laugh. Oh and … he's got a girlfriend! How bloody hopeless is that!'

Emily, face flushed, came right back at her. 'About as bloody hopeless as you spending two fucking years running round to Bastard Ben's whenever he felt like a shag!'

'Fuck you Emily!'

'No fuck you Bella!'

Emily was first to storm into her bedroom and there followed a rally of competitive door slamming followed by a long silence.

Some time later, once Emily's convulsive sobbing had subsided, she noticed a post it note slipped under her bedroom door. She reached to pick it up.

Sorry!
Bx

She opened the door 'I'm sorry too,' she said and hugged Bella, who was standing with a filled shot glass in each hand.

20

To: *josie.t@marketmakers.com; jess226@gmail.com; raveena@deveers.co.uk*
From: *Bella.j@hothouseproductions.co.uk*
Subject: *A spot of Christmas cheer?*

Girls
Its five days till Christmas! Our dear friend Emily has suffered a triple whammy rejection blow – more later. She needs to be lifted back onto the dance podium of life. Before you all disappear off, who's free this Thursday night? Kicking off at 18.30 sharp with Rossini cocktails at Vertigo 42, then on to opening of swanky new Soho bar, which I happen to have invites for – d-list celebs guaranteed, Big Brother runners up, entire cast of Casualty, bloke who won The Apprentice six years ago, etc. Spray tan, magic pants and the usual prize for the stupidest heels...

Bella x

To: Bella.j@hothouseproductions.co.uk
From: josie.t@marketmakers.com
cc: raveena@deveers.co.uk; jess226@gmail.com
Subject: A spot of Christmas cheer?

Spray tanning as we speak. Poor old Em! See you there...
Jo

To: Bella.j@hothouseproductions.co.uk
From: jess226@gmail.com
cc: josie.t@marketmakers.com; raveena@deveers.co.uk
Subject: A spot of Christmas cheer?

I'm in!
Jess x

To: Bella.j@hothouseproductions.co.uk
From: raveena@deveers.co.uk
cc: josie.t@marketmakers.com; jess226@gmail.com
Subject: A spot of Christmas cheer?

Triple whammy??? I'm way out of date! See you on
Thursday.
Rav x

Emily and Bella teetered out of Bank tube station and up Threadneedle Street towards Vertigo 42. It was starting to rain and their heels weren't designed for walking, but trying to find a taxi on December 23rd had turned out to be virtually impossible.

Jo, Jess and Rav were all there when they walked into the bar. Raveena Kapur, tiny and beautiful, a barrister and easily the cleverest girl Emily had met at Oxford, also the filthiest. Who could forget her fine collection of 1970s porn mags, featuring unfeasibly well endowed men – all tumescent splendour and comedy, blow dried hairstyles. Then there was Josie, a St Xavier veteran. She had skipped university to go straight to the money markets, earning bonuses bigger than their combined starting salaries. No nonsense Jo, mouth like a sewer, the only girl on the currency desk. She was funny, uncompromising and tough as old boots.

And then there was hippy Jess, another St Xavier girl. Long, flowing blonde hair, lanky, charming, away with the fairies. Running a stall at Portobello Market for ten years hadn't quite paid the rent. Her long suffering parents had been so hopeful when Bella had got her a job as an assistant at Hothouse Productions. Of course after less than 3 weeks she quit. Apparently working in an office was oppressive. She was currently thinking about becoming a hat designer, but hadn't quite signed up for the course yet. Jack Russell Jo and Hippy Jess, always a dangerous combination – it would inevitably kick off between them after a couple of cocktails.

After the introductory squealing and comparison of shoes, they ordered a round of Rossinis and demanded a full run down of the 'triple whammy rejection debacle', as it had now become known.

Jo's response was predictable, 'I don't understand Emily. Why didn't you just tell him that Derek was Bella's boyfriend and Charlie's a gay.'

'You don't say 'a gay' Jo. You sound like my mother!' Emily laughed.

Rav was even more direct, 'Well, I've never understood why you don't just tell your mother to fuck off Emily.'

Bella butted in defensively. 'Well good to hear you're all on such tremendously sensitive form! I am so glad I called this gathering of caring women to help heal Emily's wounded heart!' They all howled with laughter.

'Well I think you can always sense when someone's soul is meant to be gay,' Oh, here we go, hippie Jess was off again.

'Absolute shite' Jo was on to her in seconds.

Bella interrupted, waving the drinks menu at them. 'Girls, girls! Far more important matters! Do we go for a round of Lychee Bellinis here or head straight to the new bar in Soho?'

They often liked to start the night here. Floor length windows wrapped around the bar with staggering views of London, lights flickering for miles below them. A night in London, glittering with promise, the river sweeping away from them, The Shard, Oxo Tower picked out in red, the London Eye, an arc of blue, beckoning to them to come on down.

They walked out of the lift and tottered onto Bishopsgate and up the road in no particular direction, vaguely following Rav, whose heels were a modest 3 inches. Every passing black cab was taken and Jo finally noticed which way they were heading. 'We're walking towards Shoreditch.'

'No we're not!' Rav kept going.

'Yes we bloody are! We're walking in the opposite direction to Soho. If I'm going to break my fucking neck in these heels, at least make me walk in the right direction!'

They bickered for a while about whether to turn back or keep going along Bishopsgate in search of a taxi, until Jess broke out of the huddle, screaming into the middle of the road and waving her hands like a lunatic. They all climbed into the waiting taxi.

The driver turned round. 'The traffic's solid the other way girls. I'm going to take you along Great Eastern Street and down through Clerkenwell OK?'

'Yes, sure.' They chorused, just grateful to be off their feet and heading anywhere at all.

Rav patted Emily on the knee. 'Look Emily, there's a sign for the White Cube gallery, shall we pop in and have a look at your giant fanny?' They all cackled with laughter.

The taxi was only just crawling along now and mostly at a standstill. Emily was the first to complain. 'This is a bloody joke girls. I'm sobering up fast.' And then as they edged along Shoreditch High Street, they all watched in dismay as her eyes locked onto a dingy basement bar.

'Look everyone! She shouted breathlessly. 'It's a Table Football bar! Stop the taxi!'

Jo rolled her eyes. 'No fucking way Emily, it's a dive. We'll never find another taxi, it took us half an hour to find this one.'

'Oh come on Jo!' Bella looked pleadingly. 'We can have a quick drink, let her have one game and ask the taxi to wait. We're not going anywhere in this traffic.'

Jo looked at Emily and rolled her eyes. She turned to the taxi driver. 'OK, how much to wait.'

'Depends how long you are love.'

'Just one game, Emily.' Jo handed the taxi driver a fifty pound note. 'Don't go anywhere!'

Every head turned as the five girls staggered into the dark café. The only lighting was above the row of five football tables crammed into the room. In the absence of cigarette smoke, it stank of stale beer and piss. A motley crowd of mostly men lined up on benches, waiting to play. They ordered a jug of Long Island Iced Tea and sat at the bar taking it all in.

Emily was animated. 'So how come that fifth table's not being used? The one with the pile of cash in the middle?'

'That's Terry's table,' the barman answered. 'There's £250 down, if you can match it, for anyone who can beat him.'

'Who's Terry?' The girls chorused, half expecting Paul Newman to emerge from a back room.

'Terry's a milkman from Bexley Heath. One of our best

players. Doesn't get beaten very often.'

'I'll beat him!' They all turned to Emily and raised a collective eyebrow.

'Emily, just drink up and get in the taxi.' Rav sounded exasperated.

'Seriously girls. I've never been beaten.' Emily was defiant.

'Sure, sure, Emily.' Bella reminded her. 'When you're playing against us, or a very drunk Spanish bloke who wants to shag you. This guy's a big time hustler and you've had two Champagne cocktails and half a jug of Long Island Iced Tea.'

'Fuck it, I'm in!' They all turned disbelievingly to Jo. She could never resist a bet. 'Come on girls, fifty quid each on the table. I'll sub you Jess.'

'Are you bloody joking, Jo?' Bella looked horrified.

'Well that's my money gone for the night.' Rav reached reluctantly for her purse. 'One drink in the shittiest bar in Shoreditch and home on the tube. Fucking rock and roll!'

'Which one's Terry?' Emily looked around. When he eventually emerged from the crowd, he was about as far from Paul Newman as it's possible to get. Middle aged, heavily tattooed, 5 ft 6" if that, Paul Weller haircut and a slightly nasal south London accent.

He sidled up to them. 'Alright girls? Leave your cash at the bar. Usual rules apply, best of ten balls, no spinning.' His wrists were weighed down with heavy gold chains, which he theatrically removed in preparation for the game.

He nodded to Emily to place the first ball in the centre of the table. Her hands shook a little with excitement as she placed it down. Before she could focus, they were off. His player snatched the ball away in an instant, toying with it momentarily, as if to mock her and boom, slammed it into her goal, gone, before she even really saw it. Rav groaned and Bella took a large swig of her drink.

The second ball can only have lasted a couple of seconds longer. Exactly the same move – slight nudge to one side, slam, gone.

He was taking the piss with the third ball, rolling it backwards and forwards between rows of players until he was ready for the slamdunk . She hadn't seen anything like this before. He was so fast, there was simply no time to react.

The girls had never seen Emily take quite such a hammering 'Come on Emily! Get on with it!' Jo shouted.

The fourth ball was in play now. She sucked her breath in, in an effort to sober up. He tried exactly the same move, but she was ready for him this time and slammed it back up the mid line. 'Bit better!' He was taunting her now. Patronising little twat. 'But not good enough!' he shouted as he flicked it off the side and straight into a set piece, right into the corner of her goal.

'Four, nil. Do you want to call it quits now darling?' And then something snapped in Emily, something which had been building up for quite a while. Suddenly she could see Frankie's contemptuous face, Mean Monica, the DJ from Radio Liverpool, Clare Forster-Blair, Marcus from the Economist, her mother. She could feel every nerve, twitching in her body as she shouted 'Fuck you!' loudly across the table. She hit the ball with such a force, it flew out of the table and across the bar. 'Steady on darling!' She could see that Terry looked surprised, as the barman handed the ball back to him and he placed it in the centre of the table. She'd learnt her lesson and before he could even focus, she flicked it sideways and slammed it down the side and into his goal.

'Yes!' All four girls leapt to their feet and punched the air in unison.

Terry was rattled now. There was a strange look in this girl's eyes. The other regulars hadn't seen this before. They started to shuffle over and form a circle around the table.

Emily didn't blink. Go to the left, keep it to the left, he's weaker that side. She slipped the sixth ball to her row of backs, then forward again, back again and finally hitting it with such force, it ricochetd off the side and straight into his goal.

Terry looked up at her. 'Easy tiger. Time of the month is it?'

Jo, who was used to that kind of comment, was standing on a chair now shouting. 'And again, Emily! Take the little man down!'

Four, two. She almost had him on the run, playing with the seventh ball, same routine, keep to the left, backwards, forwards, slightly to the middle and WHAM! Four, three.

Terry stood back and feigning nonchalance, took a sip of his beer. He blew on his fingers and cracked his knuckles menacingly. Emily didn't look up from the table. They started to play. Terry had the ball, played with it, passed it to the side. But she was too fast for him. He lost concentration for a second and she whipped the ball away and spanked it down the pitch. It missed his goal, but she struck again and again, until finally she slammed it in.

Four, four.

'Whip his pint sized little arse Emily!' An uncharacteristic outburst from hippy Jess and for a split second, Emily was distracted. Terry took full advantage, snatching the ball from her and repeating his set piece, to slam it once again into her open goal.

'What's the matter darling? Lost your mojo? Five, four. You can't win now, love.'

'Don't bet on it, my little friend!' She muttered, without looking up.

'Championship point I think?' Terry was busy preparing to gloat. He took his eye off the table just long enough for Emily to snatch the ball and tease it down the left hand side. She was flicking her players around wildly, desperately now, but finally she made contact. Slam, she scored again.

The barman stepped forward holding the £500 cash. 'Five all! Sudden death rules apply. One more ball, winner takes all. Are you both ready?'

Every face in the bar crowded round their table. Her palms were sweaty and she had never felt quite so sober. She reached down to remove her shoes, fighting with the straps - the same sodding pair she'd failed to remove at the polo. The girls saw her struggle and came rushing forward to undo the buckles on each ankle.

Terry attempted some feeble sledging, but she couldn't hear him. All she could see and hear now, were the scornful characters in her head, there they all were again, the growing cast list, waiting to bring her down. Jem's face snarling abuse, Henry from Hamilton's laughing and winking at Charlie, Clare Forster-Blair 'you're on such thin ice Emily', Marcus from the Economist 'what is it that you do exactly?', Mean Monica, her foot out, waiting to trip her up and now Terry, some little twat milkman called Terry, whose lips were forming insults she couldn't even hear.

The barman placed the ball in the centre. No noise now, but the sound of her own breathing. Terry was off. He smashed it straight towards her goal. She saved it and her goalie sent it flying up the side of the table. But Terry struck again, blasting it at her goal. There was nothing she could do to withstand this force. Sooner or later he was going to score. But then she remembered - La Bofetada. Could she still do it? Nothing to lose now. At last she had control of the ball, she flipped it up into the air, but backwards, towards her own goal. Terry was caught off guard. As it fell she flicked her wrist in reverse – the player did a perfect back flip and sent the ball flying off its heels, into the air and smack into Terry's waiting goal.

'The girl wins!' Emily stood stunned and motionless

and only the combined screaming and jumping up and down of the four girls, who now lifted her in the air, finally brought her round. The barman handed her a wad of cash.

'What the hell was that?' Terry looked awestruck.

'That was La Bofetada.' She turned away from him. 'Girls! I need a drink.'

Jo was there in a second with a shot of tequila and a slice of lemon. 'Emily girl, you were awesome. Get that down you and let's get out of this dive!'

Giggling and screaming they ran out of the bar and piled into the waiting taxi. They didn't stop laughing until they were almost at Bloomsbury. It was at this point that Rav spotted Terry on a moped, pulling up beside them. 'Oh shit girls, it's him!' He was knocking on the window. 'He's probably going to kill us. Do you think he wants his money back?'

'Well he can't bloody have it.' Jo lowered the window an inch. 'What the hell do you want?'

'Girls!' He called out in nasal drawl. 'Can I tag along?'

They looked at each other, with such relief. Jo spoke for all of them. 'Yes sure Terry, we're going to a new bar on Dean Street called Shag! Meet us outside.'

'Right on, girls!' Terry sped off.

They were hysterical once more. 'What did you go and say that for?' Bella mouthed at Jo.

'Oh my God he thinks he's Austin Powers,' Jess giggled.

Emily's phone buzzed in her bag. It was a text from Charlie.

Hey gorgeous! how r u doing? If I don't c u b4 Xmas, have a great time in Paris! Cx

Emily read it out and there was a collective sigh, followed by a chorus of 'such a shame he's gay!'

Suddenly Rav piped up. 'Get him to meet us the bar!'

They all shouted approval, as Emily texted him back.

gaggle of pissed girls, desperate to meet u... come to Shag! bar on Dean St asap! don't even try to resist? Ex

The entrance was packed as they wrestled their way up the stairs. The waiters were mostly pretty Eastern European boys, with very tight, white T-shirts with Shag! emblazoned on the front. The free Champagne was long gone, but Terry spotted a vodka luge in the corner and they jostled their way through the crowd towards it. The huge ice sculpture was a life sized replica of a very well endowed Greek God. Anyone shameless enough to lie beneath its frozen member with their mouth open, could choose to have chocolate, chilli or lemongrass vodka shot into their mouth. Rav was the first one in.

Emily noticed that Terry and Jess had disappeared into an alcove behind a thick purple curtain. At the other end of the room, she could see a smattering of d-listers sitting in a cordoned off area - Jedward, a daytime TV chef and a couple of girls from TOWIE. She only prayed Rav hadn't spotted Jedward. Oh God, it was too late. Emily looked on helplessly as she watched Rav, stumbling around. She had already found the VIP area and now she had her arm around each of the Jedwards.

'I bloody love you two!' She slurred as she pulled them closer to her.

'Well it's always lovely to meet our fans!' It was hard to tell which of the Jedwards looked more petrified.

'No I mean it.' Rav persisted. 'I'd shag you both.' She squeezed them both.

'That's very flattering I'm sure, but we're just here for a quick drink, thanks anyway though.' One of the twins replied, politely, but clearly terrified.

'Oh come on boys! Make hay while the sun shines! You won't be famous for long, you know.' Rav tightened her grip.

'Security!' One of the boys waved towards the bar.

Before the bouncer could get anywhere near the VIP area, Rav disappeared into Jess and Terry's curtained alcove, from where large clouds of smoke now billowed with the unmistakeable aroma of a gargantuan spliff.

'Charlie!' Across the bar, Emily could see him struggling through the crowd, to get over to her. 'I didn't think you'd come.' She couldn't hear his reply above the sound of the music. 'Here.' She shouted. 'Have a vodka shot. You've got a bit of catching up to do.'

Rav re-emerged, giggling from the alcove. The vodka or spliff had seriously kicked in because by now, she was using her lipstick to write 'Me!' underneath 'Shag!' in giant letters on one of the prettier waiters' T-shirts. The bouncer spotted her again and they played cat and mouse all round the club, Rav giggling and hiding behind waiters. She darted in and out of the VIP area and then back into the alcove. Moments later, they all watched as three beefy, shaven headed bouncers, black puffa jackets and walkie talkies, whipped back the purple curtain, to reveal Terry, Rav and Jess wrapped in a cloud of smoke.

'It's a shite club anyway.' Rav shouted over the music, as the three of them were frog marched out of the building. 'Who thought of a crap name like Shag!'

'I guess we're off then.' Emily and Charlie put down their shot glasses and Bella and Jo followed.

They found Jess, green and throwing up at the foot of the entrance steps.

Emily knelt down beside her, 'Here have some tissues. Do you want us to drop you home, Jess?'

'God, no way!' She replied, wiping her mouth. 'I'm having a blast. Where to next?'

Jess and Jo climbed into the back of a tuc-tuc, which followed the taxi carrying Charlie, Bella, Emily and Rav.

Terry was bringing up the rear on his moped.

Jess pulled one of Terry's pre-rolled spliffs out of her pocket and offered it to Jo. They were horizontal now in the back of the tuc-tuc, shrieking and giggling their way through the streets of Soho, no idea where they were going, as the convoy followed the taxi.

'You know Jess,' Jo struggled to form the words. 'One thing that's been bugging me for eleven years now.'

'A bug up your arse?'

'No, you stupid cow! When you went out with Danny Calvert at school, only the best looking boy in the known universe?'

'God, you've got a good memory!' Jess inhaled deeply.

'None of us ever understood why you dumped him?' Jo looked wistful. 'I would have gnawed my legs off to go out with him.'

'Danny Calvert? Jess snorted. 'I dumped him…' She paused for effect and took another drag. '…because he had a cocktail sausage in his M&S pants.'

'You're joking.' Jo screamed. 'You're so shallow!'

'I wouldn't joke about something like that.' Jess replied. 'I ditched him, on account of his diminutive trouser snake.'

Jo was exultant. 'And I thought you were a sensitive hippie! Have you no feelings?'

'As it turned out,' Jess struggled to get the words out. 'I could feel nothing whatsoever.' They both snorted with laughter.

'Who'd have thought, Danny Calvert, puny pecker!' They were shrieking and shouting at passers by.

'Teeny weiner!', 'Slender fender!' 'Dwarfish dipstick!' 'Danny Calvert and his miniscule meat muscle!' 'Stumpy shlong! Stunted stiffie! Derisory dick!'

The convoy stopped at the lights and the Croatian tuc-tuc driver turned round. 'Hey girls, can I have a drag on your puny pecker? That smells like good shit.'

Jess was laughing too much to speak. 'What's your name and where d'you come from?' Jo asked, sounding like a pissed game show host.

'Miho, I'm from Croatia.'

She handed him her spliff. 'Sure Miho. Have a puff!'

In the taxi, up ahead, Charlie turned to Rav and Emily. 'Does anyone know where we're actually going?'

'The House of Love!' Rav replied. 'Only the best gay club in London!'

'No way.' Charlie looked horrified.

'Oh come on Charlie, Emily laughed. 'It's only window shopping.' He sat, sulking in the back of the taxi.

Once they had finally made it to the front of the queue, they all stood briefly awestruck in front of the stadium sized dance floor, a 20 foot high pink neon heart suspended above the crowd and cages either side of the stage, with leather clad dancers writhing against the bars. Around them danced the most glamorous mass of people Emily had ever seen. Two black guys with matching platinum blond hair, joined at their gyrating hips. The sweaty throng now punching the air in time to the music 'Everybody in the House of Love.' Shaved heads and lipstick, fishnets and feathers, pink string vests, studded gloves, a couple of girls kissing passionately as they danced on the seven foot high podium. Emily's eye was drawn to an enormous swing, hanging down from the neon loveheart.

Rav was in raptures. 'Now THIS is what I call a club!'

Miho, the tuc-tuc driver was the first on the dance floor, doing a passable impression of East 17, the accent less convincing. 'Everybody, everybody in the house of love! Everybody, everybody in the house of love, hey!'

Charlie was the most sober and the least at ease. 'Right.

What does everyone want to drink?' But none of them heard him as the House of Love morphed into Blondie.

'Cover me with kisses, baby
Cover me with love'

Emily and Bella were on the dance floor in seconds.

'Roll me in designer sheets
I'll never get enough.
Emotions come, I don't know why
Cover up love's alibi.'

Miho helped them onto separate podiums on opposite sides of the stage and they blasted into imaginary microphones, as they teetered above the throng.

'Call me, call me on the line
Call me, call me any, anytime
Call me!'

Emily could just about make out Terry in the middle of the crowd, like a human dance handbag, encircled by Jo, Jess and Rav. Charlie appeared at the side of the dance floor with a tray of drinks. He handed a vodka and tonic up to Emily and she didn't stop dancing as she knocked it back. The crowd was swimming beneath her now.

She whooped and gyrated as they swarmed at the base of the podium. Then suddenly, perhaps carried away with the excitement and sheer amount of booze she had quaffed, she was unexpectedly air borne.

As she soared through the air, towards the middle of the dancing crowd, her landing was broken by a 6ft burlesque show girl, arms outstretched. His courageous attempt to catch her was only partially hindered by thigh length silver platform boots and red feather headdress.

They crashed to the floor together and she barely felt her ankle twist as she hit the ground.

He lifted her to her feet. 'My hero!' She shouted over the music. 'What's your name and how can I ever thank you?'

'It's Vince.' He leaned down and shouted in her ear. 'And you can buy me a drink.'

Emily limped off towards the bar. She noticed Charlie deep in conversation in the corridor, his back to the wall, the other guy's arm on the wall above his shoulder. She smiled slightly smugly to herself as she stood in the queue.

At 3.10 am, they finally departed. Emily, Charlie, Jo and Bella in a taxi, Rav and Vince in Miho's tuc-tuc and Terry on his Vespa, with Jess on the back. The convoy made painfully slow progress, as the taxi slowed down to wait for the tuc-tuc and Vespa. Somewhere along the line, Emily had shouted 'Everyone back to Fulham!'

'Who's the transvestite?' Terry had asked as they left the club. He was slightly miffed that he was no longer the only bloke.

'Actually I'm a transsexual, my name's Vince and you can address me to my face.'

'Hey Charlie, did we see you pull?'

'Not exactly, but I did get his phone number!' He looked coy.

Much shrieking and whooping. 'Alright girls, calm down!'

Charlie had bought most of the drinks at the House of Love, so Emily's wad of winnings was still more or less intact. The convoy waited outside as she and Bella stumbled into the Cromwell Road 24 hour off licence, singing 'everybody in the house of love.' Five minutes later they emerged, carrying a skull shaped bottle of vodka, a Jeroboam of champagne and a litre of tequila gold. Now they were singing, 'Club Tropicana drinks are freeeeeeeeee, fun and sunnnnshine, there's eenough for everyone…'

Back home and House of Love was booming out of the speakers, as they cleared the furniture in the sitting room, to make a bigger dance floor. Jo shouted across to Emily who was dancing on the coffee table, 'Hey Emily, why don't you phone Jem? Come on, let's phone him right now!'

'I don't have his number.' Emily shouted back.

Terry was rolling joints for Jo and Jess. Emily hadn't seen Charlie for a while, probably fallen asleep.

She carried on dancing, but once the thought was in her head, it wouldn't go away. She disappeared off into her bedroom. It was a struggle to plug in her laptop and her fingers couldn't seem to work the mouse. It was good to do these things when you were in the right mood, just the right mix of funny and heartfelt.

To: Jem.im.a@RadioNorth.com
From: EBrighouse@Hobbs&Parker.com
Subject: evrybody in the huse of love…

Hey Jem
Happy chrismas, I jist want u to now that I really really lik u. I can't stop thinking about you, mostly dreaming actually alot and Charlie is gay it turns out and so….call me, call me any, any, anytime! Call me, any any time, I mean pleeaaasse call me…
Em xoxooxoxooxxoxxoxxxoxxxxoxoxxxx

She'd only just pressed 'send', when they all came bursting into her bedroom. Charlie had instructed them to wait at the window, with the curtains closed and the lights off, until he gave the signal. They could hear Vince outside, counting down from 10.

'Three, two, one, lift off…'

They pulled back the curtain. And there was Charlie, balancing on the wall, butt naked, apart from a set of battery powered fairly lights, wrapped around every inch of his body, a Christmas star perched on his head, his leg balanced on Vince's shoulder as he re-enacted Bruce Forsythe's classic, knuckle to forehead pose in dazzling LED brilliance.

What none of them could see as they clapped and hollered at the window, was Mrs Vassiliadis' livid, white face as she looked out through the net curtains and watched a six foot drag queen showgirl, pissing on her sculpted conifers.

21

She woke up and was immediately aware that her tongue was stuck to the roof of her mouth. As she slowly opened one eye and then the other, the nausea kicked in, along with a pinching pain in the temples. Charlie snored lightly beside her. She tried to piece together the wreckage of last night, but thinking made her feel more sick and dizzy. The table football, Terry the milkman, getting thrown out of Shag! Visions of Rav and Jedward. Her ankle felt painful and swollen, oh God yes and Vince the Showgirl and Charlie leaving the club, looking a bit pleased with himself, a tuc-tuc and a skull of vodka…

The white pillowcase was stained with black mascara print. She was at least wearing her pyjamas, but her clothes lay scattered around the room, pants inside tights. Her stomach turned as she spotted half a bottle of tequila gold sitting on the window sill, the light shining through it from the half open curtain. And suddenly she was gripped with something even worse than her hangover – the kind of panic that leaves you physically sick – blinding horror. She remembered her email to Jem…

Leaping out of bed, she grabbed her laptop from the floor, stabbing at the keys and waiting, barely breathing, as it slowly booted up. God knows what rubbish she had written in her email. Please God, she was so technically pathetic, just maybe she had forgotten to press send, maybe there was some way to recall the email. Right now, she would pay some techno geek her entire year's salary, if they would just make it go away. No chance, there it was. Sent at 4.16am. And oh shit, he had already replied. At 4.21am. This was now officially too awful to bear.

Bella poked her head round the door. 'Emily, that Croatian bloke is face down in the bath. And his tuc tuc's blocking the Vassiliadis' front door.'

Emily didn't look up. 'I'll come and sort it in a minute. I just have to read something.' She clicked on her inbox, hardly daring to open her eyes. Why couldn't she have just left it alone, at least kept her dignity.

To: EBrighouse@Hobbs&Parker.com
From: Jem.im.a@RadioNorth.com
Subject: evrybody in the huse of love...

Thank you for your email. Jerome Armstrong has now left Radio North for an opportunity with a Canadian news channel. He can be contacted via the TV Montreal Network.

In the meantime, any enquiries or news concerning Radio North should be forwarded to Frankie Blake at Frankie.b@RadioNorth.com or telephone her direct line 0191 252 6121.

She closed her eyes, desolate but strangely relieved. Well, at least he hadn't seen her email. So that was that then. End of story. Jerome Armstrong had left the country. If there had been a little flicker of hope, it had just been royally snuffed out. She was used to disappointment. Maybe it was better like this, Jem on the other side of the world, out of reach and well away from humiliating attempts to contact him. This way at least, she had to face the fact that they were never going to get together. Even Hector would be hard pushed to offer any words of encouragement.

Bella came in again. 'Oh my God, Em, come and look at the size of the crucifix tattoo on Terry's back? It's just like Robert de Niro's in Cape Fear?' He was asleep on the floor in the hallway and they both bent over him to get a closer look. You had to admit, it was seriously creepy. Emily stepped over him and went to the kitchen to put the kettle on.

She came back with a mug of tea and two Nurofen for Charlie, who was now awake, sitting on the side of the bed and in a state of serious agitation. 'Morning Charlie! How are you feeling? Better than me I hope. I'll put this by the bed.' But Charlie was oblivious, rooting through his trouser pockets like a man possessed, literally turning them inside out and the jacket and then back to the trousers.

Emily sat on the bed watching him. 'What exactly are you looking for?'

'Nothing, really.' He carried on rifling through every pocket.

'Oh come on Charlie, what's the matter?' She was curious – he was obviously very agitated about something. 'Tell me what you've lost and I'll help you look.'

'OK.' He stopped for a moment. 'But I'm warning you now. Don't take the piss, OK? I've lost a phone number from last night.'

'Oh I see.' Emily smiled. 'You mean THE phone number.' She went round to her side of the bed and suddenly burst out laughing.

Charlie looked at her. 'I'm sorry, I thought I heard myself say don't take the piss, Emily.'

Emily opened the bedroom door. 'Bella, you've got to come in here and help!' She was snorting with laughter now as Bella came in looking confused. 'Charlie's lost a very important phone number.' She turned back to Charlie. 'Do you think you could have left it in the taxi?'

Charlie looked furious now as they both laughed uncontrollably. 'I can't remember. I just remember that I had the number somewhere.' He stood up and looked at her. 'I must say, Emily, you are being remarkably insensitive about this, considering you are someone I thought I could trust.'

'I'm sorry Charlie.' The laughter subsided and Emily opened up her cupboard door with a full length mirror inside. 'Come over here for a second!' She led Charlie towards the mirror. He was only wearing his boxers and she spun him round, so that his back was facing the mirror. 'Eh Voila!' She shouted triumphantly. 'I think we've found your phone number.'

Written in large black letters across Charlie's naked back were the words:

HEY GORGEOUS! ALEX 078835 69114 CALL ME!

Emily finally stopped laughing. 'Hey gorgeous, where's your phone? You need to save that number before you go and rub it off.'

'Alright, alright. Over there by the bed.' Charlie was grinning a little sheepishly as she read out the number. 'Thanks Em.'

'You're welcome, gorgeous.'

Bella and Emily sidled out of the front door in their dressing gowns and with some difficulty, pushed the tuc-tuc over to their side of the shared entrance. They had three hours to shower, pack, clear the house of empty bottles and party guests and get to the station – not impossible. They had tickets for the 12.57 from Victoria to Cobham. Charlie was just leaving, but Terry was on his third cup of tea and Miho was showing no signs of going home.

For some reason, she delayed telling Bella about the email. What with the hangover and everything, she wasn't quite ready for another round of 'oh Em, why don't you just go out with some nice, ugly guy'.

Instead, she had forwarded the email to Hector, taking care of course to delete her own drunken message, from the bottom. She knew he would be on his way out of London by now, but he was bound to have something to say. Sure enough, he replied from his car.

To: EBrighouse@Hobbs&Parker.com
From: hectorbraun@levoisier.com
Subject: evrybody in the huse of love...

Emily

Are you a quitter or wilfully obtuse, I'm not sure which? You are missing the point completely. This surely means he has split up with 'bitch troll canter girl'. The baroness has left the building. Hurrah! And we all know what happens next...
Edelweiss, Edelweiss...
Happy Christmas darling!

Hector x

PS. What's the 'huse of love' – sounds fun...
Sent from my iphone

God Hector was wonderful! Misguided but wonderful!

By now, Bella's OCD packing was beginning to get to her. 'Em, should I wear the taupe moleskins with the matching wrap or do you think that's too contrived?' Bella was going straight from Surrey on Boxing Day to join Derek and his family in Cumbria. A momentous relationship milestone and one which was understandably, prompting significant clothing angst.

Emily was actually thinking 'I don't really give a shit which shade of cashmere would best suit you, because my heart is breaking.' But Bella was her best friend and had met the man of her dreams. She wasn't going to rain on her parade. She mustered a smile and followed her into her room. In fact the utter trivia of it was strangely distracting.

Bella was preoccupied, standing in front of a large pile of clothes, neatly folded on her bed. 'I'll get there late afternoon and then there'll be dinner with his parents. Should I change into something else for dinner, or just wear something quite smart on the train? I think we're going to church on Sunday.' Dear God! You'd think she was going to Balmoral.

'Em, I don't suppose I could borrow your plum hunter wellies and biker Barbour could I?' She sounded a little apologetic.

'Yes, sure.' Emily was stoical. She may as well. She couldn't imagine she would be wearing them again. She pulled a bag from under her bed and brought out the boots and jacket. At least they were a little worn in by now. She also gave her the cashmere snood.

'Are you sure Ems?' Bella looked concerned.

'Of course. I'll feel better if they get some use.'

'Oh Emily.' Bella was all compassion, which had never made Emily feel very comfortable. Thank goodness she hadn't shown her the email.

Emily surveyed the enormous pile of clothes and looked at her watch. 'Come on Bels, we need to get going. I thought you wanted to be in Surrey by lunchtime.'

This wouldn't be her first Christmas with the Jenkins. She was grateful for the invitation and she loved Bella's family as much as her own, but part of her wished she could just stay in London on her own, play some sad ballads, eat crisps and wallow. In the first ten minutes, Bella's dad would ask her how business was going and if she had a boyfriend. They would have a stocking for her and Bella's mum would bring her marmite soldiers in the pink fluffy spare room, surrounded by a sea of satin cushions and soft toys.

The Jenkins were a proper family – they had pictures of Bella and her brother all over the house, those cheesy ones in school uniform, gappy teeth and fake sky in the background. Bella as a brownie, Bella's swimming awards, holidays, birthdays – loud declarations of happiness everywhere. They also had pictures of Emily on the mantelpiece, including her graduation photo, featuring platinum blonde hair and a glowing fake tan. As far as Emily was aware, her own mother had never ordered a school photo.

Emily busied herself with the clearing up. The contents of the Jeroboam smelt sickly as she poured it down the sink – the recycling bin was going to look particularly shameful this week. As the last of it glugged out of the bottle, she reassured herself that a true alcoholic surely wouldn't be pouring it away like this. She mopped the sticky kitchen floor and went round the flat chucking fag ends and broken glasses into a bin liner. It amazed her, the stuff that 9 drunken people can think of to do in 2 hours.

Emily had tried and failed to get Terry to move. Bella went into the sitting room, where Terry was flicking through the TV channels. They really were going to have to ask him to leave. 'So how long will it take you to get back to Bexley Heath, Terry?' She asked, hopefully, looking at her watch.

'No time at all.' He replied, feet up on the coffee table.

'Do you have family there?' She sounded like a politician's wife talking to a constituent.

'Divorced.' He didn't look up from the telly. 'Two girls actually, about your age.'

Bella tried a different tack. 'What about your milk round? Are you off over Christmas?'

'Supposed to be, only I expect I'll have to do a bit of overtime now.' His laugh turned into a hacking cough. 'You girls totally cleaned me out. How did your friend get so good anyway?'

Bella opened the curtains. 'She lived with her father in Spain one summer when she was 10. Apparently she sat in a bar and did nothing but play table football for a couple of months.' He wasn't shifting from the sofa. She tried again. 'OK, well we're off in a minute.'

Bella gave up and went to the hall to phone some minicab firms. They had planned to get the tube, but Bella's outfit indecision meant that they now had five heavy bags and a vanity case and Emily's ankle was still throbbing. Every mini cab company said the same thing, 'No chance love it's Christmas Eve!'

Miho emerged yawning from the bathroom. 'Don't worry girls! I can take you to Victoria station.' They looked at each other. It was less than one hour before the train was due to leave. This was their only chance of making it.

Emily finally got into the bathroom, showered and dressed in under 12 minutes. She had one bag, to Bella's five, but then Bella had taken most of her clothes. Once they had manoeuvred the tuc-tuc out of the gate and onto the pavement, they piled Bella's bags in and attempted to squeeze in themselves. It was no good, the only way was to balance two bags on the roof of the tuc-tuc and sit on top of the remaining bags, with their heads bent under the sagging canopy. Miho, with Herculean strength, started to pedal. The poor guy looked like he might break his back. It was agonisingly slow and in the cold light of day, deeply embarrassing, but this was the only way they were going to make it. To add to the shame, Terry followed behind, carrying another of Bella's bags and the vanity case and weaving around on his Vespa.

'Bella, we're still in convoy!' Emily laughed. She could hear the music in her head. Everybody in the house of love. A melancholy thought struck her, that almost everybody else had found love, a seasonal lovefest, Hector and John speeding down the M4 to Babbington House for Christmas, her mother in Paris, reunited with Benoit, Bella off to Cumbria for New Year with Derek and the pork billionaires and now even Charlie. How did she get left behind?

'Just look at us, Emily!' Bella started to giggle as Miho struggled to turn the corner into the Kings Road.

Emily leant forward. 'Are you OK Miho? Do we need to throw a few bags off? Not mine obviously!'

'Yes fine girls, no problem!' But he was clearly feeling the strain.

They smiled and waved at the inevitable smart arse comments as they creaked their way up the busy streets. 'Room for me in there girls!' 'Where's the kithen sink!' Haha, hilarious. Every window was packed with Christmas decorations and panicked shoppers, jostling as they grabbed last minute gifts.

They passed by a Salvation Army band playing Christmas carols. 'Happy Christmas Bella!' Emily shouted over the chorus of 'O Come All Ye Faithful'. 'I'm so glad it's all worked out with Derek and everything.'

'Oh Gosh Ems! Happy Christmas to you! And thank you for finding me the man!' They hugged each other with some difficulty, heads bent under the canvas roof. 'I just wish things could have worked out for you as well. At least let's hope you have a happier New Year.' They bounced along silently for a couple of minutes, before

Bella added. 'Em, I'm so bloody nervous about meeting the Dewsbury's.'

Emily squeezed her hand. 'It'll be fine. You're bound to be nervous Bels. Anyway, you don't need to say too much. What is it you always tell me? Lots of open questions. Just be your polite, charming self and they'll love you!'

All things considered, Miho had gathered an impressive pace as they scooted round Sloane Square. He took a right down Eaton Terrace. 12.36pm, 19 minutes till the train left. They would easily make it.

As they turned left up Ebury Street, the tuc-tuc creaked badly and the righthand wheels were several inches off the ground. The girls shifted right to compensate. It was now pretty much a straight line all the way to Victoria station.

They both saw the leopard skin coat at the same time, lying next to a wall, on the pavement up ahead. It was only when they were closer that they could see a girl was lying under it, face down on the pavement, blonde hair like a birds nest at the back. She had obviously been there all night.

'See Em. We're not that bad', Bella pointed.

'There but for the grace of God.' Emily muttered and with that, Bella knew exactly what she was going to do next.

'Miho, stop the tuc-tuc!' Emily shouted, leaning forward to pat him on the shoulder.

'No Emily, no! What are you doing? We've got less than 15 minutes!'

'Stop Miho!' Emily was insistent. 'We can't just leave her lying there.'

'This is insane, we'll miss the bloody train!' But Bella knew it was useless as the tuc-tuc ground to a screeching halt, bags spilling off the roof and onto the road.

Emily crouched down next to the girl, not knowing quite what to expect. She felt a little silly as she spoke.

'Excuse me.'

No response.

She tried again. 'Hello! Are you OK?' My God, was she unconscious? Choked on her own vomit? She felt the back of her neck, still warm thank God. There was nothing for it, she lifted one shoulder and rolled her over quite roughly, at which point she groaned loudly and Emily was face to face with the wreck of a woman, lipstick smeared down her chin, eyes like a panda and a couple of love bites under the left ear. And then she realised.

'Oh my God, Monica?'

More groaning and squinting, at the sudden intrusion of daylight. Finally, the wreck of a woman spoke. 'Where am I?'

'Ebury Street, Victoria.'

Massive yawn, giving off an unfortunate waft of stale alcohol. She blinked again and focused on the familiar face in front of her. 'Emily? Emily Brighouse? What on earth are you doing here?' Typically, she sounded almost affronted.

'I just happened to be passing.' Emily replied, shifting away a bit.

'What day is it?'

'It's Friday, Monica. Christmas Eve.'

'Have we got work today?'

'No Monica, the office is closed today.' Emily wondered if she was planning on going straight to work, to place a couple of magazine, hamper offers before Christmas.

'Wow, I don't remember how I got here at all.'

'Clearly not.' Emily couldn't help replying with a hint of disapproval, even though, a few hours earlier, she had been in a woefully similar state. If the tables were turned she knew damn well, Monica wouldn't have even crossed the road to help her out.

She reached in her bag for some face wipes and a bottle of water. Bella, who had finished re-stacking the tuc-tuc, helped her pull Monica up to a sitting position. 'Come on Em, this is ridiculous. We've only got 10 minutes to get there.'

Emily pulled a face. 'Bella, this is Monica from the office.'

Bella's expression changed. 'What! Blimey. Hi Monica. Emily's told me all about you. Good night was it?'

Bella pulled Emily aside. 'Listen Florence Bloody Nightingale! From what you've told me, that little cow wouldn't piss on you if you were on fire, so just give her your water bottle and get in the sodding tuc-tuc, before we go and miss Christmas Eve altogether.'

'Alright, alright.' Emily turned to Terry, who had lit a fag and was watching the scene from a safe distance. 'Terry, would you come over here and do us a massive favour?' Terry sauntered over. 'This is Monica. I think she lives in Lewisham. You couldn't get her home could you?'

He stubbed out his cigarette. 'Sure girls. No problem. It's on my way.'

They were in convoy again. The rickety cavalcade now made even more colourful with the arrival of the leopard skin coated Monica, bouncing on the back of the Vespa and clutching Terry's waist. He still had Bella's bag and vanity case on either handle, but was weaving around less now, with the added ballast behind.

This time, to save his back, they let Miho get a running start and when he was underway, leapt on like bob sleigh riders, either side of the moving tuc-tuc. Once they had both recovered and found a good position to balance, Emily tried to coax a smile from a steely faced Bella. 'Well.' she said breathlessly. 'Another farcical episode in the life of Emily and Bella!'

Bella wasn't ready to see the funny side. 'Emily, we have less than four minutes to make it. Do me a favour and save the jokes until we're safely on the train, OK!'

'OK.'

Three minutes and forty eight seconds later, they fell panting, hearts pounding, into their seats, as the train pulled out of Victoria station. They blew kisses through the window and mouthed 'thank you' to Miho, who had insisted on carrying their bags right up to the train door.

Bella waved at him. 'You know Em, that man's a saint.' She paused for a moment. 'Did you know he's a dentist in Dubrovnik? Not bad looking either.'

'Stop it Bella!' Emily shot her a warning look.

'I'm just saying…'

'I know what you're saying and you can just shut up.' Emily started to smile. 'More to the point, flipping heck! Complete shocker. Mean Monica, face down on the pavement. I can't believe it.'

Bella raised her eyebrows. 'No, well, she won't be quite such a smug little, 'stab you in the back' madam when she sees you at work after Christmas, Ems.'

'Oh, I wouldn't count on it.' Emily replied. 'I expect she'll conveniently forget that little incident pretty quickly.'

Bella reached in her bag for her iphone and held it up in front of Emily. 'Oh, I shouldn't think so Em. Not when she sees these pictures!'

22

NOTICE TO QUIT

TO: Ms E Brighouse and Miss I Jenkins, Tenants in Possession:

Take notice that your month to month tenancy of the herein described premises is hereby terminated at the expiration of 30 days after service of this notice on you,and that you are hereby required to quit and on said date deliver up to me the possession of the premises now held and occupied by you under such tenancy.

Said premises are known as:

[53 Latimer Road]

[Fulham London SW69BY]

This is intended as a 30 days' notice to quit, for the purpose of terminating your tenancy aforesaid.

Dated: December 30th, 2010

For and on behalf of: Mrs C Vasilliadis

Landlord

Messrs Blake, Williams and Jones
The Quadrant
60 Fulham High Street, SW6 7PT

Ms Emily Brighouse and Ms Isabella Jenkins
53 Latimer Road
Fulham
London SW6 9BY

December 30th 2010

Dear Ms Brighouse and Ms Jenkins

Further to your appearance at Hammersmith and
Fulham Magistrates Court on July 29th of this year
and the issuing on that date of an Anti Social
Behaviour Order, we are writing to you on behalf
of our clients, your landlords, Mr & Mrs Costas
Vasilliadis. Our client informs us, that on the
night of Thursday December 23rd, you were in breach
of the terms of the aforementioned order, for
which they have gathered substantial photographic
evidence. We remind you that should the Court find
you in breach of the Anti Social Behaviour Order,
you will be liable for a conviction and subsequent
criminal record. To avoid this course of action,
we enclose a Notice to Quit, allowing both parties
to terminate the tenancy agreement with no further
action. We highly recommend that you abide by this
notice and vacate the property within 30 days, to
avoid further legal action.

Emily sat at her desk. She tried to keep calm as she folded up the letter and put it back in her handbag. There was no point telling Bella yet. Besides, she was still in Cumbria, at the Dewsbury family 'love-in', probably mid way through a wholesome family walk. Emily pictured the scene, Bella's arm linked with Mrs D, laughing about something hysterical Derek said when he was four. No point spoiling her fun with the threat of imminent homelessness. Anyway, they had 30 days to find somewhere to live, weeks away.

Emily had volunteered to work between Christmas and New Year, a soft option or so she had thought. Flicking through the 'Get The Look!' pages of every January magazine issue, lunch with Hector, followed by some light internet shopping. It was all looking fairly relaxed, until she found out that the other 'skeleton staff' in the consumer division would be two grad trainees, Anoushka and Clare Bloody Forster Blair.

Talk of the devil, Clare popped her head over the partition. 'How are we getting along with signing up those journalists for the Territorial Army, Emily? I need to update the Major General next week.' God, she had hardly had a chance to log on to her computer and the bloody woman was hounding her. Since when, in any case, had this become her sole responsibility? As far as she could remember, when this particular PR fantasy was being pitched by the rest of the team, she was dangling outside the 7th floor window, attached to a piece of nylon rope.

'I think it's all sorted Clare.' Emily replied breezily. 'Monica told me that she had at least 5 really high quality journalists signed up before she went off for Christmas. I expect she can update us fully when she gets back.'

'Great, well keep at it and let's smash those targets!' Clare's head popped back behind the partition.

'Yes, let's!' Smash them yourself, stupid cow.

Damn, now she would have to come back to the office after lunch with Hector. She managed to sneak out, undetected at 12.00.

Hector was already there. 'Darling girl! I ordered you a glass of Champagne.'

Of course, he wanted a full run down of the Girls Night Out. She gave him the quick version, but it wasn't good enough. He wanted to wring out every last detail. 'The House of Love.' He sighed wistfully. 'Such happy memories! So did you jump or fall off the podium?'

Emily shook her head. 'Can't remember.'

'And the tuc-tuc driver is a dentist?' This detail seemed to particularly tickle him. 'How marvellous!'

'Oh don't you start.' Emily laughed. 'Bella was trying to hook me up with him.'

'Could be worse. Free dental work and you'd save a fortune on taxis.' He put on his reading glasses and scanned the menu. 'And what about Colonel Queer? How did he get on?'

'Well that's the best bit.' Emily was animated. She knew it was disloyal to Charlie, telling Hector about the fairy lights and the phone number, but it was too good to leave out.

'Fabulous!' Hector clapped his hands. 'And the email from Jem?' He took off his glasses and looked at her reproachfully. 'John and I couldn't help noticing that it was a response to one you had sent at 4 in the morning? We could only imagine it was too awful, even for us to see it?'

She looked down at her napkin. 'Correct.'

He raised an eyebrow. *'Let me guess. I think about you all the time… I think I love you… I want to bear your children?* Standard pissed girl stuff? '

She didn't look up. 'More or less.'

'Oh dear. Well, hopefully he won't have seen it, unless he's having his emails forwarded to him, of course.'

'Oh God.' The thought hadn't occurred to her. She felt slightly sick.

'And I suppose the Grand Finale is this,' she said, pulling the Eviction Notice out of her handbag.

He put his glasses back on and read both pages. He looked up. 'What will you do?'

'We'll sort something out I expect,' she tried to sound nonchalant. 'It's funny though, it might be a complete dive, but we're actually quite fond of it now. So many adventures started off in that flat. It'll be sad to leave.'

When she left the restaurant it was starting to sleet, but even so, she decided to walk. Anything to delay her return to the office. There was no one around when she sat down at her desk, no sign of Clare, or Mean Monica with one of her standard greetings. It would usually be, 'Oh there you are Emily, Clare and I were wondering when you'd get back from your lunch.' It was almost lonely without her. She opened her inbox.

To: EBrighouse@Hobbs&Parker.com
From: RoisinOD@yourliving.com
Subject: OMG...

Emily,
Who'd have thought. This TA lark is an absolute craic. When I signed up I thought it would be all jogging up mountains with bricks in my rucksack, but this week I learned to drive a tank and blew up a car in a controlled explosion. And I'm 'under', as they say, a very understanding physical training instructor. Next week it's scuba diving...I'm actually quite glad I puked on your pashmina now...
All the best!

Roisin

Who would have thought. Emily pictured her at the polo, passed out, with her face on a side plate. She forwarded the email to Clare, editing out the pashmina bit.

The phone hardly rang, no angry client emails, nothing for it but a cup of tea. As she walked up the corridor to the kitchen, she only just heard it, a gentle, rhythmic sobbing coming from the ladies' loo. She stopped and opened the door and then stood, foolish and dumbfounded. Clare Forster-Blair was doubled up over the sink, weeping and retching into the basin.

'God, Clare, what's the matter?' Emily moved awkwardly towards her, but stopped halfway. Normal, instinctive reactions felt wrong. It certainly wouldn't have been right to put an arm round her.

'This!' Clare spat at her, in between convulsions, 'if it's not already obvious.' She waved a pregnancy test at Emily. Even from where she was standing, she could see the double lines.

'Wow, congratulations!' She now felt even more awkward and tongue tied, but what else could she say.

Clare heaved again. 'You can keep your congratulations.'

'But that's good news isn't it?' Emily was confused.

Clare tried to stand up. 'Of course it bloody isn't.'

'But I thought you were engaged to Rupe... Rupert?' She couldn't quite bring herself to call him Rupey. 'And you're going to have his baby, isn't that good?'

'It's a disaster, Emily!' Clare's knuckles were white, as she clutched the rim of the sink.

'I mean, isn't it just a question of doing things in a slightly different order?' Emily knew she sounded foolish.

'No it's not.' Clare snapped at her. 'Believe me, it's not. In case you didn't know, if you don't get to Divisional Director in this place, before you get pregnant, you are finished, sidelined, washed up, on the proverbial PR rubbish tip.' She retched again. There were small beads of sweat forming on her usually flawless forehead. 'No one gets so much as a four day week unless you get to Divisional Director.' She took a deep breath and dabbed her mouth with a tissue. 'I was only six months away from a promotion, for God's sake.'

Emily was rooted to the spot, unable to leave or think of an appropriate thing to say. 'Can I get you a glass of water?'

Clare ignored her. 'You see, I've been here long enough to know what happens.' She addressed her own reflection in the mirror as she spoke. 'You get back from Maternity Leave and they start asking you to go to the 4pm pitch in Manchester, the drinks after the client meeting that you really should attend, the networking dinner. 'Oh, but don't worry if you can't make it, they say, one of the boys can always go.' Of course they bloody can, their wives probably sacrificed their career long ago.'

The retching had subsided and she was on a roll.

'And when the child's sick, who do you think will take a day off work, Emily? Me or Rupey?'

Emily didn't know the correct answer. 'I see.' She replied meekly.

'I doubt it. None of this will have even occurred to you, Emily, in your carefree single state, but it will.' That's not quite how Emily would have described her own status, but still.

Clare turned to look at her. 'I've worked my fingers to the bone for this sodding Company, Emily. I've sweated blood for every one of those clients.' She had never heard Clare use any kind of expletive before. This was magnificent.

Clare reached into her handbag and began vigorously brushing her hair. 'Did you know that I won the H&P trainee of the year award, I was the first of my graduate intake to reach account director level. And I've consistently grown my client base every year since.'

'Wow, no I didn't know that.' All of this was quite enlightening for Emily, who had always found the promotion process something of a mystery.

Clare was off again. 'And I've watched, year after year, mediocre male bastards waft in here and get the best accounts and the best teams. Average, talentless blokes in suits, full of crap, playing at business, sitting in meetings, zero aptitude or application. But they get promoted Emily, oh God yes and you can bet every one of them earns more than you! And do you know why?'

'No Clare.' Once again, Emily had the feeling that she didn't really need to reply.

'Because they haven't got a fucking womb!' If it hadn't been too obvious a thing to do, Emily would have pinched herself, not only to check that this was real, but to cause herself enough pain to stave off the inappropriate hysteria, gathering in her stomach, threatening any second, to launch itself out of her mouth.

'But you're so much better than them, Clare. Everyone knows that.' Emily was at least sincere.

'Oh wake up Emily!' She sounded weary. 'They don't need to be half as good as me or you. All they need to do is keep turning up. How many women are there on the Board Emily, answer me that?

'I don't actually know Clare.' Emily answered helplessly.

'Two Emily, surrounded by a further 19 mediocre male bastards! Do you think that Tony Jennings got to his position through his PR talents? The man's a sexually incontinent moron.'

It simply wasn't possible to believe that these words were coming out of the lips of Clare F-B, until now, the standard bearer of PR professionalism.

'Did you know that Dan plays golf with Tony Jennings every weekend? Did you know that Emily? I swear to you, Pete, Dan, all of them, they will all be earning twice as much as you, on the Board of this company, when you are begging to come back as a lowly paid dogsbody.'

Emily couldn't help thinking that this rather took the edge off all those motivational team workshops that Clare had hosted. She really wanted to go now, but couldn't think of an appropriate phrase with which to exit. She tried levity. 'Right. I see your point. Well, I can only suggest that we co-write a book, Clare. How about 'Men in Business - What a Load of Shit''

Clare managed a smile. 'Listen,' she said, splashing water on her face, 'You caught me at a bad moment. I don't expect you to share a word of this with anybody, do you understand?'

'Of course not. Mum's the word!' She blushed as she said it. 'Cup of tea, then?' She asked inadequately. Emily stumbled from the ladies loo, head spinning. Her career at Hobbs & Parker had often hung in the balance, but she had at least taken for granted certain, basic workplace principles – look like you're working hard, keep your clients relatively happy and you'll get promoted. It seemed none of it could be relied upon any more. What a sap she'd been! She felt a certain loss of innocence, foolish at her own naivety. Her first instinct would usually have been, to share every word of this with Pete, but now of course she knew he was the enemy. She went to the kitchen and put the kettle on.

Anoushka was hanging around her desk when she returned. 'Any updates for me, Emily?'

'Which account.' Emily deliberately misunderstood. 'TA or Dewsbury?'

'Noooo.' Anoushka was impatient. 'Charlie, Jem, that kind of thing.'

'Oh.' Emily sat down. 'Let me think. Have I spoken to you since the Le Voisier concert, or dinner with Charlie?

'No.' Anoushka's eyes widened.

'You're way behind. You'd better pull up a chair.' After

Clare's enlightening little chat, the need to do any client work seemed rather less pressing.

When Emily had finished, Anoushka was silent for a minute. 'So Charlie was pretending to be gay all along?' Emily looked heavenwards. She had clearly just wasted half an hour.

'No, Anoushka. He actually IS gay.'

'Oh right.' Sometimes Emily wondered if Anoushka was just very thick, or whether there was perhaps a more serious issue, requiring medical intervention.

Anoushka sighed, 'Well, you're not the only one in love with someone impossible.'

'What?' This was turning into an afternoon of revelations.

'I'm in love with someone, Emily. I can't tell you who he is, just that he is way out of my league.'

'Do I know him?' Emily was genuinely intrigued.

Anoushka giggled. 'Yes, but I'm really not going to tell you who.'

'But, you know I won't rest until you tell me Anoushka. I'll get you drunk and find out.'

Anoushka gasped. 'Oh my God, I haven't done this morning's post.' She charged off, leaving Emily wondering what the hurry was. It was nearly 5pm, but she'd never been known to deliver it before 4 anyway.

Half an hour more and she could slope off home. She decided it was time for a bit of delegation. A couple of particularly keen graduate trainees followed her obediently into the meeting room. 'So all you have to do,' she explained casually, 'is sign up 3 journalists each, by the end of the week. Standard stuff really. They only need to agree to join the TA for six weeks. We need a really good spread of national newspapers, broadcast, consumer mags, a few high profile celebs...'

Typically the girl was making copious notes, which was encouraging and the boy just nodded a lot and kept saying 'yah, no problem'. Poor loves, thought Emily. You only ever off loaded the more or less impossible shite to the grad trainees, being sure to keep the easy stuff for your own personal glory.

Anoushka was back at her desk with a pile of post. 'Emily, one here for you from PR News.' It would normally go straight into the bin, but for some reason Emily opened it. Probably some boring subscription renewal.

Ms Emily Brighouse
Senior Account Director
Hobbs & Parker plc
14-16 Millhouse Street
London W1 5NP

December 27

Dear Ms Brighouse

We are delighted to inform you that Hobbs & Parker's submission for PR News campaign of the year – consumer category, on behalf of your client Dewsbury Pork Products Ltd, has been selected by our judges as a finalist in this year's competition.

Your campaign 'National Sausage Week' will be showcased in a special Awards supplement to the magazine, including a feature length case study and there will be an opportunity to advertise at preferential rates, within this high circulation issue. The winner will be announced, from the shortlist of 5 consumer campaigns, at this year's Awards, to be held at the Grosvenor House Hotel, on Thursday February 18th.

Your campaign will be presented at the awards dinner, in front of a high profile guest list, including clients, journalists and industry peers. The event is traditionally a key industry occasion for networking, as well as an opportunity to celebrate with clients and colleagues.

As a finalist you are invited to make a group booking of one or more tables of 12.

This year, we are delighted to have secured key note speaker, Deborah Meaden from Dragon's Den, as well as a diverse list of guest journalists, including Marcus Riven from The Economist, Jill Carnegie from The Evening Standard and Newsnight producer, Jerome Armstrong........

'Bloody hell!' Emily seriously thought she was going to faint. She shook her head. 'They must have got it wrong.'

Anoushka, who had grabbed the letter from her, was now squealing. 'Of course, they haven't Emily. National Sausage Week was an amazing success!'

'No, not that, the bit about Newsnight producer, Jerome Armstrong.'

'Who?' Anoushka was impossible. There was no point elaborating.

They showed the letter to Clare, tight lipped as ever, but she allowed them a satisfied little nod. 'Good, well done.'

Emily was feeling brave. 'I thought it might be good timing, you know. I mean, perhaps take this to show Tony and have a chat about that Divisional thing.'

'I shall. Thank you Emily.' Clare sounded almost taken aback.

Back at her desk and Emily went straight onto the Newsnight home page. It had to be a mistake, but how many Jerome Armstrongs could there be in the media? And he turned down a job there two years ago. She scoured the site, biogs of presenters, contact details, but no producer names. She googled him guiltily, feeling like a smutty cyber stalker as soon as she typed his name.

There he was, an old interview in Broadcast magazine and there was his biog and picture, still featured on the Radio North website. Further down, a picture of him being presented with a polo trophy, grinning in his white jeans. She paused on that one for a while, but nothing about Newsnight. She searched again, 'There are 8 professionals named Jerome Armstrong on LinkedIn…' Nothing there, this was hopeless. Time to cut to the chase.

'Anoushka, can you come here a second?' Emily knew that this was a high risk strategy, but she had to find out one way or another.

'Anoushka' Emily explained. 'I need you to phone up Newsnight and ask if you can speak to Jem Armstrong.'

'OK Emily and what if I get through to him. What do you want me to say then?' It was a good point. She hadn't thought about that.

'I really just want to know if he works there.' Emily thought for a second. 'If you get through to him, ask him if he's interested in a survey about who does the housework. That should keep it short.' Anoushka started making notes. 'And don't say you're calling from Hobbs & Parker. You are Annabel, calling from Kendall & Webb, OK?'

Anoushka looked up from her notepad. 'But why would I be calling from one of our biggest rivals, Emily?' Expecting Anoushka to retain this level of detail was madness and Emily knew it.

Emily stood behind her and read out the phone number. This was unbearable, but she just couldn't risk calling up herself. She pressed the speaker phone button and hastily adjusted the volume, as the ringer buzzed loudly across the office.

'Newsnight.' Obviously Jeremy Paxman wasn't answering the phones himself, but they sounded equally unforgiving.

'Hello, can I speak to Jem Armstrong please?' Anoushka was businesslike.

'I'm afraid not, can anyone else help?'

'Oh, no. Thanks anyway.' She put down the phone.

'For God's sake Anoushka!' Emily exclaimed. 'You could have asked if he worked there!'

'Sorry Emily, I panicked. Shall I try again?'

A couple of the grad trainees looked up from their desks. Emily turned the volume down another notch. 'Go on then.'

Anoushka dialled again. 'Hello, can I speak to Jem Armstrong please?'

It was the same voice at the other end of the phone. 'Didn't you just call?'

This was too much, she couldn't bear to listen. She walked away, up the corridor to the kitchen. Three minutes later, Anoushka appeared beaming and waving a piece of paper. She looked very pleased with herself.

Emily could hardly breathe. 'Well? Does he work there?'

'No' Anoushka explained, 'He's in Dartmouth at the moment, but he joins next month apparently!'

'Dartmouth? Are you sure?' Emily was confused.

'Yes, he's currently working there as a condiment.'

It took her a while to work it out. 'On secondment?'

'Yes, that's right, they said he's in Monty Hall until February.'

'Montreal!' Emily shouted triumphantly.

'Which I googled and apparently that's in Dartmouth?' Anoushka explained importantly.

'Canada actually, but Anoushka, you're a bloody genius!' Emily suddenly couldn't stop smiling.

'Where's that?' Anoushka looked troubled.

'Never mind.'

4pm Friday January 10th 2011

Hector's chauffeur driven, black Audi pulled silently into
Latimer Road. They were on their way out of London for
the weekend, but Hector had promised that this wouldn't
take long. John waited in the car as a beautifully tailored
Hector, wearing his sharpest Savile Row suit, walked up
the pathway to the shared entrance of No's 51 and 53.
He was carrying a black box, tied with the trademark Le
Voisier purple ribbon. He adjusted his cuffs and knocked
at the door of No 51. Sofia Vassiliadis answered the door.
There followed a short exchange on the doorstep and then
she appeared to invite him in.

Shortly afterwards, John watched as Hector and Mr
and Mrs V came out of the house and let themselves
into the house next door. He looked at his watch. They
had been in there for over 15 minutes now. When they
finally came out, Hector and Mr V shook hands. Mrs V
blushed as Hector took the hand she offered and kissed it.
The Chauffeur stood ready, by the door of the Audi and
Costas and Sofia Vassiliadis waved, as the car pulled away
down the Latimer Road and off towards the A4 out of
London.

Tuesday January 14th 2012
Desmond Winton Building Solutions
North Vale Trading Estate
Putney SW15 7PT

QUOTE

**To carry out refurbishment works –
53 Latimer Road, Fulham London SW6,
including:**

Replace orange carpets throughout with neutral tone carpet, sample provided

Remove broken louvred cupboard doors in 2 bedrooms and replace with plain painted doors with magnetic fixings

Replace net curtains and poles in both bedrooms with New England style white shutters.

Remove existing marble effect formica kitchen units and brown ceramic tiles and fit and install white Ikea kitchen, as discussed with new oven and fridge

Bathroom – replace existing orange units with plain white suite, to include walk in shower

Dispose of existing TV and replace with 46" flat screen, wall mounted

Remove old wood chip wall paper throughout, replaster as necessary and paint with 2 x coats of off white emulsion

Remove broken plastic light fittings to hallway and replace with chrome LED spotlights

GRAND TOTAL: **£8,560 plus VAT**

23

The entire flat was now a hothouse of dense steam, every mirror misted up, condensation dripping down the black grouting between missing tiles. Unconsciously she side stepped the orange peeling lino and wiped a window in the fogged up bathroom mirror. She put the plastic cup over the tap to stop it spraying up into her face as she turned it on. These were time honoured rituals, accompanied always by the blast of hairdryers and power ballads. She instinctively held her breath as she went into Bella's bedroom to borrow her hairdryer. The air was thick with the noxious fumes of perfume, nail polish, deodorant and depilatory creams.

Bella had her hair in heated rollers and was wafting around her room in the full length, grey marl, cashmere dressing gown, which Mrs Dewsbury had bought her for Christmas.

Was this the last time they would go through this familiar routine in this cruddy old flat? Maybe even the last time they might go through it together. Emily was choked at the thought. In two weeks time, they would have to pack their bags and leave this place. They would hand over their keys to the next tenants, whoever they might be. She wondered if they'd be single girls, or two boys. Bella would be fine, Derek was already talking about renting a place for her nearer her work. She would pack her clothes into her brand new set of Louis Vuitton luggage, another gift from Mrs Dewsbury and be whisked off to some boutique hotel or other, while Derek made arrangements. True to form, Emily had not exactly tackled the problem head on. She had visions of arriving at a lonely bedsit somewhere miles away, sitting next to a pile of black bin liners hastily stuffed with her belongings, a single bed, bug infested mattress and shared bathroom.

But that was for another day and tonight she would block all that out. Tonight would be champagne and dancing all the way.

Above the thumping music and the drone of the hairdryer, neither of them heard the knock on the door. The bell had long since stopped working. Emily stood in front of the full length mirror on the back of her cupboard door. She wore black knickers and a bra trimmed in pink ribbon, a matching pair for once. Her upper half was barely concealed by an unflattering red and white satin, three quarter length boxing gown, once worn by featherweight Barry McGuigan for a cherry aid photo shoot. He had autographed it down the sleeve of one arm. Bella hated it of course and occasionally tried to hide it.

Emily turned her head upside down and aimed the hairdryer at the roots, singing loudly as she did so.

'We're on the edge of glory, and I'm hanging on a moment with you.'

She flipped the hair back again, eyes closed.

'The edge, the edge, the edge, the edge, the edge, the edge, the edge…'

'We're on the edge of 'FUCKING HELL!' She screamed loudly at the sight of a man's face, pressed up against her bedroom window and lit up eerily in orange, by the street lamp. Still screaming, she dropped the hair dryer on her foot. Ignoring the intense shooting pain, she grabbed the satin belt and tied the flimsy material, tightly around her waist.

It was hard to judge who was more horrified, Emily or Mr Vasilliadis, who was still standing outside the window and had screamed in horror at exactly the same time. He had tried to knock, but the music was too loud. Pulling down the hem of her boxing gown, which only just covered her pants, she went to open the front door.

'Girls!' It was that familiar, defeated tone.

Emily interrupted, hoping to avoid another lecture. 'Sorry Mr V, we'll turn the music down. Just going out to a work dinner. We'll be gone in half an hour.'

'No, girls.' He shook his head.

He sounded resolute. This wasn't the usual routine and she realised she'd forgotten to order another case of Greek wine. What if he decided to chuck them out there and then.

'No girls.' He broke into a grin. 'I came to tell you, you can stay.'

'What? Tonight?' Emily was confused.

'Mrs Vasilliadis.' He nodded his head towards the location of his wife next door. 'She has had a change of mind about you leaving. We are going to make some repairs.'

'Do you mean we don't have to move out at all?' By this time, Bella, a contrasting vision in floor length cashmere, was standing behind a shivering Emily who was still struggling to keep the satin stretched down over her pants.

'Mrs V says she will give you second chance. If you can just try to behave.' He added, pleadingly. 'We will bring the flat up to better standard. But no more parties girls, no nakedness.' He had to look away from Emily when he said this. 'And no strange people in the flat doing their business on Mrs V's cypress firs. Do you understand?'

'Yes, Mr V.' They mouthed in unison.

Shutting the door behind them, they were silenced by the shock of the reprieve. No explanation, no mention of the ASBO or Eviction Notice. Neither of them could take it in. Bella was the first to speak.

'What do you think changed their minds?'

'God knows.' Emily looked baffled. 'Maybe they couldn't find anyone to rent the flat?'

'No way.' Bella was unconvinced. 'There'd be a queue of people I promise you. And didn't he say they were going to do it up.'

'I can't believe it.' They both stood in the hallway, trying to make sense of it. Emily shrugged. 'We'll have to work it out later Bels, I haven't even dried my hair yet.'

In less than an hour, she would be in the same room as Jem. She felt sick. Sick with excitement? Sick with something. Everyone who was anyone in the PR industry would be there, clients, competitors, journalists and the usual smattering of low grade celebs. She didn't have a plan, no great speech prepared and certainly no hopes of making him like her. But if she could just turn it round, enough perhaps to convince him that she wasn't a total slapper. It might be too late for undying love, but if she could just claw back a bit of respect, that would be something. It was already humiliating enough, that she was up for an award that in fact, he should be claiming.

Tonight she could honestly say, that nothing had been spared in the quest for physical perfection. Gel nails, eyelashes dyed, every inch of her waxed, tweezed, flossed, threaded and spray tanned. Bella had suggested they go for a subtler shade of light mocha spray tan this time, instead of the deep umber hue Emily normally favoured.

Regaining your dignity was an expensive business. She didn't dare to think about the cost of all of this. And that was before the dress was even added to the bill. There it was, hanging on the wardrobe door. It made her sigh just to look at it. The sexiest LBD she had ever seen, a week's salary in fact. Three quarter length black sleeves in some kind of sheer material, expensive satin v-neck, nipped in at the waist and ending just above the knee.

Bella gasped when she saw her. 'Oh yes Emily, sophisticated yet sexy.' The shoes brought her almost to six foot and Bella had lent her an oversized clutch bag and sparkling drop ear rings to match. Bella was jaw dropping in a long red dress. She really was magnificent, Emily decided. What a catch! But then Emily was sure that Derek already knew that.

As their taxi pulled up at the entrance to the Grosvenor House Hotel, she took a very deep breath. Bella heard her and briefly squeezed her hand.

The foyer was buzzing. A lot of theatrical greetings, nervous glances and the mock hilarity of the ill at ease. They took their coats to the cloakroom.

They were meeting Derek at the hotel bar, there he was, looking all devastating and handsome, chatting to Hector and John.

'Oh Em, I could swoon every time I look at him.' Bella muttered as they walked towards him.

'You're making me feel sick Bella. Don't worry, he's probably about to dump you.'

'You're vicious.' Bella laughed.

'No, just bitter and slightly tragic. It's my new look.'

'You're wearing it well,' she whispered as Derek approached.

Hector and John were drinking Caipirinhas at the bar and dishing out merciless fashion abuse. They raised their eyebrows in stunned unison. The most extraordinary confection of pink taffeta strutted past, shiny material stretched to splitting point over generous bottom. The swathe of pink barely containing bright orange, spray tanned boobs, which were spilling out over the top, like freshly baked buns.

Hector turned to John, 'Do you think she's in there alone?'

John shook his head in response. 'Good God, someone needs to tell these girls. Just because you can get into a dress, doesn't mean it fits you.'

Hector had spotted another fashion crime. 'Oh Glory, look at that one!'

Emily laughed. 'Now, now boys! What did you expect, Paris Fashion Week?' She could see that the Caipirinhas were taking effect.

Hector looked appalled. 'Yes, but leopard skin Emily, really? Just about workable on a svelte Italian model, catastrophic on a fat, middle aged blonde.' He looked her up and down. 'You, on the other hand, my darling, look absolutely stunning. New dress?'

'Of course.' She smiled. 'Black Satin body armour!'

He looked over her shoulder. 'Is Captain Von Trapp here yet?'

'I haven't seen him.' She attempted to sound blasé, but no one was fooled.

They were all assembled at the bar now, Anoushka, gorgeous in a little cream strapless dress, Mean Monica, looking pale and uninteresting in a rather unfortunate beige tunic. She had apparently made it herself.

Everybody was hanging around nervously, desperate for a drink, but reluctant to buy one before Tony Jennings arrived with the Company Credit card. Clare Forster Blair was glamorous but professional, a picture of propriety, no cleavage, expensive ear rings, long dress in jade green velvet.

And here was Tony at last, big hair, fake tan. She was sure she detected just a whiff of hair spray as he kissed her cheek. 'Well, hello there Brighouse!' He held onto her for slightly too long. 'Looking forward to your big moment?'

'I don't think it's quite in the bag Tony.' She got annoyingly flustered when she talked to him. It was always hard to reply to his cheesy one liners. Mrs Jennings stood behind him, wearing a lot of gold lace and huge amounts of bling. Emily wondered if it was real.

Pete and Dan arrived at the bar, just as Tony ordered five bottles of Champagne. She scanned the room. No sign of Jem yet. This was petrifying. She would have to try hard not to drink away her nerves. She took a glass over to Anoushka.

'So, come on Anoushka, who is this man you really like? Is he here?'

'Yes he is.' Anoushka giggled.

'Come on, tell me who it is!' Emily held up her glass. 'Or I'll accidentally throw this drink down your dress?'

Anoushka didn't flinch. 'You'd never waste a full glass of Champagne Emily.'

'No, actually you're right. How well you know me!' Emily was quite surprised. 'So how long have you liked him then?'

Anoushka sighed. 'I guess I only really knew how much I liked him, when we thought the three of us were going to get sacked. I just couldn't bear him to lose his job because of me.' Seeing Emily's face she put her hand to her mouth. 'Oh Emily! I'm such a durr brain! Will you keep it to yourself?'

Emily smiled. 'Well, maybe. Anyway, what was all that rubbish about him not being in your league?'

Anoushka looked wistful. 'He's just so clever and witty and gorgeous!' Emily's eyes widened. It seemed there really was someone for everyone.

Oh my God, sharp intake of breath. There was Jem, just walking in. She retreated to the bar and found Hector.

'He's here!'

'OK my darling, stay calm. Drink this!' He said, handing her another glass of Champagne. 'Don't get hysterical, but he appears to be heading this way.' All that careful grooming and preparation would amount to nothing. She was going to faint on sight. God he was beautiful. All shiny black hair and green eyes.

He was at the bar beside them. 'Hello Hector! Hi Emily! How are you?' How could he look so cool and calm? She wondered if he remembered the last words he had said to her a few months ago. She clutched her glass to stop her hand from shaking, barely able look up and meet his eye.

'I'm great thanks.' She tried to keep her voice steady.

'And how's Charlie?'

'He's good.' She wished she could add, 'even better since he's started seeing Alessandro', but what was the point.

Derek stepped into the group, nudged forward by Bella. He held out his hand. 'It's Jem isn't it? Emily are you going to introduce us?' There was a flicker of recognition from Jem, but he said nothing. Emily was too flustered to speak and stood nonplussed, staring straight ahead.

'I'm Derek, Derek Dewsbury.' He continued, rather awkwardly. 'And this is Bella. We've not met properly, although obviously we spoke on the phone about the Sausage Week promotion last year.'

'You were at the Albert Hall?' Jem sounded nonplussed.

'That's right, Hector invited me with Bella, my girlfriend.' Derek put particular emphasis on the last two words. Emily looked at the floor.

'Very good to meet you Derek.' Jem's expression had changed and they shook hands vigorously.

The familiar voice of Clare F-B broke in. 'Emily, can I have a word?'

What now? Some God-awful prospective client Clare would force her to go and talk to. Emily was hopeless at networking. It was boring and the awful insincerity of mixing business with pleasure made her feel rather uncomfortable.

They stood away from the rest of the group. 'Yes, Clare?' She awaited her instructions.

'I just wanted to tell you that they've made me Divisional Director. Tony told me this afternoon.'

'I'm so pleased for you Clare, I really am. You deserve it more than anyone.' Emily was genuinely happy for her.

'And I wanted to acknowledge that you played a part in my promotion Emily. I know I'm tough on you sometimes, but only because I don't want you to waste your potential. If we win tonight, I want you to go up and get the award.'

Emily was appalled. 'No please, really. Dewsbury's your client. And I'd really rather not if it's OK with you.'

Clare smiled impassively. 'No, it's not OK. If we win, you go up.'

'OK, Clare.' You didn't argue with her. She walked off and Emily exhaled deeply. She didn't really like Clare being nice to her. It wasn't right somehow.

A gaggle of girls from Kendall and Webb walked past her. They looked at the Hobbs & Parker group at the bar and all started to giggle. Even though most of them would be working for different PR companies by this time next year, these bizarre events brought out some kind of tribal instinct. They walked around in little competitive colonies. All you needed to do, to bring about complete corporate mayhem, was add a little alcohol into the mix.

Emily didn't dare go back to the bar. She could see Derek and Jem, now deep in conversation. She studied the seating plan instead. Miss E Brighouse, Table No 10. Where was Jem? She scoured the list. Mr J Armstrong Table No 3. Nowhere near, thank God. At least she could relax during dinner. Who did she have on her table? Derek on one side and bloody hell, Tony Jennings on the other.

Ladies and Gentleman, would you please take your seats, dinner is about to be served.

Derek pulled Emily's chair out. 'Thanks Derek. Looks like you and Jem had a good chat then?' She couldn't resist asking.

'Well I thought I should try and clear things up a bit, after that misunderstanding at the concert.' He saw her horrified expression. 'Without being too obvious of course.'

'I hope not.'

'Trust me! I think he likes you Emily, I really do.'

'Well, thanks for trying Derek.' Emily smiled.

On the other side of the vast ball room, Anoushka took her place, next to one of the guest journalists. He turned to her and held out his hand. 'Hi, I'm Jerome Armstrong.'

She smiled impassively. 'I'm Anoushka Marchwood from Hobbs & Parker. Which agency do you work for?'

'Actually I'm a journalist. I've just started working on a news programme here in London. He stood up and pulled out her chair for her. 'You know, I spoke to your lot all the time, when I was at Radio North.'

'I thought your name sounded familiar and you look kind of familiar as well.' Anoushka giggled. 'God, that's going to bug me for the rest of the evening! Radio North have done loads of our surveys.'

'Yes, we did. Some of the finest we were sent came from Hobbs & Parker.' He laughed. 'I seem to remember a particularly good household appliance one.'

'Oh my God, that was me!' Anoushka squealed. 'Funnily enough, there's a girl in my office who's totally besotted with this guy at Radio North!'

'Is that right?' He paused and looked at her intently. 'Well, let me get you some wine and you can sit down and tell me all about it...'

Across the room, Emily pretended to have dropped her napkin on the floor, in order to remove Tony's hand from her knee. You could tell that Mrs Jennings was very much taken with Derek on her right, which left Bella to fend off the dubious charms of Dan O'Shag-me Shaunessy. Emily sat up in her seat again and looked around the table. She was having one of those, 'what am I doing here, in this place, with these people' moments and she wasn't even hungover. Clare was sitting next to Hector, two tables away. Probably just as well he wasn't on her table. He'd only get her all stirred up about the importance of passion and she'd end up making a fool of herself. Over on the top table, she could see Deborah Meaden from Dragon's Den chatting earnestly to the editor of PR News and the chairman of the industry association.

When the main course plates were removed, a few people got up to stretch their legs or go for a cigarette. Anoushka and Jem stayed where they were. They were still deep in conversation.

Anoushka was in full flow. 'So, having been all excited about the weekend in Northumberland, she decided she couldn't go, because he suddenly announced that his girlfriend would be there. Can you imagine the disappointment! But then Hector persuaded her that she should go. And it was his idea that she should take Charlie and pretend to be going out with him. Isn't that hilarious?'

'Yes I suppose it is.' Jem looked thoughtful.

'But...and here's the best bit...' Anoushka was thoroughly enjoying the rapt attentions of a proper journalist. 'Charlie is actually gay you see.' She saw the confused look on his face. 'Yes, it took me a while to get my head around that one.'

'He can't be.' Jem muttered.

'Yes he is.' Anoushka gabbled on. 'She even thought she slept with him once, but actually she hadn't at all.'

'Yes, well, that would confuse most people.' He frowned as he topped up her glass. 'What's his name anyway, this journalist she likes at Radio North?'

Anoushka snorted. 'I'm not going to tell you that! How stupid do you think I am?'

Ladies and Gentlemen, will you please all return to your seats. The awards presentation is about to begin.

Jem turned to Anoushka, 'Actually, I think that means I've got to go and present one of those awards. It was really lovely to meet you Anoushka. I expect I'll see you later. It's been enlightening!'

As he walked off, Anoushka wracked her brains, trying to remember where she'd seen him before. When realisation finally came, it caused her to blush from her stomach to the tips of her ears. 'Oh Shit!' She mouthed. 'She's going to kill me!'

Over on table No. 10, Emily decided that a menthol might calm her nerves. She headed for the cloakroom to retrieve the packet in her coat pocket. As she walked round past the next table, she edged past the back of Pete's chair.

He looked up at her. 'Hi Emily. Have you seen Anoushka anywhere?'

'Hey Pete. No, I haven't. She's not on my table.' Emily stopped for a second and almost without thinking, carried on. 'Talking of Anoushka Pete, you know she's in love with you, don't you.' She left him staring after her, looking as if someone had just walloped him on the back of his head.

Bloody hell, what did she do that for? She did wonder about herself sometimes.

At the same time, Anoushka, seized with guilt, was overwhelmed by the thought that she had to warn Emily. She saw her leaving and followed her out of the main dining room.

'Emily!' She ran up to her. 'You'll never guess what I've gone and done now.'

'No Anoushka. Surprise me!' They carried on walking.

'Well you know that guy you really liked? In actual fact, did you know his real name's Jerome?'

Emily stopped dead and looked at her. 'Anoushka, what have you done?'

'I've gone and told him everything Emily.'

'Oh God, really?' She closed her eye. 'Everything?'

'Well, only what you told me.' Anoushka reassured her.

'Anoushka, that IS everything!' Emily gasped and held her hands over her face.

'Will you ever forgive me Emily?'

She looked out from behind her hands. 'Only if you forgive me, for telling Pete you're in love with him.'

'What? Emily!'

They both started to giggle slightly hysterically.

'Emily, can I have one of your menthols?'

'Of course, let's go outside.'

Dragon's Den presenter was already in full flow when they sidled back to their tables. Clare shot Emily a disapproving look.

Deborah Meaden addressed the crowd. 'Reading through the list of finalists, there were some truly innovative campaigns, none of which I'd be prepared to invest in of course!' Canned laughter all round the room.

Emily stopped listening. She was staring at Jem, who was sitting on stage, lined up with the other guest journalists. She might not see him again. At least she could spend the next half hour staring at him.

'And the finalists in the 'Over-the-Counter pharmaceuticals' category are Shillbrook Healthcare

PR for the launch of Zemtax anti-inflammatory, Drek Pharmaceuticals in-house team for 'Arthritis Aware' and Kendall & Webb's campaign for Sayers Ltd, 'Erectile Dysfunction in the over 70s' '. Inevitable ripple of sniggers around the room.

And the winner is… 'Drek Pharmaceuticals'. The rest of the words drowned out by the whooping and screaming from the winning table. Emily stifled a yawn. God, these people really did think they were at the Oscars. Either that or they thought there was some kind of cash prize.

Emily looked at the programme. There was still Education, Government, Personal Finance and Business to Business to go, before they even got onto the Consumer campaign. At least there was Jem to look at. He was doing a passable job of looking interested. Emily found herself musing over the phrase 'die of boredom'. Was it actually possible? Probably not. You could almost certainly slip into a deep coma though. Hector, who had moved himself into a spare seat on Emily's table, was heckling quite badly now. He really was as pissed as Emily had ever seen him. You could tell that Clare was on the verge of telling him off, but held herself back. Instead she leant towards Emily and whispered loudly.

'Emily, if we win, have you thought about what you might say in your speech? Something about Hobbs & Parker?'

'Speech?' Emily's mouth dropped open.

Please God, don't let us win.

'And the three remaining finalists in the Consumer PR Campaign are…'

Please God, not us.

' *Let's make some noise!'* a campaign by Kendall & Webb, for the Skiandu Motor Company. A genuinely deconstructive campaign, which really pushed the creative envelope. A Skiandu car was taken apart to make orchestral instruments and Gareth Malone, formed a band for under privileged children.' Loud hollering from the girls on the Kendall & Webb table.

There followed a video of children brandishing windscreen wipers and banging wheel hubs. 'The song went on to become a top 10 hit and raise valuable funds for music in schools.'

'Pathetic', Hector mouthed.

Across the room, Anoushka dabbed her eyes, 'God that's so sweet.'

'*We're jammin!* by Imagine That PR, for Riverdale organic jam.' A cheer went up from the table behind. 'Bringing top class innovation to the sweet spreads market. The PR team created an art roadshow, encouraging kids to get creative with jam. Jam art literally spread around the country and the winning entry, judged by Bruce Foxton from The Jam, was displayed on the forth plinth at Trafalgar Square, followed by a highly successful, nationwide, 'We're jammin' pop up exhibition.'

A collage of jam art, featuring under privileged children, appeared on a white screen behind Deborah Meaden's head.

Emily stared at the screen. She wondered about PR sometimes. Without surveys, the forth plinth at Trafalgar Square and under privileged children, much of the PR industry would probably just shut down.

'And finally, 'National Sausage Week', Hobbs & Parker for Dewsbury Pork Products.'

She was feeling relatively calm now, confident that they couldn't win, having benefited absolutely no underprivileged children in the course of their campaign.

'A daring campaign that saw Cumbria based, Dewsbury Pork Products achieve front page headlines overnight and achieve listings for their products in every Sainsburys across the Country. The dramatic rise in profile not only drove sales, but led to a tenfold increase in the Dewsbury Pork Products share price.

And the winner is…'

I'll do anything, but please God don't let us win.

"National Sausage Week' for Dewsbury Pork Products!'

Bugger, fuck, shit.

She thought she might actually be sick. She didn't even hear the rest of the announcement. All she was aware of was Clare mouthing at her, 'Well go on then.'

Her legs shook as she went up towards the stage. Somebody helped her up the stairs and clipped a mike to the top of her dress. Oh my God, what was she going to say? Keep calm. Sober, dignified, professional. Right now, she was none of those things.

As Deborah Meaden handed her the plastic trophy, she gestured for Emily to go to the microphone.

An interminable pause, she looked straight ahead, for fear of seeing Jem looking at her.

From somewhere, the words came…

'I'd just like to thank Pete Neville for his creative input and editing skills, especially at the concept stage, Anoushka Marchwood for her rigorous research and outstanding media contacts, it's fair to say, she genuinely left no stone unturned, Clare Forster Blair for keeping us all on track and not forgetting all the people at Radio North, you know who you are, who really made this a success.' She couldn't look at Jem.

Her knees may have wobbled but her voice sounded calm. 'And finally thanks to Derek Dewsbury, for whom, I think I can say, this project has ignited a genuine passion.'

Huge hooting and yelling from Table No 10 as she mentioned each name. And just when she thought she could make a break for it, she was wrestled into position, Deborah Meaden on one side, Jem on the other, as the cameras from PR News snapped away.

Deborah Meaden kissed her cheek, 'Well done, great campaign.' The photographer clearly thought he was working for Hello! 'Can we have a shot of the young lady and Mr Armstrong now? Thanks, that's lovely. And with your arms round each other, holding up the award. That's great and one more.'

They both kept looking straight into the camera and Jem's grip tightened slightly as he said, 'Listen Emily, I sat next to Anoushka at dinner. She explained a few things. I really need to talk to you.'

She kept smiling and looking straight ahead as she replied. 'Yes, she told me. Nothing to say really, I think you've made it perfectly clear what you think of me.'

At last, she was allowed to go. She stumbled off the stage and didn't look back, as Deborah Meaden drew the whole thing to a close. Reaching her seat, she grabbed a glass of wine and gulped it down as Bella and Derek hugged her. By this point Pete and Dan were standing on their chairs, pumping the air in the direction of the Kendall & Webb table.

And, dear God, Tony Jennings was heading her way for a grope, arms outstretched, shouting, 'Well done Brighouse, come here and give your chairman a kiss!' The music drowned him out. As the band struck up and Tony moved in, she looked pleadingly at Hector, who rose unsteadily to his feet.

'Emily darling, come and dance!'

She broke away from Tony's clinch, 'Thanks Hector!'

Out of the frying pan, into the fire…she bloody hated this song. How was she supposed to dance to Dire Straits. Hector proceeded to fling her around the dance floor like a rag doll.

Here comes johnny singing oldies, goldies
Be-bop-a-lua, baby what I say
Here comes johnny singing I gotta woman
Down in the tunnels, trying to make it pay

He had clearly been to a couple of Ceroc classes and was now twirling and releasing her, like a sprung coil, across the dance floor. Why do men always think they can rock and roll when they're pissed, she thought, as she shot like a bullet away from him and only just stopped herself from falling over.

'Through the legs Emily!' Hector bellowed. He was staggering around the dance floor now, barely able to keep himself upright, let alone Emily.

He got the action, he got the motion
Yeah, the boy can play
Dedication ,devotion
Turning all the night time into the day

'Now for the big one Emily! He shouted. 'Back to back and over the head!'

Jesus, no! But he was stronger than he looked and she was locked in position and airborne before she knew it. Suddenly, no apparent reason, his grip loosened and she was released from the backwards arm lock and catapulted through the air. She braced herself for the crash landing, but just then, a pair of strong arms caught her firmly and lifted her off the ground. She was staring, breathlessly, right into Jem's eyes, her feet, suspended two inches above the dance floor.

'There you are Emily. I want to talk to you.'

Just at that moment, they both saw John, struggling without success to lift Hector up off the dance floor, 'Get up you silly old queen!' John was yelling at him, but you could tell he was worried. Jem put her down and went to help. Emily was left standing alone on the dance floor, just as the band started playing the cheesiest of slow songs. She walked as swiftly as she could back to her table. She and Anoushka sat there alone. Everyone else was either at the bar or on the dance floor.

I've never seen you looking so lovely as you do tonight...

She grimaced and mouthed 'Cheese' at Anoushka, but just then Pete walked across the room. He leant down and kissed Anoushka on the cheek. 'Would you dance with me, Anoushka?' She stood up and they walked off together, hand in hand.

Derek and Bella were locked in a dance floor clinch, Mr and Mrs Jennings sashayed around the floor in a well practiced routine.

'The lady in red, is dancing with me, cheek to cheek…'

And there she was sitting stranded at the table, all alone. Jem, who had somehow heaved Hector off the dancefloor, was nowhere to be seen. The song seemed to go on forever. She pretended to study the programme.

Ladies and Gentlemen the band will be taking a quick break. Back in 20 minutes.

This had been a disaster. Maybe now, she could just slip off home. She looked up and Jem was towering over her. 'Right Emily. You're coming with me. Now. We're going to finish this, one way or another.' He took her hand and led her, more like pulled her across the room to the bar area in the far corner.

He held her in front of him, a hand on each of her shoulders to prevent her escaping. 'Look Emily, I just wanted to say, I am sorry, for being such a prick and getting it all so wrong.' She opened her mouth to reply but he put a finger on her lips. 'Let me just say this and I promise I will leave you alone and won't bother you ever again.' The thought made her feel sick.

He looked at her imploringly. 'In my defence, how the hell was I supposed to know you weren't going out with Charlie?' He shook his head. 'And I completely misunderstood what was going on at the Albert Hall, with Derek Dewsbury? You can't blame me for getting confused.' He looked exasperated. 'You must know how I feel about you Emily?'

Her voice wobbled as she spoke, 'Well, no I don't actually.' She was determined to keep her composure. 'I mean, you sent my emails all around your office for everyone's entertainment. And you've got a girlfriend. And what was it you said to me at the Albert Hall? 'I just don't seem to be able to help myself' and 'my life's a farce'. None of it very flattering really.' She struggled to keep the tears at bay.

His grip tightened. 'I didn't mean any of it. For God's sake, I was jealous.'

'Well anyway,' once she had started, the words just tumbled out, 'As it turns out, I haven't slept with Charlie or Derek. So that brings my number of sexual partners crashing down.' She was gabbling. 'I mean, that's near enough a 10% reduction in my current lifetime shag total, so that's a bonus.' She didn't really know what she was saying. Her voice rose as she reached her conclusion. 'I'm just delighted that you've realised I'm not quite the major league slut you first thought.'

Emily hadn't noticed a hush falling, like a slow motion Mexican wave, across the entire dining room.

In the absence of a reply, she pushed bravely on. 'God you know, I'd be prepared to bet that I've slept with less people than you. Double digits I grant you, but I'm a woman, so of course that makes me an absolute whore.' She was speaking quite loudly by now. 'Gosh, that's about 1.7 sexual partners per year since I became sexually active. What a diehard trollop I am!' On a roll now, her voice rising with every word, but Jem was staring, wide eyed at her chest.

'Emily, I really don't care how many men you've slept with. But you need to stop right now.'

Emily misunderstood. 'What and never sleep with anyone again? That's extreme.'

'No! I mean, stop talking!' He shouted.

'Do you know what?' Her eyes narrowed. 'I'm not going to stop talking.' She was slurring very slightly, but still reasonably articulate. 'You are going to let me finish for once, or are you already planning to flounce off, as usual?'

'Emily, Stop!' He reached his hand forward towards her chest, but she swatted it away like an irritating fly.

'I just want you to know,' she carried on, but now she really was rambling. 'I am really flattered, that in spite of the fact that you and your ghastly girlfriend don't think I can keep my pants on for very long, you still think you could condescend to, well I don't really know what with me, but to be honest the answer to that intriguing question is no. No, thanks very much. Look around you, look at all those fuckers. My clients, my bosses, the whole fucking PR industry. You see, I've got enough sexist pricks in my life, without getting involved with another one!'

He shook his head in disbelief.

She shrugged his hands off her shoulders. 'Don't worry, I'm done. Quite frankly Jem, you can fuck off. You and all of the rest of them. The only ones worth having are bloody gay?'

Silence

'Well what are you going to say to that Jem?' Verging on triumphant now, she was disappointed by his lack of response.

'Your mike, Emily.' He was almost whispering.

'What?'

He spoke very quietly, but deliberately. 'You didn't take your mike off and you are still hooked up to the sound system. The entire dining room is hanging on your every word.'

'Oh Fuck!'

Every woman and gay man had got to their feet. The applause rang in her ears as she slowly turned around to face them. One by one, she saw their faces, Anoushka cheering, the girls on the Kendall & Webb table, ecstatic and shouting 'Go, girl!' Even Clare F-B, whose eyebrows were raised as far as they could go, was quietly clapping. My God, Mrs Jennings was on her feet.

Deborah Meaden was nodding as if she had just received some sage business insight. And still, they didn't stop clapping and hollering.

Instinct took over and she turned and ran. Even as she fled, to the sound of wolf whistles and 'too right love', the applause continued. The waitress behind the bar shouted, 'You tell him darling!' as she shot past.

Bella got up from her table and swiftly followed her out, pursued by Derek and Jem and Hector behind them. They pushed their way through the crowded bar, but by the time they reached the foyer, she was gone.

Derek found the valet at the entrance. 'Did you see a blonde girl in a black dress? She left, literally a minute ago?'

'Yes sir. I helped her into the taxi myself.'

'Which way did they go?'

'She didn't say sir.'

Hector swayed up the corridor towards Jem. 'Ah, Captain von Trapp. Has Maria run off again? How do you keep a wave upon the sand?'

Jem looked furious. 'What are you talking about Hector?'

Hector grabbed Jem's lapel menacingly. 'Follow her up the mountain Captain! Head for the foothills and don't stop until you get to the border. Do you hear me? Chase her as far as Switzerland if you have to, but go, go!'

'What?' Jem looked at him like he was mad.

Bella stepped between them. 'No Jem, you wait right there! I know Emily better than all of you. I doubt very much she's on her way home.' She held onto Jem's sleeve with one hand, while she texted with the other.

Emily, where the hell r u? Tell me now! Bels x

Less than a minute later and her phone buzzed.

Sitting on steps of Albert Memorial, smoking menthol, like loser! x

Bella, turned to Jem and showed him the text. 'OK, now you can go.'

'

24

The white and gold arches of the Albert Memorial rose up eerily behind the lonely figure, sitting in the middle of the steps. The sky was clear and glowing a dark orange.

He walked silently up the steps and sat down beside her.

'Can I have one of those menthol cigarettes?'

She looked up at him. 'I didn't know you smoked.'

'I don't, but it's been quite a difficult evening.'

She handed him a cigarette and lit it for him. 'Bella told you I was here?'

'Yes.' He dragged on the menthol and pulled a face.

They both stared straight ahead.

'The thing is Jem….'….'I just think Emily…'

He turned to look at her. 'No, you first.'

Silence. It was bitterly cold, but neither of them noticed.

Emily didn't dare look at him. 'So, do you think I'll be sacked?' She didn't actually care that much, but it was something to say to break the silence.

He smiled. 'I shouldn't think so, not if any of the women in the room have anything to do with it.'

She carried on, skirting around the issue. 'Hector was in a bad way tonight. I don't think I've ever seen him completely lose it like that.'

'No.' Jem smiled. 'And why did he keep calling me Captain Von Trapp?'

She laughed. 'I'll explain some time.'

There was a pause. He stubbed out his cigarette and flicked it down the steps.

'Emily.' He sounded exasperated. 'Why the hell did you pretend to be going out with Charlie?'

She shrugged. 'Because you and Bertha made me feel like such a low life.' She gave a hollow laugh. 'I suppose I thought a boyfriend might lend me an air of dignity.'

He looked at her. 'I see. Well no, I don't actually. And who's Bertha anyway?'

She turned to him, surprised. 'Your dreadful girlfriend, of course. Jesus, have you not read the book? Big Bad Bertha, Mr Rochester's mad wife in the attic, in Jane Eyre. I thought that's why your dog was called Pilot.'

'It was my mother's favourite book, I can't say I've read it. Emily, Frankie and I split up 4 months before I invited you to Northumberland.'

'What?' It was her turn to look confused now. 'Then why the hell did you invite her to stay for the weekend?'

'I didn't. She invited herself. She phoned dad to ask if she could stay for the weekend of the North Hexham Hunt.'

Emily looked at him warily. 'What was all that 'I'll see you upstairs darling' bollocks then?'

'I don't know. I guess she was finding it hard to accept that we'd split up, but I thought she'd got over it. Maybe she wanted you to think that we were still together.'

She dragged on her menthol. 'Well she did a bloody fantastic job.'

'Anyway the thing that worries me most, is what I could have done to make you feel like a 'low life'?' She had never heard him sound so defeated. 'What have I actually done, Emily?'

'I guess sending my very explicit emails around the whole of your office, for their weekly entertainment. It didn't exactly make me feel great. Frankie told me you see and then she said that you'd more or less got me up there for the weekend, to get more material for your latest 'confessions of a slutty southerner' newsflash.'

Her stared at her, mystified. 'What are you talking about?'

'Oh come on. All those emails that you shared with the entire Radio North news team? You must have had a real laugh!'

'And Frankie told you all this?' He spoke quite slowly.

'Yes, that weekend.'

'Jesus, I see.' He exhaled deeply and ran his hand through his hair. 'She must have been reading my emails. Listen Emily, I swear to you, I have never shown anyone your emails. There was no weekly newsflash. I would never do that to you.'

'Oh, OK.' She could hardly breathe. She didn't know what to think.

'I'm sorry Emily.'

'Not your fault.'

They paused a while as if to take it in.

Jem turned to her as he spoke. 'Listen Emily, I just think, that if you are going to carry on living your life like this, drinking too much, insulting your entire industry, crash landing on dance floors…

She raised her hand as if to stop him. 'I know. I'll never get a nice young man. God you sound like Clare.'

'No. I was going to say, that you might be needing someone a bit stronger to catch you.'

It took her a few seconds to realise what he meant and then an irrepressible smile spread slowly across her face.

'And who would that be then?' She couldn't look at him.

'Me.'

He leaned towards her and slowly plucked her cigarette out of her mouth. 'God, how can you smoke these things, they're disgusting!' He laughed.

He stood up and was towering over her. As he reached down and pulled her up into his arms, he half spoke, half whispered in her ear, 'Emily Brighouse, what do I have to do to show you how much I want you?'

She could hardly speak, their lips were now so close. She never wanted to forget this moment. Just make it last a little longer. 'Two things,' she replied.

'Just tell me.' His voice was hoarse.

'Well the first, is that you should probably take me back to your place and show me…'

She didn't get to explain the second. He was kissing her so hard she was spinning. Their bodies locked together, the fingers of one hand woven through her hair, while the other hand held her thigh, hard against him.

They were both breathless and she nearly stumbled as he half led, half dragged her down the steps.

She had no idea where they were going as they leapt into the back of a black cab. Jem gave the driver an address in Notting Hill and pulled her over towards him, oblivious to the driver and the odd furtive glance in the mirror. He was kissing her all the way up her neck to just behind her ear, 'Just wait until I get you home, Emily.' She struggled for breath at the thought.

The taxi sped past Hyde Park and turned right up Kensington Church Street, but neither of them noticed until a few minutes later when it stopped. Jem pressed too much money into the driver's hand, who raised an eyebrow and shrugged his shoulders, but he wasn't going to argue.

He didn't stop kissing her as he carried her up the steps to the front door. He reached into his pocket for the key, slid it into the latch and pushed the door open with one foot. He kicked it shut behind him.

For just a few seconds they stopped, both breathless and held each other's gaze. He didn't break eye contact as he slowly reached behind her and unzipped her dress. He pulled her back, right into his body. She gasped as she felt him, hard against her. They pulled frenziedly at each other's clothes, falling backwards onto the hall floor. It was obvious by now that they weren't going to make it to the bedroom.

A little later, lying among their clothes and the upturned contents of her handbag, strewn across the hallway, he picked her up and carried her up the stairs to his bedroom.

She woke at 8am, unsure at first where she was, until she saw the brown, muscular arm flung loosely across her chest. When she moved her head, she could see a pair of black knickers, hanging on the light fitting, right above her head. 'Oh my God!' She gasped. She didn't remember that bit at all. She blushed at the memory of it all. She can't have been that drunk, but she really didn't remember throwing them up there.

There was no time to worry about her pants, the state of her make up or exactly where she was. He was already kissing her between the breasts, down her stomach, oh my God, here we go again, as the weight of his naked body slid on top of her.

They both lay breathless, he was still on top of her but resting on his elbows now.

'You said there were two things, Emily. So what's the second one?'

'Oh yes, that's right,' she hesitated. 'It's just that…this might sound a bit odd, but I really need you to join the TA, just for six weeks.'

'What?'

'You said you would do anything?'

'I just hadn't counted on that.' He shook his head, grinning.

'Oh OK, if the answer's no, I completely understand,' she turned away and started to get up out of the bed. He pinned her down with one elbow.

'OK, I'll do it.'

'Good, that's settled then.' She smiled.

He pulled a face. 'Do I really have to?'

'Yes, I'm sorry but I'm desperate.'

'I could tell.' He smirked.

'Fuck off! I mean desperate because I've promised the TA five decent journalists and so far I've only got the bloody Oxshott Gazette.'

'I can see that would be a problem.'

'Jem.' She eyed him suspiciously. 'Did you put my pants on the light?'

'Yes, I did. Sorry.' He laughed. 'I couldn't resist.'

He sprang out of the bed, giving her a full rear view of a tanned, muscular back. Her eyes dropped down to tight, white buttocks, the left one featuring a large black patch.

'My God is that a bruise?' She winced, imagining some spectacular fall from a horse.

'No,' he grinned. 'It's a tattoo. I'm surprised Emily, that you failed to recognise the Newcastle United Football Club coat of arms.'

'Jeez, but it's big isn't it.' It was hard to draw her eyes away.

'Yes, I got quite drunk one night in Newcastle and woke up with that on my arse.'

'Did it hurt?'

'I don't remember.'

'Oh right', she looked pleased. 'So I'm not the only one with a history of shameful, drunken episodes.'

'No, you're not.'

She flopped back on the pillow. 'Do you know, in two year's worth of emails, you hardly ever told me a bloody thing that you'd got up to.'

'I couldn't compete.' He pulled on jeans and a white shirt and walked out of the bedroom.

She looked around the room. It was huge, with tall, wooden shuttered, sash windows looking down onto the street. All very masculine, white bedlinen, leather armchair, an oil painting of a city on the wall, which looked like Rome or somewhere she couldn't work out. A door led to a bathroom in the corner. Thank God they hadn't gone back to Latimer Road. He came back in.

She looked over at the painting. 'Where is that?'

'Lisbon.'

'Oh of course, I'd forgotten where your mother came from. Do you speak Portuguese?'

'Claro que sim, minha rosa inglesa sensual.'

'Oh my God! Keep going!'

'Voce gosta quando eu falo em portugues?' He smiled wickedly as he walked towards the bed. 'Que safadinha!'

'Bloody hell!' But just as he was nearly on top of her again, a thought struck her. 'Oh my God, it's Friday! What time is it? I'm supposed to be at work!'

'It's alright, I don't start work until 2 today and you don't have to go in until after lunch.'

'Why's that?'

'Because, I just phoned your work and told them you're at Newsnight's offices, involved in complex negotiations on behalf of the TA.' He pulled her hair back and kissed her neck. 'I said you wouldn't be in until after lunch. I'm going to get us coffee. Back in 10 minutes.'

She heard the front door slam and waited for a moment. She got out of bed. Wrapping a towel around her, she crept around the house, nervously opening doors, peering into each room. There were three bedrooms upstairs and a huge double drawing room downstairs. She couldn't work it out. A house like this in central London. How the hell did a journalist afford a place like this?

There was a baby grand piano in the sitting room. The kitchen wall was covered in old, framed black and white photos, mostly featuring a very beautiful woman, which she immediately recognised as his mother. She was laughing, her head thrown back. She had the same smile as Jem, the same shaped eyes and wavy dark hair, cut into a short elfin bob. Emily remembered Jem's father talking about her, the first time he had ever seen her, dancing on a table in a Lisbon bar.

She walked back up the stairs and into the bedroom. He'd left his iPad on the bedside table. She stared at it for a moment, then almost without thinking, reached forward and touched the screen. It opened on his inbox - a couple of unopened emails and then she saw one of the subfolders on the left hand side of the screen, called simply 'Emily.' She clicked on it. My God! 247 emails, every email in fact that she had probably ever sent him – he had kept every one. She opened one up.

To: *Jem.im.a@RadioNorth.com*
From: *EBrighouse@Hobbs&Parker.com*
Subject: *disastrous dates...*

Jem
How can I begin to tell you how bad last night was. I know you warned me and I didn't listen. I have a theory that the state of your underwear dictates the success or failure of a date. It didn't start well, when I walked into the restaurant...

The front door slammed. Oh shit! She closed the folder and shot back into bed. The screen was still lit up. He was walking up the stairs and into the bedroom.

He was smiling as he opened the door. 'So, did you take the opportunity to go through the cupboards and drawers while I was out?'

His back was to the iPad, which she could see was still lit up.

'No, of course not.' God, he did know her well. 'You didn't give me quite enough time.'

And as if he could read her mind. 'The house belonged to my Portuguese grandmother. She left it to me when she died.'

'It's amazing.'

'Yes it is. Right now, I've got Berocca, Nurofen, Face wipes, a toothbrush and a latte, no sugar and a bagel with bacon. I think that's what you normally have? I didn't think you needed new shoes this time, so that should be everything.'

She glanced behind him and finally the screen went black. She could breathe again.

'The trouble is,' she replied. 'Every time you say something like that, I remember the email it relates to and it brings me out in a full body blush of shame.'

'Oh really, let's have a look?' Before she could tighten her grip, he'd ripped the sheet off her naked body. 'Oh God, I see what you mean.' He pulled off his jeans and started to kiss her.

'Bloody hell!' She gasped as he slid a hand up her thigh.

'Have you never heard of the voracious sexual appetite of the Geordie male. You can always tell me to stop.' But she didn't.

He traced a finger down her stomach. 'Have you any idea how hard it was for me to lie there, thinking about you in bed with Charlie?'

'You needn't have worried. The only thing that tried to shag me that weekend was your dog.' She was lying with her head on his arm, as they both stared at the ceiling.

'So do you really think I could learn to ride a horse?'

'Definitely. In fact it might be your only form of transport. Let's face it, you're never going to pass your driving test.'

She gasped, laughing. 'Was it really that bad trying to teach me?'

'Yes, but it was the only way I could think of, to get you on your own.'

'Oh I see.' She saw the time on his watch. 'Shit, I've really got to go!'

He helped to zip her back into her dress. 'I'll get you a taxi, I wouldn't want you to have to do the walk of shame on my account.'

She cringed. 'Oh God, you know far too much.'

'Yeah well, who told me?'

He stood at the front door, laughing as she teetered down the stone steps in tight black dress, high heels, and a birds nest of tangled blonde hair on the back of her head.

'Give my regards to Anoushka!'

'I will.'

'I'll phone you later.' He shouted as she got into the taxi.

No, she turned round and laughed, 'Send me an email!'

She sat in the back of the cab. Oh my God! Oh my God! Did that just happen? 'The voracious sexual appetite of the Geordie male!' What a fabulous thought. She couldn't wait to see Bella. Obviously there were large sections that would be somewhat glossed over, broad brush strokes only, such as the precise finer points of the scene in the hallway. Maybe just a few details, outline descriptions, number of times, that kind of thing. She was aware as she stared out of the window at passers by, that she had a very stupid grin on her face, that made her look slightly mental, but she couldn't help it. Oh my God, another full body blush of shame.

She leant forward to speak to the driver. 'Excuse me, but would you mind going past the Albert Memorial?'

'It's the opposite way, if you're heading to Fulham.'

'No I know, but would you go that way in any case?'

'Sure, it's your money love.' He said, turning the taxi around.

She gazed out of the window as they swept past the Albert Memorial. But what if he didn't call? Now that they'd finally slept together, maybe that's all he wanted. Oh my God woman, listen to yourself!

As the taxi pulled up outside no. 53, Mrs Vassiliadis was just walking past on the other side of the road. Normally at this point, Emily would have ducked down behind the seat until she has passed, but this morning, she couldn't help smiling and how strange, Mrs V was waving and smiling back at her. This was all most irregular, but then this morning it felt like nothing was ever going to be quite the same again. As Mrs V turned the corner, she could have sworn she was carrying a new season Le Voisier handbag, but she must have been mistaken – they weren't even in the shops yet.

It was just before 3pm, when she finally walked into the offices of Hobbs & Parker. A piss take by any standards, but at least she had the best alibi. She only hoped Jem wouldn't go back on his TA promise. She affected the walk of a highly confident person, who really doesn't mind that half the office is clapping and cheering as they approach their desk.

'OK, thanks everyone! That's really funny! You can stop now!'

Pete walked past her desk. 'Hey Brighouse! Listen, I don't think that's so many men to have slept with. I mean not at your age and you've been single for quite a while, haven't you!'

'Fuck off Pete.'

Anoushka was there in a flash.

'Hi Emily, just ignore him!' But she stared fondly after him.

'Don't worry. I always have Anoushka. Anyway, how did it all go with you two?'

She blushed. 'Oh, really well, thanks!' She continued to hover by the desk.

Emily just wanted some peace and quiet, to go over every detail of last night in her head. 'Yes Anoushka?'

'I was just wondering. It's been really bugging me.'

'What Anoushka?'

'I mean, how do you sleep with 1.7 men a year anyway?'

'What do you mean?' Emily was confused.

'Well, how do you sleep with .7 of a man? Is that like, just a blow job or something?'

Emily looked at her astounded. 'No, Anoushka! It was an annual average! Jesus, go and put the kettle on.'

To: EBrighouse@Hobbs&Parker.com
From: AJennings@Hobbs&Parker.com
Subject: Last night!

Well done Brighouse! Another gong in the H&P trophy cabinet - a well deserved award for you and the team. A most enlightening address to the dining room, by the way...and I don't mean your acceptance speech.

Tony - Sexist Prick...

And a little while later, another email in her inbox.

To: EBrighouse@Hobbs&Parker.com
From: Jem@newsnight.com
Subject: Your shameful behaviour...

Minha querida Emily, eu nunca vou esquecer a noite passada. Voce e linda. Sou louco por voce e preciso ve-la em breve. I'll be home by 9.30 tonight. Come over and I'll speak some more Portuguese.
J

25

Five months later…

It was Saturday June 15th – a beautiful, sunny day. Emily's 30th birthday.

Wintersbourne Park Polo Club was just as she had remembered. The huge white marquee topped by a purple Le Voisier flag, fluttering in a light breeze. Just outside the marquee, a white picket fence surrounded a square of lawn, laid out with drinks tables and chairs, opening out onto a huge expanse of perfectly mown, green polo pitch.

Clare F-B, reluctant to give up control of her more prestigious accounts, had struggled determinedly to the match. Just over 7 months pregnant now, her clothes were still resolutely professional, even if her face was a little flushed in the heat. She had already made three trips to the portaloo.

A square of thin rope cordoned off a colossal, old oak tree and polo ponies were tied all around in its shade, snorting, nuzzling and occasionally kicking one another. Along the side of the field, trailers and trucks lined up, unloading yet more frisky ponies, coats shining, legs and tails, already bandaged up in bright colours.

Emily looked around nervously. No sign of him yet. She thought he'd be here by now. On this day, of all days, she wanted to look poised and in control. She wondered if he would think she looked any different. Would he still want her? If she could just make him look at her like he did before.

Grooms and players exercised their ponies, up and down, next to the pitch. 'Hi Emily!' Two of them waved at her as they cantered past.

The memory of last year and the 'straddling incident' was still etched painfully in her mind. This time, she had opted for a slightly more solid platform wedge, so as not to sink into the grass. She was careful to look both ways before attempting to walk towards the marquee. No sign of Frankie shouting at her, another improvement on last year.

She had bought a rather flimsy, floral dress, especially for the occasion. She had fallen in love with it, but to be honest, it wasn't ideal for even the lightest of winds and on reflection, it was scarily short. Luckily though, she had found a couple of large safety pins this morning and hastily secured the skirt to her pants. This year she had planned ahead, like a smug girl guide. There wasn't much wardrobe-wise, which could go wrong.

Hector had invited Bella and Derek and they had driven down this morning from Cumbria. Bella spotted Emily on her way to the tent and rushed forward to greet her. 'Happy birthday lovely!' She said hugging her warmly. 'We've only just got here ourselves. God this place is beautiful, isn't it!'

Emily was a little distracted, looking along the line of trailers for the Hacienda team truck – no sign of it yet.

Bella saw her looking. 'Is he here?'

'I don't think so, can't see him.'

Bella was wearing the pale grey chiffon dress that Emily had worn last year. She looked slightly better in it, Emily thought, more elegant. The matching pale grey pashmina had unfortunately not survived the gastric onslaught of Roisin from Your Style.

As they looked around them, taking it all in, they both noticed the arrival of an enormous, white, stretch limo as it rounded the corner, through the gates and made its way slowly down the side of the pitch, drawing up outside the marquee. They could see Hector, standing to attention at the entrance, waiting to greet whoever was inside. A waiter stood next to him with a chilled bottle of Champagne and glasses at the ready.

Bella had never been to a polo match before and was very excited. 'God, I wonder who this is? Harry and Wills?'

'I don't think royalty travel in white stretch limos, Bels. Looks more like a dodgy hen party.'

'No, definitely a celeb, Emily! Look at Hector waiting for them. It's got to be some sort of VIP! Liz Hurley maybe?'

'Simon Cowell!'

'Elton and David.'

'The entire cast of Holby City!'

'Jedward!'

They watched, transfixed, as Hector stepped forward and opened the door.

A dark, petite, elegantly dressed woman in her early 50s took his hand as Hector gallantly helped her out of the limo and bent down to kiss her hand. She was followed by a short man, who from a distance, was the spitting image of Danny De Vito.

Emily and Bella's mouths dropped open, as they stared and turned to face each other.

'Jesus Emily, do you see what I see? What in God's name are they doing here?'

'I see what you see! Has someone just spiked our drinks with a hallucinatory drug?'

The loudspeaker spluttered and screeched as the commentator announced the new arrivals.

Ladies and Gentlemen, we are delighted to have with us today, loyal polo fans, Costas and Sophia Vassiliadis, who have kindly agreed to present the Vassiliadis Cup for Best Playing Pony of the Match, this afternoon.

As Mr and Mrs V were handed a glass of Champagne and ushered into the marquee, Emily and Bella rushed up to Hector, who was still standing at the entrance, grinning at them both, like a Cheshire cat. 'Girls! There you are! Did you see who's here?'

'Hector!' Emily was at his side. 'What's going on? How do you know Mr and Mrs V?'

He was enjoying himself. 'Did Hector do well?'

Bella kissed him on the cheek. 'I don't know exactly what you did Hector. But I think we finally have an answer, to the longstanding mystery of the 'Latimer Road non-eviction'! How did you do it?'

'Well, would you believe it,' Hector replied, barely able to conceal his delight. 'It turns out that Mrs V is a huge fan of our Royal family. She had always wanted to attend a polo match, so of course, I was delighted to oblige. Obviously there were certain conditions.'

Emily was a little slower on the uptake. 'So were you also responsible for the full refurb!' Oh my God, you didn't actually go into the flat did you?'

'Yes Emily.' Hector raised his eyebrows. 'I did take the opportunity to appraise myself of the state of your accommodation. I had a quick look around, which was frankly all I could stand.' He puffed out his cheeks theatrically. 'I have to say girls, you really are shockingly slovenly. It was in a deplorable state. I pointed out to Mr and Mrs V that it was almost certainly in breach of a landlord's legal obligations.'

'And they agreed to do it up?' Emily looked astounded.

'Yes and they'll be sitting on Pippa Middleton's table at lunch. It was the best I could do. Anyway, it seems to have done the trick!'

They both threw themselves at Hector, kissing him on either side of his cheek.

'Girls, girls! You're spilling my champagne. John only lets me have 2 glasses a day now. I can't afford to lose a drop! Anyway I trust you are keeping it in a slightly better state, now that it's all done up.'

Ladies and Gentlemen, please take your seats. Lunch is about to be served in the main marquee.

Emily looked backwards, a fleeting glance at the entrance gates as they went in with Hector and found their table. Clare F-B was on a table with the woman that looked like a horse from Polo News and a couple of magazine journalists. Emily mercifully, was off duty, sitting with Bella and Derek. Thank God she wouldn't have to look after any journalists on her birthday.

They were about to take their seats, when Emily spotted her. A glorious vision, 5 ft 10" of fashion forwardness, strutted catwalk style across the marquee, heading straight towards them. Her jet black hair cut into an uncompromising Cleopatra bob and clearly embracing the trend for colour blocking, she dazzled in purple tights and an orange and yellow harlequin mini dress. And she was balancing on a pair of patent, white Mary Janes, with probably the highest heels Emily had ever actually seen anyone walk in.

'Emily Feckin Brighouse!' She shouted and waved, as the crowd parted in front of her. 'I should hardly be talking to you!' A few of the stuffier polo wives raised their eye brows as she sashayed past them. Emily stared blankly, but as the striking vision approached and sat down at their table, she was able to sneak a furtive glance down at the woman's place card.

Roisin O'Donnell, Your Style magazine.

'Good God. Roisin! How are you doing?' What else do you say? One year later and she was literally half the size she had been. A large portion of her had simply disappeared since they last met. She was a size 14, if that.

'Will you look at me! And it's all your fault woman, for making me join the feckin TA!'

Emily hastily closed her gaping mouth. 'You look amazing Roisin! Clare told me you'd done the course, but did you really do that in six weeks?'

Roisin waved aside the waiter offering her wine and sipped a glass of sparkling water. 'Jeez no! I did the first six weeks and then I signed up for real. Your man from the TA was a blast, he's training half the girls in the Your Style office. The piece will be out in next month's issue by the way – it's a double page spread!'

Roisin sat down between Derek and John. Hector winced slightly as he caught sight of the enormous acid green maxi tote by her side – clearly not from this season's Le Voisier collection.

After the main course, emboldened by a glass of wine, Bella gestured to Emily. 'Come on, we'd better go and say hello to the landlords!'

Emily wasn't keen. 'Do we have to? I suppose we should. Come on then!'

They picked their way through the tables. Good God! Mr Vassiliadis was actually deep in conversation with Pippa Middleton. What on earth could they be talking about? They veered off and instead, with some trepidation approached Mrs V. Sofia Vassiliadis, now on her third glass of champagne, was all smiles. Emily made sure that Bella got there first. 'Mrs V. How are you?'

'Ah girls! How lovely to see you! Emily's uncle has been so generous!'

'My uncle?'

'Yes, your Uncle Hector is a very charming man, Emily. We didn't realise how well connected your family is!'

'Oh, yes, I see. Yes isn't it! Well have fun, Mrs V. Enjoy the polo. We'll see you later!'

'Call me Sofia! And girls…?' She actually winked at them. 'Don't bother with Costas in future. You talk to me.'

'Yes, Mrs V.' They chorused, giggling as they walked off.

The players were now warming their ponies up, cantering up and down the field, hitting practice balls in preparation for the start. Standing by the white picket fence, two girls were eyeing up the blue team's No. 3. The blonde one turned to her friend. 'God! Check him out! Gorgeous isn't he! Do you think he's single?' They both laughed, but stopped abruptly as they realised they had been overheard. Hector, standing next to them, smiled. 'Actually girls I'm afraid he isn't, but if you look over there, I believe that Tierra Buena's no. 2 is still available.'

Ladies and Gentlemen. Play is about to get started. Please make your way outside as we introduce the players.

Guests trickled out onto the lawn, in various stages of inebriation, a few staggering slightly. The players lined up on the field in front of the marquee, waiting for the commentator to introduce them, ponies and riders restless, Hacienda in white and blue, Tierra Buena in red.

Playing at 1 for Tierra Buena is Luis del Castillo with a handicap of 4. And at 2, Jamie Fane with a handicap of 2. Mark Addison at 3, on 1 and Tom Clayton at the back on 0. Tierra Buena there with a total handicap of 7.

Emily was right in front of the riders now and she could see him clearly.

And Hacienda now. Playing at 1, it's Dan Feldman on a handicap of 3. At 2, José Sanchez on a handicap of 2. At 3, Jerome Armstrong on 1 and at the back, patron Peter O'Donoghue with a handicap of 0, giving a total team handicap of 6.

As each player was introduced, they cantered off to the right or left, accompanied by a ripple of applause from the crowd and bawdy cheers from a group of girls near the front.

And there he was, nonchalant almost, as his pony tossed its head back and gave a small buck. He kicked it on and her gaze followed him as he cantered off up the field, detached almost, perfectly poised, eyes straight in front as he practiced his swing. When she saw him now, remote and indifferent, it felt almost impossible that they had ever been together. The players lined up opposite each other. The commentator began...

Hacienda with the lower handicap starts with a ½ goal advantage. Umpire Mark Fraser-Thomas has thrown the ball in and Ladies and Gentlemen, here we go! Del Castillo brings it forward for Tierra, but Feldman's after him, Armstrong next in line... Who's going to get there first? Feldman opens up and he's running free... Where was the marking from Tierra? You really cannot afford to leave Feldman alone...
Feldman slows down, chips it over to Armstrong... Armstrong plays a blinding nearside forehand and we've got our first score of the afternoon...

Hector came and stood beside her at the picket fence. 'You're looking a bit wistful there Emily! Can you believe it's been a year…and here we are again, gawping at No.3, like a couple of lovestruck teenagers!'

Sanchez hits a forehand, Feldman behind him, but Del Castillo clears it with a beauty of a backhand. Jamie Fane's there, looks around, hits it up. They're thundering up the field now, can they catch him, no they can't and it's a goal for Tierra Buena….
Del Castillo hooks out of it and here's a chance… through the back legs of Addison's pony.
It's Addison again, in the way of the player, he's blocked him. It'll be a hit from 60 yards, Feldman takes it and it just trickles in!

'I know Hector. I was just thinking it's been quite a year. I'm exhausted!'

'I'm not surprised, now that you're 30. Happy Birthday darling girl! You should probably start thinking about slowing down, you know. You won't age well.'

'Bugger off!' They both laughed and watched, transfixed, as Jem leapt from one pony onto another and galloped back onto the field.

Fane rides off Sanchez, leaving the field clear for Clayton. O'Donoghue's after him, but too late. Clayton scores…
Hacienda's Jerome Armstrong on a fresh mount now, 5 years old, an ex race horse and quite a handful by the looks of things…

Jem thundered past them, pursued by a Tierra player, barging against him so close, their stirrups almost locked.

And Armstrong under immense pressure here again from Addison…
He can't quite pick that up and Del Castillo is right

***behind him…a brilliant nearside backhand…the flag's
are up…it's in…***
***And at the end of the third chukka, it's 3, 2 ½, in favour
of Tierra…***

Half time now, she looked around. There was Clare
F-B, good old Clare, chatting to the journalists, tirelessly
networking, Derek and Bella, huddled together at a
corner table, Roisin, her tall frame teetering unsteadily on
the grass, as she chatted to Hector.

She looked up and suddenly there he was, walking
through the crowd, straight towards her, all leather and
white jeans, running his hand through dishevelled black
hair, that same grin, looking just as he did the first time
she had ever seen him.

Clare stepped in and blocked his path. 'Jem, come over
here! I want you to meet Tabitha and James from Shortlist
magazine.'

His eyes didn't leave Emily as he replied. 'I'll be with
you in one second Clare. Just something I have to do first.'

'Happy Birthday gorgeous!' He lifted her above him and
lowered her as he kissed her on the lips, taking his time,
before turning back to Clare and the two, spellbound
journalists. 'Hi, I'm Jem, how are you doing and this is my
girlfriend Emily.'

As they stood transfixed, watching Jem and Emily
disappear behind the marquee, Tabitha from Shortlist
turned to her colleague. 'Bloody hell, I wish it was my
birthday.'

They were alone now behind the tent and Emily
reached up and wiped a trace of mud from underneath
his eye. 'What happened to you? I was really worried.'

'I know, we only just made it in time. Straight out of the
truck and onto the field. Loading the ponies took longer
than we thought and then we hit traffic when we came off
the M1. How was Dad's driving on the way down?'

'Oh fine, no problem. He even managed to text me to say he'd arrived at your sisters!'

She had spent the night at Haydon Mill Farm with Jem's father, while Jem drove north to pick up his team mate. She and John had shared, what she had pointed out, was her last meal in her 20s, a takeaway curry and a bottle of red wine, followed of course by a couple of celebratory homemade Kumquat liqueurs.

'I missed you last night. Come here, birthday girl.' He slipped his arm around her. 'Will you drive back in the truck with me?'

'Don't you need to take Dan back?'

'No, he's going back with his ponies, on Peter's lorry. Sorry you had to come and watch me play polo on your birthday.'

She laughed. 'I know. It's been a terrible bore, eating strawberries and drinking champagne in the sun with my favourite people.'

He pulled her into his chest, kissing her neck and whispered. 'I've got you a present but you'll have to wait until we're alone at the farm tonight.' A shiver ran up her spine at the thought.

He looked her up and down. 'Have you bought another new dress Emily? Wait till I get you home.' His hand ran up the inside of her leg.

'I thought you might not like me anymore, now that I'm in my 30s. Do I look any different?'

'Yes, ancient. Tonight you will officially become the oldest woman I have ever slept with. I guess if I have enough to drink it should be ok.' He lifted her against the back of a horse trailer, kissing her deeply and pushing himself against her.

'Fuuuuuuuuuck!' Emily let out a bloodcurdling scream. Jem stepped backwards, shocked.

'My God, Emily, what's the matter?'

'I've got a one inch fucking safety pin stuck in my arse! Oh my God it hurts, Jem! Get it out! Get it out!'

She bent over and he lifted her skirt. 'Let me have a look. Shit you have too. It's big! OK. I'm going to pull it out. Hang on to the side of the truck.'

Jem bent over her and slid her pants and tights down, in order to extract the pin, which was deeply embedded towards the middle of her left buttock. Neither of them noticed as Costas Vassiliadis came out of the portaloo. His glance was drawn sideways by the sight of the bare bottomed woman, bent over, her pants and tights round her knees, holding onto the side of the truck for support. The polo player bent over her, no doubt preparing to carry out some heinous act. He stopped dead and his eyes widened in horror at the sight. Looking backwards, as she braced herself for the extraction, Emily caught sight of him staring in disbelief.

'Oh my God, Mr V. It's not what it looks like.'

'It never is with you girls.' He said, shaking his head. He hurried back to the marquee, mopping his forehead and mouthing expletives in Greek. These were strange people indeed.

'God that hurt, Jem.' She rubbed her bottom.

'I'm not surprised.' He laughed.

'And I can't believe he saw that. What am I going to say to him?'

'I wouldn't bother saying anything. Just give him a wink! It's bleeding a little bit. Here, hold that on it.' He took off his wrist band and held it over the wound, which was tiny, but causing a small trickle of blood to run down the back of her leg.

Ladies and Gentlemen, please welcome the players back onto the ground, for the second half of the Le Voisier Cup.

'Listen, I've got to go. Are you OK?'

'Yes, yes, fine. Play well!'

'I'll score you a birthday goal!' He walked backwards grinning at her, nearly tripping over a guy rope.

Emily adjusted her underwear, pulled her dress down and wandered distractedly back to the marquee. She suppressed a smile, oblivious to the slight throbbing in her bottom and reflected on how, all things considered, she really quite liked being in her 30s.

She walked through the marquee and out onto the lawned area. It was then that she spotted Roisin, stricken and floundering helplessly in the middle of the polo field. She could have been re-enacting some strange, tribal dance as she freed first one heel of her white patent Mary Janes, only to find the other stuck fast in the turf. Waving her acid green maxi tote for balance, she thrashed around wildly.

Emily hurried back into the tent. 'Bella, can you come here for a second. I'm going to need your help.'

Derek tried to follow. 'Shall I come?'

'No thanks, Derek,' Emily replied. 'Women's business.'

They approached her carefully from either side like an unpredictable, wounded animal.

'What the hell is this treading in business, anyway?' An uncompromising Roisin shouted, 'You'd think they could afford a feckin roller.'

'Just sling an arm around each of us and we'll get you back to the tent.'

They were the last people left on the pitch, apart from horse face from Polo News. Jem trotted over from the sidelines.

'Do you need a hand?'

'No thanks Jem,' Emily smiled up at him. 'It's completely under control.'

'If you say so.' He laughed and cantered off.

Roisin stared after him. 'What a beautiful creature! And the horse isn't bad either.'

Horse Face journalist walked past in sensible shoes. 'You never call it a horse, it's a pony actually.' She raised her eyebrows as she looked down at Roisin's footwear.

'Well it looks like a feckin horse, from where I'm standing.' Roisin's adrenaline was up.

Emily tried not to laugh. 'Come on Roisin. Put your arms round us and lean forward slightly as you walk.'

Would the last three spectators please clear the ground as quickly as possible, so that we can get on with the second half...

The unwieldy trio limped slowly off the pitch. Roisin giggled, 'Will you look at us girls! Are we not the very picture of upper class, English decorum?'

Under the oak tree, Jem was watching them. He smiled and shook his head, as he waited with the other players to go on.

We've got some serious horse power on display for the second half of the LeVoisier Cup. Jose Sanchez on a 9 year old Argentinian mare, Jerome Armstrong on his fastest pony, Patalita...
The ball's thrown in...it's messy but Del Castillo quickly makes a break for goal...hooked by Peter O'Donoghue, Sanchez backs it beautifully. But Del Castillo is there again...he looks around, keeps his head level, doesn't try to hit it too hard...and it's a goal for Tierra...
4-3 ½ as we go into the fifth chukka...

Even those guests who were generally more interested in the free Champagne sauntered out of the marquee, hearing the excitement in the commentator's voice. The crowd fell silent.

And that looked to me like Addison wandered over the line again, the umpire doesn't think so, Feldman and Addison clearly having some words...
O'Donoghue has the line of the ball alongside the boards, Addison has to give him room...
Sanchez hooks out of it and here's a chance...
Final chukka now and Jerome Armstrong has broken free, completely unmarked. Armstrong on Patalita is flying now as he gallops to the ball, hotly pursued by Del Castillo. Del Castillo tries to hook him.
In he comes and it's a mighty hit from Armstrong, it soars through the goalposts, the flags are up and he absolutely nails it! Ladies and Gentlemen, in the closing seconds of the last chukka, Jerome Armstrong scores what must surely be the winning goal, right from the half way line...Hacienda snatches victory from Tierra Buena by just half a point...

The crowd applauded enthusiastically as exhausted players walked their ponies back. Emily strolled over to where Jem was undoing Patalita's girth. He smiled when he saw her. 'Well, Emily? Did you like your birthday goal?'

'I'm sorry, I was looking away, I must have missed it'. She looked at him innocently.

'Oh.' He looked deflated.

'Oh, do you mean the one from the half way line? The best goal you have ever scored. Do you mean that one? Of course I bloody saw it! It was awesome!' She grinned and kissed him on the cheek.

As Emily stood at the front of the crowd, for the prize giving ceremony, she still couldn't quite reconcile herself to the sight of Sofia Vassiliadis stepping forward to present Jem and Patalita the Cup for Best Playing Pony.

It took them two hours to get back to Haydon Mill Farm. It was nearly six o'clock. Emily was sitting on a gate, inappropriately dressed for the country, still in the flimsy mini dress and Jem's leather jacket. She was at least wearing the plum mid-calf hunter wellies, by now, she noticed with satisfaction, looking almost shabby. The evening sun bathed the fields in a technicolour glow, 'magic light' her father used to call it, as Jem lead the ponies, two at a time, out to the field for the night.

Hector and John and Bella and Derek would be arriving at the farm for her birthday dinner in one hour. She watched Jem walk the length of the field, back towards her. Her eyes never left him and she knew that she had never been happier.

'Come with me, Emily, I've got a surprise for you. He led her back down the driveway towards the stables. 'I want to give you your birthday present.' He put his hands over her eyes as he led her through the main door to the stables. He released her and it took a few seconds for her eyes to adjust. She blinked in the darkness and then she saw him.

'Titan? Oh my goodness, that is Titan isn't it? Hello boy!' She walked into his stable and he nuzzled her shoulder as she rubbed his nose.'

'But he's Frankie's horse?'

'Not any more. He's yours. I bought him for you.'

She looked away and desperately didn't want him to see the tears in her eyes. He saw she couldn't speak and kept on talking. 'You see, Frankie is moving away, she's leaving Radio North and she was looking to sell a few horses.'

'You saw her?'

'Yes, we had a chat. I don't think she's proud of how she behaved. Anyway the upshot is, that she agreed to sell me Titan.'

'So, who's going to teach me to ride?'

'I am. God help me.'

He turned away and she was glad he wasn't looking at her. 'It's the best present I've ever been given. What are you doing?' He was sliding the bolts shut on the stable door.

'Locking the door. I don't want any of your ex-boyfriends bursting in this time. Happy Birthday, Emily.'

He pulled her towards him and lifted her up, her legs around his waist as they stumbled backwards, laughing as they fell onto the straw bales.

– The end –